The Chance I'll Take

Best Wishes!

MOCKINGBIRD PUBLISHING
Apalachicola, 2014

1

Jeremy A. Mutz

In loving memory of Special Agent Joe Mitchell

Part I

Fort Walton Beach
Saturday, 10/24/1953

He was full of Cuban rum, and mean. Jo Ellen sat beside him, shaking—from fear of what this man might do when he got her home and from the cold, her sleeveless evening dress doing little against the chill in the night air. He flicked on the radio, cussing while the tubes warmed up. He didn't like to wait for anything. In a moment, the music began to pour through the big speaker in the middle of the dash, blaring a "Country & Western" song. He attempted to sing along. "If you're sad and lonely, you got no place to go!" he bellowed. Smoke from two Chesterfields wafted from the ashtray as he steered and hollered—as he weaved across the dark narrow highway.

Jo Ellen could feel her lip bleeding. He'd slapped her damn near as hard as he could. The sting of the palm of his hand was still buzzing through her left cheek. He straightened his tie and fedora and lit a fresh cigarette as if nothing happened.

He pulled in her driveway, tapping his foot on the floorboards. He shoved the lever in park and grabbed Jo Ellen by the arm, dragging her across the seat and out the driver's door of the red convertible. Cussing angrily, he leaned back in the car. Jo Ellen froze, terrified; she knew he kept a gun in the car. But it was only to retrieve her handbag. He threw it at her then continued shoving her toward her front porch. She dreaded what would happen once he closed her door behind them. *The last time he was here, I woke up at Eglin Field, a military doctor stitching up the back of my head,* Jo Ellen thought to herself. She looked back at the road—Highway 98. It was dead, without so much as the flash of distant high beams to suggest the presence of another living soul. *I may die tonight, right here, and no one would know.*

This was North Florida, the rural Panhandle—vast forests dotted with the occasional whistle-stop or seaside town, the people far outnumbered by the pines that surrounded their small outposts, tiny towns strung together by two-lane roads. There was no crowd she could run to or get lost in, no cop on every street corner, just quiet, just the still night air, the scent of salt water, and the pines. The nearest law officer was about as close as the nearest television set. The things she loved about the place were at this moment adding to the danger. Tonight was quieter than normal. Jo Ellen had to survive this night on her own.

The tall man zipped his pants, glaring at Jo Ellen. "You tell me no in the car. Let's see how brave you are inside. Come on," he demanded, pulling her up the steps. She looked over at the house next door. She prayed the young air force captain, his wife, and baby might be home, but she could see their lights were dim, the windows black, their carport filled with shadows instead of the Ford sedan the couple usually parked there.

He threw her on the couch, holding her down, forcing her to kiss him. His blood hot, he began kissing her neck, trying to unzip her dress. He would hurt her and in the morning accuse her of being crazy, of imagining things. So much for gentlemanly manners. He felt her reluctance, her lack of interest, and shoved her away by the forehead. "You little whore, who else have you had over here?"

"N-no one."

"You're lyin' to me. I'll slap you again unless you stop lying!" he shouted.

She explained once more that she had invited no one else to her home. He wasn't satisfied with her answers. He grabbed the large purse and emptied out its contents, trying to find some indication she had entertained another man, tearing through her Standard Oil and grocer's receipts. He scattered her lipstick tubes and makeup, her combs and brushes, all over the living room floor. He dragged her upstairs. He opened the drawers of her dresser, going through her underwear, making sure she'd not purchased anything he didn't know about. He came downstairs and made himself another drink, cussing her.

"P-please leave," she pleaded quietly.

He didn't say anything; he just advanced toward her.

"Oh!" she cried, falling backward as he hit her again. She could not believe it was real. The *pop* his hand made sounded like a gun going off. But it wasn't the slap that shocked Jo Ellen; it was the casual way he went about it, setting down his drink on the big Philco console he had turned into a bar, stepping up to her—the same way he might step up to a bartender and order a martini—and nearly knocking her off her feet.

What could she do? Her house—the rooms dark, smoke swirling about the ashtray where she puffed nervously through two or three more Chesterfields—was no refuge. Danger was right here with her—the tall man in the suit, his hat there on the newel post. He had set in like bad weather, with no intentions of going anywhere. Even if she ran, even if she made it to her car, it wouldn't do any good. His Rocket 88 blocked her Packard from moving.

She watched him go back to the Philco, the heavy burled walnut cabinet with a glowing dial that sat along the wall. She watched as he poured another glass; he was doing his best to reach the bottom of that bottle of whiskey. She had turned on the radio, hoping it would relax him. She knew how he got when he was drinking. It wasn't working. "Half as Much" was playing now, the fiddle and steel guitar sounds echoing through the small room. Though he seemed to enjoy tapping his foot, dancing about, and mixing his drink to the up-tempo rhythm of the honky-tonk number,

5

he grew more cocky, more crude, with every drink. *He* sure was enjoying *her* birthday.

Suddenly, Jo Ellen could hear the motor of a lone fishing boat coming up the sound. She moved to the doorway of the kitchen while he danced. She could see the running lights casting a glare through the glass in the back door. She held her breath, silently praying it might mean some form of rescue. She stared at the doorknob, calculating how far she might make it in a dash. She tried to gin up the courage. She listened to the man in the other room. Then she listened as the gurgling sound of the flathead Chrysler grew farther and farther away. She grabbed her little white purse from the kitchen counter from the place she'd hidden it, behind her toaster. She held the purse behind her and moved in front of the dining room table. He continued to dance and sing, but how long would that last?

If only there was some other distraction available! She looked around the dark rooms. She had no television. Right now she wished she had, even though there was only one station, a snowy WPFA Pensacola had signed on the air two weeks before. Milton Berle or the Indian-head test pattern or something might be on, something to make him laugh and occupy his attention.

Static. The radio station signed off the air. *Oh, hell*, thought Jo Ellen. The handsome fellow cussed and flung open the cabinet, finding a 78 rpm record he liked and putting it on the turntable. It spun and crackled, and the music began to play. He turned up the volume, the sound of the jazzy record deafening in the little room. Shaking with fear, she watched him while he danced the samba, by himself, in front of the radio.

He'd left the bottle on the radio. She looked at it, the faint light glinting off the brown liquid, the firewater that was giving him so much personality. She knew what would happen if she said or did anything that would set him off. She complied when he demanded she dance with him. He held her tightly, slinging her around to the lively music, dipping her roughly, and rubbing his five o'clock shadow over her chest when he brought her back up from the dip.

He was getting more aggressive, touching her everywhere he could, kissing her, trying to pull her shoulder strap down. She knew where this would end. She resigned herself to that fate. He pressed his face to hers roughly, taking a long, drunken kiss. She let him. She kept thinking how this man put on a genteel face to the world, when they were out at the Magnolia Club earlier. How he wore a fine suit and tie. How he was perfectly groomed. The way he said "Yes, sir" and "Yes, miss." He tipped his hat and pulled out her chair for her. But it was all a lie. She had run from trouble before. She had taken the figurative hard knocks before. Now the punches and slaps were real.

He tried to walk her toward the staircase, kept kissing her neck, pulling her shoulder strap down. She kept trying to hold her dress up. He pushed her hard into the wall, her head smacking the plaster, kissing her and trying to get her zipper all the way down. He held her by the neck tightly so she could not move.

This is where it's gonna end, she told herself. She—with every bit of strength she could bring to bear—pushed him away. She knocked him back about two feet and dashed toward the kitchen. She ran to the back door and tried the knob—it was locked! Her wary eyes focused on the big man. He looked surprised; that look instantly faded into rage. "*No!*" she heard herself cry aloud, trying to unlatch the door as he lunged toward her across the little galley. He caught her and laughed. He tossed her back into the living room, onto the ungiving oak floor, where she lay like a stunned animal. He looked down at her. "You're awful clumsy, darling," he said, snatching her up by the back of her dress and slapping her face—hard— then flinging her away from him.

She caught herself on her parlor chair, stepping behind the rounded back while he lunged for her a second time. She evaded his grasp, ducking behind that chair. Leaning over in front of the seat cushion, he raised his arm, ready to backhand her across her face. He laughed as she cowered behind the furniture. He straightened up, stimulated by this little game, feeling good from all the whiskey he'd had. He staggered back to pour himself another, his appetite for bourbon stronger—at the moment—than his desire to inflict pain.

She watched him refill the tumbler. He grinned. He turned the glass up then slammed it down on the cabinet, sloshing booze on the woodwork. His grin faded; he had a look of rage and lust thoroughly mixed together, like the bourbon and Cherry Heering in the cocktails he'd made himself before dinner. She contemplated what he'd do next. Would he hit her again? Would he force himself on her one more time, right here in this room?

He watched her hiding behind the chair, waiting for her to cry, to plead with him. She made not a sound. Jo Ellen could take a slap. He nodded, sizing up the situation, savoring the fire in the bourbon as it warmed his insides. This little dance excited him; it was better than hunting down a wild animal. He'd hunted big cats once, during the war. Yes, it was just like that. It was more thrilling to conquer the lioness when she resists, when she claws and fights, when she must be pinned down and subdued. He lit a cigarette and let it dangle from his lips as he puffed on it, and the smoke swirled around in the dim light. He filled the glass once more.

Jo Ellen kept watching as he took off his tie and unbuttoned his shirt. She'd taken a couple slaps just as she'd borne the other humiliations she'd experienced at his hands—in silence. But she wouldn't take another, not tonight, not in her own place. "Get out of my house!" she snarled.

He laughed at her. He took another drink. He exhaled more smoke, his eyes aflame with desire for the beautiful prey. He took in every curve as she stood there, shaking in the tight black chiffon dress, the fair skin of her chest revealed by the low neckline, heaving as it was with rapid breaths. "Come here," he ordered, the cigarette still between his lips. He

7

laughed at her again, seeing her cling to that overstuffed chair. He took another drink, spilling a bit on his suit.

Jo Ellen backed up a step, watching him brush the liquor off his lapel with the back of the same hand he'd slapped her with. She watched the light from the kitchen reflect off his cufflinks and the dial of his silver watch when he fussed with his suit coat and drained his glass one more time. It was dark in the living room; his face was in the shadows. He put down the glass and stepped toward her. She slowly backed up toward her dining room table. The dishes from the meal she had prepared for them remained there. That was where she'd left her little purse. He looked smug; he grinned. He figured he had her right where he wanted her, her back against the table, nowhere to go, standing there in her evening dress and Roger Vivier heels, her mind second-guessing her instincts, thinking, "Maybe he does love me, maybe he does think I'm beautiful, maybe this is all right." He didn't notice her gloved right hand move behind her back. He had been drinking cocktails or straight bourbon all night. She hadn't consumed a drop.

"Come here, sweetheart," he said softly.

She wiped her lip, holding a napkin in her left hand. Her cheek was still burning from the last blow. "I've asked you to go," she repeated quietly, looking away, almost unconcerned, almost as if she'd resigned herself to what was coming. She shook her head.

He figured it was time for a little sweet talk. He sat on the arm of her divan across the room from her. He dropped his cigarette in the ashtray on the table beside him. He leaned forward, speaking as earnestly as he could in a drunken slur. "You look so good tonight, baby. You don't know ha' much you excite me, feelin' your arm, your dress brush agains' me, dancin' with you, breathin' in your perfume when I'm near ya. All night long I just kept lookin' at you and wantin' you and thinkin' how much I love you."

She looked down. She stopped shaking her head; she just looked down at the floor. He thought he was getting somewhere with her. It looked like she was thinking, the way women let a thought float around inside their heads and they get all romantic feeling.

"You know you love me, you know you need me. You know you need the same things I do. You and I are the same. We love hard, fight hard," he said, looking over at the roses, a dozen red ones scattered on the floor where she'd thrown them. "We're two people that are alive, and we're not afraid of it. I'm sorry about before. But you know it made me mad what you said. It really hurt me, baby. I know ya didn't mean what ya said. You know I don't want to do mean things, lose my temper, but you made me so mad when you threw away the flowers and told me to leave. You make me get all mixed up sometimes. I just love you so much. It's the truth. I've never been with anyone that made me feel like you. I feel safe, like I can tell you anything, be myself completely. I've never felt that before." And for the coup de grâce: "Baby, you're the best thing that's ever happened to me."

She just looked down, ignoring him. He kept talking, certain that he possessed the words that could manipulate her. He sounded like a lawyer making his closing argument. But she'd heard enough. She'd heard it all before.

"Tell me we're not through, baby. Tell me we can keep going on like before. That you'll come away with me—we'll take a trip to Cuba, anywhere," he offered, almost pleading with her.

She continued to ignore him.

"Whadya say, doll baby?"

She looked up, looking him in the eye. "Beat it," she said strongly. Her look was serious, defiant.

"Aww, you don't mean that," he told her.

"Beat it," she repeated, more forcefully this time.

"Look here, you can't just run me out. We're pals," he said, standing up.

"Not anymore."

"Aww, I didn't mean nothin' by that slap. You deserved it with that crack you made, that bit about breakin' up. It didn't hurt you anyhow," he insisted. "You can take it."

"It was *three* slaps—just about one too many. Get out!"

"Look, there's no need to get sore. You and I have always stuck together."

"We're getting *unstuck* tonight."

"You sure you wanna do that? After all this time?" he said, stepping toward her. She didn't answer. His look was menacing. He was tall; even in her heels, she had to look up at him from her position against the table. "I can make a lot of trouble for you, you know," he told her, taking another step.

"I don't like being threatened in my own house," she told him. She didn't flinch. She kept her left hand by her side. It was shaking, and she didn't want him to see it.

He took another step.

"Uh-uh," she said, raising her right hand and the .25 she had been hiding behind her. It was a tiny automatic, a Baby Browning.

He leaned back, his eyes wide with astonishment. He swallowed and looked at the gun as if it were a cobra popping up from a basket he'd just knocked

9

the lid off. Even in the dim light, the faint light reflecting off the nickel plating, there was no mistaking what she had in her hand.

"Unless you want to hear Baby go off, you better feel around for that doorknob. If you're too drunk to find it, I'll show ya," she said, motioning with the gun.

He swallowed again. "Now that ain't no way ta talk." His face turned red with anger.
"Where'd ya get that gun?" he growled.

"Oh, that ain't a gun. That's Baby. I've been hiding him. And you better move, or you may find yourself close acquaintances."

"Put that gun down!" he barked, taking another half step. She took the safety off and pulled back the slide to load the chamber. Her left hand was still shaking, but she did it, the mechanism rewarding her with a solid click that sounded like Minnesota Fats sinking the eight ball on the break. "I know how to use this thing. The next move I make is gonna be to squeeze the trigger." She looked him squarely in the eye, his chest, his unbuttoned shirt, no more than four feet from the short barrel of the gun.

He stepped back, popping the palm of his right hand with his balled left fist, rolling his eyes and cussing, red-faced and veins bulging. "Where did you ever fire a gun before? I bet you couldn't hit a thing!" he taunted.

"Don't worry, if my aim's off, I get five more chances." She gestured again toward the door.

"This isn't finished—not by a damn sight," he growled, shaking his finger at her.

"I say it's through. Don't come back here—not in a hundred years," she told him, her gloved finger still on the trigger. He nodded his head angrily; he wheeled about and stomped toward the door, snatching his silk tie from the divan, knocking over one of her end tables and a lamp, flinging the door open, and loudly descending the steps of the little porch. She heard his car roar to a start, the wheels tear out of the driveway as he gave the Rocket 88 the spurs.

Jo Ellen collapsed on the divan and set Baby beside her. She held her face in her hands, crying. After a moment, wiping away the tears from her cheeks, she began to laugh. Sometimes she felt her life might make a good script for a movie. "How did I get in this fix anyhow?" she asked herself aloud.

She didn't want trouble. She'd had enough of it—from men, mostly. Jo Ellen was quiet by nature. Sometimes she preferred to be alone. *Yeah,* she thought, looking around her empty house, *being alone ain't so bad.*

She had crossed paths with some dangerous men; tonight wasn't the first time a man had threatened her. Part of it was bum luck. She came to know some things that well-connected men didn't want anyone talking about.

Every creak from the old timbers, every car that slowed down in front on a lonely night—alone, lying in bed, her windows open in her upstairs bedroom—reminded her of some of those things from her past that she wished she hadn't lived, wished she didn't know.

It would be nice to have a *good* man around in moments like that, someone that might keep a lousy ape like Mr. Oldsmobile from dropping in whenever he felt like it. She'd let herself get fooled by a handsome face and a grin, by beautiful, insincere flattery whispered in her ear—once again! He had a way of building up her ego, making her *feel good about being lied to*. It was the damnedest thing. She felt ashamed; she wished she could erase the entire experience.

She took off her white gloves and heels and got her broom, sweeping up the rose petals and the little card. "Happy Birthday," it said. She dumped the lovely-smelling mess in the trash can under her carport. She cleaned up the glass from the lamp. She got a towel and wiped the whiskey and melted ice from the top of her radio and from the wood floor.

When she finished, she got a few ice cubes and wrapped them in a damp washcloth. She sat down and lit a cigarette, holding the ice to her face. Yeah, there were things she would like to forget, stuff she'd like to erase off the books and live a normal life. She'd forget she ever knew the man with the Olds convertible for starters.

What else would I forget? I'd forget what happened six years ago, that's for sure. That was when Henson Jamieson was killed. That one event caused her more trouble than anything else.

She came here and tried to avoid any more trouble. For five years she'd hidden from it, living quietly off the beaten path. People knew her Packard convertible around town, but she tried not to draw attention to herself if she could help it. She ran her business and was good at it. She treated people with respect—it didn't matter if they were countryfolk, the lowliest airman, or a general's wife, Jo Ellen Harbert was nice to everybody. The locals liked and respected her for that. If she didn't say much, they figured she had her reasons. She came here, it was said, from Jacksonville or Pensacola, one of the big cities. No one knew the details. She tried to forget the truth, avoid its implications. She wasn't looking for trouble.

He might come back, maybe tonight. She nodded her head, looking around the room. *That's the chance I'll take.*

2

North of Tallahassee
6:05 a.m.
Sunday, 10/25/1953

Shadows. Silence. Porch light in the fog. Miccosukee Road, away from town. Pistol loaded. Wipers clearing away the dew.

The plantation road was dark, covered with a canopy of live oak branches, falling leaves, and Spanish moss that soared overhead like the ceiling of a cathedral, scant light making it through to the path below. The new county sheriff, Frank Carter, cut his lights and steered his green and white step-down Hudson over to the side, onto the soggy, leaf-strewn shoulder. He pulled off as far as he dared, fearing the car might get stuck. Three unmarked Fords pulled in behind him in like manner, cutting their lights.

Carter looked ahead into the darkness, along that tunnel-like road. He switched off the motor. The silence was loud—louder than the idling six's low drone. A gospel quartet number poured from the radio as the country station signed on the air with its Sunday program. He shut it off. Silence. Listen. No one else was around, the only hint of human presence the smell of smoke from a woodstove permeating the cool air. He got out of the car, his Police Positive drawn from its holster. He wasn't a tall man—standing five inches shy of six feet—but he was tough-looking and well-dressed in a new brown suit and Stetson.

The doors of the Fords opened, eight men getting out of the shoebox sedans, big fellows they were, pistols and shotguns at the ready as they stood in the shadows. Carter gave the signal to move. The men quietly advanced toward Johnson's farm, hugging the red clay banks that hemmed in the road. Then silently, they climbed up, through the tree line, to the open pasture between the road and a little farmhouse in the distance.

They advanced under a sky, black and endless, filled with stars, no city lights to dim their glow. They stepped over the rusty wire fence one by one, watching that one-story house. They kept their eyes open. They stepped lightly, careful to avoid alerting the large dogs Reynolds Johnson kept. Johnson's' lights were dim, save for a glow from the kitchen window.

Closer they crept, across the field, Carter in front. Chief Deputy Dreggors was two paces behind. He was a big fellow, wearing his fedora with a turned-up brim over his reddish-blond hair, a trim mustache, collar unbuttoned, and red tie askew. He stopped, listening to the dogs stir just past the house. His gray suit coat unbuttoned, his Colt ready in his giant hands, he kept moving. The other seven men followed in turn.

Another light came on. Dreggors looked back at young Deputy Cook, who carried a Winchester pump shotgun. Cook nodded. They were awake.

After Cook came the fellows who Carter had sworn in as temporary deputy sheriffs: two hired detectives who worked for Governor Johns, two PI's who worked for the attorney general, and two men from the police department. Only the policemen wore uniforms, their dark-blue coats with shiny buttons fastened securely on this cool morning; the other men wore their "uniform" of sorts: suits, ties, wide-brimmed fedoras. The sheriff had watched the house for four days. Three people inside, possibly a fourth.

The dogs started barking. Each man knew what to do. Carter and Dreggors moved toward the front door, the policemen ran around back, and the others took their positions on either side of the porch, ready to fire through the side windows should Johnson try to make a fight.

Johnson looked through the window by the front door, his face illuminated by the dim light inside. Enough light to reveal his lips mouth the words of an expletive. Too late. Dreggors was up the front steps, kicking the door off its hinges like it was made of cardboard; the breaking of the back door could be heard simultaneously—it too imploded on itself, easy work by the six-foot-tall TPD officer. Dreggors grabbed hold of Johnson before he could get at the.45 on the kitchen table.

The thin dark-headed Johnson wasn't through. He took a swing at Dreggors, which was quickly rebuffed by the big lawman. Johnson was spun around and jammed against the wall, handcuffs slapped on both wrists before he could resist again. The woman—Johnson's paramour— swung a skillet of fried eggs at the sheriff. He caught her by the arms and clicked handcuffs on her as she screamed and kicked. He shoved her into a chair and flicked the eggs off his suit. "Looks like you burned 'em. I prefer my eggs scrambled anyhow."

Johnson's cousin, Ricky, was cuffed by the TPD men on the back-door stoop. "Where's Tommy?" asked the sheriff.

One of the policemen, a lanky fellow named Al, answered him. "He saw a feller make a run for it. He took off after him, running towards the woods— him, Jim, and ol' Billy." Al was referring to the Governor's hired men and the short, bald-headed AG investigator.

Johnson, his woman, and Ricky sat down on the divan, Cook with his shotgun aimed in the middle of them. They were sullen, angry.

"All right, boys, let's have a look," said the sheriff. The lawmen tossed the house. The dogs barked furiously but could do little, chained as they were to a dogwood tree. Al went through the little bedroom and the bathroom. He turned off the light to the toilet. "There ain't nothin' here, Sheriff." Joe, the AG investigator who stayed behind, came out of the larger bedroom. He lowered his eyes and shook his head. Nothing. There was no sign of any gambling paraphernalia, not in the cabinets, dressers, nor under the beds. Johnson smirked.

13

Carter himself went through the papers and envelopes stacked neatly on the table in the living room. Nothing. But Carter was not fooled by the tidy nature of Johnson's farmhouse. He faced the suspects and lit a cigarette. "How y'all doin' this mornin', huh?" He smiled at the spit and vinegar in their glances, the venom in their rage-distorted lips. "Y'all didn't think you'd get caught, did ya? We know you runnin' bolita out of here—where's it at?"

They glared at him silently.

He put out his cigarette. "If I have to take an ax to the plaster and rip every damn one of these floorboards, we'll find it."

"We ain't got nothin' hidden in this house. You boys ain't got a thing on us," spat Johnson.

"I guess we'll see. I got lots of time," said Carter. His men went over every nook and cranny of the house, taking down pictures, flipping mattresses, shoving furniture, and lifting rugs. They found nothing. Joe began opening kitchen cabinets, tapping on the insides of them to see if there were secret compartments. Again, nothing. Johnson laughed. The PI gave the refrigerator a shove. "Well, I'll be... Hey, come here! Look here, boys!"

The others gathered around. "Whadya got, Joe?"

"There's a panel! A little door with no knob."

Carter nodded, and Joe tugged it open with the blade of his pocketknife. "Look here," he said, pulling out a canvas bag.

Carter looked inside. "Tickets. Must be four, five hundred of 'em."

Joe pulled out a little wooden box. "Look here, there's the tally slips, cash money. Looks like close to two thousand dollars," said the PI.

They sat the evidence on the kitchen table, the sheriff, the investigator, and Cook looking it over.

Dreggors shined his flashlight in the compartment. "What about this here?" said Dreggors in his thick, rural accent, leaning far into the bottom of the compartment, as far as he could with his large belly hindering him in the small space. "Addin' machines—three of 'em. And a couple Underwoods." The big man pulled out the items one by one.

The three detectives returned from their chase, their lungs burning from the cold.

"What did that fella look like?" Carter asked as they walked in the back door. "We need to get out a broadcast on him."

"Caucasian, six feet tall, medium build, blond hair," said one of the fellows, a bit out of breath.

"All right, we'll git 'im," said Carter.

The telephone rang. The men looked at each other. The sheriff nodded to the governor's man. "Go ahead, Billy."

He picked it up. "Yeah? Okay, go ahead." It was a seller reporting ticket sales. Billy began to write. He replaced the receiver. The telephone rang again—and four more times after that. The governor's private dick and one of the TPD men took turns. They looked at each other as the information poured in, realizing what they had—they'd brought down the Florida side of a three-state bolita ring. The whole shebang.

Carter couldn't help but strut. The suspects looked restless. "Nothin' in the house, huh? Y'all fixin' to do some time at the state prison. Yes, sir!" The Johnson men looked down at their shoes; the woman shot a particularly dirty glance Carter's way. "You can expect a real nice stay at one of the women's cell blocks at Raiford. I hear you get a cell all to yourself if you a female," Carter told her. She looked away.

Ricky stared at the sheriff with an odd look on his face.

"You lookin' at me like my fly's open, son. What is it?" asked Carter.

"Uh, nothing," the kid replied, looking away.

"Just set there and be still," the sheriff told him.

"You gonna bond 'em, Will?" asked Al, grinning.

"Judge ain't set their bonds yet," replied the chief deputy, a sheepish grin on his face. "I reckon we'll hold on to 'em a while."

"Let's carry these prisoners to the jailhouse," said Carter. "Good work, boys."

The cars were moved up. The men began to take the prisoners outside. Johnson writhed loose, lunging for Dreggors, knocking over a bottle before Dreggors caught hold of him. It rolled off the counter, shattering on the floor. Johnson looked down at the broken glass, the bourbon spreading out on the linoleum. The top half was intact, its edge jagged as a razor, better than a knife. He tried to break loose and get at it. Dreggors yanked him away, popping him in the face with his fist. "You fat cop!" snarled the prisoner. "It was a full bottle. I shoulda least got somethin' out of it."

"It's illegal anyway," Dreggors told him, shoving him through the door. The prisoner turned to curse Dreggors, his face red with rage. It didn't faze the big man. "Aww, shut up," said the chief deputy, giving him a kick down the front steps. The man had a blue suit on, wrinkled from sleeping in it, his

15

tie over his shoulder from the struggle. Dreggors pushed him toward the car. He tried to pull away, looking back at Dreggors. "I want my hat, you mug!" Dreggors shoved him in the backseat of the Ford.

"Sure, I'll get it for ya, Mr. Johnson," said Carter. "Don't want ya to catch cold." Cook and Dreggors got in on each side of Johnson, guarding him, as there were no prisoner cages in the automobiles. Joe started the car. Johnson cussed them all but shut his mouth when Dreggors shot him a telling glance. Johnson knew what the big cop would do. *Give him half a reason, and he'll work me over. Yeah, he'll work me over, but good. Don't push it, fella.*

Carter brought the hat over, tossing it through the window and into Johnson's lap. He patted the trunk of the car, the signal to take off. Dreggors stuck Johnson's hat on his head as the car sped toward the jail downtown. Johnson thought of escape; it'd be a while before they got back to town, open country, and woods to hide in. He glanced to either side and thought better of it—these were big ol' boys that he knew he could not get away from. He shook his head and silently cussed. *Fate. Bad luck. Son of a bitch.*

Only Carter remained at the farm. He sat behind the big steering wheel. A shotgun mount and a Motorola was the extent of the car's police equipment, except for the thermos of coffee. "One got away," he thought aloud.

He reached for the coffee, listening to Bobby the dispatcher and one of his deputies on the radio. Suspicious car on US 90. Traffic stop. *Was it the third man?* Bobby read out the description one more time.

Carter started the car and got moving—fast. The deputy came back on. "Five foot six. One-twenty. Black hair. 10-4." Okay. Not him. Carter backed off the throttle. "One got away." The sheriff didn't like that one bit.

3

St. Vincent's Hospital
Jacksonville
Monday, 10/26/1953

Fulton listened as the priest moved from room to room, checking on the other patients in the cardiology ward, his vestments ready for comforting prayer—or last rites—as the case dictated. He could hear the padre cheerfully greet the sick and dying, whether they were well enough to respond or not. Those pleasant "Good evenings" drifted their way down the hallway to Fulton's ears, growing louder as the priest worked his way toward Fulton's end of the hall. He followed the priest's movements as much as he could, flat on his back, unable to move around, his eyes watching through the doorway, observing the father step in the room just across the clean tiled hall.

Fulton forgot about the padre momentarily. He strained to sit up and put the pillows behind his back. Marlene was coming. He wanted to be sitting up when she arrived.
He managed to prop himself up all right. A bit out of breath from the exertion, he listened as the priest finished his prayer as his footsteps tapped across the hall. *He seems surprised to see me sitting up,* Fulton thought. The priest appeared roughly the same age as he and seemed an affable fellow. "Good evenin', Detective Fulton. Are ya feelin' better?"

"Evenin', Father." Fulton was the youngest patient in the ward at thirty-three and was not feeling better. Not at all. He didn't say so, just asked the priest for a cigarette. The father handed him one, chatted with him, and invoked the saints on his behalf. In a moment, an attractive blonde appeared at the door. She looked in on the dim, depressing room, her man with wires and oxygen and an IV attached, a priest in black at his bedside. She leaned against the doorframe with her hand behind her head, her elbow against the doorjamb; despite her worried, anguished thoughts, it was a becoming pose. Fulton saw her and smiled. "How ya feelin', baby?" she asked quietly.

"Oh, excuse me," said the padre, turning around.

"It's all right, just here to look in on my man."

The priest excused himself, and the little 5'2" knockout walked over to the bed. Trying to be as strong as he could for his wife, Fulton smiled cheerfully and told her he was fine. He reached out to her and hugged her tightly. He cracked a couple jokes for her benefit. Underneath the cheerful expression and wisecracks and put-on confidence, he wasn't so sure the next stop wouldn't be the morgue downstairs.

She kissed his cheek and took his hand. No words passed her lips, but she seemed to say a million things with her eyes. They were hazel blue. Pretty as Jean Harlow's. Marlene was never one to sob, but she could not help the

17

flow of tears down her cheeks, looking at the twelve electrical leads attached to her best friend, watching the simple little ECG heart monitor, the frightening machine in a wooden box scratching her man's heart rate on a roll of paper. She wiped her cheeks with her hand and held on to her husband.

The old doctor, white-haired and grandfatherly, came in and listened to the policeman's chest one more time. "Please tell me something, Doctor. Please tell me," Marlene implored.

The doc pulled the stethoscope from his ears and lit a cigarette. He offered Marlene one, and she shook her head. "An attack—it's always serious. Besides that, he has this irregular heart rhythm."

Marlene looked up at the doctor. "So what's it all mean? Can you fix it?"

The doc stabbed his cigarette into the ashtray. "It may continue to occur. I can't say. I do know there's little to be done about it."

Fulton squeezed Marlene's hand as tears flowed down her cheeks. "I'll be fine, baby. You'll see," he told her, mustering a smile to encourage her.

The nurse, in a gray habit of the Daughters of Charity, made Marlene leave. Visiting was over for the day. Marlene kissed her husband on the lips, which seemed to shock the nun. As the nurse gently pulled her away, Marlene handed her husband a picture of the two of them at the beach from the summer.

After Marlene left, Fulton drew the trash can toward his bed and vomited until he nearly passed out. Sweat poured from his brow, and he collapsed on his pillow.

"You havin' chest pains now, are ya, Detective Fulton?" asked the nurse in her faint Irish accent. He nodded. The ECG's pen swept a frenzied track across the strip of paper. The nurse brought in a nitroglycerin pill to place beneath his tongue. "There ya are." She nodded as he closed his mouth.

Sister Sereptha rarely spoke in anything more than grunts or "Hmms"; she stood by as the pain subsided and the doctor returned, listening once more. Sereptha dabbed some alcohol on a rag and held it to the patient's nose. "For the nausea. Old nurse's trick," she told him as he breathed the fumes. The nun covered him with another blanket before leaving to check on a patient down the hall.

Fulton looked at the photo, thinking of his wife. Her perfume lingered near him. He wondered if he'd grow old with "the Doll," like they'd always said, or if he'd leave her a widow, aged thirty. He looked at the JPD badge and gun on the table beside him, the fedora hanging opposite his bed, doubting if he would ever work as a policeman again. He fought back tears of his own, gritting his teeth. He'd not feel sorry for himself. The only way to get out of here would be to hang tough.

18

The doctor returned with a pack of Chesterfields. "In case you run out, son."

Fulton thanked him and smoked one.

4

Fort Walton Beach
Monday, 10/26/1953

She heard a noise outside. She stepped out of the shower, wrapping herself
in a blue towel, tucking it in so it would stay over her breasts. She shut off
the faucet. Water off, it was quiet in the room. She stood still, listening.
She heard the sound of a car door slam in front of her house. *Oh, hell!* She
proceeded into the bedroom. She picked up Baby from the night table and
went to the little windows that looked out over the lawn. There was a red
car out there. She moved the shutters a bit so she could see. There was a
man. She opened the shutters a bit more. She breathed a sigh of relief. It
was just someone with a flat tire. Sleeves rolled up, '39 Plymouth up on a
jack.

She closed the shutters and slipped the gun in her purse. Her father had
given her the pistol. It was a rather smart-looking gun—shiny, nickel, her
initials carved in the ivory grips: J. H. The old man taught her to be a fair
shot. She didn't make a habit of showing it around, but if the situation got
desperate, it could surely put a few holes in a man.

She combed her dark hair in front of the mirror. It had been an eventful
weekend, to say the least. An *uneventful*, dull week—after Saturday and
Sunday's festivities—would suit her fine. She dressed for work. Just as she
was about to pour herself a cup of coffee, the telephone rang.

"Well, who could that be?" she asked aloud, putting the coffeepot back on
the stove. She picked up the receiver. On the other end was a shaky voice,
one trying to fight back sobs, the voice of a woman with a rural accent—the
voice of Clara Jamieson. That voice she hadn't heard in five years.

"Miss Jo Ellen?" she implored, sniffling.

"Why, Mrs. Jamieson!"

"Do you remember me?"

"Of course! Whatever's wrong? You sound terribly upset." *The woman must
be about forty now*, thought Jo Ellen. She'd never heard her like this. Even
when she buried Mr. Jamieson in the old Chestnut Street cemetery in
Apalachicola, she didn't sound as distraught as she did now.

"I hope I didn't call too early. I wasn't sure if y'all were on slow time or not,
so I waited.
I'm just *beside* myself. Sadie Phillips found your number for me," said the
older woman. "I hope it's all right."

"Why, yes, what can I do for you?" asked Jo Ellen, stepping back into the
kitchen, carrying the heavy phone—the cord could reach from the hall—

20

and filling her cup. She was glad Mrs. Jamieson didn't get her number by calling information; she'd paid to keep it unlisted.

"I'm in trouble. The man that owns the shop here plans on selling it. He done stopped payin' the bills, and I ain't had no pay for a week. I was just wonderin' if you knew somebody that might have some work for me." Jo Ellen had helped her get the job years before, when her husband was killed.

"Well, I'm not sure. I may know someone over here."

"I will surely go where the work is. Anything will do. Christina and Elizabeth are so hungry when they go to bed. Sarah, she's not mindin' me no more. She's not goin' to school. I fear for what she's goin' to do—take off for some big town, and I won't ever see her ag'in. I ain't so proud I won't beg if it will keep them in somethin' to eat. There ain't nothin' 'round here. They say I'm too old, I don't have no diploma. But you, Miss Jo Ellen, you got me this job, and I'm so grateful, I just know you could help me ag'in."

"Well, I will try."

"I ain't never done no other type of work, that's the thing that's hard. I went from cookin' and cleanin' and farm chores with my daddy, to bein' merr'it, cookin' and cleanin' for Henson. I didn't have no skills. Well, you know that. But, Miss Jo Ellen, I've done everything for that business, for that Sam Nowak. I even learned how to keep the figures for Mr. Nowak. He's so lazy, he doesn't do anything. Now he just wants to sell the buildin' and close the business. He's so mean, Miss Jo Ellen," said the woman, starting to cry.

"Hmm, this fella wants to sell, does he?"

"Yes'm, he wants to sell and wash his hands off it, me and the girls, after we worked for him these last five years."

"What's his name again?"

"Sam Nowak. He's a Yankee, not that I'm sayin' they're all bad or anything. But he's from up north somewhere."

"Well, you know this business. How are the profits?"

"Real good, Miss Jo Ellen." The woman described how much cash they took in and what she thought Mr. Nowak wanted for the business. "Ol' Sam just doesn't want to pay for new machines or fix the roof. He'd rather sell the place and open a shop where folks put coins in the machines and do their own washin'."

"How do you get in touch with this Sam?"

"Miss Jo Ellen, here is his number. 2-8557," she said, reading Jo Ellen the five-digit Tallahassee number. "Can you help us?"

"Well, let me do some checking on this," said Jo Ellen, writing down the number. "I'll need to make some telephone calls."

"Thank you, ma'am. Thank you, Lord!" she said, looking up. "You know I don't ever ask for handouts, just a chance to work and take care of my girls."

"I know."

Mrs. Jamieson thanked her again and said good-bye; Jo Ellen returned the telephone to its spot in the hall and sat down with her coffee, thinking as she stirred. She could ignore Jamieson; that would be easy, safe. Jo Ellen's father had always told her to mind her own business. And she had found that, more often than not, to be damn good advice. Still, Mrs. Jamieson was *owed* something. Jo Ellen felt that in her soul. She decided she might buy the business and let Jamieson run it. She had the operator connect the number Clara gave her. She found Nowak gruff, but he could meet her on the thirtieth, in the evening.

Jo Ellen telephoned her father. She talked it over with him, that this business was for sale, she had someone to run it, everything except how she came to know the Jamiesons. She'd have to take out a loan for most of the purchase price, but it seemed like a good investment. Her father—always one to ask about anything financial—agreed.

She called her banker. It would be no trouble to borrow the money, but she would have to go to Crestview to make the loan. Tomorrow she'd let Mrs. Lindgren run her shop, and she'd drive up there.

Of course, this business would take her to the capital—a city she never wished to lay eyes on again. She assured her father it was fine. She hoped she was right.

Near Tallahassee
Monday, 10/26/1953

Four men met on the back porch of the large wood-framed house along an isolated stretch of the Ochlockonee River. They hadn't expected the *bolita* raid.

The oldest, with wire glasses and a jar of moonshine in his hand, sat in his rocker, listening as the younger men discussed who might have betrayed them, who might threaten more damage, what might be done about it. The old man sipped whiskey as the young fellers talked; they were talking big, twelve-gauge talk, when a squirrel gun would do. Finally, he put his two cents in. "So they made a few arrests in Atlanta, a couple fellers spill what they know, and that tips off Frank Carter. He got lucky, that's all." He leaned back in his rocker and looked at his colleagues with his icy-blue eyes. He spoke slowly, in a North Florida drawl; he was a man wise in his years, wise in his dealings that happened to run "a tad again the law." "I don't think we have much to worry about. The sheriff hasn't learned the true players—here nor in Alabama. No need to stir up a wasp's nest when they ain't nowheres near the house."

"What if Johnson talks?" asked the middle-aged lawyer. He was the best-dressed—new suit, hand-sewn tie. It was his white Lincoln that sat, mud-caked from the drive through the woods, beside the house. He perched nervously on a rocker, facing the old man.

"Carter's a hick sheriff with a tenth-grade education. He won't get anything outta Johnson," said the youngest, blond-haired and handsome. Hat down over his eyes, he tilted the bottle of Straight Eight to his lips.

"We're damn lucky they didn't get you," said the old man.

The young tough nodded, still drinking. The young fellow sat beside the lawyer, talking and imbibing while the attorney worried. He was pleased to talk about his narrow miss. "I noticed the dogs acting funny and started out the back door. I tried to warn Johnson. Three men chased me, but I was able to get away, back to where I'd hidden my car." He leaned back, his jacket on the back of the chair, his automatic and holster naked at his left shoulder. He grinned, satisfied with his ability to evade the slower private dicks, hired men with bellies and wives to slow them down.

"Mighty lucky, son," said the old man, looking out over the slow-moving river. "You can't be too careful."

It was quiet for a moment, the river silent in its flow, the only sound a squirrel scurrying up a pine. The old man watched a mockingbird swoop in and land on an oak branch, driving away a cardinal; the feisty little bird made him grin. The blond took another swig of beer. The lawyer lit another cigarette.

"What else did you hear?" asked the old man, turning to the fellow at his right—the fourth man balding, heavyset, and potbellied, but a man of intelligence, a hard case that wore bow ties and smoked Pall Mall cigarettes like they were going out of fashion.

"They swore in Johns' private investigators and a couple city cops," he replied. "A couple of those boys drove their own cars, no radios, nothin'." The four men laughed at the rag-tag nature of the sheriff's operation. There was no state law enforcement—and that suited these fellows just fine. It was the portly man's business to keep tabs on the law, to minimize its reach. He had his ear open to every rumor, he had his friendships, and he had family ties, which ran as deep in these parts as any kinship in the Scottish clans of old; he did "favors," whatever it took.

"So things go on pretty much the way we please," said the blond fellow, adjusting his hat.

"We just gotta make sure we keep a few of our boys in the legislature," said the old man, taking a sip of whiskey. "We don't need a lot of unnecessary laws passed or any kind of state police nosin' around our bidness. There's always talk of it."

"But we always fight it off. And we got a good fella set to run for the house. Nothin' gonna interfere with that," replied the fat man, taking a puff on his cigarette.

"Yessir," said the old man. "I know who you mean. I don't think anyone will cause us problems there. But don't get cocksure. And when can I expect to see you again, nephew?" he asked, turning to the youngest.

"Got a train ticket in my pocket. I'll be in Jacksonville for a while. I expect I'll be back this way soon—sooner if y'all need me for somethin'."

Fort Walton Beach
Thursday, 10/29/1953

She was walking by the lake. Someone was following. She tried to walk faster. She looked back. The shadow was still there. She tried to run, but her legs felt like they were wrapped in lead. He was getting closer! He—

"Hah!" she gasped, waking with a start. She looked at the clock. Five thirty. Almost time to get up anyway. Baby was ready, in the purse where he belonged. Next to Baby was a blue envelope with $5,000 in it. Money talked where she was going. And that kind of money would say a lot.

She got under the shower, the steam and heat helping her wake up. She dried off with the blue towel. She put on her underwear; she was still a twenty-six-inch waist. She hadn't gained a pound since college. *Well, that's what being broke—and working hard to keep from staying that way—will do for your figure. I work too damn hard to get fat.* She pulled on her brassiere and fastened it behind her, taking a minute to adjust it so that it provided some modicum of comfort. "Damn thing," she muttered, moving the straps on her shoulders. That was about as good as it was going to get. She stepped into the gray skirt she had laid out, then sat on the bed to tug her nylons on.

She wound her watch. There'd be time for coffee and breakfast. She ate quietly in her kitchen and washed the dishes, leaving the place spotless. She put on her silk blouse and the suit jacket. It was a nice Dior suit that accentuated her slim waist. There were seventeen pairs of shoes in the rack beside the dresser with the mirror. She picked up some blue ones, sat on the bed, and worked her feet into them. In the top drawer were the pair of white gloves she liked to wear when she was driving, and a floppy, wide-brimmed hat was in the box she'd placed on the bed.

She dragged the suitcase down the narrow staircase, to the side door in the kitchen. "Damn it," she muttered, tugging the case over the threshold. She didn't realize it was that heavy. It must have weighed seventy-five pounds. She lugged it out to her car. Its smooth lines, vertical grill, and winged cormorant at the end of the long hood identified it as a Packard. The blue '49 she'd backed in beneath the carport. She lifted the big case into the trunk. She had to go back for her purse, more hats, and a leather bag with a worn two-inch-thick journal that she kept.

The journal wouldn't interest most people. The last entry she wrote was about the sour milk left by the milkman last Thursday. Oh, it had a few "salacious" details about her college days that might amuse and entertain, but it was mostly what she felt at various times, struggles she faced, things only she cared about—except four or five pages at damn near the beginning of the book. *These pages could send a few men to Raiford Prison,* she thought. No, there would probably be some *statute of limitations.* But it could certainly end the political aspirations of a few prominent families in

Tallahassee. She made sure it was secure in her leather case. She had borne the weight of that secret long enough.

She had come to this little town when there was nowhere else to go. It was either quit boozing, come here, and get to work, or they would find her body floating in the St. John's. Her father knew Mrs. Silver; he talked the elderly woman into giving Jo Ellen a job. It was the only help she would take from the old man. He dropped her off in his black Clipper, as silent as he always was. He gave her a copy of the Alcoholics Anonymous book. He wished her luck. That was really all he'd said. And she set to work; she must have tailored half the uniforms at the air force base on the north shore of Choctawhatchee Bay. She cried every night the first two weeks; the work was so hard. Her AA sponsors made her read more than she had since her days at the Florida State College for Women. She thought about Mrs. Jamieson sometimes; it helped her keep going. Why, if Jamieson—all alone—could struggle and support her three girls, there was no reason she couldn't support herself.

After two years hemming britches for GIs, or now and again letting out the waist for a general, or sewing a wedding dress for the bride of some lieutenant, she saved enough to buy out Mrs. Silver and be her own boss. She made enough to rent this cottage, put $200 down on a used Packard, and keep food in the noisy old refrigerator, a 1920s thing with a Monitor top and a pedal that opened the door. She made rent on the store and hired a woman to help with the work. The out-of-the-way town was just that—out of the way of *trouble*. And she was happy for the first time in her life.

She shut the trunk lid and looked out over the backyard. She could see across the Santa Rosa sound, over to the island, the white sand dunes, the old casino at Tower Beach, which was a wooden dance pavilion and boardwalk. *Tower* and *casino* were, perhaps, somewhat misleading, the former having been blown away by a hurricane years earlier. Nor did the latter offer gambling anymore; sporting ventures weren't carried out in the open any longer. You had to know the right places to find a slot machine or a roulette wheel. The white sands and the ice cream and burger stands were the main draw now. In the summertime, she could hear the music from the pavilion from her open windows. Today the only sound was the rustle of a rather strong breeze from the gulf.

She got in the car, pressing the accelerator to the floor with her toe, the motor turning over and settling into a nearly silent whir. She backed out onto the main road. She noticed a monarch butterfly land on the hood ornament, the little creature opening and closing its colorful wings, moving its antennae as if it were trying to take its bearings, trying to get back on course. She paused for a moment, watching it until it flew away, back on its proper heading—south. She pulled the column gear lever down toward her knee and into first, letting out the clutch, the big motor tugging the car toward downtown, a couple blocks east of her driveway. US 98 became Main Street as it ran through the business district of her little town.

26

Locals and tourists alike spent their money along six blocks of shops, restaurants, bars, and package stores that ran down both sides of Main. Her shop was in between a bar and a cocktail lounge. The bars didn't bother her. She didn't want a drink, hadn't wanted one in four years. Maybe it was a little ironic that she learned to drink in a dry county over in the capital city, but found sobriety in a place that had enough booze to float an aircraft carrier—or a coast guard cutter at any rate.

That wasn't to say downtown wasn't nice. It had everything you'd expect in a small town: Robert's Rexall drugstore, Echol's Furniture Store, a shoe store, clean sidewalks, and blasted five-cent parking meters. The Spindthrift Restaurant was down at the western end of Main, not far from Jo Ellen's house. It was a typical small town where respectable citizens traded on a Saturday. It just happened to have a few nightclubs and strippers mixed in to please the tourists. The place was crowded with out-of-state visitors in the summer, but dead quiet this time of year. She lived close enough to walk to work. She felt safe.

She didn't feel safe where she was going 170 miles away. It might as well have been 17,000. She passed her shop, the Closed sign in the window after eight o'clock a rare sight. She came to the prominent fork in the road. Straight, she'd cross the Brooks Bridge and end up on the beach. Turn left, she'd be on State Highway 85 and one step closer to confronting her past.

She pressed the clutch and let the car coast. Was she making a mistake? Should she turn around, enjoy what she had here, and stay away from the capital? She looked in her rearview mirror back toward home. No—she had to go. Letting out the clutch, her small gloved hands wound the wheel of the big car, making the turn on the highway, passing the little nameless gas station. The car picked up speed, the butterflies in her stomach fading away. It was thirty miles to the county seat, going through Shalimar— home of the infamous Shalimar Club—and skirting the edge of the military base. Up through endless pinewoods ran the two-lane road. *Up* was an accurate description as the road climbed from sea level to 250 feet in elevation.

The highway was once a trail for ox-drawn wagons from Camp Walton to Crestview. It seemed scarcely wider now as she steered the big car. She looked over the hood, through the *V* of the cormorant's wings, out at the pretty evergreen forest along both sides of the road. The sky was a perfect blue. A large truck went by, the wind whistling as it shoved its way past. Several miles passed without seeing another car. There was little traffic this early on a Wednesday in the off-season.

After a forty-minute drive, she pulled up in front of the old Bank of Crestview. The town was aptly named; there was a lovely view of forests and valleys from the high ridges there. Highway 85 was Main Street through town, the town boasting a hotel, two cafes, and a package whiskey store, along with an old wooden L&N depot that looked like it was straight from a Hollywood movie set. A proper Southern courthouse with four ionic columns stood at the dead end of Main. The bank—the only one in town—was at 361 North Main, across from the Fox Theatre.

Jo Ellen parked at the front door of the bank. It too was like something from a movie set with its brass cages at the teller windows, high ceilings, and ornate tables to write out deposit slips. The banker, old Mr. Maynard, knew her well, rising from his rolltop desk, greeting her by name when she came in.

"No, don't have my key with me." That, she had hidden.

"Oh, that's all right, Ms. Harbert," said the old-timer, leading her back inside the vault, the iron door already open and propped with a wastepaper basket. He unlocked the box and carried it to a table for her. She put a bound copy of those pages from her journal in the safe deposit box, and he locked it and returned it to its place in the vault. "Thank you, Mr. Maynard," she told him, smiling, her heels clicking across the polished floors out to the sidewalk. The old man waved to the glamorous-looking woman as she pulled away and went back to watching the cars go by.

She made a right on James Lee Boulevard—US 90—the town quickly fading into open country. The highway would take her through whistle-stops like Mossy Head and old railroad towns such as DeFuniak Springs and Chipley, with little restaurants and filling stations that catered to tourists and truckers. This was the part of Florida the tourists hurried through to get somewhere else. No interstate ran through the Panhandle. These "back roads" were the main roads. They could be narrow, without lines to mark the edge or divide east and west traffic. Some stretches could be quite lonely.

7

Near River Junction
Thursday, 10/29/1953

Leaves turning vibrant shades of orange and yellow shaded the road, making the approach to the river resemble a fall landscape painting. Rounding the curve at forty miles an hour, she noticed the wood-framed bridge tender's house and the beginning of the ornate railings of the Victory Bridge. It was very beautiful, but once she crossed, there would be no turning back.

The Apalachicola split the state in two. The railroad once dead-ended here; travelers had to ferry across. Such was the obstacle posed by the river. She slowed for a semi laboring to get going from a dead stop. The tender must have just lowered the drawbridge to let traffic through. He waved to her from his window. She looked ahead at the bridge, at the river below the bluffs. The long viaduct stretched out in front of her, on into the woods. It seemed narrower than it did the first time she had set eyes on it when she was a little girl, peering out over the front seat of Milo Harbert's '27 Packard. It was the first span built for automobiles to cross the river, opening up the state like never before, her father had said. She wondered what she was opening up for herself now. Those butterflies returned.

The truck was picking up speed, but she hesitated. *All right, I'll play this hand through.* She nudged the accelerator, following the truck at twenty-five miles an hour, the tires buzzing as they rolled across the concrete. She looked down at the shallow bronze water; downriver, in between the high banks, the famous bluffs, an old steamboat fought against the current, the slow-moving paddle wheeler soon to pass beneath the ornate arches of the bridge. She wondered about the days when such boats were as common as corn bread, plying the waters from Columbus to the coast, carrying cotton and probably hosting their share of card games in smoky saloons.

She steered close to the railing, allowing room for the Trailways Dixieland bus coming the other way. No materials were wasted in the bridge's construction; it seemed that it was built just wide enough for two Model Ts to pass each other, with mere inches between running boards and the Art Deco asterisk pattern of the balustrades.

The central time zone ended in the middle. It was now 2:05 p.m. She heard a steam whistle ahead; the L&N, American Coast Line, and Seaboard rail lines all converged in River Junction. Just another car-length to go.

The little sign said Gadsden County. She proceeded slowly. The concrete road was not wide; it had changed little since the late '20s—no center line, no fog lines to aid tired drivers in staying on the roadway. US 90, the main road across the state, remained a two-lane highway—a long, lonely two-lane highway.

With the town constable behind her, she sped up. The faint hum of the engine was drowned out completely by the whistle of the wind through the vent window and her racing thoughts. Her mind kept going back to what she had to do. It was over an hour to Tallahassee through forest and farmland and slowing down through towns and settlements like Quincy and Midway. It all passed in a blur. Her mind went back to what she had written in the beginning of her diary. She turned on the radio to drown out her thoughts, but these things had troubled her for too long.

She thought about the laundry business. Could she pull off this deal for herself and Mrs. Jamieson? She'd borrowed a lot of money; Maynard had trusted her. She didn't want to let him down. It made her think about the past, how she'd been run out of Tallahassee. She was a nobody then. She thought it was time she owned something there, had some say there. And it was time to make the truth known after all these years. She had to confront the people that killed Jamieson; that was the tricky part. It was time they pay something for what they did. She hoped to squeeze them a bit and get some money for the widow and her three girls.

She went alone; she didn't want to mix anyone up in this. The people she was dealing with liked to think of themselves as local mafia. They had money and connections, and they weren't above bending the rules if it meant making a buck; they were a far cry from the real syndicates in New York, Chicago, or Tampa, but still dangerous. She couldn't be sure if the local law could be trusted, so she brought Baby. Six years ago, these people threatened her, got rid of her. She was just a young girl.

Running away was easy. The going back was hard. Whatever happened, she'd be afraid no longer. She'd carry the guilt and the shame from crawling away on her belly no more. She'd stand up to them and stand with the decent people that might, someday, be strong enough, cognizant enough, to run out the rats that hid in their midst.

Rats, she thought. *Rats can be dangerous. Well, that is the chance I'll take.*

8

Along US 90
Thursday, 10/29/1953

One last river to cross. That dense covering of gray clouds finally decided to open up, tapping her windshield with heavy droplets as soon as the little two-lane bridge came into view. A truck sped toward her, shaking her car and fading away in the side mirror.

The Ochlockonee—the little coffee-colored river. The lazy water trickled down from Georgia, skirting around the capital city. It separated tobacco-growing Gadsden County from Leon County, home of the state capital, Jo Ellen's alma mater, and a few characters from her past. Jo Ellen reached the end of the bridge, noting the sad little bent-up sign that announced Leon County on the east bank. Up ahead, a much larger and nicer sign for the Tallahassee Motor Motel loomed over the road at the edge of the dark pinewoods. It was very rural this far from town; for the next three or four miles, she saw nothing but the dancing branches of pine trees in the rain.

The road rose steadily as she drove away from the river. Several minutes passed before she encountered traffic. She stopped, waiting for the wrecker to pull a smashed Cadillac from the road near the *Y* where State Highway 20 met US 90. A highway patrolman in a Stetson hat and a man in a brown suit helped push a banged-up Ford from the other lane. The road was concrete, narrow, with no lane markers, no shoulders, no traffic signals. The rain made it hard to see. The Pontiac FHP car had a flashing red light on its tall roof. She noticed a couple motels, little ones—the Talquin Inn inside the *Y*, the Gulf Wind Motel out her left window.

The country that rolled past her windows was quite hilly the closer to town she got, rather different than Fort Walton where everything lived at beach level. A prop plane flew low over the highway, on final for Dale Mabry airport—the old military airfield—that was just south of Highway 90. There wasn't much west of the college. The Capital Truck Center, a big truck stop, was near Dixie Drive. A couple rigs had pulled in to the pumps. Beyond that was the Gandy Motor Hotel, little cabins on a hill overlooking the highway. The Vacancy sign glowed red in dramatic contrast with the gray surroundings, everything—the pines, the City Limits sign—gray and dreary in the rain.

There was farmland along 90 next to the campus, cows grazing in the damp grass along the fence line. An imposing ten-story dormitory, West Hall, had been built in the open fields next to the highway, and a new student center had gone up at Woodward Avenue. *They must have raised tuition since the class of '47*, she thought. Farther ahead, she could see some of the old red-brick Gothic-style halls she'd lived in.

A row of weather-beaten houses closely spaced along the road marked the edge of French Town. US 90 was more like a side street than a highway, a narrow two-lane avenue into town. It rolled up and down over hills that gradually grew taller as she neared Monroe Street. Ahead, she caught her first glimpse of the larger buildings: the brick hotel with its name Floridan painted on the façade and a couple church steeples. The doors of little storefronts clung to the steep sidewalk as it sloped considerably up to Monroe, the threshold of each door a bit higher than the next. Just across the intersection on the left, there was a seven-story building going up, the Duval Hotel according to the sign; it had scaffolding around it, no windows yet. There were gas stations on three corners and a Cadillac showroom on the fourth, beside the Floridan. She pulled into the Standard Oil station at the southeast corner of Monroe and Tennessee, and a young man came over to fill the gas tank of the convertible. The kid was curious about the whistling coming from the tank.

"That's so you know when it's full," she told him. "See?" she said, looking back from her window, her gloved hand resting on the door. "The whistling has stopped. That lets you know to stop—"

"Oh!" he exclaimed, shutting off the pump just in time before gasoline splashed all over the car. "Say, that's pretty neat! I don't see too many Packards," he said, wiping the fender with his rag. He cleaned her windshield and checked the oil on the massive straight-eight. He closed the hood, the chromed swan ornament ready to feel the rush of air around its wings once again. She handed the kid a five dollar bill for the tank of gas and tip. He gave her a glass candy dish and told her there were matching cups if she came back again. She put it on the seat.

She drove around the corner, taking Calhoun down to the Hotel Cherokee. She checked in, and an old man carried her heavy suitcase to her room. Jo Ellen held on to her attaché. She didn't stay long before doubling back to Tennessee Street, turning behind the Greyhound station where Mrs. Jamieson lived. The rain had stopped; a bit of sunlight was coming through the gray clouds. Jo Ellen climbed the rickety staircase, walking past laundry hanging out on the balcony and a shiftless-looking man hanging out in front of his door. He looked Jo Ellen up and down as she passed. A honky-tonk Hank Snow tune blared from the open windows next door. Apartment 9 was last. She knocked. A little girl with pigtails appeared. She had a broom in her hands; she'd been cleaning. She looked at the well-dressed visitor curiously. "Do you remember me?" asked Jo Ellen, smiling.

The girl looked down at her feet bashfully. She shook her head. She looked up at the visitor, cocking her head, trying to remember. Her eyes lit up in recognition. She smiled, and without saying anything, she stepped toward Jo Ellen and hugged her.

"Oh, you *do* remember me?" she said, pleased. "You were only a baby when I saw you last."

"I seen your picture," said the little girl, Mrs. Jamieson's youngest.

32

"Oh, you have? You're so pretty," she said, stepping back and looking at the child's face.

"Hello," came a rather grown-up voice as an older girl with french-braided hair came out of the bedroom, a high stack of folded clothes in her arms. "You're Miss Jo Ellen," she said, putting them in the dresser that sat on one side of the tiny living room/kitchen/dining room. She extended her hand, very formally, to Jo Ellen.

"Yes, I am," said the visitor, taking the girl's hand and giving it a businesslike shake. "And you must be Elizabeth, but I'd hardly recognize you. You've grown into quite the young lady."

"I'm almost grown up. I'm in the fifth grade. We just got home from school. That's Christina. She's six."

"Yes, I see," she replied, turning back to Christina. "Well, you were small enough to sleep in that dresser drawer when I saw you last," she said, brushing the little girl's hair back, nodding toward the battered chest. The place had linoleum that was probably put there in the Harding administration; it certainly hadn't been updated since Jo Ellen found the apartment for Mrs. Jamieson. Despite their poverty, the place had been swept clean and the dishes washed, the girls were clean, and it was obvious someone had recently brushed or beat the cushions of the shabby davenport to get the dust from them. The eleven-year-old picked up a mop and went to work in front of the icebox.

"My mama's at work. We've been doin' our chores," said the oldest, the fourteen-year- old, coming out of the bedroom with a sweeper and a bandana around her head. "My job is to git the rug clean. That's the guest wing through there. Our butler has the day off," she said sarcastically, jerking the sweeper back and forth. Jo Ellen laughed, and it made the teenager laugh too.

"Oh, and it looks like you've done a good job," said Jo Ellen, peering into the bedroom and the throw rug covering the middle of the linoleum floor. She smiled and patted Sarah on the shoulder. She had a blue dress on, one probably made by Mrs. Jamieson; it had a lighter-colored patch in the front where it had been mended. All the girls had aprons that seemed to have been made from a tablecloth. All three resembled their daddy, Henson—auburn hair, blue eyes. Sarah was tall, like her father, and good-looking—a fact that must have added to Mom's worrying. The littlest scurried into the bedroom and began rustling through something.

"What are you *doin'*, Chris?" inquired big sister Sarah in a rather deep voice. The girl returned, smiling, holding something behind her back.

"Whadyagot?" demanded Sarah, trying to grab it. The agile child evaded her, stepping up to Jo Ellen and thrusting something toward her hand.

"This is your picture," she said softly.

33

"Why, yes, that was a few years ago," she said, looking at the small black-and-white snapshot of herself standing in front of her '38 Ford near the front steps of Leon High. She'd given the photo to Sarah. "That was when I was a teacher." She'd taught school for six months.

"We've all missed you. It's been really awful around here, Miss Jo Ellen," said Sarah, starting to shed tears.

"Well, it's gonna be all right, don't you worry none," said Jo Ellen, putting her arm around the teenager's shoulders, looking out at her sisters with their cleaning equipment. "Do you girls like helping your mother?"

"Yes, ma'am," replied the two youngest in unison. Jo Ellen looked around. There wasn't much—just a sink in the kitchen, an old card table they ate on, four chairs that didn't match. No refrigerator. They had a wooden icebox. A black-and-white picture of Henson and Clara, each with a small child in their arms, hung over the sofa, alongside one of Henson in a sort of quasi-uniform, khaki shirt with a sheriff's badge pinned on his chest. There was a single bare bulb hanging in the center of the room, no outlets; Jo Ellen saw an adapter they could twist into the light socket and plug in an old radio, which had a few missing knobs. The light off, it was a little dark in the room.

"We ain't got no 'tricity, the city done turned it off," said Elizabeth, noticing Jo Ellen look at the unlit bulb. They had the curtains, which appeared to be made from old bedsheets, pulled back so as to bring in as much light as possible.

"Do y'all have food in there?" asked Jo Ellen, her eyes glancing towards the icebox.

"No, ma'am. Mama hasn't any money for ice," said Christina.

"Do you want to come see your mama with me?" asked Jo Ellen.

"Can we ride in that?" asked the little girl, pointing to the shiny car below.

"Sure!" replied Jo Ellen. The girls put up their mops and brooms and aprons and followed Jo Ellen to the convertible. The girls smiled when they saw their faces in the paint and big mirrorlike hubcaps with cloisonné emblems. The two eldest got in back while Christina slid across to ride beside Jo Ellen.

"What happened to your lip?" asked the little girl.

Jo Ellen started the car and looked over from underneath her sunglasses, wondering how she'd answer that. *What do you say to a kid?*

The oldest intervened. "Mind your own business, Chris," she said, flicking the little girl on her shoulder.

"Hey!" cried the six-year-old, shoving her sister's hand away.

Jo Ellen backed away from the apartments, taking Adams past the Greyhound station and turning right on Tennessee. West four blocks, then a quick turn down Macomb, driving past the cemetery with its big trees and obelisks. The girls showed the way, down through the colored neighborhood—Lincoln Valley—and on to Sam Nowak's laundry.

Jo Ellen pulled up to a plain-looking building with a tin roof, a big fan turning in a vent above the open doorway. The place was near the brick clock tower that poked up through the trees, looming over the shabby low-roofed buildings in the area, the way Big Ben must stand out above the Thames. A wealthy eccentric built it, Jo Ellen recalled.

A freight train was rolling by, the roar of the diesels and the *click-clack* of the wheels drowning out the fan and everything else. Jo Ellen set the brake and opened her door.

"Well, I never saw such a purty car!" yelled Mrs. Jamieson, practically running outside to meet the visitor. "I wasn't sure who it was, but then I saw you through the winder of the car!" She stepped toward Jo Ellen and hugged her.

The locomotive had passed; just the *click-clack* of the freight cars remained. "Hello, Clara! My, how your girls have grown!"

"Yes, ma'am, they look like their daddy. I just can't believe you're here!"

Jo Ellen nodded, looking around. "Some things have changed—a lot's the same."

"My, how purty the suit you're wearin'. Would you look at that! I reckon you don't teach school no more?"

"No."

"Well, come on in, take a look at the place."

Jo Ellen followed with the girls in tow. It was a large room with open rafters, with several tables stacked with laundry and canvas laundry carts with squeaky wheels. Big washers were noisily spinning loads of dirty clothes and sheets. It was stuffy, despite the fans. A few barrels were placed strategically about the place to catch the rainwater from the leaky roof. It was still dripping in one or two places.

"You run all this?"

"We got a colored man that does pickup and deliveries, but I do all the washin' and foldin' and sometimes the girls hep, there's so much. Ol' Sam is so cheap, he don't want to pay no one nothin'."

35

A couple came in to drop off laundry. Mrs. Jamieson went to wait on them while Jo Ellen looked around. Clara wore a skirt, a denim jacket, and a scarf tied in her hair. She came back a moment later. "The chief of police is my landlord. He sends one of his officers to collect the rent on the first of the month. I'm afraid this time he's gonna tell me to pack up and go. When I told Sam about not having my rent money, he went crazy. I thought he was gonna hit me. He started yellin' about me botherin' him for money."

"It really is a shame. It looks like you do a good job here."

"Thank you. I even got to where I can fix the machines," said Mrs. Jamieson. "I got my tool bag in the office. Ain't much I can't fix with a wrench, screwdriver, and a swift kick to the sides of these old things!" Clara must have made some repairs today, thought Jo Ellen, noting a few smudges of dirt on her nose and cheeks. Clara had struggled; she was still pretty, but she was aging, with strands of gray appearing in her wavy red hair. Mrs. Jamieson noticed the younger woman's busted lip and bruise under her eye; she didn't say anything. She knew Jo Ellen had her share of trouble too.

There were some black ladies waiting to use a washer in the corner. "Sam got that automatic coin machine. It's got 'em lined up, waiting to use it." Jo Ellen looked out the side door and saw more ladies carrying baskets, ready to take their turn at the wash house. "Sam wants to sell this place and put a whole bunch of them coin-operated machines in a new building he's got."

Jo Ellen nodded.

"He could still have something here if he wanted it. I reckon ol' Sam made all his money, doesn't want to put none back," said Jamieson.

"Now, I've got some hagglin' to do, but I think maybe I can buy this place," said Jo Ellen.

"Oh, that would be so wonderful! Wouldn't it, girls?" she asked, hugging Elizabeth toward her. The youngest girls were smiling, playing. Sarah was sullen, looking through a magazine, ignoring the conversation. She caught Clara's eye; Jo Ellen could see the worry in the mother's face. She turned back to Jo Ellen. "It would be an answer to my prayers!"

"Well...I want to loan you this money," said Jo Ellen, pulling fifteen dollars from her purse. "You go pay the rent with this."

"But—"

"No, ma'am, you pay the rent money—down there at the police station or wherever you got to go—and you buy these girls some food. And you can pay me back when we get this business deal worked out."

Mrs. Jamieson hugged her neck, tears in her eyes. "Can you come with me to the police station?"

"I got to try to meet with Mr. Nowak. He said he couldn't see me until Friday, but I'm gonna find him today. I'll be back, then we can go to the police department," said Jo Ellen, walking back to the car.

"Be careful around him, Miss Jo Ellen. He gets madder'n a hornet, has these fits where he turns redder'n a fire truck over nothin' at all."

Jo Ellen nodded.

Mrs. Jamieson leaned in closer and whispered, "Miss Jo Ellen, I seen somethin' I shouldn't have—I seen it in his car, he said he'd break my neck if I told."

"What did you see?" asked Jo Ellen, raising an eyebrow.

"Whiskey—not moonshine, but still agin' the law 'round here. A whole case. He'd get in a lot of trouble if anyone knew. You be careful around him."

"I will." The girls wanted to know when she'd be back. "In an hour," she promised. She stepped outside to the deafening roar of another passing freight. She found a telephone booth at Mike's Texaco at Copeland and Tennessee. Sam didn't answer. She drove to his office. She crept along past her hotel, trying to read the address numbers. She found 407 Calhoun: the Mayo building. *So the address he gave me is a state office building.* She shook her head.

She parallel-parked in front. She looked up at the little high-rise; taller than anything else around it, it guarded the woods and open country to the east like a medieval tower. A block away, up Pensacola Street, was Culley's funeral home and ambulance service. She could see a fellow washing a hearse. *Stiffs. Gives me the heebie-jeebies*, she thought, shivering. She shook it off and went up the stairs to the main doors of the Art Deco structure. The entrance was ornate, the words *State Chemist* molded in the little frieze that capped the entryway. She asked the receptionist where she might find Sam Nowak. She was directed to the fourth floor, where she waited twenty-five minutes, passing the time with a year-old *Life* magazine. His secretary was certain he'd be back. He never showed.

Jo Ellen drove back to South Macomb and picked up the Jamiesons, running by the small police station on Adams Street. The curious building had once been a restaurant and the Union bus station; they found a plain-black two-door Chevy and a motorcycle parked along the street, and the chief was sitting inside, eating supper, no other cops in sight. The pale, gaunt-looking man took the money and went back to his chicken.

Jo Ellen dropped the family off behind the terminal. It was dark, just a bit of color left on the western horizon. It was noisy where the Jamiesons lived, the racket of the diesel buses idling close by. She drove back to the

37

Standard Oil dealer. She found the telephone number in the city directory the young man had inside the service station. She went outside to the booth, pulling the door closed behind her. She glanced at her watch. It was getting late. She wanted to call before supper. She dropped in a dime, the bell ringing once upon receipt of the coin. She spun the dial.

"Hello! Who is this?" demanded the impatient man on the other end of the line.

"Jo Ellen Harbert."

He was silent.

She was sure she heard the sound of a teakettle, a kitchen timer going off, so she knew the line wasn't dead. Perhaps she might have heard his beating heart. She smiled. "You didn't think you'd ever hear from me, did you?"

"Are you in town?"

Jo Ellen sensed the apprehension in his voice, like her call had pushed him off balance. *He hadn't counted on this. He hadn't planned on the fact that I might turn up one day. Good.*

"You're not *supposed* to be here," he insisted, sounding even more uneasy.

"Well, the Jamiesons are in trouble. I wanted to see if you'd do the right thing and set up an account for them."

"No! There's no need in that. I can't have anything to do with them."

"It's time you paid something for what you did."

"Oh, you don't think I have?"

"Don't tell me your conscience has bothered you, that you lost sleep at night. Save that for your girlfriends. You still have a few of those, don't ya?"

"Shhh. Not so damn loud."

"Look, I ain't got all night. How 'bout it?"

"It sounds like you're threatening me?"

"Yeah?"

"Yes, like you're trying to extort money."

"If I wanted to make a threat, you'd know it. I can still go to the attorney general."

"I don't think that'll get you anywhere."

"Then the *Times-Union*. They'd run the story. Don't think I won't do it."

"You better have something to back up those kinds of threats. Something more than your word. Remember how you had to leave town five years ago? We can dust off a few old memories."

"Oh? You'll find I'm not the shy twenty-two-year-old I was back then."

"Look, it's been five years. Why are you involved with this family again? Why can't this woman remarry, find someone to provide for her?"

"Maybe their ain't too many men that want a forty-year-old woman with three kids and no money."

He sighed. "Well, maybe I could spare a little. I want to see you though. I'm not writing a check nor setting up any accounts. I'll meet you somewhere."

"I'm not that stupid."

"That's the only way. In person."

"When?"

"How about tonight."

"No—I want daylight."

"All right, how about eleven o'clock tomorrow morning, out at the river house?"

"Still like to sleep in, eh?"

He laughed. "Never was an early riser."

"I'll call you. And I'll pick the place." She didn't trust him or his friends. "Will you have the money together?"

"Sure. Say five or six hundred."

"No, let's say fifteen hundred."

He sighed. "I can get it."

"No tricks."

"No tricks—just you and me."

Jo Ellen hung up. She waved good-bye to the attendant and got back in her car. She undressed in the comfortable room at the Cherokee. She made sure the door was locked and Baby was beside her. She doubled over the pillow under her arm and fell fast asleep.

XXXXX

"Wake up, Jo Ellen! Son of a bitch, this is no time to sleep!" he cried, shaking her by the arms. She was groggy, full of Cuban rum—they all were.

"I am 'wake!" she insisted, trying to stand up, hitting her head on the doorframe of the car. "Let go of me!" she cried, flopping back into the seat. She cussed, rubbing her forehead. She pulled herself up again, the task made difficult by the car listing awkwardly to one side. The driver leaned back in, shaking her once more, pulling her up by her arm. "I can do it, let go!" she demanded as he pulled her out.

"Come on!"

"All right, all right, I am!" she replied, grabbing a hold of the door, smacking his hand away. She tried to focus her eyes, clinging to the door to steady herself. They struck something. She heard the brakes squeal. They skidded toward the edge. *What had they hit?* She couldn't see a thing. It was dark as ten feet down, the road disappearing into the blackness, the dim headlights on the '38 Ford doing pitifully little to penetrate that utter darkness, even on their high setting. A flurry of moths and other insects swarmed in the brightest part of the light, two or three feet from the car. It was about the most isolated stretch of US 98 she could imagine, between the state capital and Carrabelle.

She slid along the front door of the car, the mashed front fender. The Ford was stuck, tires sunk in the soggy shoulder, one wheel nearly over the edge. She looked down at the shimmering water of the St. George Sound. Another two feet, and they'd have plunged down that bluff. *Damn, that was close!* She sobered up fast at that realization. She lost sight of the driver. She heard him puke in the tall weeds in front of the car.

She could hear their two friends doing something behind them, somewhere back along the road. She staggered toward their voices. Her balance poor, no line to mark where the pavement ended, she was cautious to avoid the edge. She could see them leaning over something in the middle of the road. She couldn't tell what it was. She took another step. "Oh god!" she exclaimed, seeing that they were looking at a man lying on the pavement. *That's what we hit*, she realized.

She returned to the car. The driver was pacing beside it; the others came back, shaking their heads. The driver began to panic. "Do you know what this means? My future, everything is ruined! I'll probably be jailed!" he cried. He took another drink from the bottle.

The oldest, a bit potbellied, tucked in his shirt where it had come loose. He lit a cigarette and tried to decide what they should do. The driver and the other young man paced frantically. The driver took another swig from the bottle.

"You need to lay off that stuff," Jo Ellen told him, grabbing his wrist.

He looked at her blankly and pulled away, raising the bottle to his lips once more. She shook her head in disgust. She retrieved her purse and stepped into the darkness, returning to the hurt man. She got blood on her summer dress from trying to listen for his heartbeat. She could barely hear it. His pulse was weak. "We have to get him to a doctor!" Jo Ellen hollered, trying to apply pressure to his head wound with her handkerchief.

"Damn it, if we do that, they'll say it was my fault, that I killed him!" the driver yelled, tossing the bottle in the grass.

"He may live!" insisted Jo Ellen.

"Not so loud, you two! Look here—I say we just drag him over there. It ain't our fault. No doctor could help him anyway," said the older fellow.

"We don't know that," she protested. "He's breathing!" she cried, listening to his chest. His khaki shirt was covered with blood.

The driver began sobbing loudly by the car.

"What the hell are you doing?" asked Jo Ellen as the other young fellow leaned over and got the injured man's wallet. He opened it and found a driver's license, reading the name aloud. "Henson Jamieson." He stepped back, feeling something under his feet. He picked up the piece of metal—a badge! "Say, this fella's the law!"

The driver took a step closer to examine the little star. "Oh, hell!" The driver returned to the car and sat on the running board, his head in his hands, sobbing.

Jo Ellen continued to try to help the lawman. A moment later, the driver returned, kneeling over the body.

"Whadya say we just drag him over there and get the hell outta here?" said the oldest.

Jo Ellen shivered at the chilling ease in which those words had been spoken.

The driver looked up at his friends. "Yeah, you're right," he said, sniffling. "It's the only way."

The two men—the driver and the potbelly—dragged the fellow into the ditch, near the spot his banged-up motorcycle had come to rest, the back fender and tire mangled where the Ford had clipped it. The driver continued to cry, saying something about his future in slurred, rambling,

41

shrill utterances. They walked back to the car, and the other young man wiped the blood from the fender of the Ford. "Let's go."

"This is wrong," Jo Ellen told them. "We can't just leave him, damn it! That man will die unless we help him."

"Yeah? Whadyagonna do about it?" said the oldest, shoving her.

"I'll call the sheriff!" she retorted, shoving him back.

"Yeah? Seein' how this is your car and all...." He let the sentence trail off. She knew what he meant.

The two men got the sobbing driver back in the car. The older fellow picked up the bottle and Jo Ellen's handkerchief. He shoved Jo Ellen in the backseat and slammed the door. He spun tires and sawed at the steering wheel until they were out of the soft dirt, leaving Jamieson to die.

The first driver sobbed and shivered, his face turned toward the window. The older man jabbed him in the ribs and glanced back at the other fellow. "Remember, none of us was down here. We left Carrabelle and, uh, got home last night. Yeah, last night, understand? We all keep our mouths shut. *You keep your mouth shut, Jo Ellen,*" he insisted, looking back at her in the rearview mirror, his words frigid, threatening, his large face and eyes ominous in the eerie reflection. His face seemed to float in the air and get closer and closer to her. His teeth were like that of a shark, sharp and numerous. He kept saying it over and over: "Keep your mouth shut! Keep your mouth shut!"

"No! No!" she shouted. "No!" Jo Ellen sat up with a start, her heart pounding. She was dreaming of it again. Those days—the summer of '47.

Jo Ellen went over to the window. She looked through the curtains, out over the dark street. She could still see the face of that dying man. She shivered, recalling how she felt when she heard that the sheriff down there in Franklin County—silver-haired, coach gun–wielding Pratt Harlowe—was looking for the hit-and-run driver. He found his young deputy the next morning lying in the ditch beside his banged-up Indian, right where they'd left him. Harlowe had few clues—only a set of tire tracks for a Ford V8. It could have been anyone. Everyone drove Fords.

Somehow, Harlowe closed in; Jo Ellen remembered the day he arrived at the high school and asked to speak with her. She didn't know how he found her. He reminded her a little of Harry Carey with the way he talked, friendly and easygoing, an unassuming old man, drawling like he stepped from the set of a Western. But he had intense, blue, searching eyes under that broad hat. She didn't reveal a thing, but she had the idea he knew she was hiding something. He told her he'd find out what happened; he was patient.

But his strength was failing. The Tallahassee doctor said it was cancer. He searched until time finally ran out. Forty years he'd worn a badge in the small county at Florida's big bend; when he was younger, he'd tracked killers in swamps and woods that seemed prehistoric, so remote were they from human civilization. He died in a hospital, looking at his nurses with those same searching eyes.

Jo Ellen was safe, but Mrs. Jamieson and her three small girls were left on their own, without their provider, without a means to survive. That $150 a month Henson brought home included what he made oystering and fishing and any odd jobs he could find to supplement the flat fee the county paid for each man he carried to the jailhouse, plus mileage. It wasn't much, but it kept them in a rented house and enough food to get by.

Jo Ellen befriended Clara Jamieson, helping her find work in the capital city. She tried to help the family when she could—that is until she herself was beaten down by the same people that covered up what happened to the young sheriff's deputy.

Her date last Saturday had been in the car that night. Harlowe never learned his identity or that of the two other men. If only she had slept through it! If there was a drink she could pour that would make her numb to these recollections, she'd order a whole case. She tried with vodka—it didn't work. Ol' Smirnoff brought his own trouble—and bad memories.

Tallahassee
Friday, 10/30/1953

It was the same Ford. It was the second time he drove past. The gears whined; she could hear him circling around. She closed the curtains and sat on the bed for a moment. She sighed. Perhaps, this entire thing was getting out of hand. She tied a scarf over her hair, put on her sunglasses, and walked down to the lobby. She saw the car come by once more, then turn north on Monroe and disappear.

She walked to her car, which she'd left near the old library on Park Avenue. She moved the Packard to the lot beside the Centel building across the street, backing in so her Okaloosa tag wouldn't be visible. She walked back to the hotel, making sure she wasn't followed. She ordered eggs from the restaurant, which were brought up to her room. She didn't want to take a chance being seen downstairs. She watched the clock. It was 9:30 a.m. when she picked up the telephone in her room. He didn't answer. She left a message for him to call her at the Floridan. He was just waking up, apparently. She walked over to the big hotel, the one she'd seen driving into town. It was pleasant in the lobby; it was quiet. The legislature wasn't in session. She waited about twenty-five minutes; she passed the time by reading the book her friend Sadie had given her. She heard the telephone ring, and presently, the clerk notified her she had a call.

"I can't believe you left a message like that," he chided her, speaking in a rather hushed tone.

"Never mind that. You have it?"

"I got cash money."

"Good. I'll meet you at Doak Campbell Stadium tomorrow."

"But there'll be fifteen thousand people there."

"I know."

"Where should I meet you over there?"

"Don't worry about that. I'll find you. Just be there, and leave your parlor tricks at home."

XXXXX

Jo Ellen sat at the counter at Bennett's drugstore, at the corner of College and Monroe, waiting for Nowak. She finished her milkshake. It was well after 7:00 p.m., and he
hadn't showed. She sighed, put money on the table, and went to see a movie at the State theater.

Doak Campbell Stadium
Saturday, 10/31/1953

Saturday shopping. Downtown department stores. Matinee at the Florida theater. Regular routines. Only today, people moved with a bit more urgency. A sense of anticipation was in the air. One could see its manifestations everywhere. A retired couple, in front of Grant's Furniture Store, cut their window shopping shorter than usual. A young man, a new radio from Sears in his arms, hastened his pace down the sidewalk to an old Ford. A teenage girl stopped to chat in front of Bennett's, but only for a minute. Today, the hometown football team would be taking the field.

At 12:45 p.m., Jo Ellen drove to the new stadium at the far end of Pensacola Street, west of town. She could see Doak Campbell a long ways off, the steel-framed bleachers and the big lights rising up from what had recently been farmland. The uncovered stands afforded fifteen thousand fans a place to cheer for their favorite team. She followed the steady stream of Ford and Chevrolet sedans trickling into the parking lot, filling the large open field around the stadium like droplets of rainwater filling a barrel. The sidewalk along Pensacola was busier than normal—smiling faces, women in sweaters and skirts, men in button-down shirts, all walking from the small houses and apartments that bordered the college.

She parked near the end of the north bleachers, where she could look across the end zone and the goal posts on the west side of the field. She could have driven onto the field if she had wanted; both ends were open. The facility more closely resembled a high school football field than a professional stadium. FSU had no stadium when she attended; the new football team played at Centennial Field, near the jail.

Cows grazed in the meadow behind her, curious about the sudden appearance of several thousand people that interrupted a quiet Saturday afternoon. It was still fairly quiet, an orderly flow of people into the bleachers, the tranquility punctuated only by the announcers testing their PA system or the sound of a freight train passing through on the Seaboard Line to the south.

She watched the people, scanning for her "friend." She used her small binoculars. She didn't see him. A few minutes passed before a big sedan caught her eye. She focused in. She had done some checking on that too, the make and color. It was *his* car all right. It was newer, more expensive than the Ford that pulled in immediately beside him, another row of cars filling up under the direction of a beer-bellied policeman. Her fellow seemed nervous, looking around.

She pulled Baby from her purse, working the slide to put a round in the chamber; she didn't make a habit of carrying the pistol with a bullet chambered. She made sure the safety was on and that she could work it readily with her gloves on, then put it away again.

I ain't gonna let Jo Ellen off too easy, he thought, lighting a cigarette as he walked toward the bleachers. *She seems pretty sure of herself—too sure. I might have to cough up a little dough, but I haven't entirely become a pushover for a dame.*

He looked around. He didn't know what kind of automobile she was driving—not yet. The place was full of cars and people walking in, plenty of attractive women with dark hair. He didn't see her anywhere.

He'd lost none of his youthful appearance and was attired in an expensive suit. He wore a scowl under his hat to go with the rest of the ensemble. He seemed impatient; certainly he disliked getting the business from a dame. Jo Ellen opened the door and got out.

She made her way into the stands, noting where he took his seat—near the end zone closest to her car. She climbed the stairs on the opposite side of the field near the press box, taking a seat high in the uncovered bleachers. She looked over at the fellow through her binoculars. He looked at his watch, fidgeted with his tie, huffed and puffed with annoyance, grunting at a mother and her kid that had to step over him to take their seats.

The colorful players took the field, the Seminoles in gold jerseys with garnet numbers, VMI Keydets in red and yellow, twenty-two cleated feet digging into damp, olive, drab grass. The Seminoles' kicker lined up at the twenty-five-yard line under a fifteen-yard penalty for delay of game. She saw the ball fly down the field, the new coach, Nugent, commanding the sidelines like a captain on the bridge of his ship, neatly attired in suit and striped tie.

She watched as her "friend" stepped over people one at a time, making his way past shoes and knees, tipping his hat and begging ladies' pardon, out to the aisle and down. She followed with her binoculars. The Keydets got a first down at the FSU forty-eight, the sound of the VMI band and the announcer's blaring speakers echoing about the stadium. She watched the fellow approach the state trooper standing on the sidelines. The two of them scanned the crowd, looking for someone—for Jo Ellen.

Her "friend" approached a tall fellow with short hair—probably a cop—and got him in on it. Jo Ellen cussed. The Seminoles' George Boyer made an interception at the forty-yard line, sending the fans to their feet, roaring with approval, unaware of the other drama unfolding in their midst. Jo Ellen watched as the "friend" showed something to the cops; it appeared to be a photograph. The men split up, obviously to look for her. Her heart beat faster. What had he told them? The crowd to its feet, she slipped down the steps, masking herself in the midst of all the excitement, ducking after a young fellow hawking food from a concessioners' tray that seemed

46

heavier than he was. She stayed behind him all the way down the steps, keeping a careful eye on the big fellow who was taking steps two at a time, ascending the stands on the far end of the press box.

She made her way down to the washrooms without being seen. She ducked in the ladies' room. A moment later, she peered outside. She could hear the crowds cheering and the band playing as Florida State scored the first touchdown of the day. No one was about; the bathrooms were on the back side of the stadium, hardly the place to be with all the excitement of the first quarter underway. She kept watching. She saw her "friend" approach, look around, then disappear into the men's room. She waited for him to come out. "I should have known you'd be a little unpredictable," she said, walking up behind him.

He shrugged his shoulders. He looked her up and down. A scowl formed on his face. "What are you doing in this town?" he growled.

"I *thought* you'd be ecstatic to see me."

"What the hell are you doing *back in this town*? You *know* you can't be here," he insisted.

"Well, I am."

"What do you want, huh?" he demanded, taking a step closer. "Come off this thing about the Jamiesons. Do you need money for yourself? What is it, booze? Gamblin'? Well, forget it!" His face was red, his eyes burning with displeasure.

"*I* don't need money. I'm quite all right, actually," she said, gesturing with her arms to call attention to her expensive mint-green Chanel. It was sleeveless with a low neckline, which she accented with a string of pearls. Her gesture wasn't really necessary; the garment was exquisite, and the woman filled it out perfectly.

He looked her over again, lustfully. She'd been to a beautician recently. Her hair was to the neck and stylish. She had Roger Vivier shoes on her feet. They were nicer than anything he'd bought his wife. She wasn't the unadorned girl from the Panhandle that had left a few years ago. "I see that."

"You see? Then you realize how you took everything from me. You left me with nothing. It's taken me a long time, but *I'm* all right."

"I don't want to hear it, Jo Ellen. What do you want from me? What will it take to get you to leave town? For good?"

"I made quite a bit of money in business. I'm not the poor lovesick twenty-two-year-old girl I was when you ran me out of town. You won't be able to push me around that easily now. I've enough money to have some say in this town."

"The hell you do!" he replied, lunging toward her.

She backed away, raising her purse. "Careful," she warned. "Baby might get a little noisy."

"Huh? You got a gun?" he asked, continuing to come toward her.

She let him see the business end of the barrel poke up from the purse. He stopped abruptly, like someone had nailed his shoes to the ground. He was wide-eyed, his tie disheveled, his elbows out like he was on the opposing team's fifteen-yard line, men coming at him from all directions, trying to figure out which way to go. His face turned red.

She laughed. "What were you going to do, slug me? Choke me like you used to?" He didn't answer. Through all his anger and fist-clenching, he looked scared. "Come at me again, and I'll put a hole in you, right in your cold, selfish heart." Baby fit rather well in her graceful hand, which was quite steady. She was surprising herself with how coolly she was handling this. She was becoming rather adept at pointing a gun—er, purse. VMI's band fired up on the other side of the stands. The music was an odd background to the conversation taking place below.

"Let's get away from here. Over by my car," he said.

"All right. But be careful," she warned. They walked over to his gray Lincoln, a rounded-off bar of soap with suicide doors at the back. She looked it over and eyed the surrounding cars warily. No one was about, practically everyone in town focused on the game. *This would be a perfect time for a burglar to strike*, Jo Ellen thought. She looked in his car a second time, just to be sure.

"I'm alone," he assured her. His anger and arrogance faded a bit. He sat on the bumper, leaning back against one of the sunken cow's-eye headlights.

"Say, what did you tell those cops?"

"Oh, I told 'em you was my wife, and I couldn't find ya. They're probably still looking for ya in those stands—never seen so many people here." He rubbed his face, looking down, trying to think of his next move. He looked up at her with a silly expression. "What is it that you want, Jo Ellen?"

"I told you."

"Aww, I don't buy it."

"It's the truth."

"You can't come here and make these kinds of *demands*."

"Either that, or I tell what I know."

"That's not—"

"That's not 'how things are done,' is that what you were going to say? That this is your town, your family is of a certain standing here? Well, I have the money to buy that standing too," she said, leaning against the fender of a Ford. Cheers echoed from the stadium as the Seminoles got another first down, the brass band loudly whipping up enthusiasm for the hometown warriors churning up the field.

"You don't tell me what to do, Jo Ellen! You don't tell me what to do!" he hissed, pounding his fists on his knees. He got up, pacing in front of the Lincoln, his face again bright red.

"Calm down, before you throw a rod."

"Shut up!" He sat down. He looked at her and cussed then rose angrily. She raised the purse, giving him a look as if to ask, "Really?" He got the point—*she* held the gun.

He calmed, but remained scarcely amenable to satisfying her demands. "I won't negotiate with you—I won't negotiate at the barrel of your little bordello pistol." He looked at her the way he used to: a look of icy contempt mixed with a menacing power bottled up inside him, like a tidal wave of ice water, ready to overflow its containment. It filled his eyes—eyes he focused on her intently. She'd experienced it before, that unstoppable wave. He poured some for effect, the words flowing out every bit as cold, as sinister as he intended, the chill in his voice coming straight from that storehouse inside him. "Woman, don't make threats. You be careful what you demand from me."

"That doesn't scare me the way it used to."

"This isn't the last word," he growled, storming around to the door of his car, yanking the handle violently.

Jo Ellen stepped back around the front of the Ford Mainline. "I sure hope we get to talk again. I enjoyed it!" she said as he flung the door shut. He heard her laughing as he started the car.

He sat for a moment then shut off the motor. He opened the door and got out. "Aww, I guess I'm a hothead. Doggone it, I know I'm no good."

"I thought you'd see reason."

"Aww, I was just blowin' my top a little. Didn't mean nothin' by it. But—no foolin'— will ya leave town again if I give ya some money for the Jamieson woman and her brats? Are ya on the level?"

"Sure, it's on the level. *I* ain't a liar."

"I guess I deserved that. Some things ain't worth fightin' about. You and me go back a long way." He began to grin, staring at her legs.

"Look all you want 'cause that's all you're gettin' to see."

"Aww, we used to have some good times in the old days, didn't we?" he said, his grin broadening to a confident smile.

"Yeah, in the *old* days."

He nodded and looked around the lot. There wasn't another person in sight. "I got the money right here," he said, reaching inside his suit coat. She brought the pocketbook back up.

"Slow," she cautioned.

"No tricks, this really is the dough," he said, pulling out the greenbacks. "Gee, you're careful."

She nodded, watching him.

"Say, can we make it twelve-fifty? I got that amount right here," he said, holding up the folded-in-half bills.

"Look, we said fifteen hundred."

"Okay, okay! Here you are. Here's the money!" He pulled out a couple extra C-notes and a Ben Franklin. "Doggone, if you ain't a tough businesswoman!"

"Lay it there on the fender," she said, backing up around the other side of the Ford.

He frowned. "Boy, you'd think I'm Al Capone or somethin'," he protested, dropping the money on the left fender. "There ya are. No hard feelings?"

She smiled. "No hard feelings." She reached over and picked up the money; his eyes widened as she leaned over the hood to get it.

"Gee, honey, you look swell. Now that you and me are back to bein' friendly, how about a kiss for old time's sake?"

"We ain't *that* friendly," she said, tucking the money in her purse. "You have other girls for that, I'm sure."

He grinned.

"Look, I'll see ya around."
"Sure. You take care, darlin'," he said, getting back in his car.

"Aren't you going to see the rest of the game?"

He just grinned.

She lost herself among the crowd spilling out at halftime. She went back to her seat high in the stands, waiting until he left; he sat in his car for fifteen minutes. She breathed a sigh of relief as she watched him pull away. She waited well into the third quarter with the Seminoles up by two touchdowns before slipping away, getting back in her Packard, not stopping for anything until she was back in town. She put that money in the Capital City Bank on Monroe. A man named Warren Conley was the manager over the savings accounts, and he set up a passbook account for Mrs. Jamieson. Jo Ellen thanked Conley and walked outside. She stuck the receipt in her purse and, not paying attention, walked toward her car. She looked up. "Aww, hell!" she muttered, recognizing the red Oldsmobile and the mug behind the wheel. She gave the driver a frown, her right hand on her hip.

"I just missed you, that's all," he said, a stupid grin on his face.

She stepped between the cars, up to the open window of "Old Friend." "I'm flattered, seeing how you saw me only a few days ago. You left me with something to remember you by," she said, taking off her sunglasses.

"Boy, you oughta put something on that!"

"Why don't you do me a favor and go get lost."

He lit a cigarette and exhaled smoke out the window. "You're real sure of yourself now, Jo Ellen, but you'll come back to me."

"Oh, I will, will I?"

"Yeah," he said, flicking the cigarette to the brick pavement. He backed out into Monroe Street. She watched him disappear up the street before she started her car and drove back to the Cherokee. She parked in the lot behind the Midyette-Moore "skyscraper" at College and Monroe, backing in. She slipped around the corner to the hotel. The lobby was empty. She nodded to the clerk—a man with a Clark Gable mustache reading the paper—as she walked past, taking the stairs up to the fourth floor. She

51

locked herself in the room, breathing a sigh of relief behind the heavy wooden door. She laughed. She pulled it off. It was sort of thrilling. But also kind of dumb. *Why the hell am I doing this?* She stepped out of her shoes and turned on the water for the tub. A hot bath, a cheap novel, and Baby—the gun on a towel on top of the toilet seat—were all that she needed at the moment.

Tallahassee
11:30 a.m.
Saturday, 10/31/1953

She got out of the tub and looked through the window. She didn't see any familiar Fords, Lincolns, or Oldsmobiles. Good. The clerk had some coffee sent up. A towel wrapped around her and a cup of coffee on the night table, she telephoned Nowak.

"Yeah?" came the rather curt greeting.

"Hello, Mr. Nowak, this is Jo Ellen Harbert," she said pleasantly, stirring the coffee.

"Uh-huh?"

"I've given considerable thought to it, and I'd like to make an offer on the laundry, but there are some questions I have. Well, I—"

"I won't be pressured like this," he said coldly.

"Oh no, Mr. Nowak, I don't mean to—"

"You call trying to pressure me," he said, his voice sounding more agitated. "You talk to my employees! You come here and bother my secretary, you follow me around! You—"

"Mr. Nowak, I—"

"Don't interrupt me! Don't interrupt me!" he yelled at her. "You're trying to pressure me! I won't be pressured by nobody!" He was practically screaming. He went from being calm to screaming in a span of seconds.

"Mr. Nowak, I—"

"You're lucky you're not a man!" he interrupted. "I'd tell you what I think of you! You're lucky you're not a man!" He was shouting.

She was trying to have a rational conversation, but it was proving impossible. "Mr. No—"

He cussed at her, refusing to let her speak.

"Now, look here, I drove a long way. I waited for over an hour last night. Do you want to sell or not?"

"I'll meet with you on Monday, same place, four p.m., and that's it!" he screamed, slamming down his receiver so hard she thought she could hear the bells ringing on her end.

Jo Ellen calmly replaced the handset on the cradle. "Well, Baby, looks like I may need you again," she said aloud, looking down at the shiny automatic at her thigh. "Happy Halloween." She jotted a few things in her notebook; she tried to write something every day. She tried to write something positive. She sat there, the end of the pen in her mouth, mulling over this entire situation. Monday, she'd wrap things up with Nowak and get the hell out of town.

She read her dime-store novel. The telephone rang, startling her. *Who in blazes could that be?* She'd given the number to no one. She picked it up. She recognized the voice. *Damn, someone must have followed me*, she thought. "So it's you. How'd you find my hotel?"

"This is a small town."

"Yeah, and I guess it gets smaller the less money you have."

"Never mind about that. I want to talk sense with you."

"What business is it of yours?"

"Anything that concerns *him*, concerns me," said the voice. "I want to meet you, face-to-face."

"Why?"

"I want to know, for sure, what your intentions are."

"I don't think so."

"Look, I'll throw in some money for Jamieson and her brood."

"Well, that's awfully generous of you."

"Shall I come to your hotel? To the restaurant perhaps?"

"No, I'm not sure I like that."

"Don't trust me, eh?"

"No."

"Smart girl. I always thought you was a smart girl."

"Smarter than I used to be."

"Why pick on him anyway? There were three of us in the car that night."

"He was driving."

54

"Maybe we can come up with something that will work for everybody concerned. There's a lot at stake here—big plans. Big rewards for people that help, a lot of trouble for people that get in the way."

"I won't meet with you. I don't care about any of that. I got my own business to attend to, then I intend to leave. Any objections?"

"No. Like I said, I always thought you was a smart girl." *Click.*

She looked out the window, her hands shaking as she pushed the curtains aside, just enough to see below. Her breaths were rapid and short. She was scared; there was no other word for it. *Shouldn't I pack up and leave town—right now?*

12

St. Vincent's Hospital
Jacksonville
6:00 p.m.
Saturday, 10/31/1953

Fulton couldn't recall when he had been so bored. He finished the novel. He stared at the bare plaster until he memorized every nail hole and chip in the paint. He counted the tiles on the floor. He closed his eyes. He woke up from his catnap to Marlene kissing his cheek.

"You might shave, you know," she told him, rough whiskers scratching her face.

"They won't let me up to do anything."

"I brought you some things that might make you more comfortable." She reached into her large purse. "I got you this radio," she said, lifting the heavy box. "Here's another novel—just finished this one."

"Thanks, darlin'."

"And this robe. It covers your backside," she stated, laughing.

"Very funny."

She laughed again. These contraband luxuries she'd smuggled in, past the watchful eyes of the nurses. "Honest, are ya feelin' better?"

He nodded. She sat on his bed. She held his hand, running her fingers softly, lovingly, over it, the powerful but gentle hand that she loved. One of the younger sisters—a middle-aged woman from Dresden—appeared in the doorway. She began to usher the young woman out and cast a disapproving look at the radio.

"Gotta go," said Marlene, leaning down to give him a smooch and darting away like a schoolgirl caught kissing a boy at recess. The nurses let Marlene see her man for a half hour at a time. They didn't want visitors taxing their patient's strength. They didn't know that Marlene was the best medicine that could be prescribed.

Marlene had opened the blinds that he might at least see the sky. The nurses promptly closed them as soon as they came in to check on their patient. Fulton breathed the remaining traces of Marlene's perfume and tried to nap again.

When the oldest nurse, Sereptha, wasn't looking, his partner, Spence, smuggled in a report for Fulton to look over—and a coffee—hiding both under his wool overcoat.

"What's doin', Spence?"

"Oh, I'm tryin' to make a pinch in this rape case we got. Happened down by the rail yards." Spence handed Fulton the report. He pulled a chair toward the bed, which he turned backward; he took off his fedora, uncovering his dark hair and Latin features, sitting astride the chair with his arms folded across its back. He watched Fulton's eyes scan the handwritten report. They talked it over, the younger man answering questions, filling in his partner on the details. Spence noticed how tired Fulton seemed, how glassy were his eyes, sensing his partner wasn't in as good of spirits as he let on. "We could sure use you on this one, buddy."

"Thanks," replied Fulton quietly, taking a sip of coffee—his hands shaky, Spence noticed. Spence tried not to let worry show on his face; he forced a half smile. "Say, how long you gonna be hooked up to all this? Can't be too much longer, huh?"

"Not much longer, maybe. If they can't find out what's the trouble, maybe they can take me over to McLanahan's Garage and put me on the big oscilloscope—fix me up for another three thousand miles."

Spence laughed. "Sure, you'll be all right."

The nuns discovered the unauthorized visitor and politely escorted the Cuban out of the room. The ECG continued its scroll. It was back to Marlene's detective novel and having his blood pressure and temperature taken every twenty minutes. Fulton had to laugh at some of these crime stories. Solving homicides was nothing like the stuff you read in books.

13

Tallahassee
5:30 p.m.
Monday, 11/2/1953

Nowak didn't show. She found his number in the directory and spoke to his wife. Mrs. Nowak seemed pleasant and took down the number for the Cherokee. Jo Ellen desperately wanted to conclude this business and get out of town.

She called the attorney general's office. Someone could speak with her, but not until morning. She circled the time in her appointment book—8:00 a.m. It wasn't long before she heard a knock at the door. She was reluctant to open it. There was no chain or a peephole. "Who's there?" she asked. No reply came. She thought she heard footsteps on the carpeted hall.

She got on her bare knees and peered beneath the door; she expected to see a man's shoes or a shadow at least. There were none. Nor did she hear any more footsteps. She kept her ear near the door. No sign of him. That didn't mean no one was lurking a few steps down the hall. She called the clerk. "I hate to be a bother," she said with a sigh, "but might I trouble you for another coffee?"

Another knock.

"I have your coffee, miss." She recognized the voice and opened the door. "Say, there's a package here," he told her. She could plainly see a box, wrapped with red paper, there at the man's feet. She took the thermos and thanked him and also accepted the box, which he picked up and handed to her.

"Did you see who brought this?"

"No, miss, I saw no one." He excused himself, and she locked the door.

What the hell could it be? She tore away the wrapping paper. It was a plain, ordinary box. It wasn't very heavy. She opened it, finding a bottle of whiskey. "Damn it!"

She lit a Chesterfield and took a few long drags, jabbing the stub into the ashtray nervously when she had smoked it up. She looked at her journal that was on the bed and the contract she had prepared for the laundry. She looked at the fancy bottle, the amber liquid that glowed, that danced in the sunlight pouring through the window. She looked away. She wished she could leave now, but she had to wait around another day to deal with Nowak. *Damn it, I just have to pull this off.*

14

*Tallahassee
7:00 p.m.
Monday, 11/2/1953*

The telephone was ringing. Her heart beat faster. She picked it up. Nowak. "I can meet tonight, eight thirty at Bennett's."

Jo Ellen looked at her watch. She was still wearing her suit, the Dior tailored number, a charcoal skirt, and jacket. "I can meet you right now, if you like."

"If you want my shop, eight thirty's the time."

"Okay. Perhaps we can meet at the lobby of the hotel. It'll be more comfortable." *And safer*, she thought.

He refused. One last check in the mirror. She looked professional—and feminine. She felt confident and sexy; those things were naturally intertwined, she thought. She was ready to hit a home run on this deal. She drove to the drugstore, but finding no parking space, she continued another block, squeezing the car in along the curb on Jefferson. She walked back up the sidewalk and found a booth.

He was late. He came in and sat opposite her, a wild look in his eyes. She offered a fair price, and he flew off the handle. He yelled at her and pounded his fists and made a scene. *That Sam Nowak was as crazy as all get-out!*

Her mission to save Mrs. Jamieson's job was more difficult than she thought. She'd try again tomorrow. She wasn't giving up. She parked by the hotel. The hands on the big clock next to the speedometer read 8:45 p.m. She sat in the car a moment, trying to relax. She loved the smell of the leather, the same as the chairs in her father's office when she was a girl. She was so happy the day she pulled up in front of the bank and took her father to lunch in the lovely car. Her father had certainly influenced her purchase. He brought home a Packard when she was little and kept it twenty years. "A banker mustn't give the impression of being too free with his money—people will get the impression he's being free with *their* money," he'd said. "One should make a good investment with an automobile. There's no need to change them like socks." Jo Ellen laughed, remembering that. She thought of driving someplace but changed her mind. It was doubtful anything was open. She got out of the car.

The gardens that ran down the middle of Park Avenue were shadowy and quiet. There was an old mansion with a columned veranda across Calhoun and more grand houses with porches and latticework and shade trees poking from the fog along the street, which seemed to go on endlessly. Not an automobile in sight. It was a lovely place, mysterious in the darkness and fog. *Too bad I won't be here long enough to enjoy it.*

59

She left the car, walking along the dark sidewalk and around the corner to the front doors of the hotel. Occupied by her thoughts, she was startled by the long piercing cry of a locomotive. It had to be the last steam engine on the Seaboard Line. She walked across the exquisite floor of the lobby, up to the desk, to the clerk busy with paperwork.

"Yes, ma'am?" he said, looking up. He was an affable gentleman, about forty-five. He looked even more like Gable when he grinned.

"Yes, I'd like to pay for another night."

"Surely, miss," he replied, retrieving his book, writing her name and other information, filling out a receipt for her check. He recalled her name, her hometown from memory.

"Are you from Fort Walton Beach originally, Ms. Harbert?"

"No, but I've lived there for some time. I rather like living there."

"Oh, yes, ma'am, it's a lovely town! But you do look familiar, miss."

"Well, I went to school here."

"Are you here on business then?"

"In a way."

"What sort of business are you in, if I may inquire?"

"You may," answered Jo Ellen politely, shutting her purse. "I own a company that does alterations and tailoring, mostly military uniforms."

"Gee, that's interesting. Well, here's your receipt. Have a good evening."

"Thank you kindly," she said, taking it and walking away.

She looked around the serene lobby. She listened to the sound of her footsteps, the click of good shoes on that polished floor; it was comforting. Likewise, the way her suit felt on her body—comforting. It reminded her of what she had now. And how little she had before. Her mind went back to the house in Duval County where she nearly lost her life—the thin walls, the stench, the sound of beatings and creaking floorboards, wearing the same cheap dress for three days at a time. She needed to remember.

She put on these clothes, and she was somebody, even in this town. It was like putting on a uniform. Businesswoman. Prosperous. Alone, out of "uniform," she remembered what it was like to have nothing, no dignity. She needed to remember. The clothes didn't make her confident; they just reflected how much stronger she was inside. She had lost everything, but she'd fought back. She, in fact, *owned* her own business. That meant so much to her—to *own* something. It might be mundane, but she was grateful for it. She had made it into something with her hands. No one would have her on the ropes again. She'd remember that.

It was 8:55 p.m. Up the stairs, down the dim corridor. She took off her hat, gloves, and jacket, revealing her sleeveless blouse. The room had grown stuffy; she opened the window, enjoying the cool air that poured in. She used the contract as a fan then dropped it on the bed. *Arguing with that man is impossible!* She had gotten a bit red-faced too. She didn't like to lose her temper—a lady didn't do that. *This trip is turning out to be an ordeal!* She laughed and shook her head. Running a business as a young single woman wasn't always easy. Almost made her want a drink. *No—It'll be five years next month.* She got a glass of water from the bathroom.

She started to sit down when unexpectedly, the phone rang. She lifted the large receiver in her delicate hands. "Yes," she said calmly. She recognized the voice. "Fine, we can talk in the lobby," she said. She marked "9:30 p.m." in her calendar. She didn't like this meeting at night. But if that—and the appointment she had in the morning—could help the Jamiesons, then the risk was worth it. She smiled, thinking she played this pretty well. Then she shivered at the thought of the danger of it all.

Perhaps she should pack up right now. She picked up her suitcase and began filling it. The last time she was in this town, she'd had to pack her scant belongings in paper bags from the Lovetts' store on Monroe, taking the bus back to Pensacola in a cotton dress she'd worn for three days. She stopped. She sat on the bed, holding her red notebook—small it was, but it contained what had become a ton weighing on her soul. There would be little to do but wait the next half hour. She crossed her slender legs and read Sadie's novel.

A quarter hour passed; she dressed, descending the three flights to the lobby. She said hello to the clerk, the *Democrat* again unfolded on the counter before him. She looked around the lobby. It was 9:30 p.m., and no one was there; she walked out to the sidewalk and down to her car. No one was about. She returned to her room. The telephone was ringing as she unlocked the door.

"So you're downstairs? Fine, I'll be down momentarily," she said, replacing the heavy receiver.

Jo Ellen retrieved her notebook. She made sure Baby was in his spot. She took the elevator to the ground floor. Again, no one was about. She looked outside and thought she recognized a car. She walked out to the sidewalk, wet from drizzling rain. She looked around the corner. She didn't see anything. She continued toward her car, the only car on the block. The window was open—just a crack—on the passenger side. She stepped closer. *Darn it!* Water was dripping inside.

She made sure no one was lurking around. She opened the door, settling into the luxurious seat. She pressed the window switch, the hydraulics raising the glass again. Still no one about. It was cold, so she slid behind the wheel and, with white gloves grasping her key, switched on the ignition and started the car. *Is he up to something?* She'd drive around the block and find out. She adjusted her hat—the fashionable wide-brimmed saucer—and released the brake. *This is certainly a strange way to meet— out in the rain, having to circle around. Why not just get it over with?* She pulled the lever down into first. *Oh, I'll just run around the block and call it a night*, she told herself, checking her mirror. *I'll be right back.*

Part II

15

Pensacola
10:50 p.m.
Monday, 11/2/1953

"Who in blazes could it be at this hour!" exclaimed the silver-haired man as he descended the dark staircase, summoned by the loud ringing in the hall. Milo Harbert had finished this morning's *Wall Street Journal* and had made it nearly to the top of the stairs before he heard that infernal telephone and had to turn around.

He looked at the old clock that hung over the landing. It was damn near 11:00 p.m.! No telephone upstairs, but the one in the hall wasn't terribly far away in any part of the house—a small bungalow, one of many built in East Hill in the twenties. Eleven chimes meant it was time for sleeping, not talking.

A frown on his face, his tie crooked, he turned the corner from the staircase and snatched the receiver from the cradle, the phone in a little alcove in the unlit corridor. "Yes, this is Milo Harbert. What can I do for you?" he asked impatiently.

On the other end was a man with a very rural accent. "This is Sheriff Frank Carter, over here in Tallahassee."

"Yes?" replied Harbert. He didn't know the sheriff in the capital, had no business with him, but in the banking business, it wasn't unusual to get calls from lawmen.

"I'm 'fraid I have somethin' difficult to tell you, sir. I don't like to do it over the phone, but I feel you should know now, that you be told direc'ly and not have it some other way."

"What is it? State your business, sir."

"Mr. Harbert, your daughter, Jo Ellen—"

"Yes?"

The sheriff paused for a few seconds.

"Sheriff?" asked the old man, thinking the line had gone dead.

"Sir, I'm real sorry. Your daughter has had an accident."

"Is she all right?"

"Sir... " said the sheriff, pausing to find the right words. "No, sir. She's dead."

Harbert didn't answer. He looked around the dark hallway and the adjoining unlit rooms, at the black-and-white pictures of his children. *No,* he said to himself. "No, sir," he heard himself saying aloud, forcefully, as if somehow he could forbid the occurrence of this event, that he could refuse what fate intended to impose upon him. He longed for this to be some crank calling from the state hospital. He'd had some of those calls at the bank and usually got a laugh out of it. No, the gravity in this man's voice meant it had to be true. He sounded completely sincere. "No, sir," he repeated.

"It was an accident. She had a bad car wreck—up near Lake Jackson. She died 'fore we could get her to the hospital." Carter pronounced it like "*hahs*-spittle." "I'm real sorry about this, sir," said Carter, clearing his throat. The sheriff had witnessed death before, had been at bedsides with dying folk near as often as some physicians, had tried to comfort his soldiers when they died in war, but no amount of practice made these calls any easier.

The old man didn't say anything.

"Please call upon me if there's anything you need. Jo Ellen is at Culley's Funeral Home. My number is 2-4740," he told him. "It's easy to remember. If there's anything you need, you just say so."

Harbert took down the number. He replaced the large black receiver. He heard the clock chime. He found himself reaching for a drink. He reached toward the spot in the pantry where he'd once kept a bottle behind the canisters of sugar and flour. But he'd thrown away the whiskey years ago. Instead, he made coffee and packed. He'd be the first man aboard the *Gulf Wind* when she slid to a stop in front of the old Louisville & Nashville station.

16

Pensacola
Tuesday, 11/3/1953

Harbert listened as the blast of her horn grew louder, watched as the bright headlight—at first a dot in the distance—grew larger and larger, shining down the track. What a beautiful sight, the platform lights illuminating the colorful train as she coasted in, the streamlined bull-nose engine and the booster behind it, lime green with a red stripe down their sides, the blue L & N cars, the polished stainless steel coaches of the Seaboard Line. He climbed the steps; the conductor wasted no time before they "dragged."

Ninety miles an hour. Harbert stared out his window, the black canvas rolling by, nearly the entire way to Crestview. The high hills slowed them some, but twin diesels in the lead engine and two more in the cabless "booster" behind it made easy work of the climb, up to the city on the high pine ridge.

Tired but unable to rest, he rose, walking past the peacefully sleeping passengers, to the front of the car, the door. He worked his way forward to the platform behind the booster car. There he stood, feeling the rushing wind, smelling the pinewoods. Somehow the brutal intensity of the engines as they worked to pull the *Gulf Wind* to the summit of the ridge was comforting. A brief pause at the old wooden depot, and off they were again, little towns and crossings appearing for an instant then fading from view amid the mournful cries of the engine's air horns.

At 4:30 a.m., when they stopped in River Junction, the conductor led Harbert forward to sit with the engineer. It was as if looking through the slanted windshield in the cab—straight ahead along the track—could get him to the capital faster through will alone. He had ridden the train for years and knew both the engineer and conductor. The two railroad men liked Harbert; he had done them a good turn or two. The old man was never talkative, but he was even more sullen than usual, looking out the windshield, thoughts swirling beneath his wide hat. They knew something was eating at him. He seemed anxious to get to the capital. The engineer shoved the throttle to its stop, letting the train nudge ninety-five on the downhill run between Quincy and Tallahassee.

XXXXX

It was raining, water dripping from the gutters of the platform when the diesel coasted to a stop in front of the passenger depot. The steps flopped down, and Harbert climbed down from the coach. The conductor leaned down and shook his friend's hand. "So long, Milo."

"So long." The conductor, raindrops dampening his navy blue uniform and flat-topped hat, disappeared into the car. A porter in the same uniform handed Harbert his suitcase, and the train prepared to get moving again. No other passengers got off.

A green-and-white Hudson sat, idling, on the other side of the platform, wipers flicking across the flat panes of glass, headlights illuminating the droplets of water cascading down in the shower. The car had a flashing red on the roof, a seven-pointed star on the door. Harbert—with his briefcase, his suitcase—walked toward it. A man—not very tall but stocky, wearing a dark-colored jacket and a big hat on his head—got out, examining his watch. "On time. They run a pretty doggone good railroad." He extended his hand. "Frank Carter. I'm real sorry about what happened," he said sincerely, looking the older man in the eyes. He helped Harbert put his suitcase in the backseat. He shoved the Hydra-Matic into reverse, tearing away from the depot, spinning around quickly in the middle of Railroad Avenue. It was still dark and no traffic at the intersection when Carter roared across Gaines, heading north on a side street.

"Have you any suspects?" asked the old man as they squealed around a corner.

"No, sir," replied Carter, surprised. "Every indication is that this was an accident."

"And the cause?" asked Harbert, bracing himself against the door as Carter took a quick left up Boulevard Street, splashing through a large puddle.

Carter turned onto Pensacola and let the car coast to a stop, the idling engine drowned out by the wipers whooshing across the split windshield. He looked ahead into the darkness silently. "This isn't pleasant. I was gonna wait 'til we got to the office or someplace we could talk."

"I'd prefer having the facts now."

"We found a whiskey bottle in the car. We smelled the *alkeyhaul*—"

"I cannot accept that."

Slowly, Carter drove past the Supreme Court, all the windows silvery, unlit. He turned toward the old man. "It may not make a lot a sense. Things like this don't make sense. But I don't think anyone coulda done this on purpose, Mr. Harbert."

"Did you find a journal with her things?"

"No, sir, but we ain't checked her *ho*-tel room. Our chief 'tective is standin' by for that. We figured you'd like to be there to collect Miss Jo Ellen's things."

"I would. My younger daughter is on her way from Baton Rouge. She's in school there." Carter let the car pick up speed, splashing through another puddle, past the north wing of the capitol.

Harbert didn't think the book would be in the room. There was something in Jo Ellen's past that scared her, that troubled her deeply. She never would speak of it, but he had figured that whatever it was, she had written about it in that book. She was very protective of it, either locked it up in her home or carried it with her in an attaché case. She had left this town suddenly five years ago, leaving her job, everything. Now she had met her death here. Someone, perhaps someone still roaming about the little capital city, was responsible.

Monroe Street was lined with stores and restaurants, all closed at this hour. Shadows fell across the sidewalks and the quiet streets. Even the capitol was unlit, the large helmet- like dome rising out of the shadows, towering high above the mysterious live oaks—the trees decorated with Spanish moss, wet and glistening like tinsel—that surrounded the old building. There was a big Sears store and office building across the street, the department store's large windows looking out over the main drag.

The sheriff gunned the motor, racing across. He spun the wheel over, the car bouncing over the dip in the pavement as he pulled up to Culley's front steps. The funeral home occupied a small blocklike building behind Sears and next to a small law office that overlooked the corner of Pensacola and Calhoun. The hearse faced out from an open bay on the side of the building. Carter let Harbert in the unlocked front door. The lights were off. Harbert lowered his head at the sight of the coffin in the front parlor. Carter removed his Stetson and bowed his head for a moment before excusing himself, his boots echoing on the wooden floors on his way out.

Carter roared away in the Hudson then returned with a tall man identified as an assistant state attorney. Taylor was his name. He was a cordial man, apparently a former policeman; Harbert gathered as much from Carter's comments, something to the effect that he "used to arrest 'em and forget it like the rest of the city boys—now he tries to *keep 'em* arrested." Apparently, Taylor had studied the law, hung out a shingle to take civil cases, and then took prosecutions on a part-time basis in front of the circuit judges, here in town or when court was held in Quincy or Crawfordville. He appeared to be in his early thirties and wore wire glasses with his short hair. Harbert shook his hand.

"Mr. Taylor's office is in the Midyette-Moor [he pronounced it *Muh-jet More*] building up the street," said Carter, taking off his hat and shaking drops of water from the sleeve of his jacket. It was not a uniform jacket and bore no insignia, and neither did the shirt he wore underneath. The sheriff's office had no uniforms. He made a pot of coffee while Harbert talked to the prosecutor in the back room. The place smelled of embalming fluid and roses. The sheriff had been present for more than a few autopsies in the room, before the new hospital was built. Carter poured three cups; he and the lawyer tried to answer the old man's questions.

Harbert tried to impress upon the men the strange circumstances of five years ago, that Jo Ellen was there on business, and it made no sense for her to be near the lake alone. Harbert pointed out that she could walk to half a dozen bars where she lived, that it made no sense for her to come to a town without so much as a package store and decide to get herself liquored up. The sheriff and the prosecutor listened politely, cups of black coffee above their laps. They meant well but were doing nothing. Despite the *facts*—they were facts in Harbert's view—both men thought the evidence pointed in one direction: an accident attributable to drunk-driving.

The men left and allowed Harbert time with his daughter. He knelt before the coffin, silently reading from the Psalms for he could think of no words to say to God at the moment, nothing that seemed to do justice to Jo Ellen. He allowed the casket to be opened long enough to place a white rose beside her face, then without saying anything, he closed the casket and walked out.

Harbert took a room at the Dixie Hotel, a block from Culley's and across the street from the capitol. The place looked like a large house, wood-framed and added on to more times than anyone could recall. A Standard Oil station had stood alongside for many years. The rooms were beginning to look rundown—the carpets, once bright-patterned rugs, were frayed and dull. The bed sagged on one side. Harbert got another room for his younger daughter, Janine, next door to his and down the hall from the bathroom.

The sheriff drove Harbert to the airport. They waited on the flight line while the National Airlines DC-3 chirped tires and taxied back to the little terminal. The twenty-one-year-old stepped through the door of the DC-3, looking for her father; she spotted him, quickly descending the portable steps to the ramp. Harbert couldn't help thinking that she looked so much like Jo Ellen, standing in the rain with a hat on over her eyes. The sheriff noticed the resemblance too. Not quite as tall, but the same dark hair, tall and slender figure, blue eyes.

She walked over to them. No longer a girl, a grown woman in a dangerous world. Harbert made sure she carried her pistol—he'd given her one that was identical to Jo Ellen's when she left to attend college. She carried it in her luggage without any difficulties. She hugged the old man. He held on to her—longer than he ever had before.

Harbert introduced the sheriff; the lawman drove them back to town in the patrol car. Jo Ellen's room over at the Cherokee was examined with Chief Detective Holland. No book. Harbert asked them if they found Jo Ellen's gun. "Ivory handle with her initials," he explained. "It had been a present to her, and she always carried it."

"That, we ain't found no place," Carter told him.

Tallahassee
Friday, 11/6/1953

Harbert looked down Pensacola Street as it plunged away toward a valley, the road and sidewalk steep enough to be worthy of San Francisco. Tallahassee's hills took on a symbolic nature for him. He'd spent the last four days climbing up and climbing down, trying to find answers.

She wasn't some hapless accident victim in the newspaper, a headline to sell a few rags, then quickly forgotten. Jo Ellen was his firstborn, his eldest daughter. He wouldn't allow her to be filed away. The tall banker raised such a fuss that the medical examiner decided he'd better hold an inquest. The family had one more meeting with the sheriff and the assistant state attorney. When Harbert made it known he wasn't satisfied, the men agreed they would let the coroner's jury decide.

He walked back to the funeral parlor. He sat with Jo Ellen by the coffin, watching the sky turn pink and purple with the sunrise through the window that overlooked Pensacola Street. Jo Ellen lay under a heavy varnished mahogany lid while the killer was free, living it up somewhere— somewhere out *there*. He looked out at the street, shivering at the thought of a killer walking those sidewalks, enjoying a cup of coffee, going to a movie. He shook it off, his eyes going back to the casket in front of him. He prayed that today the jury might provide justice for Jo Ellen—or at least take a step in that direction.

He looked at the coffin—the somber thing—and realized it would be the last item he'd ever purchase for her. He felt tears form in his eyes, and he fought them back, walking out into the cool air on the sidewalk along Pensacola. The door clicked shut behind him. Across the street, the clerk was opening up the ticket office for the Seaboard Line. Harbert raised his wide-brimmed fedora to his head. It was uphill to the corner and just another block to his destination.

He knew these policeman and lawyers needed a *motive*. But that motive was as elusive as Diogenes's honest man. Try as he might to shine a light into the dark recesses—the dim corner booths, the back offices, the shadowy tree-covered back roads where people met and whispered in this town, where people spoke around the truth in fragmented bits and pieces— no one wished to look at what the light may uncover. No one wished to come along into the shadows with him. Content were they to leave this matter be, to let stand the simplest, most convenient explanation.

He talked to many people, anyone he thought may have come into contact with his daughter. Even Nowak. The man called the police when Harbert tried to enter his laundry. He was reticent, rather odd in his effect, coming face-to-face with an inquisitive father. There were indeed fragments and pieces. He lacked the skill to shake them out.

Harbert could see that questions must be asked, but he was no detective. He was a banker, albeit one that could smell an embezzler a mile away. If anyone *took* so much as a $2 bill from the cashier's window at his bank, he *knew* it. This was no different—he *knew* someone *took* the young woman's life. But he knew not how to *prove* it. Perhaps the coroner's jury would make sure the right questions were asked.

He'd thus far found no one among the authorities willing to sustain the effort necessary to grab hold of those fragments, to sort through and make sense of all the pieces. Someone had to fit it all together—but whom?

He continued up the hill, underneath the slender palm trees planted in a row alongside the office building. He turned the corner, walking underneath the awning that shaded the display windows of the dinnerware store. Someone switched the lights on as he walked past the big display windows at Sears, passing the little Allstate car nosed in toward the curb. He stepped down onto the red pavement bricks as he crossed South Jefferson, to the front doors of the rather plain courthouse.

He stepped inside. The illumination provided by the Art Deco fixtures hanging from the high ceilings was dim. He passed the front staircase, looking at the little signs outside the doors as he walked along. Supervisor of Elections. Tax Assessor. Superintendent of Public Instruction. He saw signs for the clerk of court and the sheriff farther down at the end. It was a typical small-town courthouse. Every county department had their office along this hall. He could hear typing coming from one of the offices, but he was alone in the hall.

He turned to go up a second staircase, the old risers creaking under his feet. He found himself in front of a holding cell, a small barred cage. It was empty. He walked past offices that belonged to judges. The old floors were solid, the walls a foot thick. The courtroom—there was only one— overlooked North Jefferson Street through large windows behind the jury box. He opened the door that led into the front of the courtroom, by the jury box and the witness chair. He looked in; it looked as one would expect a courtroom to appear: dignified and formal, lofty ceiling, this room brightly lit with Art Deco fixtures suspended fifteen feet in the air.

The room was empty. He removed his hat and chose a seat in the gallery, midway back and in front of the overhanging balcony. Presently, a middle-aged man—bald and wearing suspenders—entered, placing a file on the judge's bench, then departed. Soon, another man, dark-haired and clothed in a flannel suit, peered in then left.

That man returned wearing a black robe. It was a quarter past eight before anything began to happen. Judge Vaughn was announced by a bailiff in a brown civilian suit, a small gold sheriff's badge pinned to his lapel. Vaughn took his seat behind the bench; he noted the lone member of the audience.

Silently, the father watched, amid all the empty seats, his icy, angry eyes focused ahead—eyes that Vaughn tried hard to avoid. The affable middle-

71

aged jurist attempted to make small talk with the father, but other than a terse "Good Morning, sir," he had gotten little response from the well-dressed gentleman from the Panhandle. Only the sound of the large ticking regulator behind the bench offered relief to the awkward silence in the courtroom. He tried to look past him, out the open back doors of the courtroom. The view was unobstructed out into the hall and through the large window; he could see across Monroe and down Jefferson to the fancy Martin building. He could see people walking up the steps, probably to take care of some automobile tag problem. The judge hoped they could afford the father his day in court and conclude this business in time for supper.

It was 8:30 a.m. Janine arrived with Jack, her brother, the pair folding down the tiny wooden seat bottoms to sit on either side of their father. Jack resembled the older man greatly—tall, same facial features. Hair parted, identically, on the left. Light blue eyes. Jack had driven up from Tampa.

At 8:45 a.m., the county judge empanelled the jury in the box to his right; the men found their seats, which appeared a bit more comfortable than those in the gallery. He greeted each man and explained, "We might be a little rusty. We do so few cases like this. But I am sure we will be able to conclude the inquest today." The jurors nodded. Vaughn admonished the men they must be "fair and impartial." "Fair and impartial," the judge kept repeating, asking each man if he was a resident of Leon County and if he could be "fair and impartial." Six of these fair and impartial men were chosen; these six sat on the coroner's jury, the others dismissed for the day.

"Ladies and gentleman of the jury, you have been summoned here to inquire into the death of Josephine Ellen Harbert." The jurors followed along, serious and attentive while the judge went over the preliminaries of how the inquest should proceed. He turned to the bailiff. "All right, let's go." Witnesses were ushered in and out, law officers and the ambulance driver. Vaughn wasted no time. He sipped his coffee and paid attention to every word. It took but a morning to hear the evidence. Sheriff Carter was the last witness in the morning. When he finished his testimony and left the courtroom, Vaughn looked at his watch. It was nearly noon. He leaned forward. "Dr. Elston, how much time will you need?"

"Half an hour," answered the doctor, an older man with a trim gray mustache and crotchety demeanor.

"Good. We'll resume at one fifteen," said Vaughn, snapping his watch shut, quickly disappearing from the courtroom.

At 1:13 p.m., by Harbert's watch, the jurors were led back in. At 1:18 p.m., Vaughn returned to the bench with another cup of coffee. Harbert sat through Dr. Elston's testimony, the summations, and watched the six men leave to discuss the evidence in the jury deliberation room, one of several little rooms that opened to the hallway outside the courtroom. Harbert

72

watched as the men retired and heard the heavy paneled door of the jury room shut with a loud click.

The clock showed 2:00 p.m. He listened to it ticking. He sat there, praying.

"Could be hours. Could be a few minutes," the clerk remarked.

Janine and Jack waited in the hall—anything to get out of the oppressive courtroom. Jack lit one cigarette after another. Harbert looked out into the hall and at the closed door of the deliberation room, through the heavy glass-paned doors at the back of the courtroom. The sun shined brightly through the big window on Monroe Street. It was in his eyes as he faced the hallway. He sat alone in the courtroom.

At 2:15 p.m., there was a knock. They had a verdict. Janine and Jack resumed their seats, flanking their father. He seemed strong; he seemed every bit the man that had fought in two World Wars and built a business. He was like granite. But how much longer could he remain so? The judge made his way back to the courthouse. The jurors filed back in at twenty-five past the hour. The decision was unanimous. The large electrician was apparently the foreman, a folded piece of paper he carried in his big right hand.

The judge came in a moment later and resumed the bench. "Gentlemen, have you reached a verdict?" The father looked over at the electrician, each member of the jury, and Vaughn. Harbert's expression was one of intense interest and, obviously, a little hope.

"Yessir," said the electrician, rising, the paper still in his hand. He was dressed in a poorly buttoned collar, his tie hanging midway of the belly of his clean navy blue shirt. His hands were rough, his knuckles scarred. He was from Miccosukee and named White.

The clerk collected the verdict form, a sheet of paper folded in three like a letter—like most warrants and summons. The judge picked up his glasses and read the form that was signed by each of the jurors. He nodded and passed it back to the clerk and on to the electrician.

"Mr. Foreman, would you please announce the verdict," ordered the judge.

Jo Ellen's father stared even more intently, trying to read the jurors to see which way they had decided. Jack and his sister looked at each other, puzzled.

The electrician stood, adjusting his reading glasses to read the printed and handwritten words on the form, holding the folded paper lengthwise, struggling with the unfamiliar language. "We, the jury....summoned to inquire into the death....of Josephine...Ellen... Harbert....find as follows..." He paused for a second, trying to find the right words.

Yes? thought her father, leaning forward.

73

The foreman looked over at him for a second. So did one or two other jurors, the store owner and the man that drove for the Velda Dairy. They could rule this was a homicide and a proper investigation would be done—but would they?

The foreman looked at the paper again then looked up, continuing. "We, the jury, bring in a verdict of—accidental death."

The father grimaced, his expression in one instant cycling through hurt, disappointment, rage, and sadness.

The electrician handed the form back to the clerk and sat down in his little swivel seat in the jury box.

The clerk passed the verdict form back to Vaughn. "All right, thank you, Mr. White. The cause of death was a motor vehicle crash, the manner of death was an accident," the court announced, nodding in approval. The case was simple enough, thought Vaughn. He'd listened to the facts. The clerk recorded the verdict in the docket in flowing, cursive script.

Vaughn removed his black-framed glasses and turned toward the jurors. "Gentlemen, we thank you for the time and attention you've given this matter. I dismiss you with the appreciation and thanks of this court."

The men rose quietly and filed out of the courtroom, having done their duty as good citizens. The bailiff shut the door. Janine and Jack stood, looking around the courtroom, as if they were looking for something that would make sense of it all. The father sat for a moment, almost paralyzed; then he rose, put on his hat, and left the room.

The clerk gathered the exhibits, switched off the lights, and carried the file away, taking it down to the dusty file vault in the basement.

The Harberts silently descended the staircase. Harbert, his hands trembling, reached for the door. He was surprised to hear music; the brassy ragtime piece jarred his ears as he stepped outside.

Jack and Janine walked down the street to get the young man's car. Harbert stood there, lost in thought, as the music played. He saw White drive up to the corner. The electrician held up his hand in acknowledgement then kept going. White and the other jurors could go back to their jobs, their families, their lives. The fall term of court could end, the case forgotten—by everyone. Almost everyone. A father would not have the luxury of forgetting.

The sheriff found Harbert standing on the sidewalk, staring north up Monroe Street. He didn't have to ask what the decision was. When Jack pulled to the curb, Carter opened the back door for the old man and said good-bye. The musicians in the little band shell behind the courthouse continued their practice, a strain of "Putting on the Ritz."

74

Jack took them to a place on South Monroe, the *Silver Slipper* or something. The elder Harbert paid little attention, hardly touched his food. Jack tried to entertain them with stories from his travels to all sorts of little towns in Korea and Japan when he was in the service. The old man just stared out the window. Something about the long shadows cast by the building and the telephone poles in the orange light of the setting sun seemed to amplify the melancholy he felt inside. The sun dipped below the trees, the chill in the air grazing his cheeks as he walked to Jack's car.

Jack drove to the depot. Janine, wearing a white coat given to her by Jo Ellen, hugged her father. The old man said not a word. He shook his son's hand and boarded the *Gulf Wind*. He sat staring into the darkness, the unilluminated fields and forests and hills and tiny towns of the Panhandle. The wheels clicked along the track. Other passengers napped or read quietly. He could do neither. He had yesterday's *Wall Street Journal*. All he could do was stare at it, unable to read a single word.

Echoing in his ears, he could hear every word of the trial. They kept playing, as if a record on a broken phonograph. The driver. The decedent. Ms. Harbert.

xxxxx

"Can you tell the jury if you were able to identify the driver?"

"Yessir, I identified her as Jo Ellen Harbert."

"And you were the first deputy at the scene?"

"Yessir."

Harbert could see the face of the young officer, Charlie Haywood, as plainly as if he were sitting in the opposite aisle of the coach.

"And how did you determine her identity?"

"I found her driver's license in her purse, sir. Twenty-eight-year-old Jo Ellen Harbert."

"Twenty-eight-year-old Jo Ellen Harbert."

A name and a number. The trial was so impersonal. But this was a person, my daughter.

One juror knew her name from college, he had told the judge.

"Yes, I knew of Ms. Harbert. Not to speak to, but I knew her name. It was the first year men could attend Florida State, and she was a senior. She was a shy girl with black hair."

75

She was also very beautiful, a girl people would have certainly remembered, Harbert had thought.

"I don't know what she did after college or where she went. Yes, I can be fair and impartial."

"What do you do for a living, sir?" asked the judge.

"I own a store on Tennessee Street."

"What's the name? Might as well get some free advertising," said the judge, smiling.

"It's Acme Indian Sales. We sell appliances and Indian motorcycles."

"Oh, yes. All right. Tallahassee is a small community. It is not surprising a juror should know the decedent," said the judge, looking at the jurors, Dr. Elston, and Mr. Harbert. The judge let the store owner stay on.

"I don't know what she did after college, or where she went."

She lived in a little town along the Choctawhatchee Bay, it turned out. Mr. Harbert had recommended that she move there.

"Fort Walton. There she'd made a new start, where she'd rebuilt her life," Janine had told the jury. She came over from LSU to testify. Yes, Jo Ellen had made a new start. And now, Harbert wondered if it was for nothing.

"Dark, lonely road." Everyone on the panel knew that stretch of US 27. "The road was slick from a steady rain that night," testified the young state trooper, Weiss.

The court took notice of the weather report from November 2, 1953: "Thunderstorms and heavy rain," read the judge.

"My sister was not familiar with the area," said Janine, the third witness. She held up well. The verdict had been a hard blow. She didn't say a lot at dinner; usually she talked all the time. It left Jack to make up for it, trying to cheer them up. Harbert wondered if he could endure this much longer. He had not been the same since his wife had died right after the war. And now this. He felt numb. He was good at smiling and speaking a pleasant word when required, but inside, he was broken.

The most difficult part was the summations. When the *facts* were supposedly "summarized" for the jury. Most telling of all—it was said—was "the decedent's" .220 percent blood-alcohol level. Dr. Elston's opinion of the test baffled Harbert. Jo Ellen didn't drink like that—not anymore—but he could see the jury gave the test a lot of weight. But many facts were left out.

"Fair and impartial." "Fair and impartial," said Vaughn. Fair and impartial to whom?

xxxxx

Harbert placed the paper on the seat beside him. It was no use. He reflected on the last three or four days. They seemed like weeks.

His mind began to replay that sequence too. Monday night, of course, he had received the telephone call like no other. He didn't even recall the last train ride. It seemed like he drove himself to the station, then the very next moment, Carter was driving him to Culley's.

It was early in the morning, and the place was closed. The ambulance driver—Linton—got there a moment later. It was he who led Harbert to Jo Ellen's body lying in the dark parlor. The driver switched on the light; it was Linton who had brought her from the accident scene to that very room, although Harbert did not know it then. He didn't know it was Linton who took care of his daughter's body, that it was he who subsequently took Jo Ellen to the hospital for autopsy. Neither man spoke at the time. Harbert saw the ambulance driver again when he testified.

"I work for Culley's funeral home on Pensacola Street," he'd said. He had no medical training, but he had driven the ambulance—a hearse really—for fifteen years and could see that Jo Ellen was dead and the injuries were consistent with a bad car wreck. "The hearse nearly got stuck—the ground was soft along the highway with the rain. The patrolman helped push. Then we brought Ms. Harbert's body to the funeral home."

The accident scene was a bit more than five miles outside the city limits. Harbert insisted on taking a cab there—alone. There wasn't much between Lakeshore Drive and the Tradewinds fish camp at the lake, just long-leaf pines along both sides of US 27, a band of blacktop just wide enough for two trucks to pass without their mirrors touching. The road ran along the shore of Lake Jackson. The cab driver was talkative. Harbert could remember every word of their conversation.

"This road'll take you to the state line if you keep going—through Havana. You ever been there, sir?"

Harbert shook his head, continuing to look out the window.

"That's where I'm from. My daddy and brothers grow *tuhbaccuh* up there. It's just two lanes through pines as far as a feller can see, all the way to GA. Good huntin' woods."

"Um-huh," Harbert grunted.

"You ever see pictures of Los Angeles, all them big roads?"

Harbert nodded.

77

"Ain't no big roads like that around here."

"I see."

"Wouldn't mind seein' it. Hollywood, the big city, the sign," said the driver, looking back in the mirror.

The old man was looking out; the old man didn't seem to hear him. After a moment, Harbert replied, "I've been to California. During the war. Never did see the Hollywood sign."

"Oh, it must be somethin'! Yessir!" said the driver, pleased to find conversation.

Harbert nodded but didn't say anything else.

About half a mile from the lake, on a curve in the road near the top of a ridge, they came to a point where Harbert could see a little valley, the wide break in the pines where the blue waters of Lake Jackson began. He asked the driver to stop. Harbert got out and stood for a moment. It was isolated but beautiful, marsh and shoreline unaltered since De Soto explored four centuries earlier. Jo Ellen never got to enjoy that view.

The driver got out, walking with the old man along the side of the road. He thought perhaps the old man was looking for something.

Harbert reckoned the slope to his left was where the car plunged off the road; it would have been gathering speed, the road noticeably downhill toward the lake.

The driver lit a cigarette, unsure why the old man wanted to come here. Then it dawned on him. "Sir, you knew the gal that went off the road?" he asked, a cigarette hanging from his lips.

"Yes, son. My daughter."

"I'm real sorry," said the driver, dropping the half-smoked Marlboro.

The old man stepped into the tall grass to look down at something. The driver moved closer and saw what it was: bits of shiny chrome conspicuous on the floor of saw palmetto and weeds. A door handle and a hubcap.

"I'm ready to go now."

These thoughts swirled in his head as the train crossed the trestle over Pensacola Bay and the air horns announced the *Gulf Wind's* arrival, the echo of the horns like mournful trumpets. *The decedent. Cause of death. Alcohol. The big Packard.* That was mentioned a few times. "The big Packard had to be lifted out of the woods with a crane when the rain cleared," said Deputy Haywood. Jo Ellen was proud of that car.

78

"Forty miles an hour. That's the best we could figure. Point two-two-zero. I am certain."

Harbert could not accept the verdict. The system had struck out; the truth was nowhere to be found in the mumbo jumbo machinations of the trial. It seemed that the process was designed to smooth things over rather than get at what really happened the last day of Jo Ellen's life—what happened to her and who might be involved.

For the six gentlemen, the verdict was easy. That .220 figure was decisive. No one gave the case much thought after the reading of the verdict. It wasn't the first wreck up there; it wouldn't be the last. It was a tragic loss of life, but simply an accident. The things the family tried to bring up seemed unimportant.

The train crossed the trestle over Seventeenth Avenue; the engine's air horns and the headlights of an automobile below jarred Harbert from his thoughts. They were home. Harbert wasn't alone. Jo Ellen's coffin rode among the baggage. At the depot, he phoned for an ambulance. The big car was allowed behind the large Italianate station, and he made sure the casket was lowered carefully from the train. Harbert insisted on riding with the coffin along the dark streets to see she was properly cared for.

They drove up Palafox Hill, parking in front of the massively built First Baptist Church, the sharply pitched roof soaring high above the sidewalk. The casket was carried up the steps and placed in front of the sanctuary. He removed his hat, making his way past row after row of empty pews. Flowers were arranged and candles lit. Jack and Janine came and sat with him. The church began to fill with people, many of whom had come from Fort Walton—folks who knew Jo Ellen there, did business with her, and thought highly of her. It seemed to Harbert that there was no greater compliment than that. A middle-aged woman was there with three girls; Jo Ellen had made an impression on many. Milo was proud of that. Yet none of these people—not the pastor, her siblings, not anyone—could bury Jo Ellen knowing the *truth* of what happened to her.

Jack and some of M. K. Harbert's friends from the bank were pallbearers. The crowd descended the front steps after them, the hearse leaving for the cemetery and the burial. The woman and her girls left quickly before the old man learned who they were. Harbert and his children were the last to leave. But soon it was time for the young people to go on; Jack and Janine said good-bye and were off to the train station in Jack's car. The elder Harbert stood over the fresh dirt that covered the coffin; it didn't seem natural for someone so alive, so young, to be buried beneath the soil. Perhaps in some way, you could rationalize and say that's simply the order of things: one living being dies, returns to the ground, and lovely flowers and trees grow from that ground. He'd lived an interesting life. Why wasn't it his funeral today instead of his child's? He realized he wouldn't make sense of it.

He wondered if he was just too bullheaded to admit his daughter had fallen off the wagon, got knee-walking tight, and piled up her car; perhaps he too ought to accept that it was simply a dreadful accident. He knew what they thought over in the capital. They felt sorry for him; they shook their heads for the grief that kept an old man from accepting the obvious facts. He knew that's what they felt—that he was an old man who couldn't accept the truth—and he didn't go back.

18

St. Vincent's Hospital
Jacksonville
Thursday, 11/26/1953

Thanksgiving. Fulton could go. He could wear clothes again. Canefield and
Spence had come for the occasion. Marlene helped him with his tie; the
chief handed him his pistol and badge. Fulton looked at the shiny silver
and the words inscribed, "Jacksonville, Fla., Police Dept.," trying not to get
choked up, happy he might still carry them. He thanked the doctor and the
rather strange Sister Sereptha, who had been his nurse.

The nun placed a small bottle of nitroglycerin pills in his shirt pocket and
patted him on the shoulder. An orderly wheeled him through the corridors
of the grand red-brick hospital to the elevator and down five stories,
everyone crowded in the old lift. Fulton insisted on walking the rest of the
way to the car. He stepped through the doors, enjoying the gentle breeze
from the river, the stroll along the little side street with its lovely palms and
gracious homes.

Spence opened the door of the '47 DeSoto. "Come back to work when you
feel like it, and take it easy," said Canefield, shaking Fulton's hand. "Make
sure he does, honey," he told Marlene.

"I will."

"See ya later, fellas," said Fulton. Marlene started the car.

"Oh, almost forgot," said Canefield, leaning in the window with a pack of
cigarettes. "In case you run out."

"Thanks, chief."

Marlene turned down the side street, toward the river, so Fulton could
have a look at Memorial Park.

"A lot of people today."

She nodded. He kissed her on the cheek. She shook her head and turned,
looking into his eyes, kissing him properly. The hospital disappeared in
their rearview mirror—like magic.

19

Tallahassee
8:05 p.m.
Tuesday, 6/21/1955

The *Gulf Wind* coasted to the station, the windows fogged with condensation from the air-conditioning in the pitch-black, sultry night. Hal Martin sat alone at the back of the coach, looking through the wet glass. He silently lit a Camel cigarette. Two businessmen in the row ahead of him had been talking the entire way, ever since the fellow with the crew cut boarded the *Silver Meteor* in Waldo. Somewhere in between switching trains in Jacksonville and the last stop in Madison, the two of them had decided Stevenson would be a shoo-in for president next year and the Yankees would have the series in the bag over Brooklyn come October. They showed no signs of letting up. As the brakes squealed on the last twenty yards to the depot, the topic turned to television. "You don't say! Tallahassee's getting a station!" exclaimed Crew Cut.

"Yeah. My brother-in-law is in the television business. He's produced a couple shows in Tampa."

"Yeah?" said Crew Cut, excited about the television business.

"Sure. He says they'll be on the air in September."

The two men continued their conversation to the door of the car, carrying their suit jackets, hatless and modern, like the fellows in California. Martin followed, his broad fedora covering his full rather dark head of hair, his leather case in hand. The older man wore black-rimmed glasses and a tan suit. Even in the suffocating heat of late June, he didn't take off his coat. Martin was a descendant of Florida pioneers, well-accustomed to the summer temperatures and putting little stock in air-conditioning. To him, it was an interesting curiosity. A battered Ford was parked near the platform; the green and black taxi had met the train in search of fares. The businessmen, still chatting, grabbed the cab. Martin collected his bag and waited for the next one underneath a burned-out light.

It was a long ride from Ocala. Governor Collins had telephoned and asked him to make the trip as soon as he could. It was lonely at the depot; a couple people got on the train, the conductor scurried about, but otherwise, no one was around. Railroad Avenue was dark, devoid of traffic. Martin put a dime in the public phone and began dialing the number he'd seen on the door of the taxi. He paused, surprised by a black Cadillac approaching. A state trooper got out of the shiny car and walked toward him, swaggering a bit with the Colt at his hip and a new Stetson on his head.

Martin hung up.

"Sheriff Martin, howdy!" exclaimed the friendly trooper. He extended his hand like he'd found a lost friend.

Martin shook his hand, a little curious. He didn't know someone would be meeting him—in a Cadillac, no less.

"Oh, I was sent to meet you, sir. The governor asked me to drive you up to the Grove."

"That's mighty nice of him. Thank you, son."

"Yessir," said the trooper, taking Martin's suitcase and tugging the back door open. He pulled away from the station, heading through town while chatting about baseball and his work on the road, his kids. In just a few minutes, the driver maneuvered the big car into the driveway, up to the front steps of the Collins's home on Adams Street. "Well, here we are, sir," said the Trooper, getting out to open the door again. "The governor said just come right up to the house. He's expecting you."

Martin said good-bye. The Cadillac pulled away, leaving him alone before the mansion; he looked up at it, the veranda and the big columns. Slowly, he went up the steps, facing a very elaborate door.

He wondered if the efforts of the past six months would be in vain. Florida was being run like sixty-seven little countries. Law enforcement agencies didn't communicate. What sporadic coordination there was depended on personal relationships between sheriffs. A man picked up in one county could be released before word got around that he was wanted someplace else. There were no resources to assist with serious cases and organized crime. They needed something like a Scotland Yard or FBI. He'd spent countless hours on the phone with the governor and with state representatives, to no avail. So far, the legislature had done nothing but slam doors in his face.

He knocked. The door was opened by LeRoy Collins himself. "Hal! I'm sure glad to see you," said the governor, still a rather young man with just a bit of gray at his temples. He greeted the sheriff warmly, shaking his hand and leading the fifty-nine-year-old back to the richly furnished parlor. There he offered Martin a comfortable chair and coffee.

"The legislature is gonna pass the bill tomorrow afternoon," said Collins, stirring his china cup.

Martin was surprised. "Oh?"

"I wanted you to be in town. I think that's what did it," said Collins, hitting his newspapers—he'd laid several of them out on the table—with the back of his hand.

Martin looked at the collection of headlines. "Judge Chillingsworth Missing." "Judge Chillingsworth and Wife Murdered." "Mobster Charlie

83

Wall Slain." "Bolita King Dead." The papers referred to the murder of Judge Curtis Chillingsworth and his wife in Manalapan, near Palm Beach, just weeks before. The others referenced the day crime boss Charlie Wall got it in his bedroom in Tampa in April.

"They're finally gonna do something," said Collins, referring to the legislature. "The bill will authorize a small organization of men that can be called upon to assist with major crimes. It'll be called the Sheriff's Bureau."

The significance was in no way lost on Martin. He smiled. "We've never had anything like that, not in the one hundred and ten years we've been a state."

"It's a small start, but a start nonetheless, and I sure hope it'll give us a fighting chance to get the ball back and pick up some yards. The other sheriffs support you as director."

Martin, a man of few words, nodded. His smile faded; he knew the assignment would scarcely be easy. He sipped his coffee and set the cup down.

"Pick out some men. FBI men, murder cops."

Martin nodded. "I know two that are interested."

"Oh?"

"Jack Culver, from Deland. There's a fella named Berwin Williams, from Marianna. Both had FBI training. And there's one fella that I still need to talk to, True Fulton, with the city department in Jacksonville."

"By the way, the legislature isn't giving us any money. More cream?"

Martin nodded. "I...kinda figured that." He paused for a moment while Collins poured from the little china serving set. Martin stirred his coffee.

"So what do you think?" Collins inquired, smiling broadly.

"I think this thing will take off once the sheriffs see it will help them, once the legislature sees the results, when we work together and solve cases instead of letting 'em go cold."

Collins nodded.

"It'll be a challenge trying to keep up with it. We'll be spread mighty thin."

"Covering the whole state? That's a lot of territory."

"People talk about Texas being big! I tell people we stretch eight hundred miles from Pensacola to Key West, and they don't hardly believe it. We're a

84

big ol' state with, up til' now, no law enforcement agency to coordinate anything in a serious case going 'cross county lines."

"Yes, sir."

"The hardest part of the job will be tryin' to stretch what resources we get, as far as she'll go. And we haven't even begun to tackle some of the other problems, training and so forth."

"The battle will be in the legislature. We'll keep after them. I've thought about equipment. We'll scrounge up a few things, anything lying 'round loose. I'll find you an office, even if I have to rent something myself," said Collins, chuckling.

Martin knew the governor wasn't really joking.

"More coffee, Sheriff?" asked Collins, picking up the fancy pot.

"Yessir, it's good coffee—strong."

Part III

Pensacola
Saturday, 10/6/1956

Harbert lit a cigarette and examined the envelope he found in the mailbox. It had been taped up thoroughly. He opened his pocketknife and cut the package open. *What the devil could it be?* thought the old man, looking down inside.

His cigarette fell from his mouth. Black-and-white snapshots of Jo Ellen. They'd been torn in half to block out whomever else had been in the picture. She looked as she did when she graduated college, about twenty-two. She was dressed plainly and for the summer, sunglasses and a scarf. Two of them appeared to show the edge of a man's arm and sport coat, but no other distinguishing characteristics.

Harbert had his secretary make photostats of the fragments. He composed letters to Sheriff Carter and to the state attorney in Tallahassee, enclosing the copies. Two weeks went by, and he received his reply: form letters. The case would not be reopened.

Harbert took the letters to Janine's apartment. She read them. "They're never going to do anything, Dad. They simply don't believe there's anything amiss, or they don't care if there is."

"I think the only way is to return to that city and make enough of a ruckus that something must be done."

"Are you sure, Dad?"

"Yes, I am."

"Well, I'll go with you."

Harbert nodded, contemplating what might face them. "Perhaps we'll find someone unafraid of the search—and the answers that he might discover."

Pensacola
Monday, 10/22/1956

At 11:58 p.m., they boarded the *Gulf Wind* bound for the state capital, 196 miles into the darkness. Harbert sat by the window, falling asleep instantly. Janine suggested paying for the Pullman car, but the old man wouldn't hear of such an expenditure. So she sat next to him in the upright seat, closing her eyes and trying to get some sleep.

By the time they stopped for the L&N coaches to be switched where the *Gulf Wind* joined the Seaboard Line at River Junction, the old man was awake and restless. He went forward to look out from the open platform at the front of the car. He did so despite the frigid wind and raindrops on his cheeks.

It was a unique perspective coming into a city on the tracks; in some places, the train came right up to Main Street, the depot a proud building downtown. In others, the tracks ambled in the back way. For the capital, the "welcome" to the city offered a view of woods, low warehouses with tin roofs, that little terminal on the outskirts of town. The place had changed little since his father had brought him there as a boy.

He watched the "Tallahassee" sign appear in the headlight of the train as she slowed down to little more than a brisk walk. Even without the sign, there was no mistaking the small two-story brick station. It was about the size of a large house, much smaller than Pensacola's L&N. It was used for freight now. The wheels squealed as the engine rolled past the old building, pulling the coaches to the "newer" (circa 1905) terminal, a one-story affair across Railroad Avenue.

The train blocked the road momentarily, a few parcels were flopped to the platform, a few passengers were exchanged, and the big locomotive idled and made ready to drag again. Harbert was first to step from the train, his hair completely silver now. He was dressed in a wool coat over a dark brown suit. It was cold; he could see his breath. He helped Janine down when she appeared. She—twenty-four now—in her fashionable wide-brimmed saucer hat, cashmere coat, and white gloves looked glamorous in front of the shiny, stainless steel train cars. The sky was dark, just a dim hint of dawn on the eastern horizon.

A colored porter assisted their departure. A taxi idled beside Railroad Avenue. Janine unfurled her umbrella, and they approached the battered green and black car, a bullet-nose '49 Ford.

"Is there another hotel near the courthouse besides the Cherokee?" Harbert asked. They'd settled in Pensacola after the war, after Mr. Harbert had been stationed at the naval air station. They hadn't much occasion to come to the capital and little knowledge of its accommodations. Harbert had stayed in the old Dixie Hotel anytime he journeyed to the capital but heard it had been torn down. And Janine didn't wish to stay at the Cherokee.

"Yessir, the Floridan, just up the street," answered the driver, a fellow with a scarred face named Hiram Darley.

"That will do. Let's go there." It would do if it was close; they came to neither enjoy the sights nor to relax.

"Sure, mister, you bet," said Darley, stepping from the car. "Let me help ya with that, miss," he said, taking the suitcase. He wore the typical cabdriver "uniform": eight-point cap, windbreaker, tie. He pulled the squeaky door open for the sophisticated woman. He collected Mr. Harbert's suitcase in his other hand. "The *Floor-i-duhn* is a real nice place," he told them.

The Harberts settled in the back of the cab, which smelled of sweat and was cold—no heater in the "bean counter's special." Darley loaded the trunk, pulling the lid down by the sign advertising the "Air-Conditioned M&N Restaurant" that was bolted to the hack. It took a couple of slams to get it closed. A colored gentleman drove up in a newer Plymouth, picking up a fare and her hatboxes, dashing away before either received too much of a dampening. Darley—a white man of about forty, his jacket and cap wet from the rain—slid behind the wheel. He shoved the gear lever into first with a crunch, and they were away, moving up the little street. The noise of the diesel locomotive and the busy scene of the station faded; ahead was Gaines Street, shrouded in the early morning quiet, the darkness that yielded little to the headlights of the Ford, whose scant light was further diffused by the continuing drizzle.

The car screeched to a halt at the corner where there were little warehouses poorly lit. The driver wound the wheel, turning on Gaines. The sedan rattled terribly as it crossed over a portion of the road where the old bricks showed through. They passed the unusual clock tower, poking from the shadows of the oak trees. Burnett Park where the lawn and the oaks seemed shadowy, dark.

"Ya'll vis'tin'?" asked Darley, shifting gears. The scar ran up to his hairline, Janine could see, when light from an isolated streetlight illuminated the rearview mirror. He'd got that scar at Leyte. "We're here on business...long overdue business," said the older man, sitting uncomfortably on the seat's sagging spring.

"Okay. Well, welcome to Tallahassee. We're glad to have ya." The tires hissed through the water on the smoother sections of blacktop, past a handful of small businesses, little storefronts whose glass windows shimmered in the rain from the headlights. They saw a Texaco sign light up as the filling station opened for business, the red star shining brightly on an otherwise dark street. Two pumps. Twenty-two-cent regular. They kept going. Little houses with porches lined both sides of the street.

A driver leaned into the back of Velda Dairy truck, preparing to deliver the morning's milk. Across the street, a boy on a bicycle reached his small arm into a bundle full of fresh printings of the *Democrat* and flung one onto the porch. The rain was starting to come down harder, and the boy pulled his cap down to shield his face from the spray.

"Y'all keer fur a piece of gum?" asked Darley, looking back in the rearview. Janine nodded. The man handed the package over his shoulder. The young lady took a piece, her faint smile expressing a silent "Thank you." She chewed the gum, clutching her purse in her hands, shivering. Her father had his warm wool coat on, his long legs folded in the inelegant backseat. The cab kept going; a flash of lightning would occasionally illuminate a building or a little house, the rumble muffled by the rain beating on the roof of the car. The vacuum-driven wipers flung back and forth furiously on the high setting. *Click-click-click-click-click.*

Darley tugged the gear lever down into first. The car moaned in protest as he wrangled the steering wheel and squeezed the accelerator, rounding the corner onto Monroe, the car rattling as it crossed onto the brick pavement. The wipers slowed, the rattling drowned out, as the engine labored to pull them up to the main part of town.

They recognized the Capitol, of course. No building stood more prominently. But it offered no solution today. They'd written their representative; he sent them a nice form letter. The Dixie was gone, as was the little gas station at Lafayette Street; an open clearing remained to define the spot where they'd stood for so long.

They passed the courthouse, the lights off, the building dark and gray. The driver kept going, making an illegal U-turn to pull to the curb beneath the awning of the large red-brick building—the Hotel Floridan. The driver snatched a squeaky door open for his passengers.

"We have business at the courthouse. I expect the sheriff's office would be open at eight o'clock?" asked the old man.

"Yessir."

"Thanks," said Harbert, handing two dollar coins to the driver.

"Thank ya, sir!"

As the Harberts disappeared into the lobby, the driver helped the porter get the bags and load them on a cart. The bellhop, in a gray Confederate-looking uniform, brought them to their rooms on the fourth floor, which looked out toward the Gothic bell tower and stained glass of the old Episcopal church, its lovely garden showered by the rain. The rooms were plush, freshly renovated. Janine's had a good view of both Monroe and Tennessee Streets, the two main roads through town.

"Is everything to your liking?"

"Yes, it's very nice," said Harbert, handing the man a half dollar.

Harbert walked next door to his daughter's room. He sat on the bed. Alone, father and daughter faced each other, not knowing what the day would hold for them. Answers, perhaps? Or, quite realistically, more disappointment. Thunder crackled outside.

"Perhaps we should have breakfast, first," he said. It was only half past seven.

They rode the elevator down to the lobby. It was empty, the legislature out of session until April. When the politicians were in town, the Cypress Lounge and the Grille were the hosts of more deal making than the Capitol itself. The dining hall would be full of men in gray suits, smoking and finagling. Today the Harberts had the room to themselves.

Janine removed her gloves, revealing an engagement ring, a bright cluster of five diamonds. They ate silently. The older gentlemen barely touched his bacon and eggs and buttermilk biscuits; he did finish his coffee. The young woman finished her toast but left the steaming cup on the table half-empty. The sunlight—what little there was of it—began streaming in the fan windows with their rounded tops. Harbert looked at his watch. It was ten 'til eight. "Let's go," he said, shoving his napkin onto the table, rising; a bit impatient were his words and his movements. Janine folded her napkin and followed, trying to keep up to the quick strides of the tall man. The older gentleman wanted to be early.

They opened their umbrellas. It was drizzling, despite a bit of blue showing in the sky, despite rays of sunlight that made the sidewalk glisten and the Cadillacs at Proctor's sparkle.

A taxi was parked beside the hotel on Call Street, today's rain doing little to wash the accumulation of grime from the Ford. It had the same "400 Cabs Inc." on the door. Dented fender. Perhaps it was the same one? "Would y'all care to ride? It's still a little wet out here," said a familiar voice. He apparently wasn't busy. "Why walk when you can ride, I always say," said he, offering a sentiment that seemed perfectly appropriate at the moment.

He waited for the traffic to clear then turned—illegally—with the traffic light, mounted on a short pole jutting from the sidewalk, still red. He drove them down to the courthouse, turning down Jefferson, the little street that ran beside the building. "Here we go," said the driver, pulling to the curb.

Harbert handed Darley a half dollar and a dime. "Keep the change."

"Thanks! And the sheriff's office is right inside, sir."

It was just a minute till eight.

91

Tallahassee
Tuesday, 10/23/1956

It wasn't a typical Southern courthouse. No columns. No dome. Plain white marble, a two-story rectangle. The entrance did stand out a little, with large windows above the doors and a little clock on a raised section above the cornice. The doors were unlocked, and no one was about. Janine shook out her umbrella, and they stepped across the threshold into the dry confines, onto the clean marble in the hall. A young woman was coming the other way, carrying files in her arms, her heels echoing down the hall.

"Excuse me, miss, do you work in the building?"

"Why, yes, sir. For Mr. Hartsfield, the clerk of court. May I assist you?"

"We're looking for the sheriff's office."

"It's down at the end of the hall, just past the stairs. You can see the sign there, at the last door."

"Oh, yes. Thank you, miss."

"Of course, sir. Y'all have a nice day."

They walked down to the little sign that read Sheriff's Office, jutting from the wall. The lettering on the glass said SHERIFF FRANK CARTER. They opened the door and walked in.

"Mornin'. May I he'p you?" came the voice of Chief Deputy Dreggors, seated awkwardly at his little desk. He rose to shake hands with Harbert. The chief deputy (as well as the bondsman for the county) was cleaning his shotgun and had cotton patches and gun oil on his desk, a telephone, and little else. He wore a green tie, which hung halfway down his belly.

"We're here to see Sheriff Carter."

"Come on back," said Dreggors, leading them up steps that took them through what seemed to be an old window opening, into a part of the courthouse that had been added on. Dreggors had to lean forward to clear the little entrance. A little hall led back to two more offices. The big man turned to the first one. "Sheriff, I got Mr. and Ms. Harbert here to see ya."

"Thanks, Will," replied Carter, rising to greet the visitors. He instantly recognized the Harberts and welcomed them into his office. "Sit down. Would y'all care for some coffee?" He was just about to pour himself a cup. In his early forties, he had a friendly manner and a North Florida drawl. He was tanned from working outdoors most of his life, but he wore a white shirt, carefully starched and pressed that morning. His Stetson hung from an old wooden clothes tree in the corner.

"I'm fine, thanks," said Harbert. The sheriff took measure of Harbert, reflecting on his experience with him three years ago and the man's demeanor today. Harbert seemed wealthy, the way he carried himself. He seemed assured, yet he wasn't haughty. The sheriff reckoned he was about sixty now. Something was ailing the gentleman; he didn't act as spry as he did their last meeting.

"Ma'am?" asked Carter, turning toward the young woman.

"No, thank you," she replied.

She must be about twenty-four, thought Carter. *She's a real sport model! Clothes a tad more expensive than what the average gal wears 'round here.*

The sheriff poured himself a cup from the pot on the side table. He took it straight. "Cold, rainy out there. I reckon it'll clear out in a day or two," he said, taking a seat behind the old oak desk.

Harbert nodded.

"Where are y'all from again?" asked Carter, taking a sip of the black steaming liquid.

"Pensacola, sir. You remember my daughter, Janine."

"Yessir, I remember you both. Pensacola—that's right. I *got* your letter last week. I reckon the last time we spoke was after the inquest. Of course, the crash ain't somethin' I'd forgit."

"You called me that night. I appreciate the way you handled that."

"Yessir." Carter remembered that call. Such things a man didn't forget. He read the letter, but he listened to what Harbert had to say again, in person. He focused his gaze on the speaker, taking an occasional sip, giving an occasional glace to the inside of the cup, as if the solution to many a problem swirled at the bottom. Then the older man reached in his pocket and carefully laid out fragments of photographs, one by one.

The sheriff looked at them curiously then looked into the cup. "You know this case has been ruled an accident by the medical examiner, by our investigation, by the *high*-way patrol. The cor'ner's jury found the cause of death was an accident. Even the state's attorney's office looked at it."

"Yes, I know. We believe you could prove otherwise. My question to you, sir, is whether you will reopen the case?"

Carter took another look at the photos then arranged them in a pile. "No, sir, I can't."

"Why not?"

"I don't think we could prove that," said the lawman, looking Harbert in the eye.

"Even with everything we've told you? All the circumstances—"

"That's just it—all circumstantial. Even if we proved all 'a that, it ain't enough to take to a *grand* jury."

"Don't you think it should go to the grand jury?"

"Not when we can't *prove* it. *Who* and *why*. Not even J. Edgar himself *could*. Ol' Mr. Wilkinson will never touch it after the cor'ner's jury ruled the way they did. We have no idea who sent those photos, but they don't *prove* anything. I'm just being honest with ya."

Harbert thought for a moment. It wasn't what he hoped the sheriff would say, but he had no reason to doubt the man's sincerity. "I believe that you are, sir. Thank you for listening to us," said the old man, sweeping the photos into the envelope.

"Yes, sir. Ya'll going back to Pensacola, or you intendin' to stay a while?"

"We want to make a few more inquiries today."

"I understand."

"Is the office of the state attorney in this building?"

"No, sir. His office is 'cross the street in the Lewis State Bank building."

"Thank you."

"Course, Mr. Wilkinson is in trial. He may not be able to see ya right away."

"What about the man we met at the funeral home? Taylor?"

"Well, he's the assistant state's attorney. You'd wanna talk to Mr. Wilkinson about this here."

"Very well."

"Ya'll got a place to stay?"

"Yes, sir. We have rooms at the Floridan. It's very nice."

The sheriff nodded. "I wish y'all a pleasant stay," he said, rising to see them out. "You walk right in the front door of the bank. There's a staircase to your right. You can't miss ol' Grant Wilkinson's office up there. He's got his name up, real conspicuous-like."

They thanked him for his time, the two men shaking hands. The sheriff stared out his window for a minute, looking out over the parking lot and patrol cars and the bandstand where politicians gave speeches. He knew the man and his daughter were not at all satisfied. They hadn't been all along.

XXXXX

They crossed the street to the Lewis State Bank building. They looked up at the sign that said Law Office in the second-story windows. There were three entrances; they picked the one closest to the law office sign and went in. There was a staircase off the little lobby. Beyond that, glass doors led farther inside the bank, high ceilings and marble. They took the stairs to the second floor and turned the corner.

Janine read the signs. "Hodges and Wilkinson, Attorneys and Counselors at Law." Another just below read, "Steven G. Wilkinson, State Attorney" in gold letters. They opened the door and stepped in the little office that overlooked Monroe. There was a receptionist sitting behind a small desk. She had a pencil in her mouth, leaning over the typewriter, trying to change the ribbon. "Oh, may I help you?"

"We're here to see Mr. Wilkinson," said Harbert.

"He's in trial today. Can I help?"

"It's in regards to my daughter. Jo Ellen Harbert."

"I don't recognize the name. Are y'all sure there's a pending case?"

"It's not pending. My daughter was killed, and we hope that a case can be made against her killer."

"Oh. I'm sorry," said the woman with great sympathy in her eyes. "He's in the courtroom. The Tourville trial. Everyone's waiting to see what'll happen!"

"We came a considerable distance."

"Perhaps, if you don't mind waiting, he could speak with you when they break for lunch."

"You're sure that's all right?"

"Oh, yessir. Mr. Wilkinson will be happy to talk to you!"

XXXXX

Harbert found the gentlemen's restroom ("White only") down a darkened corridor. He splashed water on his face and looked up at the mirror; the circles under his eyes appeared darker, and his hands holding the paper

95

towel were not as steady. Inside the picture of himself was as a young man—but it was an old fellow looking back at him, haggard and weak. He turned off both faucets and found Janine out in the central hall. They climbed the stairs and soon lost their way, finding themselves by the holding cell, turning the wrong way down the disjointed hall, a confusing array of nooks and crannies in the old building, the core of which dated to 1884. Fortunately, a court reporter happened upon them; the woman stopped to ask if she could help, rubbing the back of her arthritic right hand as she determined what they needed. She led them downstairs again and then up the front staircase to the main entrance to the courtroom. She stopped by the stairs, pointing out the doors ahead. "It's right down there, where that officer is sitting."

Large bottles were lined up outside. A muffled yet powerful voice emitted from the doors. A city police officer was seated on a wooden bench.

"Is the state attorney inside?"

"Yessir," answered the officer. "You need him?"

"Yes. We've traveled a great distance. But I'm afraid he can't see us if he's in trial."

"Maybe he can talk to you on a break. I'm afraid there ain't a seat to be had."

A colored woman and a white girl with a baby were peering in through the glazed doors. Harbert joined them, looking inside into the vast courtroom. The audience was full of spectators that had folded themselves into the narrow wooden seats that flipped down like those in an old auditorium. The judge on a high bench in front was a tough-looking man in his fifties with a trim gray mustache. He had a marked solemnity, a grave countenance about him, as if presiding over the Final Judgment. The pendulum of the giant regulator clock in a large niche behind his head marked off each important second, adding to the intensity.

"That's Judge Anderson," whispered the policeman.

A man in a gray suit, forty years old and handsome, dark hair with a bit of gray above his ears, was questioning the witness. He leaned in toward the police detective to accentuate his question then straightened up and looked at the jury while the witness made an important point. The cop sat in the oak chair that was the "hot seat" in this courtroom—the chair on a raised platform but completely in the open. The detective too was about forty, with dark hair and thick eyebrows. The jurors focused keenly, their eyes moving from the handsome lawyer back to the detective. A couple jurors nodded, obviously following the thread the lawyer was trying to weave.

The handsome fellow had to be Wilkinson, Harbert thought. The prosecutor was very confident, obviously in his element in a courtroom. It was he that had the commanding voice they'd heard but a moment before.

Wilkinson was the youngest state attorney in Florida, Harbert had been told. The prosecutor stepped back toward his table and asked another question. The jurors nodded again. A nervous-looking man and an elderly fellow with a bow tie were seated at the table farthest from the jury— apparently Tourville and his attorney.

The prosecutor called one witness after another, building a mountain of proof against the moonshiner. The woman next to Harbert whispered to him. "This is the second day. Mr. Wilkinson sure is a fighter. Everything Old Man Ingleside does, he has an answer for!"

Harbert looked at his daughter. Yes, he certainly was a fighter.

The judge asked Wilkinson for another witness. "Your Honor, I'd ask the court's indulgence for a ten-minute recess to make sure the evidence has arrived."

"All right," growled Anderson. Giving a glance at both lawyers then the jury, he admonished them. "There are twenty-three clocks in this courthouse. No two of them agree! This is the one we're going to go on!" he said, pointing to the clock over his shoulder, a slightly mischievous grin forming on his face. He paused as if to let its loud ticking echo off the ivory-colored walls. "Let's have everyone back here at ten fifteen, by that clock." People rose and began to murmur. The burly judge disappeared from the courtroom.

The doors flung open, and folks poured into the hall, flowing down the staircase, the prosecutor among them.

Harbert stepped toward the fellow. "Mr. Wilkinson?"

The prosecutor leaned in to talk to the officer. "Just a few minutes, George," he said, smiling and patting the cop on the shoulder. "Gotta go back to my—"

"Excuse me, Mr. Wilkinson?" Harbert put his hand on the man's shoulder, Janine right behind him.

"Uh-huh?" The prosecutor took a step back, pulling a king size from the yellow Fatima package. "I'm Wilkinson. What can I do for you?" he said, the cigarette between his lips.

"I'm Milo Harbert."

Wilkinson paused to light his cigarette. "How do you do?"

"Just fine. This is my daughter," said Harbert, nodding in the direction of Janine.

"How do you do?" Wilkinson repeated.

"We received your letter. But we still have many questions," said the old man.

"Well, I wish I had time to visit with you folks. You seem like nice people. But I must return to my office," he said, smiling apologetically.

"Mr.—"

He held his hand up. "I can tell you no more than what's in the letter. I have closing arguments in a few minutes. I haven't the time. Excuse me," he said, hurrying toward the stairs. A man with more jugs was coming up the other way.

They wanted answers. But so far, they had none. The *criminal* justice system, it seemed, was just that—a system that worked for the *criminal*, but not the families hurt by the crime. Wilkinson could try his moonshine case to high heaven.

They left, walking outside. Oaks hung their branches over the sidewalk, their arms stretching over the lawn surrounding the courthouse. It remained a gloomy day.

A man was parking his car in front of the Sears department store next door. They approached him. "Where is the police headquarters?"

"Why, right around the corner. It's easiest to cross over there at Jefferson," he said, pointing. "Then turn right on Adams. You won't miss it. It says *poe-lease department* on the winders."

"Thank you."

Jefferson ran between the front doors of the courthouse, along a narrow row of shops, dead-ending at the front steps and shiny brass doors of a pretty three-story building with a tile roof and elegant cornices.

They turned the corner where there was a little café, passed the office for the *Democrat*, and nearly missed the police station until they noticed the lettering on the plate glass. It was a narrow storefront with a colorful awning. The one-story building stretched back a ways, an alley running alongside, a long canopy for buses to pull through and load passengers. The fire department was next door, across that alley—a red-brick two-story with room for two trucks. An old man was polishing one of them with a rag. City Hall was on the corner, a red-brick Victorian with a high-pitched roof.

A lone policeman in a light blue uniform shirt and eight-point cap was behind the desk, taking a phone call and writing down a dispatch on a pad of paper; in a moment he'd hand it to the radio dispatcher to send out to a patrolman. It was just a small desk pushed against the wall, almost too small for the tall officer. A cigarette smoldered in the ashtray by his telephone.

"Yessir, may I help you?" asked the man, rising as they entered; he was over six feet tall with a deep voice and a crew cut.

"My name is Milo Harbert. This is my daughter."

"How do you do? I'm Joe Millirons. Please sit down. Would you care for a cigarette?"

Harbert shook his head.

"Thank you, yes," replied Janine.

The officer produced one for her as they sat down. The officer returned to his little desk, his hands folded in front of him; they had his full attention.

He listened intently as the old gentleman explained, the officer making notes on a small notepad. Janine took in the little office. Typewriter. Telephone. Some chairs. The room was paneled in pine to about six feet. Plastered above that, an L&N calendar hung behind Millirons's crew cut. A door with frosted glass led farther inside. The oldest police force in the South was rather tiny.

"So there you have it. And what we want to know, sir, does the department still have a case open—"

"Yessir?"

"A case that the police department is investigating currently. And if not, could you open one?"

"Up there on twenty-seven, it sounds like a county matter."

"County?" asked the young woman.

"Yes, ma'am. Our jurisdiction ends up there past Lake Ella. Beyond that, the county has authority. And of course, FHP has the highway. I'll look in our files just to make sure."

"We got these photographs in the mail from some unknown person," said Harbert, showing them to the policeman.

"Well, that is mighty peculiar. I'll just be a minute, folks," said Millirons, opening the frosted door and disappearing. He returned a moment later. "I looked through our files. The city has no information on it. Like I said, the location is outside city limits. I'm sorry, you may want to speak to the highway patrol. They're over in the Martin building. It's that fancy place a block from here." He stepped to the window, gesturing with his hand. "You can see it from here."

"I see it," said Harbert.

99

"Well, that's where the highway patrol headquarters is. Like I said, we wouldn't have a case up there outside the city limits."

They thanked him and, umbrellas in hand, walked back outside. They passed a small hardware store on Adams then crossed to the Martin building, up a dozen steps to those shiny doors. Finely detailed and made of red brick and concrete that had the look of limestone, the building reflected the prosperity of the twenties. It sat at the crest of a ridge that dropped very sharply behind it. It had red awnings over the windows and white begonias dancing in the rain along the foundation. A janitor was busy mopping the hall, making sure no one tracked in the rain on his shoes and diminished the spotless appearance of the marble.

They found the highway patrol's main office downstairs in the basement. The lady working there could find no file. No one could see them today. Colonel Chambord would be back tomorrow. He had gold lettering on the door to his office. His large portrait graced the reception area.

XXXXX

"Ben Austin just might be the only lawyer that would talk—and not send a bill."

Harbert's bank had hired Austin last year—the best attorney in the capital city. His office was in the Midyette-Moor building, the six-story yellow-brick "skyscraper" at the corner of College and Monroe. They looked up at its Art Deco eagles and tile. It was much taller than any of the other one- or two-story businesses nearby.

They shook out their umbrellas and entered the lobby. The elevator man asked which floor they desired, but Harbert preferred the stairs. Janine thought they should take the elevator, but the old man insisted. They walked up the narrow staircase, the view from the window on each landing getting higher and higher. A woman was leading her son down, squeezing past them, the boy holding his jaw from a visit to the dentist's office on the fourth floor.

Up another flight. "There. Six-oh-one," Harbert read, rather out of breath. They opened the door, and the secretary—a young girl in a skirt and cashmere—greeted them. She offered them a seat. "My name's Hattie. Let me know if I can get you anything. Mister Ben's meeting with a client, almost done."

They sat down opposite the door to Austin's office. Harbert could hear the murmurs of the discussion inside and a few sobs—apparently a divorce case. Presently, his door opened, and the divorcée client left. Ben Austin was young—only thirty-three—but already had a successful practice. He greeted them warmly. "It's wonderful to see you, Milo."

"This is my daughter, Janine."

"I'm glad to make your acquaintance. Come on in! Please have a seat."

"Thank you." They sat on the tufted leather chairs, Harbert looking about the spacious office. He noted the diploma over in the corner: University of Florida, class of '49. One from the University of Miami Law School hung opposite. He saw a framed photograph of Austin in military uniform with some other young men, one of them wearing captain's bars. The latter he recognized to be Frank Carter. Lovely photos of Austin's wife and son were arranged on a credenza, black-and-white photos of a happy family.

"I got your letter a few days ago," noted the lawyer.

"Have you heard anything?" asked Janine.

"I haven't, unfortunately."

"Anything in regard to that man, Sam Nowak?"

"No, and I know how volatile he can be. I believe the authorities should have asked more questions about that. Can I get you a drink?"

"No, I'm fine," replied Harbert.

"We've been to the sheriff, the police, and the highway patrol. We even saw the state attorney, briefly."

"And none of them would take a second look—even with the photos?"

"I'm afraid not," replied the older man.

The lawyer shook his head. Austin offered his guests a cigarette from the silver box on his desk. Janine accepted one, which he lit for her.

"Did the sheriff suggest examining the photographs for fingerprints?" asked Austin.

"No."

"Well, they probably don't have the technicians that could do it anyway," thought Austin out loud.

"Do you know anyone we could talk to?" asked Janine.

"Perhaps my father could help. Perhaps his contacts with the FBI might help." Austin's father was the US congressman for much of North Florida.

"We'd appreciate anything that could be done," said Harbert.

"If you need anything regarding Nowak, let me know. Howard Jenkins is certainly willing to tell what he knows about that man. You know that he is rumored to have imported bootleg whiskey into the county."

"No."

Austin nodded. "He's just ornery. Associates with rough people. *Nothing* would surprise me when it comes to that man."

"What can be done to get the case reopened?" asked Harbert.

"It's hard to say. If Wilkinson won't touch it, you have a hard road to hoe. He's the only game in town."

"Well, we intend to make some more inquiries today. It was good seeing you," said Harbert, extending his hand to the lawyer. They shook hands, and the elder man turned toward the door.

Austin opened it for him. "I sure wish you luck, sir."

"I surely appreciate the time you've given us. It is a great comfort to my family."

"Good-bye," said Janine, following her father.

"Good-bye. Let me know how it goes," said the cordial Austin, seeing them to the elevator in the small landing.

This time they took the lift; the man in his uniform and cap saw them to the first floor and bid them good afternoon. It *was* nearly noon. All the walking and the scant amount he'd had for breakfast was making Harbert light-headed. They'd noticed the sign at the Dutch Kitchen on the corner of Adams and Park when they'd walked to the police station. They'd heard the food was decent. It wasn't raining hard, so they walked over.

"We should go back to the sheriff with that bit about the whiskey," said Janine.

"Yes, I think so," said Harbert as he opened the door of the tea room.

"Welcome. May I take your hat, your umbrellas?" the hostess greeted them. Another waiter approached. "Table for two?" Janine nodded. "This way please." They followed, Harbert leaving his hat and the umbrellas with the woman at the hostess's desk. They were seated at a table with a linen cloth. Coffee and hot soup quickly appeared. The tea room was in one of Tallahassee's oldest homes, the Columns, named for the columned portico in front of the red-brick mansion covered in ivy over much of the side.

A man with a short gray beard and crooked bow tie consumed a roast beef sandwich at the table beside them. He was writing something on a bit of hotel stationery. He looked up from his work, turning to face the old man.

102

"Y'all visiting?" he asked. He wore a good-natured smile on his bearded face. He had a full head of gray hair he parted on the side and swept over his forehead and neatly trimmed around his ears.

"Pardon?"

"Y'all here for a visit?"

"Yes, we are, as a matter of fact."

"This is a good place to have a meal. You folks have family here?"

"No, but we came to look into a matter concerning my daughter."

"Oh? I don't mean to ask a lot of questions. I happened to see you folks come in and heard the waiter say you had talked to the sheriff, the state attorney, and paid a visit to Ben Austin."

"Really?" asked Harbert incredulously.

"There ain't no secrets in a small town," said the man, grinning. "And I hope it ain't no secret who I am. Bill Dufour's the name."

"How do you do?" said Harbert. "It seems that I have heard your name, sir. Forgive me if I'm a little troubled that our business is so well-known."

"I guess people just tell me things. I work for the *Times-Union*, office over on College Avenue," said the man, wiping his chin with the cloth napkin. "Don't hold it against me." He winked.

"No. Of course not. You're a reporter then?"

Dufour nodded.

"Yes...William Dufour," Harbert repeated, thinking about the name. "I know your column, as a matter of fact. I'm Milo Harbert. I'm a banker. I hope you will not hold *that* against me," said the old man, a bit impish in his expression, surprising his daughter. Taking on a more serious tone, he gave Dufour an explanation for their visit. "I believe, as does my daughter, sir"—he nodded in her direction—"that there is some person or persons guilty of murder living here in the midst of this town."

The reporter set down his fork. "You folks had my attention. Now you got my *undivided* attention. I'm sorry to hear that. But whom? Who was killed? Do you know who did it?"

"It was my daughter, Janine's sister—"

"I'm truly sorry."

"And indeed, the identity of the man or *men* that did this, I do not know."

They spoke for a few minutes about the case. Dufour had not heard of it. "Have you any leads?"

"Scarcely any." Harbert told him about the photographs.

"Might I have your permission to do a story about this?" asked Dufour as the waitress brought their checks.

"Perhaps it might do some good."

"Do you think it would help?" asked Janine.

"It might. The *Times-Union* gains new readers every day. May I pay for your meal, sir?"

"No, that is quite all right. You needn't go to any trouble."

"I-I would like to, sir," said the reporter, pulling his wallet from his suit pocket. Dufour walked with them out to the sidewalk. As they were saying good-bye, the reporter had something to add. "Well, I just remembered," he said, snapping his fingers. "You might try Hal Martin's bureau."

"We've never heard of that."

"It's new. I wrote an article or two about it, but I'm not surprised it isn't well-known."

"Where is it?"

"I want to say it's on *Bruno.* That's b-r-o-n-o-u-g-h, not far from the Supreme Court, there's a little house. There's a sign. I think. They moved since I last talked to those fellas."

"We're not from here. Where's Bronough Street?"

"Oh, yes, of course. I'd show you the way, but I must get back to the Capitol for an interview. Take Jefferson, then Duval. You'll know the Supreme Court."

"Yes, I think so."

"Dome on top, six columns," he said gesturing with his hand, first arching his fingers to show a dome then holding them up to show six columns. "Bronough runs behind it. Or is the place on Gaines?" he wondered, tapping his chin, trying to remember.

"We'll find it," said Harbert.

"There's a fella over there named Fowler. No, that's not it neither," said the reporter, looking up, trying to recall the right name. "Oh yes, like the steamboat! Fulton's his name. True Fulton. Ask for him."

"True what?"

"Fulton. If there's anyone that could help, it would be him." Dufour, a bundle of nerves, dashed away toward Monroe.

True Fulton. Sheriff's Bureau. It is rather curious-sounding, thought Harbert. He'd never heard of any "Sheriff's Bureau." What good could such an unknown, obscure little agency be?

Tallahassee
Tuesday, 10/23/1956

They wondered if the reporter had made it up. They walked the way Dufour had told them, down Duval. Just houses. They walked around in a circle, finding nothing that gave any indication that this unknown department might be located there.

"True Fulton—what a funny name," thought Janine out loud.

"Yes, it is," replied Harbert.

"We know *that's* the Supreme Court," Janine said, pointing at the Monticello-like structure at the corner of Duval and Pensacola.

"That's the only building I recognize." There were houses right behind the Supreme Court, across Bronough. One had a sign on the porch.

"Perhaps that's it," remarked Janine. It wasn't. The sign advertised a cosmetologist.

It was raining harder. They walked back toward the front of the Supreme Court, uphill noticeably on Pensacola. They stopped at the corner, just a stone's throw from the steps and the portico, trying to get their bearings. It was fairly dark. Thunder crashed; the clouds appeared ready to send a torrent down on them as they turned the corner. They didn't hear the car approaching from behind. The car pulled up beside them, slowing to match their pace, the wet brakes squeaking a bit. Startled, they turned to look at it. It was a police car.

"You folks lost?" asked the man in the cap, cranking down the window of the black-and-white. It was the officer from before. A younger officer was in the car with him. Millirons hadn't heard of the Sheriff's Bureau either. Nor had he read of it in the paper.

"A man told us it was behind the court, or it might be on Gaines."

"Why don't you get in. Let me drive you down there." They gladly accepted the offer to get in the dry confines of the '54 Ford. "There are some little houses the state is leasing. We can drive over there, right quick."

He turned on St. Augustine, going around Waller Park, a large open lawn separating the Supreme Court and the back door of the capital. Harbert wondered if there was some meaning in having two branches of government overlook each other, that perhaps the legislators wished to keep an eye on the justices—and vice versa. The park had flowers and shrubs and a liberty bell in the middle. Perhaps that bell was placed in the middle as a reminder to both organs of government. Schoolchildren—it took two or three of them—would pull on a rope and attempt to ring the bell. He'd seen pictures in the paper. Harbert envisioned men in suits and black robes fighting over the bell, and it was rather amusing.

The officer turned south on Adams. Palm trees lined the street on their side, and parked cars stood along the curb on both sides of the street. The black-and-white rolled to a stop at Gaines, between the Old Supreme Court and the newer Caldwell building. There were some small houses on the other side in the shadow of the Caldwell building on a down slope away from the Capitol. "You reckon it's one of those?" asked the younger officer, pointing through the windshield.

"I can't tell," said Janine, leaning on the front-seat back, peering ahead.

Millirons turned onto Gaines slowly so they could look at the houses. "I see the sign!" he exclaimed. "There, ma'am. That's it!" It was a tiny makeshift placard. "Never noticed that before," said the young man, adjusting his hat.

"Well, we solved a local mystery, ma'am," said Millirons with a grin.

"We hope so," said Mr. Harbert.

On the low side of Gaines Street sat the wooden house. The lights were on inside the front rooms of the squat one-story, the glowing windows reflecting off the damp surface of the little porch. The porch roof was leaky and the grass soggy with puddles of water from the morning's heavy rain. The ramshackle structure looked more like a place that sold bait and tackle than a law enforcement headquarters.

The Harberts approached it, looking at each other skeptically; they waved to the policemen as they pulled away in the radio car. They stepped up to the door, the porch creaking when they walked on it, water dripping on their coats. "Cross your fingers, Dad."

XXXXX

Wanted posters hung from the mantel like Christmas stockings. There was a smell of coffee and cigarettes. Rain was dripping from the corner of the ceiling down into a metal wastepaper basket.

A woman—late thirties, plastic glasses, hair pinned up—stopped typing, took their hats, and provided them two uncomfortable chairs. She offered them a Chesterfield from the pack on her desk in what was once a living room. "It will only be a minute," she told them. They looked at the bare walls, the dull yellow linoleum on the floor.

The telephone rang. The secretary scrawled something on a pad. She read back the information. "Homicide. Need fingerprint expert right away. I will tell Mr. Fulton to pack his bag. Oh, yes. Thank you, sir, you too."

The secretary heard Fulton hang up. She leaned in the door. "I have the Harberts here to see you."

107

"Okay."

"Right this way, please," she said, gesturing for the visitors to enter the office.

The man behind the desk stood. "Mornin'," he said, shaking Harbert's hand. "Please have a seat." He gestured to two wooden chairs. Father and daughter accepted; the seats were hardly comfortable, but the best hospitality the state allowance afforded. His office was once a bedroom in the wood-sided cottage. A bit of wallpaper—flower patterned—still hung on the wall behind him. The rest of the room—walls and ceiling plaster—had been painted over in a drab gray-green. But other colors showed through where bits of paint were flaking off.

"Would y'all like some coffee?"

"No, thank you," father and daughter replied, nearly in unison. Fulton noticed Ms. Harbert glancing about the room. She could scarcely be impressed. Fulton noticed the suit Harbert wore appeared to be English. The woman was quite attractive; she had a large engagement or wedding ring underneath her glove. He noticed her shivering. "It's so cold, I'm tempted to find an old woodstove and bring it in here," said the lawman.

The old man nodded. The two visitors sized up their surroundings and this special agent in front of them. The place was hardly impressive. The man they found a bit more difficult to read. He spoke in a country accent. He seemed quiet, low-key, not at all what they thought a detective should act like or look like—certainly nothing like detectives in movies. He was over six feet tall. He had a bit of a belly held back by his belt, his hair thinning on top. His smile reminded her of Hank Williams, Janine thought. He seemed easygoing. But the gun he wore, his large hands, the scar on his cheek, and that nose angled from a break or two all seemed to suggest he was not a man to be trifled with. The same could be said of his very clear blue eyes; they seemed to suggest a genuine interest, a sympathy even, but also masked something tough and perhaps deadly.

"It's been three years since my daughter died," said Harbert, reaching into the inside pocket of his suit. "Here is her picture," he said, handing Fulton a small photograph. She was a pretty girl with dark hair and very captivating eyes, Fulton could see. "Neither one of us feel that the case was handled appropriately."

"Yessir?"

"We don't feel this was an accident like it's been told," said Ms. Harbert.

"No, sir. We feel Jo Ellen, in fact, was the victim of foul play."

Fulton could see the agony in the man's eyes. He was obviously tormented by a loss he'd been suffering with every day. "I'm not familiar with the case, Mr. Harbert. It involved a car accident?"

"Or so it would appear." Harbert reached inside his coat, drawing out the envelope. "Just a few weeks ago, some person or persons sent me this."

Fulton took out a handkerchief and accepted the envelope, then carefully emptied the contents on his desk. He studied them and looked up at Harbert inquisitively. "And you haven't any idea who sent these?"

"No, sir."

"It sure is odd. Address was typed. No return. Who else has touched all this?"

"Well, several people, I'm afraid."

"Can you tell me about the accident?"

"Surely," said the old man. He told Fulton all he knew about the spot near the lake—the DWI allegation, everything.

Fulton looked at the picture of Jo Ellen. "When was the last time you saw or spoke to your daughter before the second of November, fifty-three?"

"Well, I spoke to her a few days before. Janine would know the dates better than I."

"That would have been the week before, Dad. But we were *all* in town for my brother's wedding in Pensacola—a few days before that."

"Oh, yes," agreed Harbert.

"And I last spoke to her—I last spoke to her the day before she died," said Janine, tears appearing at the corner of her eyes.

"Can ya tell me about the conversation the day before, ma'am."

"Sure. She phoned me up Sunday. She told me about her business deal and said the fella was pretty testy. He was trying to back out of the deal. From what she described, this man was erratic and bad-tempered."

"Mr. Harbert?"

"His name was Sam Nowak," said the father.

"He threatened her," added Janine. "He accused her of trying to cheat him out of $500. That's all she would say about the trip, that she was trying to buy this laundry from Nowak. Ben Austin knows about Sam. He's a lawyer."

109

Fulton nodded. "Did she seem scared of Mr. Nowak?"

"She didn't let on that she was—but that was Jo Ellen. It sounded serious to me," said Janine.

"Anything unusual when you saw her at the wedding?"

"No," both answered.

"Did she seem like anything was bothering her?"

"No, sir."

"Any signs that she was having any trouble with alcohol?"

"No, she didn't touch a drop," said Mr. Harbert.

"Now, what about when you spoke with her? Was it by phone?" he asked the father.

"Yes. There didn't appear to be anything wrong. I knew she had a meeting with this business owner. She wanted my advice."

"And you've talked to the state's attorney?" asked Fulton.

"We've written a letter to the prosecuting attorney's office every year since Jo Ellen's death. This is his latest reply," said the old man, holding up an envelope. "Here are his two previous replies." He drew out two more envelopes from his coat pocket.

Fulton read the letters. He looked up at his visitors, somewhat confounded.

"Rather disappointing, aren't they? We were not satisfied, so we made the trip over here. I'm retired now. Janine works at my old bank, but she's to be married soon."

"Well, congratulations," Fulton said. Janine noted the picture of Fulton's wife on the table in the corner. Fulton skimmed through the letters. "Well, the state's attorney said it was a 'straightforward, unfortunate case of driving while intoxicated, or DWI.' He mentions the autopsy, the report from the deputy on scene. It seems like he thought it was open and shut."

"Do you?"

"What else can you tell me?"

"Jo Ellen had a meeting the evening of the second at nine thirty p.m.—the night she died. And another at eight a.m. the next morning. We haven't any idea with whom these appointments were made."

"Here is the calendar she kept. She always wrote down her appointments. It was still in her hotel room after...after her death," said Janine.

"She had a journal she always wrote in. She wrote nearly every day--everything she did. It was not among her things. Neither from the wreck, nor from the room at the Cherokee Hotel," added Harbert. "We think someone wanted that book, whatever may have been in it."

"She met with a Sam earlier the day she died?" asked Fulton, noting the name scrawled on the calendar: "APT, Sam," read Fulton. "Four p.m. and again at eight thirty."

"Do you know the lawyer Ben Austin?" Janine asked.

"I've heard the name," said Fulton, flipping through the calendar.

"Well, he told us something new today. Shall I tell him now?" asked Janine, looking at her father. He nodded. "Mr. Austin told us that there are rumors that Sam brings in whiskey into this county, and he knows some rough people."

Fulton nodded. "So maybe your sister got cross ways with some bad hombres." He looked serious, like the wheels were turning in his head. Illegal whiskey sales had long been the focus of the law in Florida. The only thing to draw more ire in recent years was gambling.

"Her pistol was missing, a little.25 caliber I'd given her," added Mr. Harbert.

"Oh?" remarked Fulton, raising an eyebrow.

Harbert added something for Fulton to chew on. "I spoke to the hotel clerk where Jo Ellen had stayed. He said he was on duty that night. He saw her at nine. She was, as he put it, 'sober as a Baptist preacher on Sunday morning,' had said she was going to bed or words to that effect. Then she left between nine fifteen and nine thirty, and still she seemed just fine."

"How can it be an incident of drunken driving if she wasn't drunk?" asked Janine.

"That's a good question," Fulton agreed.

"I came over after she died. My brother and I. They told us it was an accident. I was there for the inquest. But everything we learned, it just didn't make sense."

"Yes, ma'am?"

"For one thing, they said she smelled of whiskey, that the bottle in the car was a whiskey bottle."

111

"Yes, ma'am?"

"Well, I know for a fact Jo Ellen didn't like whiskey. That was what Dad used to drink."

Mr. Harbert nodded. "She liked vodka," affirmed her father.

"Okay," said Fulton.

"We have never seen a copy of the reports written by the sheriff or the autopsy," said Mr. Harbert.

"I'd be interested in reading those, same as you would. Did your daughter live in Pensacola too?"

"No, in Fort Walton. You know where that is?"

"Yessir, by Eglin?"

Harbert nodded. "She had a business that catered to Eglin Field."

Realizing that could mean a lot of things, Janine added, "A uniform alteration business."

"We haven't any idea who she may have had the early meeting with," said Harbert.

"There are other questions to consider," Fulton told them.

"Go on," replied the old man.

"Was she having any financial problems with her business?"

"No."

"What about her personal life?"

"Not recently. She ran into a bad spell at the end of her time in college. She was unhappy when she finished school. Nothing seemed to help. She began to drink."

"Yessir?"

"She lost her job here and came back home. I told her I would have no drinking in my house, and she left. I didn't see her for months. She hit rock bottom. I found her nearly dead in Jacksonville. I had to take her to a hospital where she remained for three months. She had nothing but the clothes on her back. I got her in touch with an organization I am a member of, the Alcoholics Anonymous."

"Yessir."

112

"You may surmise then that this drunken-driving accident makes perfect sense. But I tell you, Mr. Fulton, she hadn't taken a drink in five years. I've been a sponsor for that length of time. I've seen plenty of people pretend to live the twelve steps, make a show of it for their wife or their boss. Jo Ellen wasn't like that. She took her sobriety seriously."

"Okay."

"It's unusual, but her sponsor would be willing to talk to you. Here's his number," he said, handing Fulton a piece of paper where he'd written "Fort Walton Beach, 2-3380."

Fulton took the paper. "You saw no signs that she should fall off the wagon?"

"None."

"Was she pretty punctual?"

"She never missed an appointment. If she had something at eight a.m., I believe she would have made that appointment unless precluded from doing so by the hand of someone with a sinister purpose."

Fulton nodded. "Is there anyone you're aware of that knew her when she left here five years ago or when she was in Jacksonville?"

"Only the principal at the school, other teachers. I know of no one else," said the old man.

Janine agreed.

"Do you know how long she was in town?"

"Her employee said she took off Thursday and Friday, and we know she paid for her hotel room for five overnights. But we haven't any idea where she went—or with whom she associated—whilst she was here," explained the old man.

"I see. What was the name of the business she managed?"

"The Fort Walton Alterations Shop. It was very successful. She built it herself, wouldn't take any help, even though Dad offered. We are...were—" Her sister shook her head, fighting back tears. "I always looked up to her," she said, looking at her father, a bit of a glint in her eyes, though she fought back the tears and the lump in her throat. "We are so proud of her, even still."

"Yes, ma'am. Did she have any close friends that may know something?"

"Why, yes, one—Sadie Phillips, I know Jo Ellen spoke with her when she was in Tallahassee. We saw her at the funeral. I don't have her address."

"Any other friends over here?"

"She hadn't kept in touch with anyone else," said Janine.

"What about where she lived?"

"There was Mrs. Lindgren from the shop. I'll have to get you her address. I heard she left the shop."

Fulton took down the name.

"There was Sarah Morris. She lived down the street from her. I have her number," she said, handing him her address book that she'd opened to the page with the Morrises' number.

"Okay," replied Fulton, writing it down. He set the pencil down and looked up at his visitors. "Getting back to those other possibilities..."

They nodded.

"Did she have a man in her life?"

"Not for a few months. She was seeing someone up until six months before," said Janine.

"What was his name?"

"Clay Howerton," answered the young woman.

"Any problems between them?"

"Yes, there were some hard feelings, the way it ended."

"Was he ever violent towards her?"

"He...he made her do things that she...she *didn't like*. I hate to even speak of it," said Janine, nearly distraught over the recollections provided her by her sister.

"It's all right," Fulton assured her.

"He forced her to do things that made her ashamed. She was a good girl. Then"—she paused, clearing her throat—"he hit her, and that's when she ended it."

Her father was pained; Fulton could see it in his eyes. The man looked down, holding his fist to his mouth just under his nose, shaking his head

114

slightly, absorbing what he was hearing. "I didn't know everything. A father tries to protect his children...Are they ever truly safe?"

Fulton shook his head. "Do you think her former boyfriend wanted to harm her?"

"I do not. I confronted him about it. But I don't think so. She hadn't seen or heard from him in five months," said Harbert.

"Where does he live?"

"Jacksonville. He's a lawyer," replied the old man, regaining his repose.

"Do you have his number or address?"

"No, sir. I will find that too. I have an address book of Jo Ellen's. I can get it and bring it back," said her sister.

"That's all right. We'll find him. Do you think there's a chance she was close with any other men, met someone on a trip, anything like that?"

"No. Rarely did she go anywhere—almost never. She and I went to Miami after my second year of college. I had to talk her into it. She never took a vacation. She worked too hard."

"Yes, ma'am."

"There's not much to go on, is there?" asked the father.

Fulton shook his head. "But some cases have been solved with less."

"We fear the case will not be solved. Tell us your honest opinion," said Harbert.

Fulton leaned back, the old chair squeaking as he moved. "Honestly, I don't know. There'll be some discussions to see if we should handle the case. Our jurisdiction is limited, you see."

"Is that so?" replied Harbert.

Fulton nodded.

"Yes, I'm beginning to see this matter is more complicated than I could ever imagine," said the old man.

"Hardly like the motion pictures, detectives solving cases and getting a confession and all," added Janine.

"No, ma'am. Now, you said there was an inquest?"

Both nodded.

"Did any of the matters y'all are raising—the things you just told me—come before the jury?"

"No," answered her father.

"I didn't think so. They had something that looked like an accident, and it's unlikely they'd go after all the...loose ends is what I call 'em."

Harbert nodded.

"Are y'all staying in town?"

"We have rooms at the Floridan."

"I'd like to hold on to the pictures for now."

Janine nodded.

"Can we meet again at three o'clock?"

"We will be back at three exactly," Harbert assured him.

24

Tallahassee
Tuesday, 10/23/1956

He put his hat on. Buttoned his coat. He enjoyed walking. It gave him time to think. Also, it was even money whether the worn-out car would start. Leon, Dade, and Bay counties had each donated a 1952 Ford to the Sheriff's Bureau. The dark blue one had been Cliff Holland's; it was the nicest. The light blue one must have came from Dade; it came replete with a large coffee stain on the seat, stick shift, and a propensity to die on days that were rainy—or sunny for that matter. They kept their siren. The car never had emergency lights, and Miami probably realized the temperamental radio wasn't worth the trouble of removing, so they left that as the only "equipment" in the car. He walked past the Ford, crossing Gaines, heading to his favorite hole in the wall at the corner of Adams and College.

The little bell clanged as he swung the door open. The place was empty. He liked it that way. He sat down, dropping his hat on the table. A young waitress in an apron and a blue cotton dress brought him a sweet tea. "The usual?"

"Yes, ma'am."

She disappeared again. In a moment, an older waitress came over, attired in like fashion as the first, a pad of paper and a pencil in her hands. She noted the empty glass in front of him, the fedora on the tablecloth. "Are you waiting for your food, Mr. Fulton?" she asked, pushing her red hair back behind her ear.

Looking up, dead serious, he answered her. "I put in an order thirty minutes ago."

"What? I'm terribly sorry!" she apologized. "I will check and see what the trouble is!" His countenance didn't change. He just looked at her. She tried to read his expression. Knowing his sense of humor, suspecting he was pulling her leg, she put her hand on her hip and cocked her head. "Now, Mister True?"

Fulton grinned. "Actually, Sandy just got my order a couple minutes ago."

The waitress smacked his shoulder with her order pad. "Oh! Mister True, you're bad! Well, it shouldn't be too long then."

"Thank ya."

She walked away to have a cigarette. Fulton pulled the photograph from his pocket and looked at it. *What should I know about all this, gal?* he thought, asking her as if she could respond. *What's your story?*

Wipers on in the mist, the '50 Ford coupe glided to a stop at the curb along Call Street. The driver's belly was squeezed in against the steering wheel, the car was small, and he an overweight man. He lit a cigarette, noting the men busy tearing down the storefronts along Monroe, clearing the way for a new J. C. Penney's and Woolworth's. He had a good view of the entrance to the Floridan.

He watched the old gent and a young woman cross Call on their way to the front door of the big hotel. "So the banker's back in town." He cussed, flicking ashes out the window. He rolled up the window; droplets of water were falling on the sleeve of his suit. He sat for a minute, wondering what sort of problems the Harberts might cause and what might be done about it.

XXXXX

Fulton squeezed the collar of his sport coat, shielding himself from the icy wind as he walked back to his office. A black Ford was parked in front. Martin's. The director drove his own car on state business, having assigned the donated Fords to the special agents, the Bureau having no money to purchase another unmarked. Like the rest of them, he didn't dwell on the budget; he got on with the job. Too much was at stake.

Fulton walked past Mary Ann's desk, down the hall of the "shotgun" house, finding his mentor in his office; it was once a dining room. It had enough room for a desk, a file cabinet, and two chairs and had the same dingy yellow linoleum as the rest of the house.

Martin had his glasses on. He'd been reading something. "How are ya, True?"

"'Afternoon, Sheriff."

Fulton called him that even though he no longer held that post. Martin had been his boss years earlier, when he came to work for him on the advice of Pratt Harlowe. Martin was a wise old lawman. Fulton shivered; the director's office felt like a meat locker. Tallahassee's winters, though a bit more harsh than Ocala's, didn't bother Martin, who grew up outdoors handling all the tasks of ranching and sheriffing for as long as he could remember. He'd be the last to utter complaint toward today's wind and rain.

"Set down a minute, son." Martin had a cigarette in the ashtray. He brought it to his lips while Fulton sat in one of the oak chairs facing the director and the desk made by inmates of the state prison. Also donated by Bay County. "I just returned from the governor's office."

"Oh?"

118

"He thinks next year, we might get some funding. If those boys over in the legislature can spare a few dollars."

Fulton looked around at the paint peeling on the door and the water stain on the ceiling. "That sure would be nice."

Martin grinned. "He's fightin' for us. If he has his way, we oughta see things really take off around here."

"Yessir."

"Heard you had some visitors," said Martin, puffing on the cigarette.

"Yessir, some folks stopped in earlier about what may well be a homicide," said Fulton, opening his small spiral notebook.

"Here locally?"

Fulton nodded.

"Go on," said Martin, interested.

The younger man proceeded to fill him in on the details, sparse but striking as they were. "She had business appointments the day she died—intended to buy a laundry owned by a Sam Nowak. But she had an appointment at nine thirty that night and another at eight a.m. the next day. No one knows whom they were with. Her sister said she wasn't the kind that would miss an engagement. Her sister and she were close. She could think of no reason for it. No enemies they know of. But she had some difficulty with Nowak over this business deal. The ol' boy was all riled up about $500. She mentioned it to her sister."

"People can get awful riled up about money," agreed Martin.

"People have killed over less, that's for sure."

"What else?"

"Hotel clerk said she left the lobby—sober—around nine fifteen. Ends up drunk—and dead—a half hour later. Way up US 27 by herself. Family said she hadn't been drinkin' in a long time. The big thing is this missing book, journal she wrote in every day. She always had it with her." Fulton shut the notebook. "Nowhere to be found."

"The missing book is interesting."

"The sister didn't know what was in it. But she kept it locked up when she was home, took it with her when she traveled. There's also the matter of a missing gun. She had a little .25 that was never found."

119

"Hmm, well, maybe she pawned it, sold it—people do all kinda things with guns."

Fulton nodded. "And the family got some photos, torn so as to conceal who had been with the victim when they were taken. They don't know who sent 'em."

"Now, that kinda jumps right off the page at ya."

"Yes, sir."

The old man thought for a moment. "If I was lookin' at this. If I was puttin' two and two together, tryin' to pull together the pieces...whoever sent the pictures, finding that book—those are the things that you'd wanna go huntin' after." He thought about it some more without speaking, stirring the ashtray a bit. He looked up again. "What about a boyfriend?"

"She had one. They broke up. He was something less than a gentleman."

"Violent?"

"He seems to have been something of a sadist—a *sexual* sadist."

Martin raised an eyebrow. "Is that so?"

Fulton nodded.

"Someone that takes enjoyment from hurting people... That always raises a red flag with me. You think maybe the boyfriend sent the photos?"

"Maybe."

"If this was a homicide, we'd be dealing with a smart killer."

"Yessir."

"Making it look like a traffic accident. Not an accident like falling down stairs or drowning, but a drunk-driving *accident*. I've never heard of anything like it."

"No, sir."

"Yessir, this fella'd be real smart," said Martin, putting the ear of his glasses in his mouth, thinking. "Yes, real smart." Martin always warned about the sort of criminal that had brains, who would be hard to catch. He sounded the alarm about training and technical expertise as often as he could—although his advice, for years, had gone unheeded in Tallahassee. "This might be another Chillingsworth."

"A lot like that. No leads at all."

120

"Those kind are tough to prove." Martin looked at Jo Ellen's photograph and shook his head at the loss of such beauty, vitality. "It is a bit of a head-scratcher, ain't it?"

Fulton nodded.

"But don't you think the obvious explanation is the one that holds up? What was the alcohol level?"

".220 percent."

"Hard to get around that. Maybe the family just can't come to terms with it."

"It was the family that impressed me more than anything. They didn't seem the usual hysterics you get. I thought about that, the usual thing, you know, family just doesn't want to accept someone'd fall off the wagon, get plastered, and pile up into a tree. But I didn't sense that. I think they just want to *know*."

"It seems thin."

"I just get that *feeling*. I'd like to look into it some more."

Martin nodded. Fulton's hunches were generally good ones. "Culver and Williams are in Palm Beach—Chillingsworth, you know—and you've already got the Dade County investigation. You like that one?"

"Yessir."

"I *thought* it was right up your alley. And you're going back to Duval County for the bolita case," said Martin, folding his glasses and putting them down on the desk.

"Yessir."

"Well... how are we?" he asked, pausing, waving his hand over his desk a bit to emphasize his point. "Gonna work it in? You got a way of making a mimeograph copy of yourself?"

"It's been busy enough. Sometimes I don't know if I'm coming or going," said Fulton. Culver and Williams were the only other agents that Martin had to work the entire State. "I've had to change the oil twice on that Ford, and it's only been three months."

Martin nodded.

"But, the case with the hotel safe didn't take as long as I thought," Fulton added. He'd been doing fingerprint work nonstop by request from sheriffs across the state. If they needed someone to dust for fingerprints, Fulton

121

would pack his old suitcase. Most counties didn't have officers trained to collect and analyze such evidence.

"It's you that's gonna have to be on the road. It's you that Marlene's gonna be cross ways with, not me."

"Yessir."

"As long as Frank's okay with it, it's okay with me."

25

Tallahassee
2:30 p.m.
Tuesday, 10/23/1956

The green and white pulled into the circle driveway behind the courthouse. Fulton waved, and the sheriff responded with a tap on the horn. Carter pulled the '55 Chevrolet—new five-pointed star on the door, red light on top—right up to the back door. "Fulton! How are you, son?"

"Afternoon, Sheriff."

They shook hands. Carter always tried to have the toughest grip. "You comin' to see me?"

"Yeah, there's an old case I wanted to ask ya about."

"Come on in!" he said, patting Fulton on the back and showing him inside. "Penny, would you be so kind as to get ol' True Fulton some coffee?" Penny was Carter's daughter who had the office next to her father's; she handled the administrative tasks for the office, payroll, and filing.

"Yessir," said the pretty young girl.

The men walked up the steps through the old window, down the short hallway, and back to Carter's office. Penny brought them each a cup.

"I ain't seen ya in a dog's age! How's that purty wife a yours, boss?"

"Good. And Myra?" asked Fulton, stirring the cup in his lap.

"Fine, son, just fine. You hear about my boy? He's about the best dang thing that's happened to Leon since I was there myself!" Father and son both played Leon football.

"I've heard. I saw him play a couple times at Centennial Field."

Carter grinned. "Well, what's this about, son?"

"I got a visit from Milo Harbert. His daughter, Janine, came with him."

"Yeah, they saw me this mornin'. I remember the accident," said Carter, taking a sip of coffee. "Dadgum, if it wuhdint a bad one."

Fulton nodded.

"You hold on, son, I'll get you the paperwork we got." He leaned forward toward the door of his office. "Hey, Penelope? Can you pull that accident we did back in fifty-three, one up there near the lake?"

"Sure thing, Sheriff!" Presently, she appeared with a thin manila file.

"Here, let's spread this thing out." Carter did just that, spreading the reports on his desk so the special agent could read from his chair while the sheriff looked over his shoulder.

"This here's the cor'ners' report," said Carter, laying his large hand over it. "Yeah, I remember the autopsy. I didn't go. I think Holland may have. But I remember talking to Doc about it. That high amount of alkeyhaul." The sheriff continued to look over the figure that Dr. Elston had come up with. "Umm, umm, umm." He shook his head. "She was *drunk*. I had a photographer come out to the scene." He flipped through the papers. "Photos ain't in here. Doggone, we'll have to *find* 'em."

"Okay."

"You want to look into this some more?" asked Carter, sounding a little surprised.

"Uh-huh."

"The family's still sayin' it's murder?"

"They think it was," said Fulton, nodding.

"*Hell*. You believe there's anything to it?"

"There are some questions. Maybe these questions get answered, and it turns out it's nothing."

"Or it just opens us up to a bunch a headaches—every case where somebody don't like the answer, they'll git to have another investigation." The sheriff put on his cheaters and looked at the report once more. "I'm gonna have to think on it. The folks seemed reasonable, but dadgum, this was open and shut."

"Okay."

"I know there are things that seem odd. But you know well as I do, we just don't know the reason for *everything*. Take ol' Dennis Tucker, you know, killed hisself last year with a shotgun. We found out about him living in Germany, havin' a wife over there. How he had $10,000 in the bank but was living over by the bus station. A lot of things didn't make sense, but he shot himself all right. Sure, some things are gonna seem odd. There's always gonna be people questionin' what we do, wantin' to take pot shots at the quarterback 'cos they're havin' to sit on the bench. But that don't change the *facts*."

"I agree. But one thing has got me thinkin'. She had a run-in with a man over a business deal. Sam Nowak?"

"Can't say as I know him."

"He accused her of trying to cheat him. Threatened her. He supposedly has ties to some rough men, bringin' in whiskey and so on."

"Uh-huh?"

"And she was involved with the AA, hadn't drank in years."

"Well, she coulda fell off the wagon *that* night," replied the sheriff, chuckling.

"But then there's the diary—that was known to be kept by the victim at all times. She may have written things in it once she met with this fella Sam. It wasn't found. And there's these torn photos the family received. Someone out there knows something."

"Hell, if you'd seen the wreck, that coulda been thrown out in the woods, it coulda been left in the car, twisted up like it was. The photos could be coming from someone that just got out of Chattahoochee that knew this girl in school for all we know. I'm gonna have to think about this and what we're opening ourselves up for. They give you any witnesses?"

"They gave me some names. Nothing definite."

"A lot of hours runnin' that stuff down. Even with you taking lead on it, it's a lot for us to commit to over a hunch from a family. They're hurtin', they got every right. But that don't prove a *crime*. I got to think on it, True." He was serious, almost apologetic.

"I understand. It's thin."

The sheriff's smile returned as he changed the subject. "You fishin' much lately?"

"Haven't had the chance."

"Ol' Hal runnin' you ragged, ain't he?" said Carter, a sly grin on his face.

Fulton laughed.

"That rascal Holland's out fishin' today. Went down to Leesburg with his sons, fishin' them lakes. We too busy, son."

"Yeah."

The old friends rose and shook hands. Carter walked with him to the door. Fulton turned the old knob.

"I'll call you on this," said Carter.

"Thanks, Frank."

XXXXX

The telephone rang.

"Hello, I'm Lee Shelley."

"Yessir. Mr. Harbert's friend?"

"That's right. He asked me to telephone you."

"Okay."

"About Jo Ellen Harbert. My wife and I were friends of hers."

"Yessir."

"Normally, I wouldn't talk about matters of our society—to preserve anonymity, of course. But Milo Harbert's a good friend. Jo Ellen came to us at his urging when he told her about our membership in the AA and our little group in Fort Walton Beach."

"You were her sponsor?"

"I was."

"He said she took it seriously."

"Yes, she took her sobriety seriously."

"Did you know her to have any relapse?"

"No. She hadn't taken a drink in five years. I saw no signs of it. I've been involved with the twelve-step program for years. Naturally, I get calls all the time—someone at a bar tempted to drink. A wife bounces a check, so the man is tempted to get drunk, that sort of thing. I never got that with Jo Ellen. I was very surprised when I heard about...about what happened. There has to be something more—"

"Yessir?"

"There has to be some other explanation. I don't know what, precisely. It baffles my wife and I to this day."

"Was she a stable person, Mr. Shelley?"

"Why, yes. She loved her business, she worked there every day, attended our society, her church. She inspired my wife and I, so sure she was in her sobriety."

Something gnawed at Fulton. Why would a gal that never hit the sauce suddenly come to a strange town—a dry town—so she could get drunk? "Well, thank you very much, Mr. Shelley. I sure appreciate it."

"I hope the information proves helpful."

"Yessir." Fulton hung up. He looked out the window. *None of this makes a damn bit of sense.*

26

Tallahassee
3:05 p.m.
Tuesday, 10/23/1956

The aroma of the fourth pot of coffee and the eleventh Chesterfield swirled about the room. Janine paused for another light. Fulton obliged. She exhaled and fixed her intense eyes on him. "Sadie was my sister's best friend. She never would tell us anything, but she, perhaps, does know something. She works at a beauty parlor. I don't know which one."

"Is there anyone else she had business dealings with that might know something?"

"No one I'm familiar with," said Janine.

"Nor I," said the old man.

"What about neighbors—besides Mrs. Morris?"

"No, Mrs. Morris was the only one we knew," said Janine, tapping her cigarette into the ashtray on the desk.

"Anyone else at all?"

"No one she mentioned."

"Do you know any reason your sister might have had for driving up towards the state line?"

"No," replied Janine. Her father agreed that there was no reason for her to have driven that far from town.

"But she may have decided to leave town, meet up with some old friends from school that y'all don't know about?"

"It's possible," Janine admitted.

"Hmmm." Fulton's demeanor was one of trying to measure up the dimensions of the problem, but he gave no indication that he was enthusiastic about the case. Harbert and his daughter both sensed it and well knew the difficulty of the facts they were confronting this policeman with. They were visibly downcast. Fulton was quiet for a moment, his face without expression. "There is something else," he said finally.

"Yes, Mr. Fulton?"

"May I keep the pictures?"

"You may, indeed," replied Harbert, a faint smile on his face, clearly understanding then that Fulton did intend to look into the matter.

Janine's spirits buoyed as well. She too had the vagaries of a smile; her expression seemed lighter. Sensing their elation and not wanting to give false hope, he cautioned them, "It's not official yet."

"Certainly," said Miss Harbert, obtaining a fresh cigarette from her silver case.

"And I will need the ex-boyfriend's number and address if you have it."

"Yes, of course," replied the young woman.

Fulton got out his lighter again as Janine waited.

"Thank you," she said, opening her purse and retrieving the address book, the book well-worn, the pages full of entries in Jo Ellen's neat cursive. "That's funny, I don't have his address, not his Jacksonville address anyway. I thought I had. Of course, his mother lives here in an old house. His family goes back many years."

"That's all right, I'll track him down."

"I asked someone about you," she told him.

"Yes, ma'am?"

"They told me you used to investigate homicides for the city police department in Jacksonville. That you went to the FBI Academy in Washington."

"Yes, ma'am."

"I spoke to Chief Canefield. He's a friend of ours. He says you've got a great deal of experience with homicide cases."

"Well, I guess that's so," he replied modestly.

Janine's eyes—the same intense eyes Jo Ellen had—focused in on him. "I want to ask you a question."

Fulton nodded for her to proceed.

"Can you solve it?"

27

Tallahassee
Wednesday, 10/24/1956

No heater in the Miami Ford. The cabin felt like a deep freeze. The Caddies in the showroom, the lights at the gulf station, the yellow glow of streetlights all passed by in a blur. He had that *feeling* inside—something told him this was, in fact, *murder.*

Fulton twisted the wheel, sending the boxy sedan heeling over onto Gaines, into the oncoming lane, the brakes squeaking as he slid to a halt at the curb. Mary Ann set a mug with a chipped rim in front of him. The black-and-white picture of the victim, with her striking eyes, stared back at him, paper-clipped where she was to the handwritten report. Sure, it was cold in the office; he was shivering and uncomfortable. But that feeling was something else entirely. It meant something among the seemingly unimportant bits of information didn't add up.

No prints. No witnesses. The entire case file was six pages. *Three years had passed.*
The Bureau had no resources to look into accidental deaths. The entire organization was but five men and one woman set up to help the sheriffs fight organized crime. That was the focus. The new bolita bosses were raking in the money. Plenty of dough to buy off officials, judges, and cops. They were getting nasty.

Many in the legislature, even among the sheriffs, resisted giving power to anything that resembled a "state police." The Bureau had no power to initiate an investigation; it had to be invited to assist by a local authority. Fulton had not received such an invitation.

Mary Ann pounded the keys of her typewriter. *Clack-clack-clack.* She worked tirelessly at a pitiful salary. Martin had to borrow her Underwood from the attorney general so she would have a machine. Thunder rattled the windows and made the lights flicker. Fulton smiled, remembering what Marlene had said: "Gee, this place sure is *fancy!*" She warned him not to take the job; it sounded like poverty row to her. She was right.

Fulton looked at Jo Ellen's photograph. Perhaps she knew something that someone didn't want told.

Will I get the chance to solve this, or will I be obliged to file it away?

All he could do was wait.

XXXXX

Friday, 10:00 a.m.

Was he humoring them, trying to be polite like the others? Harbert thought Fulton would have called by now. He sat by the telephone anxiously. Finally, he looked through the city directory provided by the hotel. He scanned the listings for "Sheriff's Bureau," but it was no where to be found. He knocked on Janine's door.

"I'm almost ready, Dad."

"Fine," said Harbert, taking a seat by the window. The rain had stopped; he looked out at the overcast sky. Janine put on her hat and gloves. She told him she would certainly accompany him down to the little house on Gaines.

Fulton could see the agony in the man's eyes. He appeared years older than their last meeting. Janine seemed less poised. Still, he could not tell them anything definite. "At least the sun is coming out," he said, little else to say. "But it's awful cold, that kind of cold that sits in your bones."

"Yes, like it's turning colder, how it does after a rain," said Janine.

"Um-hmm," agreed Fulton. "It'll probably clear out tonight, not a cloud in the sky, but cold."

The old man nodded. They chatted for a while, Janine doing most of the talking; they all seemed to glance at the telephone, as if they expected it to ring any second, delivering them from the dreadful waiting.

Tallahassee
11:00 a.m.
Saturday, 10/27/1956

Fulton phoned the Harberts—still no word. Janine thanked him and hung up.

"Fulton was right about the weather," said the old man. "The clouds are gone."

Janine nodded. For the next five hours they sat, waiting for the telephone to ring, Janine smoking and reading, Harbert opening and closing his watch and staring into his coffee. Finally, they could wait no longer.

XXXXX

At 4:30 p.m., he heard a car pull up. A taxi.

"My daughter and I did not wish to make you wait past five," said the old man. Fulton led them to those hard chairs. Fulton sat behind his desk, the telephone between them. They all found themselves staring at it. The silence continued for what seemed like several minutes before they were jolted by the loud bell of that phone.

"Yes?" The Harberts stared at Fulton, trying to read his expression. He was obviously listening to someone; that person went on for two or three minutes. It seemed like half an hour. "I understand," said Fulton, gravely serious. "Yessir." He listened as the man on the other end of the line went on about something that was unintelligible to the Harberts. "I know, there's a lot of that," said Fulton in response. The other man kept talking; it sounded like he was talking rather fast. "Yessir," answered Fulton. The Harberts were nearly beside themselves. Fulton's faro-dealer countenance did not reveal a thing, and they could not hear one word of the man on the other end of the line.

"All right, sure. Okay, good-bye," said Fulton, carefully placing the receiver back on the cradle.

Their eyes scanned his face; they were leaning forward, asking, without speaking, "Was it a *yes*?"

Fulton looked at them for another seemingly endless second before telling them the answer: "The sheriff says go."

Harbert practically leapt from his seat, embracing his daughter.

"I can hardly believe it!" Janine exclaimed, tears filling her eyes.

Fulton shook hands with Harbert, who gave him a hearty slap on the shoulder. Janine smiled like a child on Christmas morning. "Thank you," she said, looking up at him.

"Thank you, sir!" said Harbert, still not letting loose of Fulton's hand. The older man seemed to regain his strength. "We can finally *know*."

"I think Jo Ellen would be happy," added Janine.

Harbert checked his watch. "We'd better go. We need to get back to the Floridan. Our things are there, and we must catch our train," said Harbert, smiling broadly.

Fulton followed them out. "Are y'all gonna walk all the way up there?"

"Yes, sir, and we'll be walking back much lighter," Harbert said, smiling.

"I can drive you."

"Are you sure you don't mind?" asked Miss Harbert.

"Not at all. Come on," he said, leading them to the Ford. He drove them up the street, parking alongside the Cypress Lounge on Call. He opened the door for his passengers, and they stepped out onto the sidewalk.

"Naturally, if there's anything you need from us, you have my number," said Harbert.

"Yessir."

"Good-bye," the woman said. "And thank you."

"Yes'm," said Fulton, tipping the corner of his hat. He shook the older gentleman's hand. "Good-bye, Mr. Harbert."

"Good-bye. Please stay in touch."

XXXXX

5:05 p.m.

Jo Ellen's calendar. He flipped to October. Monday the 26th had a list of things to do. "Pick up supplies. Jones wedding dress."

Tuesday the 27th: "Crestview—bank."

Thursday the 29th: "Tallahassee."

Friday the 30th, 6:00 p.m.: "APT—SAM." *No show.*

Monday the 2nd, 4:00 p.m.: "APT—SAM."

133

At 8:30 pm, in blue ink: "SAM."

"9:30 p.m." was circled.

Tuesday the 3rd: "8:00 a.m." Circled in blue.

Except for a hair appointment the following Tuesday and a note to "pay light bill," there the entries stopped. So he'd fill in the gaps.

He dialed 0. "Long distance, please." The long-distance operator came on the line, and he gave her the number.

"Hold, please, while I connect your call."

It would be 4:05 p.m. in Shalimar. It took a moment for the call to go through.

"Hello," answered a man's voice.

"I'm True Fulton. I'm working with the Sheriff's Bureau in Tallahassee. I was trying to reach Vera Lindgren."

"That's my wife, but she isn't here. She's at work. What's this about?"

"It's about a friend of your wife's, Jo Ellen Harbert."

"Oh, yes, the poor girl. Well, Vera went back to work at the alteration shop."

"I didn't know that."

"Yessir, the new owner asked her to come back. They needed the help. Anyway, here's the number for the shop. 2-4498."

"Thanks, I'll give it a try."

"Good-bye."

Mary Ann leaned in his office. "Mr. Fulton, I have a copy of the transcript from the coroner's jury." She handed it to him.

"Oh, thank you." He opened the envelope. It was eighty pages. Mary Ann, herself very curious about the case, had walked over to the courthouse to get the file. She had her coat and hat on. "Good night," she told him.

"Good night," said Fulton, looking up from the notebook and the list of telephone numbers. He called the long-distance operator again. He gave her the town and the number, and she connected the call, station to station.

"Fort Walton Alterations, may I help you?" By the sound of the woman's voice, she was in her fifties.

"I'm True Fulton. I'm workin' with the Sheriff's Bureau. I was wondering if I might speak with you about Jo Ellen Harbert."

"Oh, Jo Ellen," she said with a sigh. "I can't talk now, it's been a busy afternoon. Can you call back later?"

"Sure. What might be a good time?"

"Really, no time is good," she said, sighing again. Fulton heard the sound of a sewing machine. The noise stopped. "Look, why don't you try back tomorrow."

Click.

He dialed the number for Mrs. Phillips. It had been disconnected according to the operator. He got out the directory and found a new number. It rang without answer. Fulton called the bank in Crestview. Maynard had died. No one knew about Jo Ellen.

Fulton poured a fresh cup of coffee and began going through the reports Mary Ann had obtained: Autopsy. Transcript from the inquest. The sheriff and state attorney investigations were consistent. Holland and Wilkinson agreed it was an accident attributable to drunken driving. In that light, the jury verdict was not surprising. There were no witnesses to the crash in the SO report. Deputy Haywood had been the first at the scene. He testified at the inquest, as did Holland.

He placed a call to Sarah Morris. The operator tried the line twice. No answer.

Fulton turned down Park Avenue; there were a lot of cars at the barber shop, which was open until midnight on Saturdays for the farmers. He turned the corner on Calhoun, looking for the Howerton mansion. He found it: three stories with a porch that wrapped around, fresh white and yellow paint, lovely grounds. There was a Cadillac poking out from the carriage house. He looked for a moment then drove on.

XXXXX

It was nearly 10:00 p.m. Harbert removed Darley's card from his wallet and spun the dial for 2-5150. Presently, the 400 Cabs Ford squeaked to a stop in front of the Floridan.

Harbert approached the desk clerk with Janine. The clerk collected the key and bid the man and his daughter a safe journey home. The 150-room hotel had good service; the Confederate bellhop had their bags loaded in the taxi before they even finished saying good-bye to the clerk. Darley was

135

waiting beside the green car. The Harberts rode back to the station as quietly as they'd come, on the same darkly lit side streets.

XXXXX

They didn't notice the 1950 Ford coupe that was following, the heavyset driver reaching into the glove box. He pulled out the object—a bottle of chalky antacid tablets. He downed a mouthful. His stomach told him the Harberts' presence was ominous. It was just a dull ache when they got to town. Now, with the Sheriff's Bureau getting involved, it was full-on burning pain. *How foolish those boys were down south, drowning a judge, stabbing Wall. All they did was give Collins an excuse to put more money into law enforcement, more cops with nothing better to do than nose around like bloodhounds, digging up things that were supposed to stay buried.*

He watched them board the *Gulf Wind*, watched the train disappear into the dark of night. This meant real trouble. He lit another Pall Mall and took the rest of the antacids.

29

Tallahassee
Sunday, 10/28/1956

He drove down Gaines Street, passing the jail and down into the little valley, bouncing over the railroad tracks and up the hill to Myers Park, a swanky subdivision begun in the twenties. He turned down Country Club Drive, enjoying the lovely avenue of shade trees and fine homes and the golf course perfectly situated over plunging hills and streams. He parked in front of the wooden clubhouse that accommodated a small locker room and a large ball room. Chief Detective Cliff Holland was looking very relaxed in a golf shirt and pressed trousers.

"Hello, True! Nothing like spending a Sunday out on the golf course. You play?"

"No. Tried it once but never got the hang of it," said Fulton, shaking his hand.

Holland was a handsome fellow, six feet tall with light brown hair, which he kept carefully in place with pomade. "Oh, it's great! Gets me away from the wife and kids," he said with a wink, at the same time watching the curvy brunette in a tight cashmere sweater and skirt getting out of her car.

"I see what you mean. Well, I was wanting to talk to you about the Harbert accident."

"I thought that was put to rest three years ago. Say, I better get my gear ready. Judge Vaughn and a few of the boys and I are supposed to tee off at nine thirty."

"Sure," said Fulton, walking with Holland over to a shiny station wagon. The chief detective lowered the tailgate of the garnet and white Buick, pulling his golf clubs out from behind the rear seat. Fulton looked the car over.

"Oh, you like this buggy? Me and the missus just got it. The fella at Carr Buick gave us a good trade on our old heap. First '57 they sold."

"She looks like she's just built to take a vacation."

"Oh, lots of room," said Holland, slamming the tailgate. "But I'd prefer anything than havin' to go on one of those long trips, kids hollering in the backseat, the wife putting cold cloths on her forehead because of the strain." Holland shook his head. "We went to Marineland last summer—miserable!"

Fulton smiled at that. "Well, I was wondering if there was anything you recall about Ms. Harbert's personal effects. I understand you went over her hotel room."

"That's right. I went there to help her sister gather her things," said Holland, lifting the clubs. "Wasn't anything unusual. Clothes and stuff. Why do you ask?"

"Did you find anything like a notebook or diary?"

"Don't remember."

"Did you hear mention that she had something like that?"

Holland set the bag down, pulling out a seven iron, holding it up like he was sighting for a shot, then brought the head back and looked it over. "Well, now that you mention it, they were asking about it, wanted us to search for it."

"Her father talked to you about it?"

"Yeah. So did her sister, I don't know her name—although she had a pretty classy chassis, if you know what I mean. But we recovered the girl's leather bag, sort of an attaché, from the trunk of the car. The sister insisted it had an impression from a book, and that book was missing."

"Did it look that way, maybe worn from where she'd carried a book?"

"It coulda been, there coulda been some worn places on the leather, I don't remember." Holland waved to Vaughn as he pulled up in his Ford.

"Okay."

"We looked through everything in that room—no book was to be found there."

"Okay."

"And the sister was kinda bent outta shape over it. Probably had something in there about *her*," said Holland, winking. "I didn't think it was too important."

"Was anyone else with you?"

"No."

"Did anything else stand out to you?"

"Not really."

"No other papers or anything?"

138

"No. She had a dog-eared AA book and a Bible. The Bible wasn't nothing unusual, but I thought the Alcoholics book was. It fit the nature of the crash, what we'd found with the bottle in the car and so forth."

"Okay."

"What's going on anyway? I mean, I know the sheriff agreed to open this, but do you think there's anything to it?"

"Could be."

"I don't get it. I heard you were a hell of a cop in Jacksonville, solved some big cases. But this was cut and dry. I never saw a clearer case of a drunk going out, getting themselves killed."

"But she did have an argument just before she died, and the family swears she had this book—this missing book."

"They raised hell during the inquest too," said Holland. "I'm sorry, but I think we have better things to do."

A Bel Air pulled up in front of the country club. "Well, there's Grant. He and I play every week the weather's good. Sometimes more," said Holland, grinning.

"I'll say hello to Mr. Wilkinson. I haven't seen him in a while."

Holland nodded.

"Mr. Wilkinson, how are you, sir," said Fulton, stepping up to the prosecutor and extending his hand.

"Fulton. How are ya? We were just going to play a round. You care to join us? We can probably scrounge up some extra clubs."

"Thank you, sir, maybe another time."

"Suit yourself."

Fulton said good-bye to the men as their caddies approached to carry their clubs out to the fairway.

XXXXX

Cherokee Hotel. Maybe Norma Desmond stayed there. It looked the part, built in Florida's boom years, before the real estate bubble burst in '26. It was swank, though not as modern nor as animated with politicking as the Floridan. It was tucked away off the main drag, across from the town's telephone exchange. Fulton found a space along Park. He walked along the sidewalk, which sloped down to the entrance. He passed beneath the awning and into the gilded lobby.

The place reflected the opulence of the flapper era—high ceilings and chandeliers, an intricate hexagon mosaic on the floors. Businessmen chatted or read the paper in the chairs and sofas.

He approached the desk, with its polished woodwork. "Mornin', I'm wonderin' if you can help me," said Fulton, addressing the clerk.

"Why, yessir, what can I do for you?"

"Would you mind tellin' me somethin'?"

The man nodded.

"Were you workin' here back in fifty-three, in the fall?"

"Yessir. I just got back from Korea earlier in the year and got this job."

"Do you remember this girl?" said Fulton, showing him the picture.

The man took it and looked at the photo, studying it. Some people will just glance at a photo and hand it back, or simply shoot their eyes over and not even reach for it. But this man *studied* it.

"You know, I try to remember faces and names. The hotel wants us to call folks by name. I remember her, she was from the Panhandle. Are you a policeman?"

"I'm with the Sheriff's Bureau." Fulton showed him his ID with the small silver star.

The clerk looked at it curiously. "You know, I've never heard of that. Is that something like the FBI? I had an FBI man stay here once." He seemed excited.

"It's more like skid row."

"Pardon?"

"Oh, nothing," said Fulton.

The man studied the face some more. "Yes, her name was Jo Ellen Harland? Harlow?"

"Harbert?"

"Yes, that's it," he said, returning the photo. "Nice woman."

"So she did stay here?"

"Oh, yes, sir."

140

"Do you recall the date?"

"It was in the fall, like you said. October, I think. I would have to get the guest log from that time."

"Can you? I can come back later if you need time. I'm interested to see how long she was here."

"No, sir, I have them here." He retrieved them from a cabinet under the counter. "Okay, fifty-one, fifty-two, there it is, fifty-three," he said, coming up with the book and laying it on the counter. He flipped though until he found the pages labeled October 1953. He scanned the pages for her name. He flipped back another page, looking. On line 14 was the signature in neat cursive:

zzzzz
Jo Ellen Harbert, Ft. Walton
Zzzzz-end

"When did she check in?"

"The twenty-ninth."

"Alone?"

"Yessir. I don't recall her visiting with anyone. Let's see," said the man, flipping through pages in another book. "I don't see where she checked out."

"She didn't get a chance to."

"I'm sorry, sir?"

"She died."

"Oh no!" replied the clerk, shaking his head.

"Do you recall anyone coming to see her at any time?"

"No, sir. Of course, it was three years ago. But nothing stands out. She came and went, I suppose, like anyone traveling on business. I remember she was here on business."

"She mention anything in particular?"

The man thought about it a moment. "No, I don't recall the details."

"Was she acting strange?"

"No."

"Did she act like she'd been drinking any of the times you dealt with her?"

"On no, I would have remembered that. Sometimes we've guests that have imbibed a few too many. Sometimes it's downright funny. Not her. She paid for her room and was as close to me as you are now. I would have smelled it. She paid on two occasions because the last night she paid in advance."

"That book got anything about her car?"

"Blue Packard and the tag number, see?"

"Uh-huh."

"I remember the car."

"Yeah?"

"I remember that last night she parked it on Calhoun, right under her window, like she wanted to keep an eye on it. The other nights, I don't know where she parked it, never saw it."

"Yeah?"

"But that evening, probably right before I saw her leave, I went outside to help bring in a guest's luggage, and I saw the Packard there."

"Anyone hanging around out there? Anyone that looked out of place?"

"Umm, I don't think so."

"The family recalled someone from the hotel assisting with her belongings. Do you know who that might have been?"

"That was me."

"Do you remember anything about that?"

"Her things were neat, orderly. Her bed had not been slept in the last night. It had not been touched since the maid changed the sheets and made the bed that morning. Her suitcases were an expensive kind. Nice clothes."
"Yessir?"

"Really nice things, not sure if they had an expensive label, but I shouldn't be surprised. And she had three thousand and some odd in cash in an envelope inside there."

"Cash money?"

The clerk nodded.

"Did anything seem like it was missing?"

"Nothing stands out."

"A book maybe?

"Well—oh yes, the young woman that came to get her things. Her cousin maybe?"

"Sister."

"Yes. She said some sort of diary book was missing. It wasn't in the room."

"Yessir?"

"The young lady seemed upset about it. We searched that room from top to bottom."

"Booze?"

"No, sir. I don't remember seeing anything like that."

"And you were with Detective Holland and the sister?"

"No, there was another deputy—Charlie Haywood."

"Oh?"

"Yessir, I remember that."

"Now that last night, you're sure you were here the entire time?"

"I'm certain of that. So what happened to Ms. Harbert?"

"That's what I'm workin' on."

XXXXX

Another witness with information—one we didn't know about. Fulton had read Haywood's testimony. He didn't know he'd gone to the hotel.

He picked up the mic for the Motorola. He called Bobby the dispatcher on the Leon County frequency. Bobby was making a fresh pot of coffee. He heard the call and came back to the radio on his crutches. "True, ol' Charlie's got the night shift *tonight*. I can tell 'im you want to *talk* to him." The dispatcher had a very distinct way of talking. He probably could have worked in radio—or as a preacher.

"Sure, Bobby. Much obliged."

"Okay, ten *four*. I'll let him know when he comes in."

143

In a moment, the sheriff came on the radio. "I got something for you, hoss. I'll send it over with Will."

"What is it?"

"You just wait and see."

Dreggors. Gray fedora. Red tie. Sport coat unbuttoned for it was too snug. He got out of his five-year-old Ford coupe, clutching a large envelope. The clerk led him up to Jo Ellen's room, where he found Fulton looking around, opening the door to the bathroom, glancing in and shutting it, then the closet in the same fashion. Fulton got a peppermint from his pocket then sat on the bed, thinking.

Dreggors's eyes scanned the room, his left hand in his pocket jingling his keys. "Hey, they got a TV in here now," he noticed. He slowly moved around the set, admiring it.

"All right, you gonna keep me in suspense?" asked Fulton, eyeing the envelope under Dreggors's right arm.

"Oh yeah," said Dreggors with a sheepish grin. "Here," he said, handing over the package.

Fulton opened it. "Ha! The photos. I thought they were missing?"

"They was—they are. Frank called ol' Robert Nash and had him develop some more. You know Robert?"

Fulton nodded.

"He's got the shop up on North Monroe. He was the photographer they called to the scene that night." Fulton flipped through the photos, shots of the wrecked Packard and the body. He set them on the bed and looked around the victim's room. He sat on the bed, as if he was looking at it through the victim's eyes. What she might have seen, done.
Dreggors got a drink of water from the sink, drinking from a paper cup with the Cherokee logo.

"I checked with the clerk. There wasn't anyone staying in the room next door or across the hall," said Fulton.

"Well, these walls are thick anyway," said Dreggors. He stuck his hands in his pockets and looked out the window. "She had a good view of the street through this winder. If she parked out there, she coulda seen her car, for sure." The big fellow looked around the room, a nice room that didn't reveal much. "No chain on the door, no peephole for her to see who's knockin'."

144

"Clerk thinks she had no visitors," said Fulton as the two walked outside. Fulton reached back to shut the door and walked with Dreggors down the hall. "The corridor goes around a corner there." Fulton pointed out. "It's dark, especially with this wallpaper. If someone hid there, steps out when she goes toward the elevator..."

"Yeah, maybe." They took the stairs. "But if I get hold of her in there, how do I get her out to her car, past the clerk?" Dreggors wondered, looking over at the front desk. They continued outside to the sidewalk.

"So I gotta make my move outside someplace."

"So she parks out here. It's pretty dark out here on Calhoun," said Dreggors.

"Does she have it locked?"

"Who locks their car 'round here? I expect, her bein' from Fort Walton, she wouldn't have neither, small town and all."

"Okay. Let's say she did have it locked, it ain't hard to slip a coat hanger down and unlock a convertible, is it?"

"No, I reckon not."

"So I'm the killer. I get in the car and wait. She comes along. She doesn't look in the windows, check the backseat. He's there in the shadows."

"And you got a gun. Ya tell her ta drive."

"Wouldn't she scream?"

"Well, you do have that gun. Maybe ya cover her mouth up. You're behind her in the backseat."

They got in Dreggors's car and turned onto Monroe, crossing Tennessee with the green light. "Catholic church hadn't burned yet," said Dreggors, pointing out the shell that remained at Carolina and Monroe. "Don't think anyone woulda been around though." They passed one of the old mansions that still stood near Georgia Street, approaching McCord Point. "The Standard Oil woulda been open," said the big man, pointing at the gas station.

"Yeah, I talked to the owner. He doesn't remember anything unusual."

"You have looked into this, haven't ya? None of these other businesses would be open that time of night," said Dreggors as they continued up Monroe, the two-lane avenue with storefronts and houses and oaks. "She'd-a passed the *motel*," said Dreggors, pointing to the little stone cabins at Lake Ella.

145

"Yeah. Checked there too." They kept going, the scenery quickly changing to open pasture and woods as they neared the city limits sign at Tharpe Street. Dreggors nodded to his left, the pasture with whitewashed crossbuck fence, GMC trucks lined up in a row. "Bassett's dairy, no one around that time a night."

"Yeah." They kept going toward Bradford. "Bowman's Auto Court was called Clark's then," said Dreggors, pointing to the cabins on the bluff that overlooked the highway. "Pretty big driveway, office up front, always lights on at night."

"No one remembered anything," said Fulton. "Except it was raining hard."

"So that masks your sound if she hollered, blew her horn. I just don't know about somethin', True."

"Yeah?"

"So's you git her in the car, ya tell her ta drive."

"Yeah?"

"How ya get her ta drink? I mean, how'd ya *make* her?"

"Well, I'm behind her, I got a gun, I got her by the neck, I've hit her. I stick the bottle in her mouth and force it down. We know half of it was consumed, according to the report."

"Hmmm."

They passed Lakeshore Drive. Pinewoods on both sides. "I reckon that was the spot," he said, pointing up ahead.

"Let me see that photo. Yeah, that's it," said Dreggors pulling over onto the grass shoulder. They got out, looking down toward the lake, the quiet stretch of country highway in the distance. Dreggors opened the trunk, reaching in an ice chest. "You want a Coke-Cola?"

Fulton shook his head. Dreggors got himself one, and they began walking along the highway, crossing over to the crash scene.

"So I get out of the car, I start it rolling."

"You got a purty good hill here," added Dreggors.

"I watch her roll down into the trees," said Fulton, walking toward the ravine, looking down the steep slope off into the pines. "She crashes. Where do I go then?"

146

"The old Coe place is just a ways thataway," said Dreggors, pointing. The two men walked toward the farm, taking a dirt road until they got to a driveway nearly overrun with weeds. "This is ol' Jimmy Coe's farm. You've got an old barn up there."

They walked through the weeds and brush to the barn, which looked as if a stiff breeze could flatten the thing, more a stack of blackened wood and rusty tin than a building.

Dreggors grabbed the dilapidated door, tugging it open. "Not much in there, old saws and an old *buy-sickle* tire," noted Dreggors.

Fulton stepped inside. There were a few cigarette butts. "Probably kids left those," said Dreggors. "I seen kids up here before, every now and again."

"Just in case," said Fulton, squatting down and sweeping them into an envelope. He looked up at Dreggors. "So I hide here until the dust settles. Then I slip on back towards town."

"Maybe he had a *buy-sickle* here or somethin'."

"Was it empty three years ago?"

Dreggors took a swig of Coca-Cola, the wheels turning under his close-cropped red-blond locks. He knew everybody in the county, and little that went on among his fellow citizens escaped his knowing. "They left in nineteen-hundred-and-fifty-one. I know 'cause I got called to go to Koe-ree-uh 'bout the same time they done packed up and moved out to Cal-fornya. They just left, didn't really say much about it."

XXXXX

Haywood was coming on the night shift; he pulled in the parking lot of the high school. They got out and talked by their cars in the shadow of the ornate brick building that overlooked US 90. The sheriff's office recently got uniforms that seemed to recall Eisenhower's D-Day attire. Haywood looked smart in his khaki trousers, short brown jacket, visor hat. He still had the old shield-type badge.

"She had a leather case, worn, like somethin' was missing. Like maybe a Bible. Otherwise, normal items. Clothes and so forth. I didn't go through her suitcase. Her sister done that. Detective Holland stuck his head in for a minute, then slipped out and smoked a cigarette in the hall. She had *a lot* of cash—three or four thousand, I reckon. She had it in an envelope in the drawer. There might have been some receipts from a bank, not sure now."

"But, you do remember the imprint of that book?"

"Yessir, it was real plain. Does that hep' ya?"

"Yeah. Now, these bank receipts, were they local?"

147

"Shoot, I think so. Is it important?"

"Don't know."

"I remember she had a box or somethin', like a present. It was in the trash. I thought maybe she had an admirer. No one came forward though."

"Could you tell what was in it?"

"No, just a box so big," he said, indicating with his hands.

"Did you take it?"

"Nah, just left 'er in the trash. Holland told me we was through, the family could take what they wanted, so I left."

"Thanks, Charlie. Stay safe out there."

"10-4."

Haywood left to begin his duties—lonely duties. At night, one man patrolled the entire county.

30

Tallahassee
Sunday, 10/28/1956

The office was dark except for a dim lamp on his desk. Fulton examined the torn photos and the envelope for prints, dusting the photos and fuming the paper envelope in a glass chamber he'd made himself. He was able to lift a few fingerprints, which would have to be compared with the half dozen or so people that had handled the evidence. No prints could be recovered from the cigarettes.

He was alone at the office. He dialed 0. Martin would certainly be questioned about all the long-distance calls. The governor would probably have to intervene to see that the bill was paid. The operator looked up Clay Howerton's home number and attempted to put through a person-to-person call. She called Fulton back. "I'm sorry, sir, there's no answer at the Howerton residence." Fulton thanked her and tried Sarah Morris's number and the other ladies' numbers. No answer. He switched off the light. He was about to leave when the telephone rang.

"Fulton speakin'," he answered, loosening his tie.

"You're wasting your time, Mr. Fulton. The answer is in Jo Ellen's past."

"Who am I speaking with?"

"Never mind that. I'm tellin' ya, you need to look back a few years. Look outside your door."

"How's that?"

Click.

Fulton drew his gun and looked through the edge of the blinds. He saw no one. He walked down the hall, opening the back door slowly. He looked outside. No one was around. He walked along the side of the house but saw no one. Gaines was dead. A Chevrolet rolled by on Monroe, the street going quiet after the hum of its tires faded into the night. He walked back to the front door and there he saw it—an envelope leaning against the doorframe. He picked it up with his handkerchief and took it inside. He put on some surgical gloves and opened it.

Photos! Jo Ellen. Her face bruised and beaten. Nude from the waist up, her arms across her breasts. The photographs were frightening. She looked scared, like she expected to get hit again. Another photograph showed bruising to her arms with her head tilted back and her eyes closed, dark circles under them. They looked unnatural. It was obvious someone derived some sick pleasure from the poses. Fulton shook his head.

A bright bulb had been used to light the morbid scene, not just a flash bulb. She appeared to sit on a stool; there was a large butterfly design, some sort of a plaster, hanging on the brick wall behind her. The photograph was taken in a basement or perhaps an old house that had been added on to. There was no shortage of either in Tallahassee.

A couple of the photos had the corners burned off. Someone had tried to destroy them. One was quite badly discolored, nearly half-singed. He examined each one for fingerprints, dusting front and back. Nothing. He switched off the light.

XXXXX

Monday. Fulton spoke to the employees at the telephone company across from the Cherokee. And the employees of every law firm, office, and filling station in the vicinity, even the janitor at the Ford dealer. No one recalled the woman from the Panhandle. While he was at the phone company, he asked them to determine where his mysterious call had come from. It was local, that was all they could tell him.

He dialed 0. The operator found Howerton's work number. Downtown law firm in Jacksonville. A moment later, she connected the call.

"Lynn, Myer, Hartell, and Locklin, how may I help you?"

"May I speak with Clay Howerton, please?"

"One moment," said the secretary, putting him on hold while she checked to see if the lawyer was busy. She returned momentarily. "I'm sorry, he's with a client. May I take a message, sir?"

"Yes, ma'am." Fulton gave her his number. Fulton grabbed the keys to the Ford and started for the door. He was about to open it when the telephone rang. Mary Ann informed Fulton that the caller was asking to speak to him.

"I got a message that you were interested in speaking to one of our attorneys. I'm Clay Howerton. Do you wish to retain an attorney?"

"No, sir, not exactly. I'm not lookin' to hire a lawyer. I'm with the Sheriff's Bureau."

"Okay," he said, sounding disappointed. "I don't get many calls from Tallahassee. I thought perhaps you needed representation. My firm handles many types of cases: injury, wrongful death, hospital negligence. Do you need a lawyer for the...Sheriff's Association, you said?"

"No, sir, the Sheriff's *Bureau*. I'd like to ask you a few questions about Jo Ellen Harbert."

"Talk about memory lane. I hadn't heard her name spoken in a long time."

150

"Y'all used to go together?"

"Yessir, about a year and a half."

"Where did you meet?"

"Well, we met in Crestview. I had one or two clients there, so I would travel over there on occasion. I was just getting started, so I took cases wherever I could. Tallahassee, mostly, but some as far as Pensacola. I met her at a function with some mutual friends. They had us over for dinner, and I met Jo Ellen. We hit it off."

"Was it serious?"

"Yes, I asked her to marry me about six months later."

"You were engaged to Ms. Harbert?" Fulton didn't know that.

"Yes, sir."

"When did y'all break up?"

"Well, it must have been the end of May, the year she passed." The man seemed to answer questions in a straightforward manner, without hesitating. He seemed cordial.

"Did she break things off with you?"

"Oh, no—I broke it off. It just wasn't going to work. I decided to try to find work in Jax. She didn't want to move. We didn't have as much in common as we thought. She didn't drink—ever. And I—to be frank—enjoy a drink now and then. We just weren't compatible."

"When was the last time you saw her, sir?"

"Why, it must have been shortly after we broke up. We had lunch in Fort Walton, talked, and parted on friendly terms. We tried to leave it with no hard feelings, you know?"

"You remember the date?"

"Well, it must have been early June. These questions...I'm curious, has something happened?"

"No, we simply have some loose ends in the case. It's my job to try and tie up those loose ends."

"I didn't know there was a case... Is this something to do with insurance, or do you mean a criminal case?"

151

"I don't know where it will lead. I've been asked to look into the circumstances surrounding her death, what was going on in her life and so forth. It might not go anywhere."

"Okay, but you must have some information that makes you think there's more to it than an accident?"

"It's possible, sir."

"Well, this is really a shock. Her death may have been the result of some kind of foul play?" The lawyer's demeanor seemed to be that of genuine concern.

"We have some things that haven't been explained yet. May not be important, but I gotta look at it. I'm sure you understand."

"Okay. Well, if I can clear anything up, I'd be glad to."

"Well, as you would imagine, anything going on the last couple weeks of her life, who she had contact with, would be important."

"Sure."

"Do you recall having any contact with her during that time, the latter portion of October, into early November fifty-three?"

"No, sir."

"No telephone calls, nothing?"

"No."

"Do you remember where you were on the second of November?"

"Why, yes. I was on my way to Cuba."

"Uh-huh?"

"I boarded the *Gulf Wind* early that morning."

"Is there someone that can verify where you were?"

"Well, my mother can verify I left the house early. A friend of mine, George Webb, met me in Miami when I arrived. That was how I learned about the accident. It was terrible news. I stayed with George until it was time to board our flight. He, his wife, and I took the trip together. I didn't enjoy it much. I was a bit shaken up."

"When did you return to Tallahassee?"

"I was away three weeks. George can confirm that, of course."

152

"Okay," said Fulton, writing down the information. "Do you have Mr. Webb's number?"

"Sure. He lives in Hollywood Beach now. His number? Uh, Wabash 2-9168."

"Okay. Did you hear anything about Jo Ellen, any problems she was having at that time?"

"No, nothing that stands out."

"It's said that you and Miss Harbert had some difficulties in your relationship, disagreements about...certain things."

"No, not really."

"It's said that you got a little rough with Miss Harbert at times—maybe things of a sexual nature."

"Someone told you that?" asked Howerton, sounding unfazed by the question.

"Any truth to that?"

"No, sir, that isn't true." He sighed. "Sounds like something her father would say."

Fulton weighed that answer. Howerton was cool. Perhaps he'd save the sadism angle and confront him face-to-face. He'd see what Webb had to say. "You and her father didn't get along, I take it?"

"I don't think he liked me much. He was old-fashioned about a lot of things. Well, about everything. Is that who said it?"

"No, sir, it wasn't her father that said it."

"Hmmm. Okay."

"Is your family still in Tallahassee, your mother?"

"Yessir, my family goes way back in Tallahassee. We've had the same house since the Civil War. I spent many summers scraping and painting that front porch," he said, laughing.

Fulton chuckled at that too. He had painted his share of porches.

"If things go well for me in November, I might be coming home."

"Oh?"

153

"I'm running for the house seat that's opening up with Mr. Ballinger retiring."

"Oh, well, good luck."

"Thanks. I may need it."

"I appreciate your time, Mr. Howerton."

"I hope I helped you. I'm afraid I don't know very much about what was going on with Jo Ellen the last month or two. We drifted apart, you see. Like I said, we just didn't have so much in common as we had thought. If you need any more information, please give me a call."

"Yessir."

Fulton's gut feeling was that this fellow didn't have anything to do with Jo Ellen's death. But certainty came from the evidence, not feelings. Fulton tapped the hook of the telephone and dialed 0 again. He gave the operator Webb's number. It rang a few times before being answered by a woman. "Webb residence," came the cheerful voice.

"This is True Fulton with the Sheriff's Bureau in Tallahassee. May I talk to George Webb?"

"Of course. I'm Mrs. Webb. I'll get him for you."

"Thank you." He heard her put the receiver down. "George, it's someone from the sheriff's department," he heard the woman say. He heard a man's voice, but could not hear what he said. "I'm not sure, dear," responded Mrs. Webb.

"Okay, I'm coming, just one more bite of that steak! Hello?"

"Hello, Mr. Webb, sorry to interrupt your breakfast."

"Oh, that's all right, we're just having a little steak and eggs. If you're trying to hire me, I will caution you, I'm retired."

"Oh, no, sir. My name's Fulton. I'm with the Sheriff's Bureau. I was wondering if you could answer a few questions."

"Sure, what is this pertaining to?"

"An associate of yours, Clay Howerton, and his whereabouts November second, three years ago."

"Is he in trouble?"

"I don't think so, as long as I can confirm what he's told me?"

"I understand. What would you like to know?"

"Do you recall a visit from Mr. Howerton around that time?"

"Uh-huh. Clay came down. We were going to Cuba together. I believe he came on the train. I know I met him downtown."

"At the train station?"

"Well, I'm pretty sure. It was the evening Jo Ellen died."

"So you'd heard of her passing?"

"Yes, someone called me from Tallahassee. It was just terrible to hear. It was a shock to all of us, Clay especially."

"Uh-huh. How well did you know Miss Harbert?"

"Not well, but I knew about their engagement, being friends with Clay. I grew up with his father. We're old friends."

"So you would have met him the night of Miss Harbert's death?"

"Why, yes."

"You're sure of that, are you, Mr. Webb?"

"Well, let me think. It was a Sunday. No—a Monday. I'm sure of that."

"Who was it that informed you of the accident?"

"Well, a friend of mine in the Capitol told me. State Representative McMahon Shiver. Mr. Shiver knew Clay and Jo Ellen. He was a mutual friend. Oh, and Clay's firm had done some work for Shiver."

"Where did y'all stay in Cuba?"

"With friends in Santiago. We spent most of the time deep-sea fishing."

"Y'all come back together?"

"That's right."

"How well did Mr. Howerton get on with Jo Ellen?"

"Oh, they got along very well. My wife and I thought they'd make a fine couple. We were sorry they called off the engagement."

"Have you any idea the reason they broke it off?"

"I know Clay moving to Jacksonville was one reason. And, I hate to mention it, but I think another reason was Jo Ellen's drinking. They always got on so well though."

"Did you ever see her when she was tight?"

"No, I haven't. Just what I heard from Clay, that she drank too much at times and acted erratically and had to go to the Alcoholics Anonymous on account of it."

"Did you ever know Clay to get rough with her?"

"Never."

"Well, thank you, sir. I appreciate you speakin' to me about it."

"Surely."

The *Gulf Wind* always came through early in the morning. Fulton drove to the Seaboard ticket office across from Culley's. The clerk said he had passenger lists; if he would have a seat, he'd find the list for November 2, 1953. Ten minutes later, the clerk spread the list in front of him on his desk; Fulton scanned the handwritten names: Clayton Howerton handwritten in cursive. He was telling the truth.

He drove home, made a sandwich, and turned on the television. A commercial was playing. "It's delightful, its delovely, it's DeSoto!" went the little jingle, a happy couple motoring away in the finned beauty. He ate his sandwich and watched George Burns.

31

Tallahassee
Tuesday, 10/30/1956

"Sam Nowak was arrested last night."

Fulton nearly dropped the phone. "What?"

"Yeah," answered the sheriff. "At the commission meeting up 'ere at City Hall. Raisin' all kinda hell. They tell him to leave, and he goes into a vi'lent rage. Ol' Millirons had to drag him out, knock him in the head 'fore he cooled off. He's in the city jail right now. Just thought you should know."

"How do you like that?"

"He's a snarly cuss, ain't he?"

Click.

XXXXX

Sam's ex-wife lived in a tiny apartment cottage on Monroe, next to the Texaco at Carolina Street. She opened the door dressed in garage overalls, a pretty woman with dark hair. She invited him inside. "I think we're safe. I heard they have him downtown." She shivered.

"You all right?"

She nodded.

"He lives right behind you, doesn't he?"

"Yes, he took a room in that house right after I got this place. Would you like some coffee? I just made some."

"Thank you." Fulton removed his hat and sat on the sofa in her half-size front room.

"You may wonder why I'm dressed like this. I work next door. It's the only thing I know how to do. I'm better with motors than I am with husbands."

"Yes, ma'am."

She handed him a cup. "I knew something would happen sooner or later. Has he hurt someone?"

"No, ma'am."

"But you suspect him?"

Fulton nodded.

She didn't seemed surprised. "He went out that night, came home sweaty, his clothes soaked."

"Yes, ma'am."

"I knew something was wrong. He didn't say a word. Went down to the basement. After a while, I smell something. I go down, and he's burned something in a trash can."

"What was it?"

"I don't know. I asked about it, and he slugged me. He told me he'd done something that could get him in a lot of trouble. He had this strange look in his eyes. As soon he left for work and I could pack a few things, I left."

Fulton put his hat on. "If he wants to act tough again, call me."

XXXXX

Fulton turned onto North Ride, stopping at a modern ranch with a Sold sign in front. Until recently, it belonged to the Nowaks. He knocked; the house was empty. Fulton walked around back. He tilted open a basement window, squeezing himself through. The walls were brick, painted white like the photographs. The entire space had been scrubbed with bleach, the smell of chlorine overpowering.

XXXXX

Sam drove a little English job, a Hillman Minx. Fulton had no trouble finding it by an expired meter on Park Avenue. It had the look of a shrunken '51 Chrysler. Sam staggered out of the front doors of City Hall at the corner of Adams and Park escorted by Officer Millirons. He looked a little worse for wear, a night spent in the ancient cell in the basement, the effects of a hangover readily apparent. Shirt untucked, hat bent, belly protruding over his britches, which he tried to hold up in the absence of a belt. He waddled down the steps, lighting a cigarette and scowling at Millirons as the latter went back to the station. The municipal judge allowed Sam a bond, letting him go free until trial. Sam vowed he would make it a fight.

He got in his car, screeching around the corner to the Seabrook hardware store. He slammed the door, red-faced and cussing. Fulton parked and followed Sam inside, keeping an eye on him from an unobtrusive distance. Sam walked over to the shotguns, picking one up.

Fulton breathed a sigh of relief as Sam returned the Winchester pump to the display rack and began pawing over fishing rods. He selected one and, giving little more than a grunt to the friendly salesclerk, dropped money on

158

the counter. He stomped out to his car, jammed the pole through the open window, and took off.

32

Tallahassee
6:40 a.m.
Wednesday, 10/31/1956

He got in the Ford, the windshield covered with dew as she sat in the dark driveway. The starter gave one grunt and quit, the battery dead as one of Doc Elston's patients in the morgue. He opened the barn doors. The headlights seemed to wink at him, as if to say, "Let's go." The roof was low. The fins high. DeSoto. Just like the TV commercials. It came in a special bronze metallic with a tan top and side spear. Salesman said there wasn't another like it.

Push-button driving. He pushed *D* and rolled out of the garage, making a left on Thomasville Road, the two-lane country road. The speedometer—a red line that moved like the mercury in a thermometer—showed 45. No traffic.

Carter telephoned just before nine. From the sound of things—the hiss of a coffee percolator—the sheriff was calling from his kitchen. "You might wanna check with the *highway* patrol. They had a man there that night," said Carter, reaching for a coffee mug out of the cupboard, wearing the boxers and black socks he'd slept in.

"Thank ya, sir. I'll head over there."

"Let me know what you find."

"I will."

Click.

"Miss Mary Ann?" Fulton called.

"Yessir?"

"Can you call over to FHP and see if they have a report on the accident?"

"You got it."

Fulton held his coffee mug, leaning back in his chair. *Would it be possible to stage a crash—dose the victim with alcohol and everything? One could make a person drink. Maybe the FHP file would reveal something. Of course, the key would be motive. Just who would want to engineer such a death and why?*

Mary Ann reappeared at the door. "Oh, I wanted to tell you, I got a call from Ben Austin. He said he'd like to talk to you, if you had time. He said it wasn't urgent."

Fulton enjoyed visiting the Midyette-Moor "skyscraper." He walked the stairs, admiring the marble and the ornate light fixtures. He found Austin in his office; Miss Welton had the morning off. The fellow was on the telephone and waved for Fulton to come in. He did so, taking a seat in one of the chairs in front of the mahogany desk.

Austin listened to the caller, a woman. "Well, we didn't have try this case—and trials are expensive—so I only used half of what you gave me. How about I refund you $300 and call it a day?" The woman said something; she sounded happy. "Well, I'm glad to hear you worked things out with Tommy. Swell. Okay, good-bye."

Fulton was looking out the window, trying not to pay attention, but it was impossible. *So there are honest lawyers. Well, now I have seen it all.* Fulton rose and introduced himself.

"I've heard your name, of course. But I don't think we've ever met," said Austin, leaning across the desk and giving him a firm handshake. He was a bit younger than Fulton and had a pleasant smile. He seemed to keep fit and probably spent time outdoors, but not doing manual labor. His hands weren't rough or calloused.

"Glad to know ya."

"Please sit down. I'm glad you came by. I'm a friend of Milo Harbert's. I asked him if I could help, and he said if I'd make sure there was nothing you needed, why, that would be enough for him. So that's what I wanted to do, introduce myself and let you know that I'm here should you need anything."

"I appreciate it."

"Sure, and it seems like the situation gets stranger all the time, doesn't it? Did you hear about the thing at City Hall?"

"The sheriff told me."

"I was up there that night."

"Oh?"

"I do some work for the city. It was crazy. When Sam walked in there—as soon as he saw me—he went nuts. Millirons had to drag him out."

"I heard that."

Austin shook his head. "I don't know why it should surprise me. He's crazy!"

161

"That's what I'm hearing."

"He's a biologist, but he seems to get involved in his share of controversies—arguments with the county, now this."

Fulton nodded.

"I represented Howard Jenkins, a local builder. Sam sued my client, said there were ghosts in the house he'd bought, wanted his money back! Ghosts! Can you imagine?"

Fulton laughed.

"But he was *dead serious*. He gave Howard a hell of a time. He practically camped out on his lawn. He *haunted* my client. I heard he made threats to Jo Ellen."

"I heard that too," said Fulton. "Was that house on North Ride?"

"Yeah, that's the one. You gonna question Sam?"

"Looks that way."

"Well, if you need anything, let me know."

"Sure," said Fulton, getting up. "I appreciate it, Mr. Austin."

"Call me Ben—I 'd prefer it that way. And your first name is True, isn't it?"

"That's right."

"May I call you that?"

Fulton nodded.

"Swell," said the lawyer, extending his hand.

Fulton shook the attorney's hand and showed himself out.

33

Tallahassee
7:45 a.m.
Thursday, 11/1/1956

He gave the heavy brass door a shove. No one was about except Ol'
Clevedale, polishing the doorknobs in the quiet hall. "Mornin', Mr. True,"
he said with a broad grin.

"Mornin', *Cleve-uh-dell*. How are ya?"

"Just fine, sir, just fine," he replied, moving on to the next door.

Fulton walked down the staircase to the basement, down to the FHP office,
finding an elderly woman behind her typewriter. "I'm True Fulton, I
understand you have a report for me."

"Oh, yessir, I have it here," said the lady, rising to hand him a manila
folder.

"Thank you, ma'am."

"Certainly," she said cheerfully. The door behind her marked Director, Col.
Chambord rattled and opened. A man in a starched uniform appeared.
"Why, True Fulton. I heard it mentioned you moved to our fair city. What
does Hal Martin have on you that made you leave Jax?" he said, thrusting
his hand toward the visitor.

Fulton took it warily. "I reckon the sheriff can be pretty persuasive. I don't
believe we've met before."

"I'm Colonel Chambord." He was the head of the highway patrol. Though
Florida never had a state police force, the highway patrol, established in
1939 and having jurisdiction over state roads, arguably came the closest.

"I hear you're lookin' into this accident we worked."

"Yessir."

"Is there something we can help you with?"

"No, sir. I got a copy of the report. I thank you for that."

"Surely," said Chambord. "I've heard a lot about you, Mr. Fulton. Captain
Davis knew you in Jacksonville."

"Yessir."

"Let me know if I can help—in any way," said the colonel.

"Thank you," said Fulton, turning toward the door.

"Let me ask you something, Mr. Fulton. Is that all right?"

"Sure."

"You boys were set up for the purpose of investigating organized crime. Am I wrong?"

"No, sir, you ain't wrong."

"Does your boss not realize a DWI case is a highway matter, not racketeering?" asked Chambord, his demeanor polite and calm. He delivered the question in the same tone one might ask, "Can you pass me the hymnal from your pew please?"

Fulton didn't answer.

"I'm a bit confused. US 27 is my responsibility," said the colonel, stepping forward.

"We're not sure it was a traffic accident, sir."

"Ha! Not sure? I read the autopsy. I read the report you got there. Single vehicle crash. A .220 percent blood test. If it walks like a duck..." said the colonel, chuckling.

Fulton didn't say anything.

"I don't want this to set a bad precedent. Nothing personal," said the man, holding up his hands. "I see no reason for the Sheriff's Bureau to get involved. Who's sayin' it's somethin' other than an accident?"

Fulton didn't reply.

"Milo Harbert?" added Chambord, shaking his head. "You may want to think about his credibility in this—and if that's enough to hang your hat on. He raised a *fuss* over here three years ago. Tried to throw his weight around. Even tried to offer a reward. Be careful relying on what he tells you."

"Uh-huh."

Chambord saw that Fulton wasn't swayed. He rested his hands on the counter. "Maybe, when I go see the governor this afternoon, he'd be interested in hearing his new bureau is wasting time on traffic accidents." Chambord kept his smile, his veneer of gentility, but that bit about Governor Collins was bureaucratese for "Back off if you know what's good for you."

Fulton didn't answer.

"Well, Mr. Fulton, good luck. If any of us at the highway patrol can ever do anything for you, don't hesitate to ask." He stuck out his hand again.

Fulton paused for a moment then took it, the look on his face indicating that he was not at all intimidated by the colonel. Chambord's look was equally firm, saying, "Don't cross me, don't get in the way, or I'll bulldoze over you like one of those yellow machines working on the parkway."

The secretary shrugged and smiled as her boss disappeared behind his door. Fulton shrugged it off too and walked back up to the main floor, scanning the report as he made his way outside. Fulton looked back at the basement windows of Chambord's office. He remembered an old-timer had told him the spot was once called Rascal's Square. He smiled at that.

Damn! There were witnesses! A trucker stopped to help. He was not identified in the SO report but was in the trooper's narrative. The trucker didn't testify at the inquest. And the FHP report listed a man that drove for the Benton film company. Two witnesses!

Fulton heard an airplane, a large one by the sound of it, the roar of big piston engines and propellers. He looked up. Four engines, triple tail, tapered fuselage. A Connie on final approach for the municipal airport. She was low enough he could see her Eastern Airline markings—blue stripe and red bird over spit-polished aluminum.

He got in the DeSoto, driving down Pensacola Street, through FSU's west campus—mostly whitewashed military barracks that had been converted for use by the college, some made into housing for married students. The entire area had been a military base during the war where P-51 pilots learned their craft. He parked near the terminal.

Fulton could hear the rumble of the airliner as she taxied to the building; he walked through the little terminal and out to the flight line. The last of the Connie's giant props ground to a stop as she prepared to disembark her passengers. A man on a little tug backed a tall set of stairs over to the plane. A stewardess in blue uniform and cap swung the door open, and passengers began to descend the stairs and walk across the concrete to the little terminal. Suits and ties, dresses, hats, and gloves were the attire on this routine run from DC. Folks waited politely behind the terminal; many had watched the plane land from there, standing outside in the pleasant fall morning.

She spotted him and waved. His eyes were drawn to her immediately— platinum hair and petite. He waved back. Folks continued past him to meet loved ones or find their cars. He walked toward her. Her walk turned into a sprint; she nearly tackled him and hugged him tightly.

Marlene felt great in his arms. He'd missed having her near him, having her fall asleep pressed up against him. He missed even the silly things, like

165

the smell of the gum she liked to chew. They looked each other in the eyes and kissed and embraced tightly once more.

She looked him over. He wore a sport coat over a shoulder-holstered Police Positive and a green necktie loose at the collar. "You look awfully sporty," she said, gently tugging his lapels and kissing him. She wore a skirt with a colorful blouse under a black wool coat. She wore simple flat shoes.

Fulton helped his wife find her bags inside the terminal, a drab space with shabby carpeting and low ceilings. They walked out to the parking lot, her arm around him, her body pressed against him. Fulton opened the door for her. He looked up at the sound of a DC-3 on short final. He lifted Marlene's bags into the trunk and settled back behind the wheel. He noticed how good Marlene's perfume smelled. He'd missed that too. He started the car and looked over at her; she touched his shoulder with her soft hands.

Fulton pulled out of the parking lot, Marlene filling him in on the details of her trip, her sister, and the lieutenant commander she had married. "They have a nice house near Arlington."

Fulton nodded.

"You seem occupied?" she said, noting the way he looked out the windshield, like his mind was somewhere besides Pensacola Street. She rubbed his shoulder and his arm, looking into his eyes.

"Just thinking about a case," he said, looking over at her.

"I'm *disappointed*," she said, dragging out the word. "I was hoping you were thinking about the two of us getting reacquainted." She grinned mischievously.

"Oh!" he replied, catching her meaning, looking and sounding like Jimmy Stewart surprised by a double entendre from June Allyson.

"But you'll just have to wait," she teased. "I need to go to the shoe store. Can you drop me off like a good fella?"

"That'll be fifty cents the first mile, twenty cents after that."

"Oh, expensive!" she purred.

"I don't have to come inside, do I?"

"No," she said, laughing, aware he enjoyed shoe-shopping as much as a case of influenza.

They passed the stadium, driving back along the street of little bungalows and duplexes where students lived, Spanish moss hanging from the live oaks, cigar flowers and sage in bloom in little gardens. The capitol dome dominated the skyline in front of them, standing head and shoulders above the oaks, the stores, and the church steeples downtown.

There were beautiful lawns around the capital: Waller Park on the west side, Gray Park to the south. There were large oaks everywhere. They stopped at the busy intersection of Monroe and Pensacola. Another driver was looking for a space ahead of them; parking was always a problem, but not as bad as on a Saturday. They turned on Monroe and circled until they saw a space down Jefferson.

He crossed the street to Sears while his wife went around the corner to Strickland's Shoe Store at 115 East College, the one that had an x-ray machine so she could see if her shoes fit. Fulton hated shopping, except when browsing among the tools, lawn mowers, and televisions at Sears. Invariably, he found himself watching people. It was just the policeman in him.

It was a little too busy inside, the three levels teeming with shoppers, some sale going on, a sea of hats and purses moving about. He walked back out to the covered sidewalk in front of the store. He looked across the street; no sign of his wife. He walked toward the courthouse. A nervous-looking man was walking ahead of him and kept looking back. A young woman with all the right "attributes" was walking the other direction. She carried a bag from the Diana shop. Fulton tugged down on the corner of his hat when she went past. The woman wore a hat, a dress, and gloves. The other men and women were dressed similarly, in slacks and button-down shirts, the ladies in dresses. Most had hats.

A couple were walking together, but they weren't talking; they were looking away from each other. *They'd just had a row*, Fulton surmised. A man left the Lewis State Bank, patting the chest of his suit coat. He lit a cigarette and patted the coat again before he got into a white Lincoln angled in toward the curb. *The fellow just withdrew a good deal of cash*, Fulton reckoned.

Fulton sat on a bench under the shade trees by the courthouse, continuing his people-watching. He looked at the clock at the bank and walked across the street again. Marlene wasn't in the shoe store. He stopped to look down the hill, the distant wrought-iron gates and fountain at the Westcott Building. He could see the water sparkling and the parked cars lining the red-brick street, the trees, and houses that led to the pretty campus.

He saw Marlene through the windows at McCrory's. The store had large display windows and shiny gold letters spelling out McCrory's 5-10-25; open sash windows on the second floor let the upstairs offices take in the pleasant breeze. Men were lined up at the lunch counter with their hats and newspapers. Fulton said hello to Deputy Cook and Doc Strong, the dentist in the Midyette-Moor building. It was lunchtime, and the store was busy. Marlene had made her way toward the back of the store; he caught a glimpse of her then lost her again.

167

He tried to squeeze past the busy displays; a woman looking at the cosmetics bumped into Fulton with her bags. "Pardon me," she said. Fulton tugged the corner of his hat to her as he continued past. He looked around. He noticed a woman slip some nylons in her purse. He sighed, walking over to her and tapping her on the shoulder. He quietly showed her his badge; thus encouraged, she put the package back.

He spotted Marlene at the front of the store. Awkwardly, he made his way past the cosmetics display crowded with purses and bags, losing sight of Marlene once again. He looked around, amazed she could disappear so quickly. Just then he felt arms grabbing the back of his coat. He turned to look, and the person moved to his other side; he looked the other way, and the same thing. Marlene's laughing finally gave her away.

"I just had to do it!" She laughed.

"Oh, I knew it was you all the time!"

"Uh-huh," she said, squeezing him with a one-armed hug. "I'm all finished. Already paid for this stuff."

"Okay, good!" he said, already weary with shopping. He helped her carry her bags to the car. Fulton pulled away from the curb and, when the light changed, turned onto Monroe. They crossed Tennessee, the street constricting to two lanes just past the Duval Hotel; the place was brightly painted in tropical colors, cars were lined up in the diagonal spaces in front of the canopied entrance.

A new Plymouth with jaunty fins pulled out of the Mayo-Mingledorff dealership at 808 North Monroe, next to the Gulf Oil station. A row of DeSotos sat like modern sculptures in front of the showroom. A boy pumped gas for the driver of a '55 Chevrolet at the Standard Oil station amid the Y formed by the split in the roads. The Colonial Hotel was across from the dealer; otherwise, it was mainly houses along both sides of Monroe and Thomasville. They drove to the Motor Hotel Dining Room at Lake Ella. Burgers and fries appeared in short order.

Fulton drove Marlene home and found the couch. She got on his lap, kissing him. The telephone began ringing. Marlene sighed and got up. "Hello, Sheriff," she said, making a face at her husband. It was Martin. She handed the phone to Fulton. Marlene sat on the couch while he spoke to the boss. She unbuttoned the top of her blouse. She crossed her legs, holding them out so her husband couldn't help looking at them. "Okay," he said, hanging up. "I have to go. Assignment in Mariana. You know, you're not making this easier."

"Well, just remember, when you're done catching the holdup man, I'll be here waiting for you," she purred, standing up on her bare feet. "Tell me something. Am I a *wanted* lady?"

He nodded, enjoying her playfulness.

168

"Well then, I must caution you—I may be desperate," she said, walking slowly, provocatively, toward him. "You know, you may have to search me. I hope you're not too much of a...*gentleman* to search a girl like me, *Officer*. You may be surprised what you find." She give him a long kiss, closing her eyes, her arms tightly around him, her soft lips latched on to him in an indication of what was to come.

Fulton drove to Jackson County. They'd had a suspect, but he hadn't confessed, and no one got a good look at him. Prints on the cash register— Fulton determined—were a match. Sheriff Hughley had his man. Fulton drove back home. He'd kept Marlene waiting long enough.

34

Tallahassee
Friday, 11/2/1956

Fulton nursed the Ford over to the Sears garage. He waited, sitting on the bench outside. Presently, the mechanic came out from under the hood, shaking his head. He had a clean uniform and peaked cap, but dirty hands from trying to diagnose the ailings of the four-year-old police car. "Mr. Fulton, she's got a bad *ginerator*. The *pohwnts* are bad. So is the voltage reg'lator. You wanna leave it with us?"

"That's fine. Here's my number when y'all finish."

"Sure, boss."

XXXXX

"There's someone waiting on you," said Mary Ann.

"Yes'm?"

"Her name's Miss Madgison."

Well, that explains the fire-engine-red Studebaker.

A homely but well-dressed woman was sitting in Fulton's office next to the drip bucket, chewing gum rapidly. She wore a tailored suit, a hat with feathers, and rather high heels with double straps.

"Mornin', miss," said Fulton, taking off his hat.

"Mornin' to you too," she said, smiling. "I'm Evelyn Madgison."

"True Fulton. What can I do for you?"

She crossed her legs, which weren't bad, and drew a Phillip Morris from a gold case. Heavy eyeliner surrounded her expressive eyes, which went over Fulton from head to toe. She leaned forward, the cigarette between her oxblood lips. Fulton recognized his cue and found the Zippo in the drawer. She took a long drag and exhaled. "I hear you're asking about that girl. Jo Ellen something or another?"

"Yes, ma'am. Jo Ellen Harbert."

"Harbert. That's right. I knew her in school. I was in her class at Florida State, when it was just the College for Women."

"Oh?"

"Sure. We used to go swimming at Lake Bradford. We were on the tennis team. We weren't friends exactly, but we knew each other. She was a nice girl."

"Yes, ma'am?"

"I happened to see her in Bennett's the day she died. She didn't recognize me. I was thinner when we were in school. She hadn't changed. Dressed nicer, maybe."

"Uh-huh."

"She argued with a man. Older man with a mustache."

"Is that so?"

She nodded. "Say, you're about six-two, aren't cha?" She was leaning forward, resting her elbow on her bare knee, looking up at him.

"Yes, ma'am."

"I thought so!" said the woman, smiling and batting her long eyelashes.

"Well...you saw Jo Ellen in there."

"Sure. She was having a milkshake. I came in for some makeup and ice cream. Here's this ape, pounding his fists on her table he was. And barking at her he was." Madgison shook her head and put her right shoe down, smoothing out her skirt. She looked up at Fulton dreamily. "Jo Ellen looked scared. I could tell." She had another puff of the cigarette and crossed her right leg this time, moving it slowly, letting it swing a little, before continuing. "Aww, these seams!" she lamented, straightening her nylon stocking so the line ran correctly down her calf. "These things ain't so easy to put on straight, ya know?"

"How's that?"

"These nylons! Boy, I can never get 'em straight in back," she said, tugging on them.

"Yes, ma'am. Well, what about the fella with the mustache? Did you see when he left?"

"Why, he left rather quickly when Phil—the guy that runs the drugstore—said he'd throw him out."

"Yeah?"

"Well, it was pretty heated. I remember that because you don't see people argue, almost yell at each other out in public. And because...because it was the day she died. I still have the paper from the next morning."

171

"Do you know him?"

"Never saw him before."

"Go on."

"That's pretty much it."

"Do you remember the time?"

"Sure, just after eight o'clock."

Fulton nodded. "Did you see her leave?"

"I did, as a matter of fact. She hung around a minute or two then left. And my friend and I decided to go. I saw her get in a car."

"Do you remember what it looked like?"

"No, I guess it was big. I don't know."

"Did you send me some photos of Jo Ellen?"

"No, I haven't any photos of Jo Ellen."

"Do you know who might?"

"I haven't any idea."

"Tell me more about this fella, what he looked like."

"Well..." She thought. "He wasn't as tall as you. Probably three inches shorter," she said, eyeing Fulton again. "Wasn't in as good a' shape neither. He had a big belly. Well-dressed, nice suit and tie. He had short hair, black. A little mustache, not a Hitler mustache, but trimmed. Not a Clark Gable, but small, you know?"

"I see," said Fulton, writing it down. "Do you mind looking at some pictures for me?"

"Not at all. I love to look at pictures," she said, smiling and chewing her gum. Fulton pulled out a box from under the little table. He opened it and pulled out a foil sheet that had the shape of a human face.

"What's that?"

"It shows the shape of a face. Was it like this?"

"No, it was fatter, rounder. Like I said, he was kinda heavyset."

Fulton pulled out a rounder "face."

"I've never heard of this thing," said the woman, looking it over with her large brown eyes.

"It's new. It's called an Identi-Kit." Fulton purchased it himself as there were no funds available. He went through all the features for hairline, mouth, eyes, nose. She seemed to enjoy leaning in close, looking at the photos, building up the face. She had pleasant perfume. Fulton moved back, but she kept moving closer.

"You know, that's close," she said, studying the composite. "Well, no, he had bigger ears." Fulton put in a different ear sheet and held it up for her to see. "That's him! That's him! Does that help?"

"You know it," he said, setting the composite on his desk. "Do you remember anything else about him?"

"His name was Sam. I heard someone say that."

"Yeah?"

"Uh-huh."

"Did you stay in touch with Jo Ellen when she was teachin' school?"

"No."

"Do you know why she quit and left town?"

"I haven't any idea."

"Do you mind giving us a statement?"

"No, I don't mind, fella."

"I don't want to keep you from work or anything. You're sure you have time? We can take your statement this afternoon if that's better."

"Oh, I've got plenty of time!" she exclaimed, looking up at him with her big eyes. Fulton sighed and called for Mary Ann to step in to take the statement in shorthand. She eventually left, doing her best impression of Marilyn Monroe hip movements when she walked. When he caught Mary Ann rolling her eyes and snickering, it made him laugh.

XXXXX

The telephone was ringing. Mary Ann answered. The other line started ringing, and Fulton picked up. As soon as Mary Ann hung up, her phone began ringing again. The telephones were ringing so much it sounded like crazed Salvation Army Santas had invaded the office.

173

"Mr. Fulton, I have a call for you."

He pushed the line button. "Fulton speakin'."

"Howdy. I got a message to call ya. Bill Harney."

"Yessir, I appreciate you calling."

"I know what you're callin' about."

"Yessir?"

"The wreck. You want me to tell you everything I saw?"

"Uh-huh."

"Well, I was driving back to *Hey-vanna*, that's where I live. I drive for Benton's. They deliver the film for movie houses, you know."

"Yessir." Fulton had seen their green trucks on the road.

"I'd made deliveries all day. They let us take the trucks home, so I'm driving towards the lake, and I see a rig stopped in the road. It's raining. There's barely room to get past him even on a good day, so I slow down. I see the driver jump from his cab, and so I pull over to see what's wrong. He's got a flashlight, and that's when I see where a car had gone down in the woods. This other fella was all shook up, and he tries to go down there and help whoever was in the car. I follow and I slip, slide nearly down to the bottom of the hill. Finally we're by the car, but no one's inside. Gasoline's leaking out. We thought it might explode. And me and the other fella check them woods around the car. And the other fella, he hollers he found someone, and she's breathin'. So I stay with the woman while he goes up to try to call for help on his radio. And 'fore long, some sheriffs get there—two sheriffs and one or two highway patrol, I reckon."

"Yessir? Did anyone else come out there that you saw?"

"No, sir."

"Anyone standing around, anyone that didn't seem right?"

"No, sir, just the lawmen, the other trucker."

"Okay."

"I tried to stop her bleedin'. We had a towel or somethin', but it didn't do no good. And you wanna know the worst part?"

"Okay?"

174

"She was talkin'."

"She spoke to you?"

"Sure did. I was with her longest, waiting on the damn ambulance. She was crying. She said, 'Call my dad.' Yeah, she said that. And there wasn't nothin' I could do fur her. She sorta gasped for breath, and she wasn't breathin' no more. I'd seen men hurt like 'at in the war. Nothin' we could do. But that's what she said, 'Call my dad.'"

Fulton sat motionless for better than twenty minutes.

XXXXX

At 2:30 p.m., the mechanic brought the car over when he'd finished. Fulton tugged the choke knob and engaged the starter. The flathead purred. He drove up the hill to Ben Austin's office. He parked along the curb and took the elevator up to the sixth floor, carrying his briefcase. He found Austin's secretary, a happy-go-lucky sort of woman about thirty, he figured. "Mr. Fulton, how are you?"

"Fine, ma'am."

"Mr. Austin has a call. He'll be finished in a minute."

Fulton chatted with the secretary until he got through.

"I love it here. I'll never leave."

"Mr. Austin's a good boss?"

"Oh, yes! He's a wonderful boss."

Ben appeared in the doorway. "True! Good to see you!" he exclaimed, shaking Fulton's hand. "Come on in," beckoned the lawyer. Campaign posters—each with a different design—littered one corner of the office.

Fulton gave them a nod. "I'd heard you were running."

"Yeah, I figured that Dad ran for office when he was thirty-one, and I'll be thirty-four in January, I gotta get with it! I just never was that ambitious!" he said, chuckling. Fulton smiled at that. "This fella, Howerton, is running against me. Nice enough fella, I suppose, but I hope, for Dad's sake, that I can beat him."

"Mr. Austin, would you do me the kindness of taking a look at something?"

"Be glad to. And, please, call me Ben. Won't you sit down?"

"I'd like to show you a composite photograph."

175

"Okay."

Fulton retrieved a peculiar-looking image from his briefcase and held it up for the lawyer to examine.

"That's one of those new kits, isn't it?"

Fulton nodded.

"I hadn't seen—wait a minute! Why, that's Sam!"

"You can identify this person?"

"Sure!" He looked at the face on the stacked-together foil sheets once more. "No doubt about it, that's Sam all right."

"Okay, I appreciate it."

"You got something definite then?"

"Not sure yet."

"Okay, but you have some leads?"

"I think so."

"Gee, that's swell. I guess you got to keep it under your hat 'til you're sure, but boy-oh- boy, won't the Harberts be pleased!"

"Yessir. There's still a lot to look into."

"Sure, sure. But let me know if there's anything more I can help with."

"I will."

Austin saw him to the door. He patted Fulton on the back, still pleased for what this would mean for the Harberts. "Oh, and, True, my campaign is having a little barbeque tomorrow. I'd be pleased to see you and your wife if y'all have time to come by. Lots of food, if you like Southern cookin'."

"I do. My britches are a bit tight on me for it. Yessir, I'll stop by if I get the chance."

"Swell."

XXXXX

The directory had several Phillipses. One entry for a Mr. and Mrs. Wm. Phillips matched the number and address given to him by Janine. But their telephone was disconnected. Fulton drove up Monroe until houses faded into open country. He made a right opposite the dairy farm, turning

176

onto Glenview, a narrow two lane. The area, Glendale, was on the outskirts of town, though not quite two miles from his office. Bowman's Auto Court was just north of there, overlooking the country highway. Glendale was beginning to build up. Houses, shops. He found 103. The house was close to Monroe. Thousand square feet. Good-sized house for a family.

There was a moving van backed into the driveway. Two workmen sprang from the van, carrying a mattress toward the front door. A woman was unloading a large lamp from the trunk of a Kaiser Manhattan. A Sold placard was hung over the realtor's For Sale sign that protruded from the lawn.

Fulton pulled in the driveway, behind the van. A young man walked out of the house. "Good afternoon," said Fulton.

"Oh, hello. Are you the man we spoke to about the insurance policy, Mr. Maxwell?"

"No, I'm not sellin' anything," said Fulton with a grin. "I would like to ask you something though."

"Okay, what's that, sir?" answered the young man. He and his wife stepped under the shade of the front porch, which ran most of the way across the front of the house. Fulton noticed the home was freshly painted, bright white, over the asbestos siding common after the war. Similar houses were generously spaced down the rest of the street.

Fulton rested his foot on the step. "Did you know the people that lived here?"

"No, sir. You see, this house was foreclosed," said the man. He was about twenty-five, as was his wife; he wore a sweatshirt and khaki trousers.

"Yes, we bought it from the bank," said the woman. She wore a house dress, a bandana on her head.

"We didn't know them. I heard they left town," said the man.

"Did you happen to hear where they've gone?"

"No, sir."

"Well, thanks anyway, I hope you enjoy your new home. It's real nice."

"Thank you, sir."

The couple went back to their unpacking as he backed out of the driveway. He stopped at a pay phone by the ice cream parlor at Bradford Road and called the city electric company. "Hey, Glenda? This is True."

177

"Well, howdy, Mister True. How are you and the lovely missus? Marlene enjoyin' this fine weather for her roses?"

"Yes, ma'am. How are you?"

"If I was any better I'd be twins."

"Ha! Listen, can you do me a favor?"

"Um-hmm."

"Can you see if a William and Sadie Phillips have an account with y'all?"

"Hold on. I got to get up and go look through that file cabinet." The woman put the phone
down, looked through the index cards, then walked back to the telephone. "Mr. True?"

"Uh-huh."

"I see it here, darlin'. Fourteen-thirteen Colonial. They're two months past due. I may have to cut their power soon," she said with a sigh.

"Yes'm. I sure appreciate it."

"Sure."

"Say hello to Jack for me."

"I will!"

Bradford to Thomasville, down the hill to Colonial, a dirt road with small wood-framed duplexes. He pulled in the driveway at 1413. No one home. He had no business cards, no money for them. He did the same as when he was a young rookie in Jacksonville—he wrote his number on a page torn from his notebook and stuck it in the doorframe.

35

Tallahassee
Saturday, 11/3/1956

"They don't live here anymore," said the landlady.

"Okay."

"But I have their new number someplace," the woman added.

"That's fine!"

He wrote it down and thanked her.

The operator connected the Alabama residence.

"Hello?"

"I'm trying to reach Dave Everett."

"Yessir? This is he. What can I do fur ya?"

Fulton was surprised Everett answered, that he wasn't on the road. "Well, I'm wondering if I can talk to you about a car wreck that happened near Tallahassee three years ago. My name's Fulton. I'm with the Sheriff's Bureau."

"Never heard of that. But I bet I know what accident you're callin' about."

"Yessir?"

"Why, the one near Lake Jackson. Ain't likely to forget it."

"Uh-huh?"

"I was drivin' for myself then. I was coming back from a job haulin' for the Elberta Crate Company up to Bainbridge and Albany. I broke down and got to a late start coming back. It's real dark and rainin' hard. It's foggy as hell, I can barely see, nearly run off the edge there by the lake. Couldn't run more'n twenty-five miles an hour. I'm coming up the hill, and I can see a good ways there. I see lights crossing my lane and fly off the road into the woods. I hit my brakes and stop up 'ere, and twenty feet down the hill—smokin', makin' noises—is a big car. It's hard to get down there. Another truck stops, and we get down and can't even see the driver. Then we find her farther in them woods. Little bitty thing."

"Yessir?"

"That was the awful part. She was breathin', weren't nothin' we could do for her."

"Yeah."

"About that time a little car and trailer stops. And they try to help the woman."

"Oh?"

"Yeah, little 'ol car pullin' a travel trailer."

"Do you know what kind?"

"No, sir. I know it was smaller than a Ford or Chevy."

"Do you remember the color?"

"No. I'm just back from a two-day run. I'm not thinking too clear...Well, I think it was yellow."

"Anything about the trailer?"

"It was just a small silver thing. Couldn't a' been more'n fifteen feet. One a' them streamlined drag-behinds. Didn't pay too much attention. But there was one thing I remember."

"Yessir?"

"Them folks carryin' on about a man runnin'. He kinda skeered 'em."

"How's that?"

"They saw a man runnin'! Yessir, they told me that. They was coming north. They done passed the trailer park. They parked in front of my truck. They had raincoats and flashlights and all. They was kinda startled by this feller, and I agreed it seemed odd—in that weather—for someone to be malingerin' in them woods. I assumed they told the highway patrolman. His car was parked by 'em."

"Did they describe the fella to you?"

"No, sir. They may have said something to the patrolman."

"The other trucker—was that the film truck driver?"

"That's right, he just had a small truck."

"Was there anyone else you remember?"

"A couple sheriff cars."

"Did you hear the woman say anything?"

"No, sir. The other feller said he heard her say somethin'. He was kinda shaken up too. But I didn't hear nothin'. That's when I left her to try to call the highway patrol."

"If you think of anything else, will you give me a call?"

"Yessir, I sure will. I hated seeing that woman there, nothing we could do for her. The ambulance came, and it almost got stuck in the mud. It was just a miserable night."

"Yessir." Fulton gave him the number and hung up.

None of that was in the report. No one talked to the couple. No one knew about the couple. Could it be Sam? I still don't have enough for a grand jury. But if I can find this couple, get an identification or at least a description that matches Sam Nowak—maybe.

A few startling shards of truth just got put back together.

XXXXX

Sunday. The telephone rang. Marlene answered it in the kitchen—the one telephone they had.

"Who was that?"

"Spence. He's coming here." Fulton's old partner. His colleagues at the department called him Cuban Spence.

"It'll be nice to see him."

"I told him not to eat on the road. We'd at least attempt to feed him here." She laughed.

"Knowing him, he might stop beforehand *and* still have an appetite once he gets here."

"That boy can *eat*. I hope I have enough."

"Should I go to Lovett's?"

"Well, maybe we could use some more potatoes."

"Roger. I'm on my way," said Fulton, grabbing his hat and keys.

When he returned, Marlene had chicken in the frying pan and was sitting at the counter on a stool, peeling potatoes to mash. "Why, thank you, True."

181

Fulton set the bag down and gave her a kiss. "Peel plenty of 'em. You know how us menfolk love your mashed potatoes."

She smiled, her focus on the peeler, which she wound around the large potato, removing one unbroken peeling. "I am. Even Spence will have enough."

Fulton helped set the table in the irregularly-shaped dining room. She came up behind him while he was stirring the sweet tea, kissing his neck. He took her in his arms. They heard the sound of a car in the driveway. Marlene smiled. "Never fails."

Fulton walked out onto the porch that wrapped around the house. Late-model Ford, solid color, with plain blackwall tires—had to be a cop car.

"True Fulton!" roared the visitor, climbing out of the Ford.

"Why, Juan Spencer, it's been a long time."

"How are you, *hermano*?" He gave Fulton's hand a powerful tug. He was a defensive tackle in college but only played for a year before he was injured. Deciding academics wasn't for him, he became a cop. A man had to stand six feet tall and look tough to get a job from Canefield. Spence fit the bill at six-foot-one and husky. And a Southern accent to go with those dark Latin eyes. The young man looked up at the little house, the pointy roof. "I never seen an octagon-shaped house before. Dang, it's quiet here!" said Spence, listening for horns blowing and buses going by and hearing nothing but a bird chirping from a sweet gum tree. "It's kind of pretty," he said, looking around at the canopy road, the house and barn, Marlene's roses. "No neighbors?"

"A few—but not so close you have to hear 'em."

"Where I grew up near the Ford plant, you could practically touch my neighbor's house from the front porch. I had an education listening to Mr. and Mrs. Willis fight—and make up."

Both men doffed their hats as they walked in. "They're building a lot of houses, South Ride, North Ride. There's talk they're going to build in the old plantation between North Ride and here."

"I can't imagine very many people wanting to live out so far from everything—no offense, LT."

"Why, hello, Spence!"

"Hey, Mrs. Fulton."

Marlene gave him a hug and took his hat.

"I missed that," he told her.

"Oh, you!" she said, swatting at his arm. "We're next to the Velda Dairy," said Marlene. "We like the quiet. True and I both grew up in the country. We lived a half mile from each other growing up. You could say we were neighbors."

"Y'all ever miss Jax?"

"I do miss the stores," said Marlene. "What about you, True?"

Fulton thought about it for a moment. "I miss the river."

"You boys sit down, and I'll have supper in a minute."

"Yes, ma'am," the boys answered in unison.

"Do you miss the department?"

Fulton just smiled at that.

"Hey, you wanna know something? I made sergeant!" Spence exclaimed.

"Well, that's great!"

"It sure is," said Marlene, carrying the chicken to the table. "We're proud of you!"

"You still living on the beach?" asked Fulton, getting up to help her.

"Yeah."

"Does Canefield know?"

"No," replied the detective, shaking his head. Officers were supposed to live in the jurisdiction. Neptune Beach was outside city limits by a good distance.

Fulton brought the platter of mashed potatoes out while Marlene brought the gravy and her own homemade green bean recipe. The talk turned to policing, as it always did, with an occasional question about family or girlfriends thrown in by Marlene. The young fellow had just broken up with another girl.

"I didn't see anyone for a year after Sylvia—I know that's hard to believe."

Fulton and Marlene looked at each other. They had lived the Sylvia experience with him; it nearly cost the young man his career.

"Anyway, Patty decided to get married to this insurance fella," he said, taking another piece of chicken.

"Well, True knows all about broken hearts," said Marlene.

"That's right. You cured me of the one I had—never had another," replied Fulton, looking at Marlene. Her look back at him reminded him of why he never would.

"Maybe someday, I'll find a girl that looks at me like that—and keeps right on lookin'," said the younger man. "If I could steal you away, I would—friends or no friends."

They laughed.

"Say, what's this big case you're on?" asked Spence.

"You heard about that?"

"I'm friends with Dreggors. He told me." Spence scooped up a massive helping of mashed potatoes and poured gravy over the mountain he'd formed on the china plate.

"Hmm," said Fulton, getting a spoonful of potatoes before they were gone.

"I hear the dead woman came from a wealthy family, had some troubles in her past."

"Then you know as much as I do. I did find a friend of hers. I'm hoping she knows something. You know, the gal I was looking for, Mrs. Phillips?" he said, turning to Marlene.

She nodded. "You found her?"

"She works at Mae's Beauty Shop. I finally got a hold of her."

"She's a beauty operator?" asked Marlene.

"Yeah, I'm gonna go talk to her."

"I bet you're gonna love that!" said Spence, knowing that shopping, hair salons, and anything of that sort wasn't something Fulton enjoyed.

"Not exactly," said Fulton, a sort of stern frown forming on his face.

"Well, if she's any good, maybe I'll get my hair done there! You be sure to ask the other girls in the waiting area how they like it," said Marlene, teasing.

Fulton shook his head, looking down at his chicken and green beans.

After dinner, the Fultons washed dishes and turned on the little Philco for their guest, the picture tube making a faint buzz as the set warmed up and the black-and-white WCTV picture came in view. The set resembled a little

184

rectangular wood box. It sat on a small table. Spence adjusted the rabbit ears. Then he moved the pillows out of the way and sat on the couch with his arms stretched out on the seat back, watching Sullivan and talking to his friends.

Spence had to keep getting up to adjust the picture. It was fuzzy, no matter how he adjusted the knobs or the antenna. He got up three times but finally gave up. "Say, why don't ya'll get a bigger set? One 'a them big twenty-one inchers?"

"We've only one station here, Spence. It didn't seem like it would do much good."

36

Tallahassee
Monday, 11/5/1956

Fulton dropped Marlene in front of Brown's Menswear, at the corner of Park and Monroe—she was starting a new job at the law office above the store. She kissed him and hurried inside.

XXXXX

Fulton called Mrs. Lindgren. "Ma'am, I'd like to talk to you about Jo Ellen."

"It upsets me to think about it. This is bringing up a lot of things, unpleasant things," she replied, her voice shaky.

"Y'all were close?"

"I'm sorry I was abrupt with you earlier. Yes, we were close. When she started this business, I was her only employee. When it's just two people doing the work, you get to know each other. She struggled at first. I was there with her through all of that."

"Yes, ma'am."

"I got to know her well, almost like a daughter. Her death was a terrible shock."

"I understand. Did she tell you much about her trip to Tallahassee?"

"No, sir. Just said it was about a shop she was interested in. She wanted me to run things the end of that week."

"Yes, ma'am?"

"Then she called me at home, Saturday, I believe it was, said she wouldn't be back on account of this fella she was trying to buy the shop from."

"Sam?"

"That's right. She sounded worried."

"Did she say anything more?"

"No, she didn't say much at all. I could just tell she was nervous, and that wasn't like her."

"Yes, ma'am."

"You know, Detective Fulton, something happened that scared me at the time, but I didn't think much about it, with the funeral and then coming back—all the work—I just didn't focus on it."

186

"Yes, ma'am?"

"Now to have a policeman call, it makes me wonder."

"What's that, Mrs. Lindgren?"

"Well, you know, someone came in the office right after she died. It scared me.
Papers were moved, a couple drawers were opened to her desk, boxes had been gone through, like they was lookin' for somethin'. It scared me. Now that you're calling, maybe it really meant something. I'm scared all over again."

"What do you think they were looking for?"

"I'm not sure."

"Did Miss Harbert keep any valuables in there? Cash, savings bonds?"

"Oh no, the cash till had some money in it, of course. Below the front counter. But it hadn't been touched. As I recall, there was twenty dollars left in there. She had a few war bonds, but those old things weren't worth the trouble of getting in. If they wanted something, the till was right there, plain as day."

"Enough money to interest a thief, certainly."

"That's what I thought too. I didn't know. Maybe it was just kids looking to steal something, and they got scared. So much happened with the business, who would run it, Jo Ellen's will, the new owner. I forgot all about the whole episode—until your call reminded me of it."

"But it appeared someone was looking for something?"

"Yes, sir."

"Did she have a diary or anything she kept there?"

"Not here, no."

"Did she leave anything there, anything at all?"

"No, sir, nothing."

"Do you know why she left Tallahassee and came to Fort Walton?"

"I do not."

XXXXX

Wilkinson agreed to meet with the sheriff and Fulton at 9:30 a.m. It was the only time he had before he left town to go hunting in Alabama. He was dressed in slacks and a tan shirt and boots. He had a .30-06 on the desk, a box of cartridges. He listened to Fulton for a moment then shook his head. "Why are we going through all this at the whim of Milo Harbert?"

Fulton explained there was quite a bit of circumstantial evidence.

"You don't have enough for a search warrant—not one I'd sign off on. And no judge around here will approve one without something from me," said the state attorney emphatically. "Now is that all?"

"I reckon so," said Carter. "Deer huntin' any good up in Eufaula?"

"It sure is. You boys should come with me sometime."

"Thank you for your time," said Fulton.

The two men left the SA's office disappointed, but determined to solve the case. "Ol' Grant wants a tape-recorded confession 'fore he'll file anything. Don't worry," said Carter, slapping Fulton on the back. "Let's go git breakfast at the Busy Bee, come on!"

They crossed Monroe. They ran into ASA Taylor, who joined them at their table.

"Why don't you give ol' Taylor here a rundown of your case, True," said Carter, taking a sip of coffee.

Fulton told him everything he knew.

"Well, I think you're on to something," said the ex-cop.

"We all know how ol' Grant is," offered the sheriff.

XXXXX

Fulton went by Sam's office. His car wasn't there. Fulton drove back to Gaines Street and got himself a peppermint out of the stash in his desk and waited. A few minutes passed, and he spun the dial. *He should be at work by now.*

"Oh, yes, Mr. Fulton. He has taken leave again. I'm not sure what's wrong. We're all worried."

Sam sure is being cagey—like he's aware of our efforts to keep tabs on him. Fulton called Carter; the sheriff didn't think Sam had gotten in any more trouble.

188

"At least no more arrests I'm aware of," said Carter, chuckling. "Looks like we just had a couple speedin' tickets. 'Is all the crime we've had the last twenty-four hours."

In a half hour, Fulton's telephone rang. Carter. "Someone that works with Sam called me. Said he boxed up some stuff, didn't tell no one where he was goin'."

"Yeah?"

"So I drove to that roomin' house to check on him, and he got in the car and drove away, zippin' his britches, tuckin' his shirt in, and getting in the car, acting like he was skeered, said he had to go someplace."

"Uh-huh."

"I didn't have no reason to stop him, so I just followed, and he pulled into Norman and Osweiler's fillin' station. Ol' Sam sure looked funny squeezing in that little car with his hat on and his ol' belly and shirttail hangin' out."

"I reckon it's time to bring him in," said Fulton.

XXXXX

It was 10:30 a.m. and the sheriff had already come around. He expected to see the big cop, Fulton, any minute. He climbed the stairs—around and around—up to the roof of the Mayo building. There was a four-foot-high parapet, so no one would see him up there, but he could look out, his view endless in every direction.

It was cold; he could hear the traffic and the cars sixty feet below. He heard the construction workers begin their labor. He pulled the doll from his shirt, grasping it in his hands. He'd taken a voodoo doll with him—a protection doll. His wife was from New Orleans. She had gone, but he'd kept the doll. He peered over the ledge. *That lawyer Austin is after me. The sheriff too. Yeah, and that big cop, Fulton.* He sat on the roof, his head in his knees, twitching, those thoughts repeating over and over in his mind. He clutched the doll. Every car that passed seemed to have the look of a police Ford or that fancy car Fulton drove.

XXXXX

Fulton pulled over by a pay phone and dialed the sheriff. "Did you try callin' me a minute ago?"

"Yeah, I just missed hearin' your voice, son," he said, chuckling. "You miss *me*?"

Fulton laughed.

189

"Anywho, I found out something. Ol' boy's still in town. Somebody seen him gassing up his car at Mike's and let me know."

"Anything else?"

"No, that's it. You expect me to have the whole thing solved for ya?"

"That'll do for now. Thanks, Sheriff."

"Sure thing, buddy."

Fulton found Sam's Minx at the bus station. He inspected the unusual car. The backseat was filled with boxes. He talked to the clerk. Sam hadn't purchased a ticket. The sheriff met him in his patrol car. He had a deputy out looking. No one could find Sam.

Fulton drove to the Mayo building, parking at a meter in front. Built in the '30s on the outskirts of town, it was a narrow five-story with a basement, which made it appear seven stories from the bottom of the hill, where Pensacola plunged down so sharply. Workmen were painting the tan bricks white. At the back, men were completing an addition that would nearly double the size of the department. It was not as elegant as the original. Bulldozers were working on the parkway, churning up dust.

He looked up at the roof. He walked in the fancy silver doors. He took the stairs, opening the door to the roof. "Howdy, Sam."

"What gave me away?"

"You're smoking, Sam. I saw the cigarette smoke."

Angrily, Sam flung the cigarette down and stomped it with his heel. "Whadya want?" He had short black hair, was a bit chubby, and had a small mustache. He wore a nice suit but had spilled something on his shirt, which was untucked.

"Just wanna talk to ya."

"Let's go to my office."

They walked down a flight of stairs, parading past Sam's poor secretary. Sam cussing like a sailor. The doll. The grave lawman in a hat. Sam had the windows cranked open. They looked out over open country—woodlands as far one could see, altered only by the swath cut by the caterpillars working below.

Fulton noticed the boxes of books on Sam's desk. "You look like you're leaving."

"So? What of it?"

190

"Just wonderin'."

"I hear you been asking of me," he said over the noise outside.

"Just wanna talk to ya about a few things."

"You're blocking the door. So I guess so. Might as well sit."

Fulton moved a plaque and sat in the upholstered chair.

"You know who I am. Well, who do you work for, True Fulton? You're some kind of law officer, I take it?"

Fulton showed him the little Sheriff's Bureau star. Sam looked up, noticing the secretary peering in from her desk.

"We can do this at my office, if you'd be more comfortable."

"I'm comfortable *here*, and I'm busy," he snapped, shoving biology journals in a box. "But you could close the door."

"Okay," said Fulton, tugging the brass knob, the paneled wood door clicking shut. "You've got quite a view," Fulton remarked, casting another glance at the blanket of fall-colored trees over rolling hills.

"Well, get on with it, whadya wanna know."

"Do you recall a young woman by the name of Jo Ellen Harbert?"

"I do not. I've known a good many ladies in my time, but that one doesn't bring back any memories." His mustached upper lip twitched some; he patted his large hand on the desk, nervous.

"How about a face to go with that name?" said Fulton, pulling the photo from his coat pocket.

"Just another doe-eyed girl. She ain't bad. So what?" He barely looked at the photo, turning away to his papers.

"She died three years ago, that's what," replied Fulton, looking Sam in the eye, his tone more firm. "You were the last person she was seen with prior to her demise."

"Uh...uh, I'm-I'm sure I wasn't the last with her. I don't keep company with dead women, not ones I don't know."

"Look, I know you argued with her, over at Bennett's, an hour before she died. Something about a business deal—that bring back any memories?"

"Yeah, well," he grumbled, looking down at his feet. "Now that you say that, yeah, she wanted to buy one of my laundry places. Had cash to buy it, but

191

I didn't agree to her price. We negotiated. She was a tough broad. Surprised me 'cause she's young, pretty." He motioned toward Fulton, who still had the picture in his hands. "But she stuck to 'er guns. And I wasn't sellin' at the price she wanted to pay me, see? I didn't have to, see?" He was insistent, getting red in the face. "No argument, really." He was trying to calm himself.

Fulton nodded, still keeping his eyes locked on Sam's face. "Well, someone said it got heated, that you threatened her."

"People like to throw things my way," snapped Nowak.

"How's that?"

"Look, Clyde, I've stood up for my rights in this town, in court. Some people don't like that. The city commission don't like it. I ain't from here neither. Some people resent that too."

"No need to get sore about it. Is that all?"

"I ain't getting sore!" he growled. "Look, maybe people don't like me 'cause I own things—my coin Laundromats. I don't know. I know I ain't killed no lady."

"Did it bother you? That she stuck to her guns?"

"N-no. Why should it?"

"Okay," Fulton nodded. "You just seemed bothered by it, what you said a minute ago."

"Look, I never did like doing business with dames. Am I alone in that?" Fulton just observed him. He was twitching. "Look, I had nothing against her, okay? We just couldn't get to an agreeable price. It wasn't anything more than that."

"Where did you go after you met with her?"

"How should I know? That was three years ago, buddy!"

"It might be in your interest to remember."

"I don't think I like the way you mean that."

"Then start remembering. Start remembering and start talking," said Fulton more forcefully. "You were with her. You left. She left there in her car. Did you follow her?"

"No. I-uh, I-uh—" he stammered.

"Where'd you go?" interrupted Fulton.

"I'm trying to think! I was with friends. Chet and Jeanne, his wife."

"They got a last name?"

"Yeah, uh, sure. Canning, it is."

"You went over to their house?"

"S-sure, about eight thirty, stayed until ten, maybe ten thirty, then I went home."

"After you met Miss Harbert?

"Yes."

"What did you do at their house?"

"Uh, play cards. The Cannings like to play cards."

"You got their address?"

"Yeah, sure. The Cannings have a store on Adams Street, the little gift shop, you know? They live on Marion Avenue now. Give me a second, and I'll think of the number. Uh, fourteen-sixty, they just built the house. Sure, you go see them. They'll tell ya where I was. Yeah, ask them, boy!"

"I'm asking you. Did you follow that girl, maybe on your way to the Cannings you went and followed her to the lake? How about it?"

"No, I tell ya!" Sam snapped. He looked toward the door, sighing, certain the secretary could hear him.

"Where did the Cannings live three years ago?"

"On Hollywood Drive," Sam answered quietly.

"That's going toward the lake, ain't it?"

"What is this! I didn't do anything, I'm tellin' ya!" shouted Sam. Remembering himself, he lowered his voice again. "Check with them. I wasn't nowheres near her."

"Oh, I'll do that. You can rest assured I'll be calling them."

"Okay," said Sam, standing and throwing more things in a box.

"Why you leavin', Sam?"

"'Cause I quit! Not that it's any of your concern. Why do ya wanna know?"

193

"Well, it seems like you heard about the law maybe wantin' to talk to ya, then ya start acting nervous, start packing up like you're leavin' town. Looks kinda suspicious, wouldn't you agree?"

"I don't see eye to eye with the commissioner, that's all. And, uh, I-I thought you might be after me for those whiskey rumors."

"Yeah?"

"Well, yeah. People are talking. It ain't true, but people are talking. Then I hear you—not that it's true, mind you—I ain't never transported no whiskey, I—"

"Oh, hell, I don't care about the damn whiskey. But you better start tellin' me the truth about this other thing."

"Oh, I am, I am."

"Did you think she found out about the booze? Is that it?"

"No, no, she didn't know about it. How could she? We just talked about the laundry—that's all."

"And you didn't see her again?"

"N-no."

"Positive?" asked Fulton, getting up. Sam could see the holster with Fulton's coat unbuttoned. Fulton crossed his arms and stood in front of the closed door, looking at Sam.

Sam nodded. His hands were shaking. He slapped his pocket nervously, rattling his keys. He swallowed, thinking about the gun.

"You're awful nervous, Sam."

"Am-am I?"

Fulton nodded.

"Am I-am I under arrest?"

"You ain't under arrest," said Fulton, turning the doorknob. "But if I want to find ya, don't make me have to look too far." Fulton walked past the secretary, wide-eyed from what she'd just heard.

37

Tallahassee
Monday, 11/5/1956

The telephone rang. Carter at a pay phone. "Sam is acting strange—even for him. He done loaded up his little car, drove to his coin laundry down on Macomb, then home. Then he leaves agin. We followed him back down there *twice*. The boy's as nervous as a virgin in a whorehouse."

"Ha! I'm not surprised."

"We'll keep watching him. How was he when you cornered him?"

"Nervous."

"Sam sure acts guilty. Maybe you get enough, we take this thing to the state's attorney agin."

XXXXX

Fulton drove up Adams Street, parking between two 400 Cab, Inc. taxis. The Cannings' gift shop was in the old Union Bank building, a small brick cube of a structure. The fan windows above recalled the elegance the building had when new—in 1841—when Adams was a dirt path with little more than the bank, a plantation house, and the old Presbyterian Church. It had been whitewashed and the fan windows painted over, but somehow, the ivy that engulfed the Dutch kitchen on the corner was held at bay by the narrow gap that separated the tea room from the old bank. He opened the ancient door.

A man was standing behind a giant brass cash register. "Hello," he said cheerfully. A woman was arranging some new trinkets on a shelf behind the counter. "Hello," she said, looking up.

"Afternoon," answered Fulton, taking off his hat.

Every sort of basket and flower arrangement imaginable, postcards of Tallahassee and Wakulla Gardens, filled the shelves and counters. The shelves reached the top of the high ceiling; shelves with glassware even stood in front of the windows. The room was small. Tallahassee's first bankers must have made equally efficient use of space. It smelled the way old buildings do—a mixture of old varnish and paint and musty papers.

"Are you Mr. and Mrs. Canning?"

"Yessir, may we help you?" replied Mrs. Canning.

"I was wondering if I might ask about a friend of yours," said Fulton, walking over to the counter.

They looked at him, his sport coat and hat. "Why, you're like that *Dragnet* fella, aren't you?" asked Mr. Canning, enthused. "Yes—Friday!" Both Mr. and Mrs. Canning appeared to be in their midforties, the woman handsome, with auburn hair held in place with clips; the man graying, but with a full head of hair. Both seemed fit, had suntans.

"Well...sorta."

"We see the show when we stay in Atlantic Beach, " said the man. Their show wasn't broadcast in the capitol. No NBC station.

"Y'all enjoy visiting the coast then?"

"Oh, yes! We love to walk along the beach and swim." It made sense, given their appearance.

"Now, this is what I wanted to ask you. Sam Nowak—he's a friend of yours?"

"Well, yes. Is there something wrong?"

"I'm wondering if you remember—around this time three years ago—he might have mentioned meeting a woman about a business deal? Maybe he called you and told you about it?" Fulton wasn't going to tip them off to what Sam had told him; he wanted to see what they remembered and if they were going to be honest.

"Oh, yes, I remember," said the woman. "But I don't remember him calling."

"Do you remember talking to him about it?"

"Yes, we ran into him, as a matter of fact," said Mr. Canning.

"Where was that?"

"Why, Sam came out of Bennett's madder than a wet hen," said the wife. "We were going to see a show. We were walking from the Seven Seas after dinner. We ran into him on the sidewalk. A woman came out of Bennett's— maybe that's the woman you mean—and he argued with her. It was awful. Both were shouting. She left, then he left."

"Did you see him again that night?"

"No."

"Did he visit your home?"

"Oh, no, I'm sure of that," said the woman. Fulton kept a poker face; obviously, Sam had lied.

"Y'all didn't play cards that night?"

"No. We love to play bridge, but that was a Monday night. It was too late by the time we got home."

"What's this about?" the husband asked.

"The woman died a short time later."

"Oh my! That's terrible," said Mrs. Canning. She was holding a lighter; her hand began to tremble. "Oh, darn this thing," she said, unable to get the flame to light.

Fulton reached in his pocket, removing the old Zippo.

"Oh, have you a light?"

"Sure," said Fulton, lighting the woman's L&M. "Did he get in a car?"

"Thank you. Yes, he got in his car," replied Mrs. Canning, fidgeting with the little turntable with Welcome to Tallahassee and FSU postcards that was beside her.

"Did you see the woman get in a car?"

"Why, yes, a big Packard," said the man.

"He likes cars," noted Mrs. Canning.

"I remember pointing out the Packard. You didn't see a lot of them at the time, don't see *any* now."

"Which way did she go?"

"Gosh, it was a long time ago. Do you remember, Chet?" asked the woman, turning to her husband.

"I think she backed out and went towards Tennessee."

"What about Sam?" asked Fulton.

"Same thing."

"You think Sam did something to her? Oh my!" exclaimed the woman.

"I'm not sure, I have to look at everything."

"Oh, I hate this for Sam."

"What time was it?" asked Fulton.

"About eight, a bit later perhaps," said Mr. Canning.

"Now, there's one last thing. Do you remember what the woman looked like?"

"She had dark hair, I remember that," said Mrs. Canning.

Mr. Canning thought about it. "I didn't really get a look at her. She had a hat on, dark hair—like Jeanne said."

"Yes, black hair, a suit—maybe gray. Well-dressed," added the woman.

"Does this look like her?" asked Fulton, showing them the picture.

"Why, yes!" agreed Mrs. Canning.

"It does look like her, but I didn't look too close."

"You'd better not be looking close," noted Mrs. Canning, lightly backhanding Chet's shoulder. They laughed about that. "Oh, she *was* a pretty girl. It's so sad," said Mrs. Canning.

"Yes, ma'am."

"How old was she?"

"Twenty-eight."

"Oh, that's a shame," said the woman, sighing. "Did we help you?"

"Yes, ma'am. I appreciate it," said Fulton, picking up his hat.

"Have a good evenin', Mr. Fulton."

"Good-bye."

A taxi was pulling away. The dispatch office was next door to the gift shop, a tiny building nearly overshadowed by the Dr. Pepper advertisement painted on an adjoining brick wall. The large antenna behind the old bank was for the taxi dispatcher.

He'd caught Sam in a lie. He was getting that *feeling* in his stomach.

38

Tallahassee
Tuesday, 11/6/1956

Fulton drove to the little F&T restaurant on Monroe, parking alongside a black and tan. The car had Collins's new state seal on the door. Inside, he found a young man at the lunch counter in a tan uniform and Stetson.

"Trooper Weiss?"

"Mr. Fulton, how are ya?" he replied, shaking the older man's hand. "Gil Weiss."

"Glad to know ya," said Fulton, taking the stool beside him. Weiss was the FHP officer that stopped at the crash scene. He was twenty then and one of the first highway patrolmen to be called Trooper and earn the fantastic salary of $275 dollars a month. He still looked like a kid, but Fulton—from the moment he shook his hand—was struck with the impression that Weiss was a good man.

"It was one of my first wrecks. The first fatality I worked. You ever work a car crash with a death?"

The older policeman nodded.

"I reckon you don't forget it, do you?"

Fulton shook his head. The somber moment was interrupted when the waitress set a cup of coffee in front of Fulton, smiling. "I'll come back to take your order."

"Oh, just coffee, thanks," said Fulton.

"I helped the ambulance driver and his son get the body. It was terrible, blood everywhere," said the trooper, downing some coffee. He put the cup back on its saucer amid the salt and pepper shakers and leftover breakfast plates on the crowded counter. He pushed away his napkin. "It smelled like alcohol and gasoline everywhere. You know somethin', Mr. Fulton?"

"What's that?"

"I can still smell it. I can think about it and smell that smell. I had to get the truck driver's fire extinguisher and spray around the car so she didn't blow up on us."

"I wanted to ask you something about a car and a trailer."

"Yessir, I saw a car, not sure what kind. It was white, maybe yellow. Hard to tell colors at night, the ambulance lights on, my flashing red, the trucks and their headlights. No streetlights. They's pullin' a travel trailer, I do remember that. Honestly, I didn't pay that much attention. We were trying to remove the body and all. You mean the lieutenant didn't put anything in his report?"

"No," replied Fulton.

The young officer seemed surprised.

"Do you think the driver hit her brakes at all?"

"No. I saw no skid marks on the road. I took my flashlight and looked. There should have been something, even in the rain. At least, that's my experience."

"Did the people tell you about seeing a man running along the woods?"

"Sure. Isn't that in the report?"

The look on Fulton's face revealed the answer. "Did anyone process the car for fingerprints?"

"No, sir."

"Okay."

"Well, what does it all mean? I heard she had a lot of alcohol in her blood. Isn't it cut and dry, with these other things just a sideshow?"

"I think, in this case, the sideshow is the main act. I just haven't been able to put it all together."

"Oh," replied Weiss, nodding. "Well, if there's anything I can do to help, I'd like to. Like I said, this ain't one I'm gonna forget."

XXXXX

Fulton called Mrs. Phillips. "Listen, I can barely hear you. I got a shop full of girls chatting their heads off. Why don't you come on over here around one thirty. I got a break then. I don't have any more appointments until two."

"Okay. I'll see you then."

"Swell."

211 South Monroe. The Lewis State Bank. Mae's Beauty Shop was upstairs. He parked along the curb; he could hear someone giving a speech behind the courthouse. It was election day. He couldn't tell if it was Austin or Howerton.

Fulton paused at the door; he sighed and grimaced and reached for the knob, opening the door to an uncertain fate. He could hear the women inside talking and laughing as he climbed the stairs. It went dead quiet as soon as he walked in. *A man. One that looks like a cop at that.* He took off his hat. They looked him over, from his polished Florsheims to the top of his nearly shaved head. They seemed puzzled; he looked like a flatfoot, but it wasn't that he wore stereotypical off-the-rack suits; on the contrary, he dressed well. It was just the *presence,* as if the gun and badge sent out signals that people could pick up like television—cop.

Two beauticians were at work. One was washing a brunette's hair, the woman's head reclined into a sink. She stopped, the water dripping in the sink. Fulton swore he could hear each drop; it was so quiet in the shop. The gal had turned off the spigot, watching. The other woman, a bit older, was cutting the blonde's hair. She paused only for a second, then went back to snipping the hair she held between her fingers.

"Mornin'. Is Mrs. Phillips around?" asked Fulton, mustering a weak smile. He wasn't sure if Mrs. Phillips was the older woman, who he assumed to be the owner, or the younger, which he assumed to be an employee.

"I'm Mrs. Phillips, big fella," replied the older lady with the scissors, which she continued to work. The other ladies snickered. Fulton blushed. "I'll be done in a few minutes," she told him, still not looking up from her work.

"Yes'm, I don't mean to rush you none, ma'am. I can wait right here, I reckon," he said, sounding a bit uncertain, perhaps hoping she would hurry and he wouldn't have to endure a long wait in the parlor. The walls were pink. Fulton sat down on the pink plastic chair. He wasn't one to get nervous, but this was a bit awkward. He crossed his legs. *These gals are starin' at me like I might have leopard spots on my face,* he thought to himself, looking around for a magazine or newspaper. One in particular was *staring* at him. She was right across from him, a copy of *Look* in her lap. Fulton nodded and half smiled. He uncrossed his legs. Another woman, a little older, was sitting next to her. They noticed how he was sitting in the pink plastic chair and looked uncomfortable. They snickered, holding their hands to their mouths and turning toward each other.

"Why, we don't see too many men in here," the younger one said. She spoke in the drawl common to the area. She was about thirty-five and wore a skirt with a pink sleeveless blouse and had golden hair, which was coming out of her clips and hanging down in strands; she had darker roots and had a few lines on her face, but she was an attractive woman. "Are you a policeman?"

He recrossed his legs. He was clutching his hat in his hands. They certainly noticed his balding head. "You gonna get Miss Leah to give you a shampoo?" the older woman asked, laughing.

Fulton had to laugh at the joke, even though it was at his expense. "That's very funny," he said, grinning. The rather overweight brunette smiled back

201

at him, a copy of *Southern Living* in her hands. "You'd look cute with one of those capes with flowers on 'em!" she said, motioning to the girl getting the shampoo; she was wrapped in a flowered smock to keep her clothes from getting wet.

"Don't pick on him. He's handsome! And look at that suit and tie!" said the younger woman. Fulton blushed. "That's the nicest tie, Mr. Officer. I bet your wife bought that tie. Did she?"

"Yes, ma'am," said Fulton, feeling rather shy.

"I knew it! I just knew it!" She seemed so pleased she was right, the way she grinned and shook her fists with triumph. Her strands of hair moved around as she spoke and gestured in very animated fashion.

Yeah, Marlene bought the tie. Not that I can't buy my own, thought Fulton.

"It is a nice tie," acknowledged the brunette, going back to her *Southern Living*. Fulton checked his watch. It was 1:30 p.m. A soap opera began—*As the World Turns*—the dramatic organ music coming from the little set with a snowy picture.

"Oh, turn it up a tad," said the friendly one. Fulton was closest, so he obliged.

"Thank you, Mr. Officer."

"*Are* you a policeman?" asked Miss Leah, excited and curious.

"Yes'm, I'm with the Sheriff's Bureau."

"Oh!"

"*Bue*-row? You mean like the F-B-*eye*?" asked the woman across from him. She, in fact, had more of a drawl than the other women in the shop.

"Kind of."

"How *interestin'*. I've never met a *Bue*-row man before! My name is Iris Colene, by the way," she said, even more of her hair coming loose from the metal clips as she talked.

"My name's True Fulton. How do you do?"

"That is interestin'. And my, I never heard the name *True* before. Do they call you a detective, Mr. True?"

"I was a detective in Jacksonville. They call us special agents. With the Sheriff's Bureau. It's much the same thing. Probably sounds more important than it is," Fulton said with a shy half smile.

202

"How interestin'! A real detective, like in the movies! Is it really like that, the movies I mean?"

"Well, sometimes it's more about talking to people than anything. Being a good listener."

She thought about that for a moment. "Oh. I can see how that might be. You know, policemen really should concentrate on a beauty parlah," said Iris, leaning forward in a whisper.

"Yes, ma'am?"

"Listen to him—how polite!" she exclaimed, turning toward the woman with the *Southern Living*. "Yeah, we could tell you all kinds of things!"

"We sure could," added the other woman. "Why, I work over at the bank for old Mr. Mavis? And do you know that he told his wife that he was going to a meeting in Pensacola, but he actually went down to Fort Myers!"

"No! He didn't!" asked Miss Iris.

"But tell him about the things he'd be interested in," said the younger beautician, looking up from the sink. "You know, about Mr. Simmons and the new car every year."

"Yes, he's got to be *stealin'* from that Savings and Loan," said Iris.

"And what about Miss Madgison and all the furs she wears?" added Mrs. Phillips. She was almost done with the haircut, Fulton observed. He hoped she'd hurry. But he had to concede, this *was* getting interesting.

"That's ol' Mr. Simmons's secretary," said Iris, a look of incredulity on her face.

"Evelyn Madgison?" asked Fulton.

"Umm-hmm," answered Iris.

"I bet there's *somethin'* goin' on," said the brunette.

"I think you're right!" said the woman getting her hair rinsed.

"Well, that is interesting," Fulton had to admit. Maybe there was something to all this gossiping.

"Yes!" exclaimed Miss Leah. The women went back to whispering, and the brunette got interested in the show. Fulton looked for something to read. No newspapers. There were magazines on a little table. Mostly *McCall's*. Certainly not the *Mechanix Illustrated* one might find in a barber shop. Finally, he found a *Life* magazine from July 1952.

203

Mrs. Phillips was finished; her customer pulled three dollar coins from her change purse and paid her. "Mr. Fulton, wanna walk outside with me? I got a few minutes. I could use some air." It was hot in the upstairs shop with no AC, even with all the windows opened.

"Sure," said Fulton, eagerly putting the magazine down.

Phillips took off her smock and grabbed her relatively plain, cloth coat. "Come on, handsome."

The brunette snickered.

"Good-bye ladies," Fulton said, following Phillips.

"Oh, good-bye, Mr. True," said friendly Iris, looking a little disappointed. "Come back sometime."

"Yes'm."

The brunette snickered as they walked out. Fulton shook his head. *What have I got myself into.* He put his hat on as they went down the steps. "I don't mean to interrupt your work. I tried to call a few times."

"Sorry about that, I'm just so busy."

"You own the shop?"

"No, I work for Miss Eubanks. She rents the place. I've worked for her three years."

They went out the side door, crossing over to the bench on the courthouse lawn.

Fulton had his notebook and pencil in his lap. "Well, I'd like to talk to you about Miss Harbert."

"Jo Ellen," she repeated in a rather peculiar manner, as if she was pondering the name, great sadness coming over her face.

"How did y'all know each other?"

"She was a client of mine at first. She was a teacher at Leon. She came in often, and we got to be friends."

"Do you know why she left the school?"

"No, sir."

"Do you know why she came to town three years ago?"

204

"No. Not exactly. She stopped in to see me—just for a minute. It seemed she had something important to do."

"Do you remember what day of the week that was?"

"No, but it was in the afternoon. I was getting ready to close the shop. I was alone that day. I remember the particular day because we lived on Glenview then—103 Glenview—and I heard the sirens, the ambulance and sheriff cars going up Monroe. It was late. We thought there must have been some accident. Then the next day, I found out who it was."

"So she saw you the day of the accident."

"Well, yes."

"She didn't say anything about meeting someone?"

"No. I guess she had some business to tend to. She'd told me about her shop. We'd talked about that a few times in the year or so before she died because I was considering going into business for myself."

"Did she act strange in any way?"

"She acted serious. But Jo Ellen could be like that. She had to, running a business. We try to keep it lighthearted in the shop, but it's still business. I know how Jo Ellen must have felt with her shop."

"She tell you much about it? I mean, any problems?"

"Just the usual things. No, wait," said Mrs. Phillips, thinking, getting up to put on her jacket. "It's hot in there, but a little chilly out here. She did say something, as I recall. She was having trouble with a man she had spoken to about buying some shop, some store. He threatened her."

"Yes, ma'am?"

"He blew up at her. She was a little shaken up about it."

XXXXX

The telephone was ringing. "Fulton speakin'."

It was Marlene. "How'd you like your appointment at the hair salon?"

Fulton sighed and rolled his eyes. "It could have been worse."

Marlene started laughing. That made him laugh. "I'll see you tonight, baby doll," she told him.

XXXXX

205

The telephone rang. It was Carter calling from the pay phone at the truck stop west of town. "I think you got him, son. I think he knows it. He's scootin' all over town. Finally, I saw him loading fishing tackle, rod, and reel in that li'l English thing. He stuck the pole out through the *win-der.*"

"Yeah?"

"I don't know if he's really goin' fishin' or that's just a put-on. So I followed him out to a cabin on Lake Talquin near the dam. It was back in the woods. I had to get out, trail him up there afoot. I must a' picked up a hundred cockaburrs. By the time I got there, Sam was fishing, looked like he was beside himself, jumpy, looking around every time a squirrel picked up an acorn. Scaring away everything in the water. Damn, son, the striped bass gotta be jumpin' in your hands this time of year, but he wasn't catchin' a dadgum thing."

Fulton laughed.

"You and me gotta get out on that lake. Them stripers like the cold water."

"Maybe that would be a way to keep an eye on our suspect."

"Say, that's all right! I've always tried to figure how I could get paid for sheriffin' and mix a little fishin' in too!"

"Did he go back home?"

"He did. I follered him all the way, damn near run outta gas comin' back, but I didn't have no cash money for it."

Fulton laughed.

"Son, it ain't funny. The county won't let us charge nothin'. But I'll keep watchin' him as much as I can tomorrow."

As soon as he put the telephone down, it started ringing again. Sam. "I-I-I'm not leaving town. I went fishing. I tried calling from Rudd's store earlier, but you were out of the office."

Fulton looked over at his messages. There was a little pink paper, a phone message Mary Ann took that said, "Sam."

"I'm home now. I'm not leaving town."

"Okay. I may need to talk to you again."

"I know."

"I'd like to meet with you the end of the week."

"Okay. I'll be home. I ain't working at the department anymore."

206

"Fine."

"Well, good-bye."

"Good night." Fulton hung up the receiver. He thought it odd. The man seemed resigned to being arrested.

39

Tallahassee
Tuesday, 11/6/1956

Fulton was about to turn off the light when the telephone rang. "Fulton speakin'."

"This is Mr. Canning. From the gift shop?"

"Sure, I remember. How are you?"

"Fine. Say, I remembered something. The woman did drive away from there—from Bennett's? But Sam had a flat tire."

"What?"

"Yes. We saw him stopped on Park Avenue. We spoke to him as we went along to the Florida Theatre. He didn't have a spare with him for some reason. He had to get a tow truck."

"Is that so?"

"Come to think of it, the lady came there and talked to Sam. And he'd calmed down. And they sort of said, 'No hard feelings.' She wished him luck with finding a buyer. And he said he'd have liked to have sold it to her, he just couldn't do so for that price—five hundred too low or something. We all chatted for a minute. Then the woman went on her way. We offered Sam a ride, but he declined. Then we went along to the show. It was starting by then."

"Well, this certainly changes things."

"You know something, Mr. Fulton?"

"Yessir?"

"She seemed like she didn't want to go. She looked at her watch. She acted like she had somewhere to go and excused herself. But she seemed nervous."

"Did you see which way she went?"

"I tried to think of that too. I just don't remember. I thought about this thing last week, after we spoke. The wife and I spoke of it at length, trying to remember more. But it just dawned on me that we ran into Sam again, the whole thing with the flat tire."

"Do you know which wrecker company came?"

"No, sir. Was I of help to you?"

208

"Yessir. If you think of anything else, don't hesitate to call."

Fulton telephoned the wrecker companies. Only one of them had records from that long ago, and the owner was out of town. Still, Sam's "alibi" was starting to hold water.

A person can act guilty, but that may not mean it's so. So did Sam do it or not?

40

Tallahassee
3:00 p.m.
Wednesday, 11/7/1956

Headline: "Austin Defeats Howerton." The telephone rang, and he set the paper aside.

It was George Pickett Mumford. He worked out of the Capital Truck Center on Tennessee Street. "What was it you needed to know, young fella?"

"Well, sir, it's a long shot, but I was told you had records of customers going back a few years, and I was trying to find out if you had something from November fifty-three."

"You betcha. I have all those records filed away in this office. If I towed the car, there's a record of it, yes, sir! That's the right way to do business. It's here for sure!"

"Yessir."

"Now, let me see, no, it's not in the file cabinet," said the old man, slamming the drawer. "I stopped using that. It got too full. No, it ain't in the desk. The rolltop is busted on that. Here, let me put the phone down a minute."

"I don't want to put you on the spot. If you need time to find it, I—"

"No, sir, it's no trouble. You just wait." Fulton heard what seemed like five solid minutes of rustling papers, drawers slamming, and the old man cussing the paperwork scattered about the office. "Wait a minute, wait a ding-dong minute," Fulton heard in the background. "Hey, mister?" asked the old man, picking up the receiver.

"Yessir?"

"I found the stuff from that year. Now, did you say the name?"

"Sam Nowak."

"Sam Nowak, Sam Nowak," said the old man, flipping through papers. "Does that say Sam? Hard to tell." Fulton could hear more rustling as the man rummaged through invoices. "Don't see it. Got a Sam Crenshaw, but not a Nowak. Got a *Sam*antha Davis. Maybe I didn't write out no invoice."

"This guy had a flat, no spare."

"Well, sir, I get a lot of those. More than you think. That's the one thing folks never check, is their spare! Or they use it and don't put nothing back. Now you take my wife for instance. Goes out of town, has to get her brother to put the spare on, then doesn't tell me about it! We get another flat, near Blountstown it was, and I go to get the spare, and it ain't no good neither—both tires deader'n a doornail."

"Well—"

"So that don't call it to no mind."

"Well," said Fulton, trying to get a word in. "This was an unusual car—little English car, cream with a black roof?"

"One a' them foreign numbers? Well, why didn't you tell me that? I got a special file for 'em. Sure, right over here." More rustling. "We're startin' to see a lot more a' them. If them fellers in Detroit ain't careful, there'll be them little French and English cars in every garage, and *Shiverlay* and Ford'll be out of business."

"Yessir. Do you see Sam Nowak?"

"No. I know what's wrong. I need my glasses. Oh, fiddle! Were are they at?"

Fulton put the phone down, running his hands over his face then chuckling. You couldn't be mad at the old coot.

"Here they are."

"That's good, Mr. Mumford. Do you see Sam?"

"By golly! It was here all the time!"

"Good! Can you tell me anything about it?"

"It says, 'Towed car, Monroe to Capital Truck Center. Patched tire.' And it's got the price. November second, nineteen-hundred-and-fifty-three."

"Any time noted?"

"Well, mister, I knew you was gonna ask that!" He laughed. "I always write the time on these late-night calls. I don't remember it to save my life. Not the car, nor this Nowak feller, nothin'! But by golly I got the time on there. We finished up at ten o'clock."

"Nowak would have paid you and been on his way at ten?"

"Yessir, I guaran-damn-tee that." Fulton started to say good-bye when the old gentleman interrupted. "You know, I do remember something. By Joe, I'm not one to tell tales, I wouldn't tell no one else, but I reckon it's okay since you the law," he said in an odd, high-pitched laugh. "By dog!"

"Yessir?"

"But a woman came and met him here. She seemed real nervous."

"What?" said Fulton, nearly dropping the phone.

"She acted real friendly-like, like a lady friend to him. But she kept acting like she was worried about someone seein' them together. He asked to use my telephone. I reckon he called her to come get him. But then I had the tire patched, and it was holdin' air, and she got there for nothin'."

"Who was she?" Fulton didn't know who this woman was. It could be Lana Turner, for all he knew. Or even Jo Ellen.

"I don't know, but I think she was a married woman because they made me promise not to say anything about her bein' there. I told 'em I didn't care what was their business. It didn't make no difference to me."

"What did she look like?"

"Oh, now let me think for a minute, mister. Well, she had black hair, for starters. Real dark hair."

"Yeah?" said Fulton, his stomach churning.

"Nicely dressed."

"Yeah? What else?"

"How do I say this without bein' too hard on the gal? She was about the homeliest woman I've seen."

"Come again?"

The old man cackled again. "I tell you, it's a fact. She must have weighed in heavier than a big ol' straight-eight motor."

"Okay," said Fulton, his stomach returning to normal. "You *sure* about what she looked like?"

"Uh-*huh.* Sure, I'm sure."

Fulton said good-bye to the old man and called Sam. "I'd like you to come to my office. Can you be here in a half hour?"

"S-Sure, I can. Am-am I going to jail?"

"Just get here," said Fulton angrily.

"Yessir."

Fulton hung up. It wasn't long before Sam pulled up in his car. He hadn't shaved in two or three days, the armpits of his blue shirt were sweaty, and he smelled of beer. Mary Ann smiled and said, "Good afternoon," clutching the telephone to her ear as she spoke to a detective in Duval County. Sam hesitated in the doorway.

Fulton waved for him to come in. "You look like hell. I'm glad you kept your word and stayed in town. I'd be even more hackled up if I had to hunt you down."

"No, sir, I wasn't going nowhere."

"Sit down," said Fulton roughly.

"S-Sure," said Sam, sitting down hesitantly; the sun was bright behind him, coming in through the broken venetian blinds.

"Why'd you lie to me about where you were? Didn't you think I'd find out? You almost got yourself arrested."

"I-I," stammered Sam.

"Giving me a cock-and-bull story about a card game. When you were prob'ly playing backseat bingo with Mrs. Engine Block," said Fulton, standing up.

"Huh?"

"The woman," said Fulton, sitting on the front of his desk.

"There was no woman."

Fulton looked at him as if to ask, "Really? You're going to keep lying? You think I'm stupid?"

"Maybe I got mixed up about the card game. I just got mixed up, that's all."

"Mixed up, huh?"

Sam realized he was caught—again. He hung his head. "S-sorry. I didn't think you'd check with the Cannings. I guess I didn't know how serious a jam I'm in. I know I'm a dope. I let my temper get the best of me. I get myself in these jams."

"Who's the girl?"

"I'm sorry for lying, Mr. Fulton. I didn't know what to do. I didn't want to mix Eunice up in all this."

"If I ask her, is she gonna say you were with her?"

"We listened to records at her house, drank some wine—white wine. It was about ten thirty. I stayed there until midnight and then went home. Her

213

husband was due back in the morning. He works for the railroad. I'm telling you the gospel truth, Mr. Fulton."

"It's about time you started quoting chapter and verse—from the truth. It's a lot easier to keep track of. Doggone, it goes a whole lot easier if you tell things straight! How are we supposed to put the right people in jail when we gotta sort though a pack of lies?"

"I don't know," said Sam, looking down. "What's gonna happen to me?"

"I oughta put you in jail for obstructing a law officer." Fulton got up and looked out the window and shook his head. Then he started toward the door.

"Uh, Mr. Fulton, where are you going?" asked Sam timidly, fearing Fulton might be going to get handcuffs—or a gun. Fulton sure looked mad! Mary Ann also looked on with interest, sensing Fulton's irritation.

Fulton paused for a moment, crossing his arms. He looked at Sam, sensing he was scared. "Well, do you want some coffee or not?" he said impatiently, a bit of a grin forming on his face.

"Huh?" asked Sam, his eyes darting back and forth between Fulton and the secretary. "Oh! Oh, yessir, thank you."

Fulton poured a cup for Nowak and another for himself with an extra spoonful of sugar. He needed it.

XXXXX

3:30 p.m.

He called the sheriff. "We better find another suspect."

"Huh?"

Fulton told the sheriff what he'd learned.

"Dadgummit! I was sure hopin' you'd have it solved. You sure it's not Sam?"

"I'm sure."

XXXXX

The telephone rang again. "If it's old man Mumford, I'm not here!" said Fulton.

"It's Ben Austin," said Mary Ann.

Fulton took the call.

214

"Well, True, I felt like I should call on the Harberts' behalf. They phoned me earlier in the week."

"Sure."

"Do you need anything on the Sam front? Do you need to talk to Howard Jenkins?"

"I don't think Sam did this. We're at a dead end."

"Don't give up so easy on him. He gave me fits on the civil case, trying to disprove his claims. He's a sly one. He proved himself an adept liar in our trial."

"I can see that. He's certainly a character."

"He's a known gun aficionado, believes in a lot of crazy right-wing ideas."

"Owning a gun isn't a crime. Anyway, his alibi holds up. He was way out on West 90. He couldn't have got all the way up Monroe."

"Well, I'm sorry it's not solved. I guess they can't all be easy. That's why we got you. I know the family appreciates all you're doing. If I can help or if you need me to do anything, you have my number."

"Thanks. And congratulations."

"Oh, thank you. I'm trying to tidy up a few things so I can be ready for the new session in April."

"Sure. Well, thanks again."

Tallahassee
4:15 p.m.
Friday, 11/9/1956

Doc Elston was a character. Fulton didn't know how old the doc was—
sixty-five, he reckoned. The ME liked to tell stories, and those from his
World War I days were ribald indeed.

Fulton got in the Ford, taking Tennessee Street away from town. He turned
onto two-lane Magnolia Drive, heading toward the hospital. Magnolia
ended in front of the five-story building, which rose from a clearing in the
woods. Fulton paused at the stoplight that was suspended over the middle
of the intersection where three country roads came together—Centerville,
Miccosukee, Magnolia. There wasn't much this far outside of town,
pinewoods on all sides except the clearing where the hospital stood.

Fulton spun the wheel over, pulling into the parking lot. He walked in the
front doors and up to the receptionist's desk. "I'm here to see Dr. Elston,"
he told the middle-aged nurse with glasses.

"Oh, Mr. Fulton! He's expecting you. Please follow me." The woman started
to show him the way to the morgue.

"It's okay, ma'am. I know the way."

"Certainly. Well, let me know if you need anything."

"Thanks," he said, heading down the hall. He turned, taking the staircase
down to the basement. It was not a large building, fairly new, replacing a
wooden Baptist Memorial that was closer to town. He found the doctor
leaning over the counter, a cigarette burning in his ashtray while he looked
through his microscope. He was the ME, but he was also an emergency
room doctor and made house calls in a rattly Pontiac; there wasn't that
much work for a coroner in these parts. He often hung out in the morgue
when the ER wasn't busy. He ate his lunch there so no one would bother
him, he said.

"Hey, True! You care for a cigarette?" he asked, holding up the pack.

"No thanks, Doc. I don't smoke anymore."

"Well, these are supposed to be good for the T-zone, help you relax. How
have you been? I never see you anymore."

"Just fine, Doc. Busy?"

"Oh, you know, people are just dying for my services." He laughed. Fulton
laughed too, even though Doc had said that a few times before. The doc

had a full head of silver hair and a neatly trimmed mustache. He generally frowned, but could be rather humorous when he wished.

"Whatcha lookin' at?"

"Just some slides. Got to try to keep up to date in case you boys need me for somethin'." He lit a fresh cigarette and looked up curiously. "Do you?"

"Well, Doc, I wanted to talk to you about a case from a few years back."

"Yeah?" said the doctor, savoring the smoke he was inhaling.

"Jo Ellen Harbert, crash off of US 27," said Fulton, pulling up a chair.

"Sure, I remember. One of the highest alcohol levels I've seen."

"I got a copy of your report here," he said, handing it to the doctor.

"Yeah, .220 percent, I remember it well."

"So I'm led to believe someone with that much alcohol would be showing its effects. Am I wrong?"

"True, the deceased was only five-six, a hundred fifteen pounds. She was as high as a pine tree in Thomasville! Shoot yeah, she'd be sloppy drunk." No, the doctor wasn't reading from his report—he remembered those numbers.

"What are we talkin' about in terms of how much she had to drink?"

"There's a way to calculate that, by golly."

Fulton nodded. "How accurate is the blood test you used?"

"You ever use the drunkometer?"

"We had one in Jacksonville, but I never had any real trainin' behind it. You had your driver, you pretty well knew they were drunk when you brought 'em in, and they blew up the balloon. It more or less confirmed what you knew. The defense attorneys always tried to kick it out," said Fulton, chuckling.

"Well, it's a good guide. It was invented by a doctor, yessir, back in thirty-six. But it's a *breath* test. It measures the alcohol a person expels when they *breathe*. Here, we had a blood test."

"Which you conducted?"

"Yes, personally. And that *is*, most definitely, *accurate*. The most accurate test that exists. Generally, anything above .150 percent is considered under the influence. They'd be showing the effects of the alcohol they'd

217

consumed. I've testified in court that I would expect someone at that level to be showing signs of impairment."

"Of course, the law doesn't set a legal limit, a number," said Fulton.

"No, but it is understood that someone at a high dosage would be showing signs that their *normal faculties* are impaired. That's the term, isn't it?"

"That's in the statute," Fulton remembered.

"I thought it was in the law somewhere."

"How long would it take to get that drunk?"

"Depends on a lot of things. Height and weight, of course. The person's tolerance. Whether they consumed food. What they had to drink. Depending on those things, it could take a couple hours to get that drunk. Now, I know she did eat—the gastric contents, you know." The doctor scribbled some figures on a prescription pad. "Six drinks—shot-size doses," he said, showing the size with his index finger and thumb, indicating a measurement of two inches. "Shot-size doses, I should think. Yessir!"

"That's quite a bit."

"It smelled like a distillery in my examination room!"

"I've been to autopsies like that."

"It's like you're standing in a dadgum barrel 'a whiskey."

"What's the least amount of time you'd need to get up to her level?"

"Plannin' to try it?" Doc asked, grinning.

"Oh no, Doc," Fulton chuckled, holding up his hand. "Marlene would have my hide."

"An hour. Could be over the course of forty-five minutes. Could be less."

"What about her injuries?"

"Uh-huh. Skull fractured. A massive internal hemorrhage. Best I could determine she hit a pine tree before landing on the ground. Fractured sternum from the steering wheel, of course."

"I saw on there bruises on the back of her head, possible older laceration on her lip, and older contusion on her bicep," said Fulton, motioning toward the report. "Anything unusual about those?"

"Bruises on her head could be from a lot of things. It was a very violent crash. She was thrown from the car. You had trees, you had the windshield and windshield post, the steering wheel in that Packard, all things that could have caused the injury."

"The possible laceration—old laceration—can you say how old?"

"I can't be sure about the laceration inside her lip—how old it was—and you know as well as I do that could be a lot of things. Same with the contusion on her arm."

"Could she have been attacked shortly before she died?"

"You think she was?"

"Family does. They suspect foul play of some sort."

"Hmm, I remember the family. Her sister and brother were here for the coroner's jury. And her father, I could scarcely forget him, by golly. I remember they asked *a lot* of questions," said Elston, rolling his eyes. "Of me, of the detective. They even tracked him down on the golf course at one point. But we simply had no facts to lead us there."

"She had a scar on the back of her head. It had been stitched."

"Yeah."

"An older injury."

"Yeah, could mean she accidentally hit her head. Could be just a coincidence."

"Could be."

The doctor watched Fulton, the wheels turning in his head. "But what do you make of that as a policeman?"

"Too many coincidences. Maybe someone hurt her before. But you can't tell me that for sure."

"No."

"Okay. Is it possible she was attacked, that this was staged to look like she passed out or ran off the road?"

"It's possible. But I could never conclude it was a homicide. Not enough evidence. Yes, it's *possible*. But nothing else supported that as manner of death. Let's say you have someone fall from a building—take this building, someone falls from the roof. Five stories. He breaks his neck. *Cause* of death is easy, isn't it?"

Fulton nodded.

219

"Sure! The human spine doesn't interact well with cement, colliding head-on at fifty miles an hour. Well, what if someone came up behind him just a moment before, grabs him, and twists his neck, snapping it. And *then*," emphasized the doctor, holding up his index finger, "pushes him off. Looking at the body, the two scenarios might look the same. They might be equally plausible. But the surrounding circumstances step in, and we get a plausible manner of death. Like a suicide note. Or the sucker's wife just left and the bank picked up his car. You see?"

"Sure."

"That's what the coroner's jury does. It may not make sense for laypeople—plumbers and electricians and store clerks—to decide cause and manner of death, but I think they reached the only permissible verdict in this case."

"Is it possible she passed out from the amount of alcohol she consumed?"

"Easily! As long as she was not a chronic heavy drinker, where one might build up a heavy tolerance, it's very possible."

"Okay."

"A lot of the evidence could fit more than one theory. Like the bruises. Or the old stitches. Or her clothes. She had a lot of blood on them. There was blood on her glove. Maybe she got that from touching her face after someone slugged her, or maybe she got that getting moved around by people trying to help her. But you got to have more to tip it one way or the other."

"So maybe someone hits her, or she passed out. They put the car in gear, let it crash, and she sustains the injuries you documented."

"Yes, that would be *possible*. Unusual and unlikely—but possible."

"Well, this is an unusual case."

The doctor nodded.

"She had some cuts on her arms, her right hand?"

"Uh-huh."

"I wanted to ask you about one of the photos."

"Yeah?"

Fulton held up an interior shot of the car. "This one shows a glass dish, a broken bowl. It appears to have blood on it."

The doctor put on his glasses and examined the photo. "Well, yes, it does."

"Did she have any cuts that might correspond to that bowl?"

"That's hard to say. Those lacerations on her arms, her hand, might."

"Is it possible someone else got cut with that bowl? I mean, there's the big piece in the front, a little piece behind the seat back, in this other photo."

"I don't know. I wasn't given that piece to test for blood type. I just don't know," said the doctor, thinking about it intently, his fingers steepled beneath his lips. "Hmm."

"Thanks, Doc."

"Certainly. Now that'll be five bucks for the consultation."

"Charge it to Frank Carter," said Fulton, opening the door.

Elston laughed.

XXXXX

Dave Everett pulled in to Ed's Truck Stop on Highway 90 near Pedrick Road. He climbed down from the high green-and-white cab of the White Freightliner tractor. He walked in the Harrison Café and relaxed at the counter, waiting for the cop to show up.

Two rigs were filling up on diesel as Fulton pulled in, the Ford's antenna flicking back and forth as the car bounced over the dip in the driveway. He walked inside. A fellow waved him over to the lunch counter. "Howdy, Mr. Fulton. Dave Everett," said the man, extending his hand. Everett was in his early thirties. He wore a cap and a bow tie with his uniform—gray trousers and long-sleeve shirt that were clean and pressed—and new cowboy boots.

"Hello," said Fulton, shaking his hand, joining him at the counter. Dave had a cup of coffee already.

"Say, would you rather sit in a booth, Mr. Fulton?"

"Sure. I have some pictures I'd like you to look at."

"Okay." They moved to an empty spot at the far end of the diner. Dave took off his cap and put it on the seat beside him. He had thick dark brown hair, which he had parted and combed in a low pompadour.

"You heading back to Jacksonville?"

"Yessir, gotta pick up another load. I stay gone from home for two days at a time, back and forth, one little town after another, from Jacksonville to Mobile. My company is growing—we haul for Winn-Dixie. They own the Lovett stores, you know."

221

"You like it?"

"Sure. You get to see a lot of things, a lot of places most people never will, lookin' out through that windshield. It's a beautiful country. It just amazes me sometimes."

"Yeah, I see what you mean." Fulton had a file folder with him, which he opened. "I made a lineup of cars. Gateway Motors in Jacksonville and another dealer over there sent me a few photos of their small imported cars. I also included an American small car." Fulton's lineup sheet included an English Ford, a Simca, and a Rambler, the Ford and Rambler being two of the most popular small cars on the market. "Now, just take a look at these. If you see one you recognize, let me know. If you don't, that's okay too. I can get more pictures."

The waitress set glasses of Coca-Cola between them.

"Yes, sir. I'd be glad to." The trucker looked over the lineup, comparing each photo. The waitress brought their burgers. Dave poured some ketchup for his fries while he continued to study on the photos. "Defin'tely wasn't a Ford or a Rambler. Dang, those Fords are small! It had a shape sorta like that, but rounder," he said, pointing to one of the cars, chewing a mouthful of greasy hamburger. "I just don't know the foreign cars that well. It was rounded off in back, where the trunk is—kind of like a '48 Hudson. My father-in-law had one, you see. But it wasn't a Hudson, not a standard-size car, I know that. It was a small sedan, like this one." He tapped the picture. "It had a weird grille, like a fish's mouth. No, none of these is the car." He pushed the lineup sheet toward Fulton's side of the table.

Fulton's hope sank a little. "Okay, I'll get some more pictures." Fulton hated to do that; he didn't have that kind of time.

"Yessir. It was very round. It wasn't like the Ford you came in," he said, turning and looking toward Fulton's car in the dark lot. "It wasn't squared off like that, but rounded off front *and* back. And it had that fish mouth, like I said." He took another mouthful of fries and washed it down with the glass of Coca-Cola.

"Wait a minute," said Fulton. "Wait just a minute!" He opened his briefcase and pulled out a magazine. He flipped through the pages. He knew he'd seen it. He held up the magazine. "Is this the car?"

"Okay," said Everett. "It was rounded off like that, sure." He took the magazine and looked at it while he chewed the hamburger. "That grille— yes, that's it!"

"You sure?"

Dave continued to examine it, nodding.

222

"How sure are you?"

"I'm pos'tive that's the car." Dave had pointed out the Dyna Z, a French model from Panhard. "Look here—the doors open from the front like a '34 Ford. I remember those doors from that night, when the driver got out!"

"And it was yellow?"

"Yessir."

"Florida tag?"

"Don't know. I don't think there was a plate on the front, and I'm not sure I saw the one on the back."

"If you remember anything, you have my number."

The trucker nodded.

"I appreciate it very much."

"Sure thing. Say, I'm gonna have a milkshake. You want one? If ya got the time?"

"Don't mind if I do."

XXXXX

Fulton drove to the Motor Vehicle Commission in the Martin building. It was on the first floor, to the left as one came in the front door. It was closed, no one there except Clevedale mopping the floor. He let Fulton in.

Fulton opened a drawer and began thumbing through the 3 × 5 index cards. It took several minutes, but he found there were four of the 1954 model-year cars in the state. He pulled open the file drawers, looking at the registration cards. The first three weren't registered until well into '54. He opened another drawer, walking his fingers back to the final card.

"Ha!" said Fulton, tapping the card with his finger. There was only one registered in fifty-three—to an Anders Ferguson from Miami!

Fulton dug a little deeper with the card catalog. Ferguson also had a '55 Jaguar and a house trailer. *This had to be the guy! He had the name of the elusive Panhard owner.*

He drove back to Gaines. "Operator, get me information in Miami."

"I'm connecting you now."

"Okay, thanks." Fulton waited. "Oh, operator, I need the number for an Anders Ferguson. Sure, I'll wait." In a moment, she had the number for him. She transferred him to the long-distance operator, who rang the Fergusons.

"May I speak with Anders Ferguson?"

"This is Mrs. Ferguson."

"Evenin', ma'am," he said, identifying himself and the purpose of his call. She thought about it for a moment. "I'd prefer if you call my husband at work. I've never had a policeman call before. I'd rather you speak to Anders."

"Sure, thank you for your time." Fulton put another call through to the number she provided, a car dealer in Miami. He could hear a receptionist paging Ferguson.

"Yes, I'm Ferguson," came the voice on the other end of the line. Fulton could hear more names being paged. *Busy dealership.*

"I'm True Fulton with the Sheriff's Bureau in Tallahassee."

"Okay, what can I do for you? Do you wish to order some cars?"

"We could prob'ly use some, but no, sir, I'd like to ask you about something you were a witness to three years ago, November fifty-three."

"In Tallahassee? It sure can't be about the small fish we caught! Well, that must have been that wreck," said Ferguson, his voice taking on a more somber tone. "I'm not sure how much I can help. It's been some time."

"Yessir. I'd like to hear as much as you can remember, but especially, I want to talk to you about anyone you saw out there."

"Okay. Well, we were driving to California. We had a car that wasn't on sale yet. The US distributor wanted to do some testing. We'd been stationed in San Diego in the war and wanted to go back, see things along the way. We got a good vacation out of the 'shake-down cruise' on this car."

"The Panhard?"

"That's right. I'm looking at that very car outside my showroom. I kept it to drive to work. She made it to *Los An-gel-ease* without any problems—but *slow* going in the mountains! We must have went through a couple hundred little towns."

"Yessir."

"Well, back to the Tallahassee situation. We stopped for some fishing at the lake with some friends. Then we followed them back to town for dinner. Everyone wanted to see the trailer, so we didn't unhook."

"Uh-huh."

"After dinner, we intended to check into the trailer park and stay the night, but then we missed it and had to find a place to turn around. It isn't so easy with the narrow road and trailer. It was pretty dark up there. We figured we'd go back to the Tradewinds camp if we had to. But then we saw a truck stopped in the road, and as we got closer—his lights shining into the trees—we could see a car had gone down into the woods."

"Okay."

"Two truckers were checking on the woman. She was nearly dead, there's no other way to describe it. A sheriff got there and a patrolman. Then the ambulance came, and we left."

"Did you see anyone else?"

"Why, yes we did! We saw a man running. It was right after we had missed the turn for the park. We were looking for a good place to turn around. We started to pull down a dirt road, and then we saw this fella in the woods. Our lights illuminated him, and he seemed to run farther into the woods. We had to back out and keep going because it was so narrow, we couldn't get turned around. When we came upon the wreck, why, we just forgot about that fella."

"Yessir?"

"So when we leave the wreck, we thought about it some more. Just the way he looked, I don't know, something didn't seem right. So we went back and tried to tell someone. Had to turn around *again!*" The man chuckled. "We told the patrolman."

"Do you remember if there was more than one highway patrol officer?"

"There may have been."

"What didn't seem right about him?"

"Well, the rain, the cold, someone loitering out there in the woods. I don't know, maybe he knew something, maybe he was driving another car and caused the accident. We even talked about it, my wife and I, and thought perhaps he'd been walking along and the woman swerved to avoid him. It was a strange place for a wreck. Way out there, no cross street or anything."

"Can you describe the man?"

"Dark clothes. Thin, athletic, I guess you'd say. Tall."

Sam is heavyset. Sam isn't tall, Fulton thought. "Are you sure, Mr. Ferguson?"

225

"Yes. I'm six-one, and I'd say that he was at least that tall. He seemed like he was in good shape—definitely not overweight."

"Could you see his face?"

"No, I'm afraid not. I mean, I could tell he wasn't colored, but in terms of recognizing him, no."

"Was it dark up there?"

"Yes, very."

"And how far away was he?"

"Thirty or forty feet."

"Which direction was he going?"

"Well now ,let me see. We were going north, back towards the lake. This man was on the left side of the highway, moving away from the road, so going west, roughly."

"Thank you, sir. You've been a big help." *That description doesn't match Sam.*

42

Tallahassee
Sunday, 11/11/1956

At 1:15 p.m., the telephone rang. Sam. He wasn't as nervous. "Happy Veteran's Day."

"Thank you, Sam."

"I-I was in the navy too."

"Yeah?"

"S-Sure. I was a cook, Commissary Man Second Class. I sorta got that job by mistake 'cause I'm really a lousy cook. I was supposed to be a bosun's mate, but there was a snafu with the paperwork, and once the navy types something on a form, they don't change it."

They both laughed at that.

"Well, I was driving down to my laundry, and I happened to notice your car at your office. I remembered something that I thought might help you. I kept thinking about that night. You know, I spoke to the girl again—a little after nine it was."

"When you got into your car?"

"Well, I-I did talk to her then too. Yeah, I cooled off a little. But I mean I talked to her *after* that."

"Oh?"

"Yeah, I thought of a dry cleaner in Thomasville that I was wanting to sell, thought she might be interested. I called from a payphone at the Pure Station at Park Avenue. I stopped to put air in my tire. After I hung up with her, I realized it wasn't gonna do no good, the tire was flat."

"Yeah?"

"She said she had to go, like she was meeting someone, and she hangs up."

"Uh-huh."

"You know, I did sell some whiskey one time. I wanted to come clean about that. Just the cheap stuff, see? And only one time. A guy in Perry talked me into it."

"Yeah. Well, thanks for the information."

"Sure thing."

Fulton said good-bye and got a peppermint from his desk. Sam's story reaffirmed that Jo Ellen, in fact, had a 9:30 p.m. meeting—with someone.

Maybe Sam's all right. The movies and television made detective work glamorous—professional killers lurking in the shadows, gangsters shooting up places from moving cars. But it's really about talking to people, listening, not being afraid to get in your car and ask questions.

Fulton went to pick up something from the fruit stand near the railroad overpass. One end of the store had a little pyramid-shaped roof, which was once part of a bowling alley and dance hall. The rest was a low, covered building with the side open and overflowing with fruits and vegetables. They had coolers with meat in the back. It was the only store open on Sunday, most of the lights and windows dark up and down the hill. Fulton pulled right up to the open front and began loading up a sack. He thanked the clerk and got in the car with the paper bag. Marlene wanted tomatoes for a salad; she'd end up with a few other items. He watched a train roll by on the Seaboard Line before driving back up the hill.

43

Tallahassee
Friday, 11/16/1956

At 4:30 p.m., Fulton drove to the high school to meet the principal. Leon had an away game. The team was loading its bus, which was painted red and white originally, but had faded to the point it appeared *pink* and white. Fulton noticed the football coach looking over at him from the door of the bus. He was smoking a cigarette, taking quick puffs. Fulton waved to him and the man turned away, disappearing inside.

Fulton walked down the empty hall. Dr. Truston offered Fulton a seat in his office. "Ms. Harbert resigned because had she not done so, I would have had no choice but to fire her."

"Why was that?"

"Her drinking."

"It interfered with her work?"

"I wasn't going to let it get that far, Mr. Fulton. She would go to parties in the evening and get plastered. She'd stay out all night. She'd run that car of hers all over town while in a state of drunkenness. The school simply could not tolerate those sort of indiscretions."

"Did you have firsthand knowledge of Ms. Harbert acting like that?"

"No, but I got it on good authority. I was provided photographs that showed Ms. Harbert in a less than complimentary condition."

"Didn't it strike you as odd, or a little too convenient, that there'd be photographs?"

"No. I took it as a matter of public service that someone would turn over the information --out of an altruistic motive."

"You never suspected a more *personal* motive?"

"I saw no evidence of that."

"Who gave you the pictures?"

The principal smiled slightly. "That confidence I cannot reveal."

"You mean you *won't* reveal." Fulton watched the principal's growing look of irritation and wondered how forceful he might be in pressing the matter. He decided to let it go for now.

The principal stood. "Well, if that's all, I'll show you to the door."

229

"Is there anyone else that knew Jo Ellen?"

"Mrs. Addley was a friend of hers. I can show you to her classroom. I expect she's preparing to leave for the day. As a word of advice, detective, you're not from here. Folks don't like outsiders coming over, stirring up what's at the bottom of the outhouse. Don't be surprised if no one wants to talk about Jo Ellen. This way please."

He led Fulton down the hall, quiet with students gone for the day; he stopped at a door where the lights were still on, and seeing Mrs. Addley through the glass, he opened it. The principal introduced him to the teacher, who appeared to be in her early thirties with brown hair she had pinned back, a blue skirt, and a simple long-sleeve blouse. "Mrs. Addley, this is Detective Fulton. He has a question or two about Jo Ellen Harbert."

"Oh, how do you do?"

"Evenin', ma'am."

The principal excused himself, shutting the door behind him.

"I understand Jo Ellen was a friend of yours."

"There's not much I can tell you. She was a nice girl."

"Well, anything you can tell me might help."

The woman said nothing.

"Did you like her?"

"Of course. She was my friend."

"Did you know anyone that didn't like her?"

"No."

"Did she have a fella?"

"Not when she was here, no."

"Did she have a drinking problem?"

"I-I wouldn't know, detective."

"Why did she leave?"

"I-I don't know. Please excuse me, sir."

There were far more questions than answers. Fulton walked down the dark hall. He put his hat on. He walked down the steps, back to his car.

XXXXX

He switched off the light and left the office. He took Calhoun north. He noted the Ford sedan in the rearview. It was dark around there, under the canopy of trees, but he could distinguish the round parking lights of a Ford. Law enforcement used them. But so did every John Q. Citizen and his brother—Fords were ubiquitous in the South. In fact, Calhoun took Fulton past the Ford dealership, the lights on, salesmen eager to do business should anyone stop in after work, a down payment in hand. There were nice '57 models in the showroom with two-tone paint jobs and stubby fins. Perhaps it was a city car. Maybe the tag had fallen off his '52 or a taillight was out. It made him chuckle, the possibility of getting pulled over. At least the radio still worked in this thing! The other car glided to a stop behind him as he waited at the traffic light.

The light changed. Fulton crossed Tennessee Street; the other car followed, four car lengths behind. No red light on top. It wasn't a city or county car. He knew the car Holland drove and the couple other unmarked cars they had, and they were plain-jane '55 Chevrolets. It might be an FHP unmarked. He was approaching Thomasville Road, the lights still glowing in his rearview.

Fulton made a right on Thomasville; the Ford followed. He could see the neon sign poking up at Carr Buick, the showroom windows glowing brightly, a salesman on the lot ready to convince his prospect that he had plenty of good deals remaining on big chromey '57s. There were houses behind the dealer and all along Bradford, the other side of Glendale. Fulton held out his arm to signal and turned down the quiet side street. The driver of the other car put his blinkers on and followed. It was definitely a '55 Ford, a two-door.

Fulton spun the wheel over, plowing onto Forest Drive and screeching to a stop. The other car screamed in passing gear as it accelerated up Bradford. He got a good view of the Ford as it sped past—dark blue, blackwall tires. He couldn't read the tag number. It was too dark—almost no daylight left— and the back of the car was dirty. But it was a Florida plate. The windows were dirty too; all he could see was a fedora hat inside. Fulton circled around Forest, through the neighborhood of little brick cottages, looping around to Florida Avenue. He stopped at the Thomasville Road intersection. No sign of the other car. He made a left and drove home.

44

Tallahassee
Saturday, 11/17/1956

Jo Ellen's students were eighteen or nineteen now. They'd graduated, begun careers, got married. Away from the school and the principal, still they revealed nothing. Only things like "Ms. Harbert was a swell teacher." If they knew anything, they weren't talking. Fulton drew a line through the last name on the list and got back in the car.

College Avenue. FSU's "Main Street." He parked and sat for a moment, watching the young fellows and their dates walking up the hill, going to the movies or Bennett's. Past the TV repair shop and the dry cleaners and little stores, they came. Some drove, parking used Chevys and Fords, opening doors for young ladies. A young woman, alone, clutched a box, coming out of the Bertha Cook Dress Shop below the main floor of Shaw's Furniture.

Bennett's. Kids under the striped awnings socializing, talking about what movie they'd see at the State Theatre. Shoppers browsing the display windows, advertisements for hair products taped to the glass, sundry items crowded in for passersby to see. The jukebox playing "Making Believe."

A young man behind the counter was busily working the soda machine. "Yeah, I'm Billy Macklin." He wiped his hands on his apron and looked at the picture. He wore a white soda jerk hat, apron, and a bow tie, black hair framing his round face. "Sure, I remember her. I was busboy at the Cherokee. I remember her 'cause she ate breakfast a coupla times." He frowned. "But that ain't it neither. You see, there was a guy that I saw coming in the back way of the hotel. He had a box all wrapped up like Christmas. It seemed odd that he didn't just take it to the front desk, but he sneaks in around by the kitchen, see?"

"Okay."

"He had a funny look, like he was up to somethin'. So I'm a dumb kid, only sixteen, I follow him. There's no one around, the place is dead, but he's sneaking—sneaking," said the young man, using his fingers to show how deliberate the man tiptoed his way in. "Up the stairs. Down the hall. Like a cat burglar. And he goes up to her room and knocks—and leaves it. I hide around the corner and wait 'til he leaves, and then it ain't but a minute or two, and the desk clerk comes up there, and I see that's this lady's room."

"Do you know this fella?"

"No, sir."

"Ever see him before?"

"No, sir."

"Can you tell me what he looked like?"

"Sorta stocky, heavyset."

"See his face?"

"No, sir. He had a hat and a coat, bow tie. I probably couldn't recognize him."

"Hair color?"

"Dark."

"All right."

"One other thing—I saw her throw away a bottle of whiskey later. Maybe that was what was in the box?"

"I don't know, son. Could be."

XXXXX

He drove down the tree-lined avenue of small bungalows and old mansions that dead-ended at the gates of the Westcott building, that imposing fortress with its ivy-covered brick towers and battlements that rose from the ridge once referred to as Hangman's Hill. A man was washing his car in his driveway, near the corner of College and Copeland. Fulton coasted to the stop sign, waiting for students to pass, on their way to the Amber House and the Mecca. He crossed Copeland, pulling through the gates. He swung around the circle driveway that encompassed the water fountain, parking at the ornate entrance.

He walked up the steps, finding the doors unlocked. The old night watchman was coming in to work; he carried a flashlight, no gun. He said hello. Fulton told him who he was and that he wanted to have a look around. The old man continued on his rounds, one man guarding the dorms and classrooms, everything from the gates out to the dairy and the stadium.

Fulton walked along the dim hallway, looking up at the high ceilings and the polished woodwork. He wandered about, taking it in. He passed offices, their lights off, typewriters silent, no one working today. He noted the archways and thick walls, a little post office with brass mailboxes for students. There was an auditorium with a giant pipe organ. Jo Ellen had walked these corridors, picked up letters from her father and sister here. But there was nothing that told him who she knew, what she did, what she thought when she was here.

He took the stairs to the second floor. There were photos in the halls near the administration offices. He walked along, looking at them, as if they were exhibits in a gallery. Various classes and years, some class photos even from the thirties and early forties. All women, of course. He looked for a class photo from 1947. There was none, but there were many photographs documenting the first year of FSU's football program from the same year, when men were admitted for the first time in a generation.

He looked for more photographs of the athletes. It took a few turns down some side halls before he spotted something. A photograph of women playing tennis. Jo Ellen. And a girl with a familiar face—Evelyn Madgison. There were two men in white trousers and sweaters watching that match. Their faces were blurred—if only he knew who they were.

Fulton returned to his car and found Janine's number in the case file. He tried the pay phone near the back door of the Amber House. It was too noisy, so he drove down to SchwoBilt's at the southeast corner of College and Adams and placed a call from the payphone upstairs. It was a booth and quiet, despite the crowd present in the department store. "Miss Harbert?"

"Oh, yes, Mr. Fulton! How are you?"

"Fine, ma'am, just fine. I was over here at the college trying to find some photos, maybe something from your sister's class."

"Oh. Was there anything?"

"No, there sure wasn't." He told her about the blurred faces. "I was wondering if you had any photographs from her things?"

"Gee, I don't know. I will certainly look. I'll call you if I find anything."

"Thank you."

"Surely. Have a good night, Mr. Fulton."

Fulton tried to find Marlene, searching everywhere. He found her looking at the displays in the open-air Hick's Drugstore on Jefferson. The entire wall was open, facing the sidewalk, accordion-like doors folded to the sides when the store was open for business. It was a way to keep the store reasonably cool in the summer. There was a giant scale by the folded-up doors on the left side.

Fulton pulled to the curb and went up the steps to the high sidewalk. Marlene was buying aspirin. She smiled when she saw him. He pointed to the bottle. "Get two of those, darlin'. I may need them."

XXXXX

He was getting, perhaps, one piece of a puzzle—just one at a time. A corner piece, the piece next to that. There was no way to predict what the completed picture would look like—or when he'd get the next piece.

The pieces he'd seen so far led him to conclude Jo Ellen had been murdered—but the pieces weren't revealing who did it. He had to shine his spotlight on a wider area. He needed to know precisely what was going on in Tallahassee in November 1953 and who was here.

He began with arrest reports. Any strangers in town? Who was in jail at that time? He could rule out persons that might have the propensity for such a crime if he knew they were in jail. He looked at records at the jail and Sheriff Carter's office in the courthouse, poring through dusty files. He went over to the city police. Their records—in a back room amid stolen bicycles and old orange crates—didn't reveal much. No rapists or drifters in town that week, it seemed.

45

Tallahassee
Sunday, 11/18/1956

"I mailed the package like I said I would. But I also learned something that might help you," said Janine.

"Yes, ma'am?"

"Yes, from my cousin, Virginia. She saw Jo Ellen the afternoon she got into town."

"Oh?"

"Yes, sir, she'd visited with Virginia at Florida State. I don't know that she said anything important, but they were close. Perhaps she confided in her. Virginia never liked me much, the little sow. I couldn't get anything from her."

"Where is she now?"

"Still in school. About to finish. She'll take her exams soon, in another month, I suppose. She lives in Jennie Murphree Hall. I have the number where you can reach her."

Fulton drew a line across the page of the little notebook, breaking the point in the process. Janine could hear him moving things on his desk, trying to find another pencil. "Have you something to write with?"

"Yes, ma'am. I'm in my office, but I broke the point on this pencil."

"Now, that always happens at the worst of times, doesn't it?"

"Yes'm, but"—he reached into the back of the drawer—"here's another one."

"Oh, good! Ready?"

"Uh-huh." He wrote down the number.

"I thought you should know."

"Sure, much obliged."

Fulton called and was able to speak with Miss Virginia Harbert of New Orleans. She said she could meet him at nine. She was studying.

Virginia walked out in the hall to take the call. It was unusual that she'd receive a telephone call. And from a man! The matron gave her a suspicious look as she picked up the receiver. *A policeman?* The older woman stood by, listening.

"Yessir. Yessir, that'll be fine." She hung up, returning to the military-like room with polished asbestos tile on the floors and bare white walls she shared with a girl from Tampa. The austere room had little more than a table, dresser, and two small beds. Virginia had one luxury—a television. That was a big hit with the other girls, a little portable that Uncle Milo had bought her. Sally was still asleep, so Virginia tiptoed around the room, getting a dress from the tiny closet. She changed from her bermuda shorts and blouse to a dress so she'd be properly attired to meet with the policeman; girls weren't allowed to wear shorts outside of the dorm rooms. She pulled the dress over her head and buttoned it then took her hair out of a ponytail, fixing it to be presentable.

XXXXX

Fulton pulled up in front, squeezing between the old pontoon-fendered Chevys and Fords parked along Ivy Way. Most of the buildings in the old part of campus matched the gothic red-brick style of Westcott Hall. Jennie Murphree Hall was no exception—one of those old red-brick halls built in the twenties.

Three girls in skirts and sweaters walked out of the churchlike entrance carrying books, heading toward a battered Chevy. Another young woman came out and looked at him inquisitively. She had dark hair and was very attractive and wore a dark blue dress and heeled shoes. She resembled Jo Ellen. She approached him.

"Miss Harbert?"

"Yes. Are you Mr. Fulton?"

"That's right. How do you do?"

"How do you do," she answered, shaking his hand. She was in a sorority; she had made her debut in great fashion, in a Southern hoop dress, three years before.

"I'm sorry to call so early."

"Oh, that's all right."

"It's okay to talk here?"

"We can go to the library," she suggested. They walked around the corner toward the Strozier Library—a modern brick building that had opened in June. A large lawn—the Landis Green—separated the library and the other red-brick buildings, forming a large quadrangle.

They climbed the steps and went inside. Students were studying at long rectangular tables in stiff-looking chairs. Fulton and Virginia crossed the checkerboard pattern of asbestos tiles to the last remaining table.

"I hear this is your last semester?"

"Yessir. I'm preparing to graduate. I've a big paper that's due, then examinations. My last one is on the fourteenth of December, and I'm all done," she said, smiling. She seemed full of optimism, a young woman with a lifetime ahead of her. She seemed free of cares, which was something Fulton marveled at, trying to recall the time when he had no responsibilities.

"I'd like to ask you about Jo Ellen."

"Okay," she said, taking on a more somber expression.

"Do you remember visiting with her when she came to Tallahassee?"

"Yes, sir, she came to see me."

"Did she act unusual?"

She looked up, thinking. "No, sir."

"Do you remember what the date was or the day of the week?"

"Um—I think it was a Thursday, maybe a Friday. It was the end of October, right before Halloween, I know that."

"Did anything seem to be troubling her?"

"Well," said Virginia, biting her lip slightly and looking up, turning her head, almost as if she was looking at different parts of the ceiling as she thought. "She was always a bit serious."

"Was she having any problems with anybody? Maybe in her business?"

"None that she mentioned."

"Friends?"

"I don't think so. Nothing in particular."

"Did she say anything about meeting anyone in town?"

"No, sir."

"Did you know her boyfriend?"

"Oh, yes. He gave her an awful time!"

"He did?"

"Yessir."

"Anything in particular?"

"You know, she did mention something to me—when she was here."

"Yeah?"

"She mentioned Mr. Howerton. He was her *ex*-boyfriend then. They had broken up, of course. But she argued with him a few days before she came over here."

"Oh?"

"That's what she told me. She had some bruises or something, maybe something with her lip. And I asked her about it, and she said it was nothing. But I told her it was *something*. And she told me they'd argued, but everything was fine now. He wouldn't be bothering her again."

"She said that?"

"Um-hmm."

"Do you know what they argued about?"

"Well, she didn't want to talk about it. But apparently, he wanted to get back together and she didn't."

"Do you know what time you saw her?"

"Here?"

Fulton nodded.

"In the afternoon, I can't say for sure."

"Do you know where she was coming from, where she was going?"

"No."

"And she had a bruise or something."

"Yes."

"And the argument was just a few days before?"

"Uh-huh."

"Are you sure about that?"

"Yessir."

"Did she say anything about seeing him here, maybe getting a gift from him, anything like that?"

"No, sir."

"Thank you, Miss Harbert. You've been very helpful."

"Don't mention it," she said with a smile. "But what does this mean exactly?"

"I can't be sure yet."

"But you're a detective?" she asked, resting her chin on her left hand, looking at him inquisitively.

"Yeah."

"So doesn't that mean somebody committed a crime if a detective comes around asking questions?"

"Or somebody got away with one."

She looked up at him quizzically. He excused himself and made his way back to the car.

46

Tallahassee
Monday, 11/19/1956

Fulton waited for the operator to connect him to Mrs. Lindgren.

"Oh, hello, Mr. Fulton. What can I do for you?"

"I was wondering if you recall Jo Ellen mentioning Clay Howerton the week before she died?"

"Clay?" she repeated, thinking about it. "Well, let me see. You mean maybe him coming to see her?"

"Yes, ma'am. Did she mention him paying her a visit?"

"No, Mr. Fulton, I don't think so. As you may have gathered, she kept things to herself. She didn't say why she was going to Tallahassee. She certainly didn't talk about her Mr. Clay."

"Can you think of anyone that might have saw something? A neighbor?"

"This may not help any, but her landlord did have a colored man that worked for her. He took care of the yard when Jo Ellen lived there."

"Do you know his name or the landlord's name?"

"Well, the landlord was named Sheffield. He still owns the house."

"Thank you, ma'am. You've been very helpful."

Fulton dialed 0 and asked to be put through to the courthouse in Crestview. Sheriff Isle Enzor was pleased to hear from him. Fulton explained why he would be visiting the county. The sheriff would meet him in Shalimar.

"That's kind of you, Sheriff."

"Don't mention it, son. I am glad to help. Always glad to help you fellers. I knew Hal Martin way back. Pratt Harlowe too."

"Yessir."

Fulton left, driving as fast as he dared on four recaps.

XXXXX

State Highway 85. Endless sea of pines. He tried to tune in the Okaloosa SO frequency, but the signal was weak, and the long antenna whipping about the right fender had been damaged while in Dade County service.

He met Sheriff Enzor at the tiny court annex. The Ford was steaming when he pulled into the parking lot. Shalimar was mostly inhabited by air force personnel who rented the nearly identical cottages that went up quickly during the war; the town was founded to get around the law that forbade clubs staying open past midnight in unincorporated areas.

Enzor was sixty-three, with gray wispy hair on top of his round face; he wore suspenders and a red-and-white checked shirt and was moving slowly. He was not feeling well. He talked slow, in the country drawl common to the Panhandle. He led Fulton inside to an office. They called Mr. Sheffield, and he told them Hollis Jones took care of his rentals. In fact, Hollis was working on Jo Ellen's old place today. Enzor hung up the phone and looked over at Fulton.

"I know Hollis pretty well, True. He drinks a mite, but he's a good, hardworkin' sorta colored fella." They got in Enzor's marked 1954 Ford and took Highway 85 through town, across the narrow bridges held up by timber pilings, over Garnier and Cinco bayous. Enzor was an amiable fellow. He had been relieved of duty a few years ago when Governor Warren got a little "hot and bothered" about gambling in Okaloosa County; he soon had his job back and made a greater effort to enforce the gaming laws. But the county was quiet, with few serious crimes.

They reached Fort Walton, turning onto Main Street. They saw a mule and two-wheeled wagon in front of Jo Ellen's old house. They drove on two more houses, intending to see Jo Ellen's neighbor first, parking along the road. It was a small woodframe, not unlike Jo Ellen's. It was the home of the elusive Sarah Morris. The two men walked up to the door and knocked. A woman in a dress and heels answered. She had a towel in her hands, drying a large glass bowl.

"Howdy," said the old man, taking his hat off.

"Hello. Now if you're soliciting for something, I'm not interested," she told them, holding the heavy bowl, a scowl on her face as she looked down at them from her doorway.

"No, ma'am. We ain't here for a c'lection. I'm Sheriff Enzor, ma'am. This 'ere's True Fulton, with the Sheriff's *Bue*-row, over in the capitol," he said, gesturing toward the east, with his age-spotted and leathery hand.

"Mornin', ma'am," said Fulton.

"Yes, how do you do?"

"We was wonder'n' if we could ask ya some questions," said the sheriff.

"Well, what is this about?" said the woman. She spoke with a Northern accent, probably from the northeast—a Yankee. "I'm busy."

242

"Well, I reckon it won't take real long," said the sheriff. He spoke slowly, softly, rather humbly in his demeanor. "We'll try and keep it short, I expect."

"Well, all right," she said, sighing.

"Mr. Fulton wanted to ask you about your old neighbor two houses down that-a-way," said the sheriff, gesturing toward the house.

"Yes, ma'am, Miss Harbert," added Fulton. "I understand you were friends with her?"

"I was. I didn't know her real well, but we talked occasionally. Once, we invited her and her fiancé to dinner with us, and they went to a movie with us on another occasion."

"Was there anything odd about her boyfriend?" asked Fulton.

"No," said the woman, looking at the watch on her small wrist.

"Do you happen to remember his name?"

"Clay," she said impatiently.

"Did you ever know them to argue?"

"No, I didn't. Clay seemed nice."

"Well, ma'am—"

"Look, I got a lunch for the women's club. I have to get ready. I'm sorry, but I really must get back to it. Excuse me."

"But—"

"Good-bye," she said, shoving the door shut.

Fulton and Enzor just looked at each other. They hoped the next one might be more hospitable. They raised their hats to their heads and started down the steps of the porch. They noticed the mule was still at Jo Ellen's, the animal eating a bit of grass under the shade of a magnolia near the driveway. Enzor was in pain, his movements slow, labored, as he stepped down onto the walkway and back to the street. He started the car and pulled into the next driveway. The little white house was right next door to Jo Ellen's; Jo Ellen had no neighbors to the east nor across the road.

Enzor pulled himself up from the car, holding onto the roof post. The house was another bungalow, half the porch enclosed and turned into a sitting room. They stepped up on the porch. They could hear a radio, a woman singing along with "Just One More."

243

"Well, I reckon we try another'n," said Enzor, grimacing as he raised his knee. He rapped on the door with the back of his hand.

It was opened by a woman in a housedress and a bandana over her hair, her face flushed from packing. Boxes filled the little foyer. "Hello!" she said, smiling.

"Mornin', ma'am. I'm Sheriff Enzor. This 'ere's True Fulton from the Sheriff's *Bue*-row over in Tallahassee."

"Yessir? How are y'all doin'?"

"We're fine, ma'am, just fine. We was hopin' you could hep' us. It's concernin' your old neighbor, Miss Jo Ellen," Enzor told her.

"Yessir, I'll try. You see, we've only been here a short time. We moved in three years ago. We're moving again. My husband flies B-29s."

"Yes, ma'am, she would have lived here three years ago—Jo Ellen Harbert," said Fulton.

The woman nodded. "I didn't know her. I heard that she passed, that she owned the alterations shop, but that's all, really."

"Do you remember anything out of the ordinary, anything stand out at all?" asked Fulton.

"No, sir. I'm sorry I can't help. We just never had a chance to get to know her or see anything, really."

"Well, we 'preciate it anyway, ma'am," said Enzor, holding his hat.

"Yes, sir. Y'all have a good day."

"If you remember something, this is my number. Give me a call," said Fulton, handing her a slip of notebook paper.

"Yessir. Y'all take care now."

The little canvass of the area wasn't turning up much. They crossed the lawn to Jo Ellen's house, a cottage with orange daisies in flower boxes under the windows, baskets hanging from the porch with white geraniums. Even the tiny dormer windows had boxes with pink aster. A colored man about forty was watering the geraniums with a big metal can. He was singing and staggering a bit.

"You been drinkin' today, Hollis?" asked the sheriff.

"Suh?"

244

"You doin' a little...drinkin' this mornin'?" repeated the sheriff, taking a step closer, Fulton slightly behind him.

"No, suh," said the man, holding the water can in his hands.

"Huh?"

"Not that much, boss!"

"Hollis, does Miss Della know?"

"Aww, Sheriff, you don't have to tell her nothin' 'bout dat!" Della was Hollis's wife, who disapproved of his imbibing and had, herself, hauled him to Enzor once or twice before when he had returned home inebriated.

The sheriff grinned. "This here's True Fulton with the Sheriff's *Bue*-row."

"Mornin's, suh. I 'spect it must be real 'portant, must be somethin' big, the sheriff got a whole burah now."

"Mornin'," replied Fulton.

Enzor stepped over to the man. "Lord, I smell that whiskey, son. Phew! And its only eleven thirty. You got to quit that, son!"

"I don't drink, drink, drink all the time!" he said, waving his hands. "But I had a little this moanin'." He was very animated, talking with his hands and gesturing. "It helps with the joints and the arth-right-us."

The sheriff shook his head. "Shoot, you ain't got arthritis, Hollis, ha!"

"I ain't drunk though. Ain't that good?" asked Hollis, coming down from the porch, refilling the watering can and fiddling with the spigot.

"I reckon so. But Mr. Fulton has somethin' he wants to talk to ya about."

"I don't mind talkin', but I mind my own bidness, that's what I'm good at." He set the watering can in his cart and began fiddling with the rakes and shovels. He pulled out a pair of work gloves. "Mind you, I had me a little, but I ain't drunk." Hollis held up two fingers, showing how much he'd drank, and returned to the porch. He put on gloves and pulled a poison ivy vine off the first step, plucking it from the ground. Hollis had an answer for everything. It was hard to get him to settle down as he paced and moved around, busy as a bee.

"All right, Hollis," said Enzor.

"That last time when you carried me to jail to sleep it off, I just had a little bit. Only reason I hit that boy was he made me mad when he pulled that knife on the other boy. I was like, 'You put it down, and y'all fight fair.' I know what you fittin' to say, I shuna hit him so hard and busted him up.

245

But he made me mad, Mr. Isle." Hollis stooped down to pull some weeds from the flower bed. "I works all the time. All the time," he muttered.

"Hollis, I need to ask you about Jo Ellen Harbert," said Fulton.

He looked up, his face sad. "It's terrible. Terrible the way Miss Jo Ellen died. I picture it. I dream of it—her lying in that car or in the weeds somewhere. I plant these gardenias fur her after dat. I say she liked flowers, and these'll always be here for huh," he said, tears forming in his eyes. He turned his head. "Don't want y'all to see me cryin'. That's the whiskey makin' me do that."

"Do you remember seeing anything at her house before she died? Anyone unusual come by, any strange cars?" asked Fulton.

"No, suh. No strangers, but the boy here," said Hollis, pointing to the driveway, "he almost hit my ol' mule. He was being rough wi' huh. I was ready to put some sport on him, if you know what I mean."

"Who was it?"

"Hold on," he said, wiping tears from his cheeks. Hollis sighed and shook his head. He stood up to his full frame, six feet tall, looking Fulton and the sheriff in the eye, contemplating what sort of trouble it would mean if he told what he knew.

"Who was it, son?" asked Enzor.

"I mind my own bidness, Sheriff."

"Hollis?" said the sheriff more forcefully.

Hollis went back to the flower bed.

"Hollis, you liked Miss Jo Ellen, didn't you?" asked Fulton.

"Now you gonna try to get at me," he said, shaking the little weed claws he was using. "Like they do in them television shows."

"Did he hurt her?"

Hollis nodded. "It was Mistuh Clay…that came here that day."

"Yeah?" replied Fulton.

"He was hollerin' at Miss Jo Ellen. He grabbed her arm. I was thinkin' I best mind my own bidness, these was white folks. But then…he slapped huh."

"He did?"

246

"Yessuh! Right in huh face," said Hollis, turning his head and pointing to his jaw. "He hit her again. I hate to see it. I can see it now, if'n I was to close my eyes. He kep' on, like he wailin' on her. I says to myseff, 'Only so much a woman can take.' So finally I say, 'Let her go!'"

"Okay."

"He comes at me. He says he'll get me thrown in jail for not mindin' my own bidness, that there were folks that take care of niggers that minded white folks' bidness. Mr. True, I don't want no sheets in my yard nor da fellas that ride around in 'em!"

Fulton nodded.

"Well, he picks up my blade, the one I got over there," said Hollis, pointing to his cart. "He picks it up and comes up on me. I say, 'Put da blade down if you want ta fight. I ain't afraid.' He just shakes his finger at me and tosses it into the trees."

"Okay. What happens then?"

"Miss Jo Ellen *come out wit' a gun*! I swear on my mammy's grave, Mr. True! She say, 'I don't want to see yo ugly mug around here again.' That was what she say, like in a *gangstuh* movie, she don't want to see his ugly *mug* again. I couln' believe what I see, wit' that gun. I never *knowed* she kep' one!"

"Okay," said Fulton, taking notes in his spiral book.

"He—Mr. Clay—backs up towards his car. He says to Miss Jo Ellen he'd be back. He say he wouldn't be run off, it would be hell to pay if she broke it off with him. He tore outta here in that Rocket '88, dust flyin', almost hit my mule with his kah."

"Go on."

"I ax huh, 'You all right, Miss Jo Ellen?' She says yes. Then she says, 'I want you to put an extra lock on my doe—can you do that?' I says, 'Yes'm, I can do that. I show can.' It was Sunday though. I ax huh, 'You gonna be all right if he come back befoe I git da lock Monday moanin' when da stow open up?' She says she got a gun, and he wouldn't be hittin' huh again. That was the last Sunday she was in town, befoe she went over there and died, Mr. True."

"You sure about the date, are you, Hollis?"

"Yessir, I knows when it was. I'd swear to it on my mammy's grave. Yessuh."

Clay Howerton's story had fallen apart like a cheap suitcase. "Do you own a car, Mr. Jones?" asked Fulton.

247

"No, suh, they took my license. Yessuh, they took 'em," he said, looking at the sheriff.

"Don't look at me. Ol' Judge Middleton done that," replied the sheriff, spitting some tobacco juice in the grass. "You got what you needed, True?"

"Yeah, let's go."

Tallahassee
Monday, 11/19/1956

Clay hadn't set foot on the *Gulf Wind*.

"No, he missed the train. He tried to get his money back on his ticket."

"You remember his face?"

"Sure, he was a jerk."

Fulton thanked the conductor, the train already rolling from the station.

XXXXX

At 5:30 p.m., there was a package on his desk. He set it aside and called George Webb. "I just wanted to ask you about that trip Mr. Howerton made, back in November of fifty-three."

"Okay."

"Do you remember what time it was when he got into town?"

"Well now, let me think for a minute. Hmmm."

"Are you positive you picked him up at the station that evening?"

"Well...I'm thinking about it. I *thought* I did. Now, I'm not so sure. I'm sorry, I'm just trying to remember."

"Yessir, that's all right. Try to remember the best you can."

"Come to think of it, I met him at the Alcazar Hotel. It wasn't the train station at all! In fact, I attempted to call Clay long distance but couldn't reach him. He wasn't on the train. And I'd heard about the accident and thought he might have stayed in Tallahassee. I just wanted to tell him, well, I was here if there was anything I could do. I tried to reach him at his mother's house. His family is old Tallahassee. They have a grand house on Calhoun Street that they'd put a lot of money in to restore. He wasn't there. Then Clay called and said he'd be arriving the next day. I'd forgotten that. I didn't think much about it at the time."

"Do you know when he got into Miami?"

"No, I guess I just assumed he came on the train, but now that I think of it, I don't know that positively."

"How was he acting at the hotel?"

"Golly, you're thorough. Let me think about that. I recall he'd been drinking. Quite heavily. I hadn't seen him like that before."

"And you've known him a long time."

"Why, yes, quite a while."

"Did he say when he got to the hotel?"

"No. Again, I wish I could be more helpful. At the time, I really didn't think about those events. We were getting ready for the trip, we heard about Jo Ellen—it was all rather hectic."

"That's all right. I appreciate you thinking about it and being honest."

"Surely. I hope this doesn't hurt Clay. I'm sure he was where he said he was. Well, I'm not sure what this is about anyway, but I hope he's not in any trouble. I mean, maybe he needs legal advice. Should I call him? Is he in trouble?"

"Not if we can confirm where he was."

"Hmmm. I wish I could be of more help."

"Thank you, sir. I appreciate you talkin' to me about it."

Fulton set the phone down.

Immediately, it began to ring. Virginia Harbert. "I just wanted to let you know—a friend of mine from Jacksonville that knew Clay overheard him say things: 'She was a drunk, she deserved what happened to her.' That sort of thing. Her name is Glennis Warren. Her father's in the same firm as he."

"You have her number?"

"Sure, right here." She read it to him.

"Thanks, Miss Harbert."

"Sure. I hope you get your man."

Fulton confirmed the story with the Warren girl. Howerton had been drinking and got mouthy with her and had, in fact, made the comments Virginia referred to.

"That was exactly what he said," recalled Miss Warren. "And he said something else."

"Yes, ma'am?"

250

"Yes, he said he didn't 'take anything from any woman, nohow.'" She also recalled that he'd said, "The only lip I want from you is on my zipper."

XXXXX

Fulton picked up the envelope. He examined the return address—the Southeastern Telephone Company office in the Old Supreme Court Building on Adams. He tore it open, pulling out the typewritten lists of calls. There were two person-to-person long-distance calls to a residence located at 2016 East Forest Drive, with the second party none other than Clayton Howerton of Tallahassee, Florida—*Monday*, November 2, 1953. At 8:47 a.m. and 9:23 a.m. respectively. Just to be doubly sure, Fulton called Miss Glenda—Howerton had utilities at 2016 East Forest from July 1952 to December 1953. Howerton's alibi was a smoldering wreck.

48

Tallahassee
Tuesday, 11/20/1956

Another package. He opened it, finding a book inside. And a note.

zzzzz
November 10, 1956

Mr. Fulton,

There were missing photographs. Someone must have removed them.
I haven't any idea whom. We took the book from her house just four days
after her funeral, when we packed up her things.

I hope it helps.

Janine
Zzzzz-end

Fulton put on surgical gloves. He flipped though the album of small black-
and-white photos. He'd dust later. Toward the end, there was a picture of
Jo Ellen in shorts in front of the Packard. There were pictures of Jo Ellen
and Janine at Miami Beach. There were some pictures of the girls
waterskiing, at Lake Placid perhaps. No boyfriends.

He returned to the beginning of the book. Photographs of Jo Ellen playing
tennis, some of her girlfriends. And places where photographs had been
but, quite obviously, had been removed. The photos had been pulled from
the little white tabs that held the corners. He wondered why they'd remove
photos—why not simply discard the entire album?

He flipped forward a few pages. Shots of Jo Ellen standing next to a
handsome young man. Another shot of Jo Ellen sitting beside the same
fellow at a booth—looked like it was taken at The Sweet Shop. In another,
Jo Ellen and the man at what appeared to be Alligator Point. The bottom of
the photo—on the white border—she had dated: "March '47." Fulton
studied the photo. The two were certainly more than acquaintances. *So he
lied about when he met her.* The young man was none other than Clay
Howerton.

On the next page, more photos of Clay and Jo Ellen. One was loose, simply
stuck in between the pages of the book. Clay was smiling broadly, his arm
around Jo Ellen. She didn't seem so happy. They looked older. On the back
was scrawled, "Clay and J. E., June '53."

XXXXX

Dreggors was talking to someone about a bond; he waved to Fulton as he
walked in.

Penny brought out a fresh pot of coffee, leaving it on Dreggors's desk. "Hello, Mr. True," she said.

"Hello, Penny. I was wonderin' if I could look through the arrest records."

"Sure thing!" she said, disappearing up the little staircase and back toward her own office. Fulton went to the file cabinet in the front of the office and began flipping through arrest reports.

Penny returned in a moment. "You find what you needed, Mr. True?"

"Well, this is interesting," said Fulton, pulling the document from the drawer. "A ticket from Monday, November 2, 1953. Written by F. M. Carter. Charges Clayton Howerton with speeding. Red Olds two-door. Florida tag 13-761. 6:05 p.m."

Carter came in the front door. "True, you find what you needed?"

"Yessir, I got a ticket you wrote."

Carter examined it. "Well, I hope you can make something of my scribblin'. I don't recall this. But it's my handwritin'. Looks like I wrote a ticket to the Howerton boy doing seventy-five miles an hour on Mahan. He was going eastbound. Ummh, ummh, *ummh*," he said, shaking his head. "What does this do for the case?"

"I got my suspect in town three hours from the time of the crash."

XXXXX

At 8:45 a.m., the telephone rang. "Hell-o."

"Mr. Fulton, I got it on good authority that Howerton purchased airline tickets to Cuba. He may be trying to run."

"Who is this?"

The caller was quiet, unwilling to reveal his identity.

"You're the fella that sent the photographs, aren't ya?"

"Good-bye, Mr. Fulton."

Fulton telephoned Howerton at 8:55 a.m. The secretary said she didn't think he was coming in today. Fulton called the Duval sheriff, Rex Sweat, and told him what was going on, that Howerton was a suspect and might try to run. Sweat would send a man to Imeson Field.

At 9:45 a.m., the telephone rang. Howerton was at work. Fulton asked if he could see the lawyer this afternoon. The woman told him that Howerton

253

came in and had already rushed off to court; the secretary made an appointment for 3:45 p.m.

XXXXX

Fulton stopped to see Sheriff Sweat and let him know his purpose in Duval County. Fulton had no arrest powers. Sweat promised to help if Fulton needed anything. Fulton drove to the Florida Life Building on Laura Street. He stood on the sidewalk, looking up at the old skyscraper; narrow and delicate, it seemed to reach for the clouds, the top floors soaring over the street, the structure a product of a time when man was proud of his newfound ability to build upward and the buildings were as much art, sculpture as they were practical office space. There was a penthouse; a wealthy eccentric owned it. His work as a beat flatfoot or murder cop didn't see him frequenting that kind of altitude. The elevator man carried him to the ninth floor.

At 3:40 p.m., Fulton sat near the steam radiator; it was chilly today, but the steam heat made it quite warm in the room. It seemed apparent that Clay still had aspirations for elected office; a man in a gray suit was there, chatting up the secretary. He said he'd helped Governor McCarty get elected, and he'd sure like to work with Clay. And something about "attorney general." Fulton couldn't make it out. But Clay Howerton seemed to have ambition—and connections. Fulton had a magazine in front of him, but he watched the man—balding and in a nice suit—out of the corner of his eye. The man was ushered into Clay's office. The secretary gave Fulton an apologetic look. The lawyer was thirty-five minutes late for their appointment.

At 4:25 p.m., the secretary announced that Howerton would see him. "I'm sorry to keep you waiting," said the handsome lawyer, showing Fulton inside. They both knew that was a lie. Howerton had intended to make him wait.

"I take it you're not here to hire our firm," said Howerton with a grin, trying to be charming.

"No, sir."

"Please sit down," said the lawyer, taking his own seat behind his desk. It was pushed against the large windows on one side. He could look down over busy Laura Street, the taxis, people going into the big Barnett Bank building across the street, or around the corner to the Kress store. He wore an expensive tie and silver cufflinks.

Fulton sat in one of the tufted chairs, crossing his legs. "Mr. Howerton, I'd like to ask some more questions about Jo Ellen."

"That I surmised. But whatever for? What can possibly be said that hasn't been covered already? Boy, you fellas must have nothing to do in Tallahassee! Who did you say you were with? The bureau of what?"

254

Fulton didn't respond.

"I don't mean to be flippant or rude to you. You've come a long way. Would you like some coffee?"

"No, sir. I had a cup earlier in the waiting room."

The man nodded. "Please, proceed with what you wanted to say."

"There are some questions about the events leading up to her demise."

"Okay," said Howerton, chuckling and shaking his head.

"When did you see her last, Mr. Howerton?"

"I told you that."

"I recall what you said."

"Is someone telling you something different?"

"Yessir."

"Well, you need to ask yourself what agenda they may have—whomever it is that's telling you lies. I've nothing to hide, Mr. Fulton. I didn't see her for several weeks."

"You had no contact with her on November second?"

"No, sir—nor any time leading up to the second."

"You didn't go to Fort Walton Beach Saturday and Sunday, the twenty-fourth and twenty-fifth of October?"

"Why's this so important? Fort Walton," he scoffed. "Does anything important happen there? This was three years ago, pal." The lawyer was getting testy.

"These are just routine questions, I assure you, sir."

"Routine? You talk to me like I'm a *suspect*. Are you looking into a cause of death? That sounds rather unroutine."

"I'm just tying up some loose ends." Fulton noticed Howerton's diploma from FSU—class of '49.

"I'm sure that must keep you very busy," replied the lawyer sarcastically.

"So you don't recall going to Fort Walton?" asked Fulton, ignoring the younger man's arrogance.

255

"No, I do not."

"Where were you on the second of November three years ago?"

"Say, what's this about anyhow? I don't get it."

"Where you were on certain days and what was going on between you and Miss Harbert. That's what this is about. So far, you've been evading the question."

"I told you I was on the train," Howerton snapped.

"Conductor says you missed it."

"He needs a calendar."

"How about this speeding ticket on the second?" said Fulton, holding up a photostat copy of the citation.

"Carter probably got the date wrong, that's all," said Howerton, dismissing it with a flick of his hand.

"How about these phone calls from that morning?" Fulton set the records from Southeastern Telephone, one page at a time, on the lawyer's desk. "Is the phone company wrong too?"

"Look, let me explain something to you. I was happy—see? She wasn't happy, apparently. Never was. We broke up because of that. She went back to whatever it was that she did. You want to know about November 1953? Okay. I was focusing on more important things than Jo Ellen. I got this job. Things were looking up for me. I was making more money than I could spend. Can you imagine making twenty thousand a year? No, you can't. I had no reason to dwell on the past. Whatever you've been hearing, it's not what you're trying to make it out to be!"

"I'm not making anything. But you've been lyin' to me—you were in town on the second, the day she died. You lied about it."

"Oh, I see how this is gonna be—a frame-up."

"No, sir, but you still haven't come clean with me."

"Look—"

"I know you went over there on Sunday the twenty-fifth and confronted Jo Ellen at her house. I got witnesses that saw you. You lied about that too. How about it?"

"I'm not gonna take—"

"You're not gonna take what? You went to her house, argued with her, and threatened her. I got two witnesses."

The lawyer scoffed. "You've got nothing. There ain't no witnesses. I was mistaken about the times, that's all." He started to stand up.

"Sit down. I'm just getting started. I did a little checking with Eastern Airlines. Here's a photostat of their passenger manifest for flight 625, departed Jacksonville four-oh-five a.m. November the third. Your name's on it."

"So I missed my train. That don't prove I did anything to Jo Ellen."

"You had plenty of time to have it out with Jo Ellen Monday night, then catch a plane to Miami in the morning. Your friend Webb says he met you at the Alcazar, you were drinking heavily, like he'd never seen before. I know you're lyin'. You can do yourself some good, but time's runnin' out."

Howerton just looked out the window. A horn honked below.

"Howerton, you're in real trouble. Either you start talkin', or I go back to Tallahassee and get a warrant."

"This whole thing is nuts."

"How's that?" replied the lawman, standing by Howerton's desk.

"That any of this needs to be looked into. It's pretty damn open and shut if you ask me."

"Oh?"

"I say she might have done it on purpose. She always was a sad sack. Had the blues much of the time. Probably did the day she died."

"You know that firsthand, do you?"

"No! Like I said, I hadn't seen her...for a while."

"You mean six or seven days? You want to set the record straight?"

"I tell you she had the blues! She drank to cover it up! That's how she was when we were together. Sometimes she'd be all right. She was a swell girl to be around. Then sometimes she'd get sullen, morose. The fact she killed herself in a car shouldn't be a surprise. Is her father behind this?"

"What about her father?" asked Fulton, sitting down.

"He's never been able to accept the truth about his *wonderful* daughter."

"You seem a mite bitter towards Miss Harbert."

"Why shouldn't I be? Sure, I'm bitter. She ran my name through the mud. She left me, gave me back my ring, told everyone I was a heel," said the lawyer, lighting a cigarette.

"Weren't you?"

"No!"

"Did you have something to do with her death? You argued with her, roughed her up,
then she ends up dead a week later. How about it?"

"You hick cop, you'd love to pin something on me, wouldn't you? You probably have a seventh grade education. It'll probably mean a lousy ten-buck raise if you can make a case on me, huh?"

"Answer my questions, quit stallin', or this is gonna get sporty real quick."

"Look, I'm sorry, okay? I'm not sure what you mean. You mean foul play? Look, Mr. Fulton, she drank a lot. I'm tryin' to tell ya. You think maybe I was mad at her, killed her—I'm tellin' ya, she drank a lot. She was driving. I read it in the paper, that's how it happened, doggonit! I never laid a hand on her!"

Fulton read from his notebook. "This from the military hospital, Eglin Field. June 17, 1953, patient Jo Ellen Harbert. Records show she was treated for a head injury. Seven stitches. Robert Fields, captain. MD. He sewed her up. Ann Paulson, lieutenant nurse. She bandaged her. Both thought somebody worked her over."

"So?"

"Fella that brought her in matched your description."

"Like I said, mister, I never laid a hand on her."

Fulton took out one of the posed photos of Jo Ellen, placing it in front of Howerton. The lawyer grew pale. He looked away. "You're really tryin' to frame me. I...didn't do that. Whoever took photographs like that must be psycho."

"Umm-hmm. Where were you Monday evening, the night she died?"

"Now, wait a minute!"

"Where were ya?"

"Now, I. Uh. Well...I had an emergency come up with a client of mine. I had to stick around town. I guess I made a mistake about that."

258

"Yeah?"

"Yeah," said the lawyer, trying to think. "I remember now—sure!" he said nervously. "I just got it mixed up, that's all!" He tried to force a smile, the pen in his hands shaking. He noticed it and set it down, then tried to figure out what to do with his hands. Fulton's cool blue eyes were fixed on the attorney; that and the lawman's relaxed demeanor seemed to make the lawyer even more self-conscious.

Howerton picked up a paper clip then set it down--twice. "I had this client I had to meet. I met him, took care a what he wanted. Then I got my secretary to book me an airline ticket. You can ask her—you can ask her, boy!" cried the lawyer, now fidgeting with his cufflink. Finally, he put his face in his hands, running his hands back over his ears. "Boy, this is a nightmare. Who do you think you are anyway? I'm not some bum sleeping behind the bus station, you know."

"Yeah, sure. What's this client's name?"

Howerton sighed. "I don't remember. I'd have to look at my old files."

"What time did you meet him?"

"About three p.m. He wanted to meet earlier, but I was stallin' him, see? I was a bit hung over, if you must know."

"What time did your meeting conclude?"

"Late. About six."

"Anyone else see you at your office that can verify that?"

"My secretary had the afternoon off," he said, irritated with himself that he'd let her go early that day.

"What did you do after that?"

"I remember that. I drove down to Georges Café. I had dinner with a young lady—Elisabeth, who's my wife now. It was the night we met. We went out, and then I hear about this car wreck thing. I get a call at George's, and Elisabeth gets a little upset. It put a damper on the whole night."

"You don't seem very sad about Miss Harbert's passing."

"Look, I was at George's in Panacea. It's a nice place. I don't suppose you've been there on your $125 bucks a week. I don't suppose you go out much, but maybe you heard of it? We were having a nice dinner. Then the waiter says I got a call. Well, it's from a friend of mine telling me Jo Ellen 'bought the farm.'" Howerton's temper was beginning to flare again.

"Who called ya?"

259

"I don't remember! Look, you can call the waiter and the bartender. They'll tell ya I got the call."

"They got names?"

Howerton rolled his eyes. "Yeah, the waiter's named Doolin. Bartender's named Thompson."

"They got first names?"

"George and Bill."

"How late did you stay?"

"I took Elisabeth home about ten—her folks have a place on the river. After that, I went with my friends back to Wilson's Beach, got there about ten thirty. They'd rented a beach cottage. My best friend, his wife, and his folks. I was too drunk to drive all the way home, so I drove to the beach. I got a couple hours sleep and drove to Jacksonville to catch my plane. You can check it out, doggonit!"

"I will."

"Well, you do that! I was at the beach, I tell ya! You need to look in *her* past—not at me. I know you cops want to frame someone."

"This ain't no frame-up. If the evidence shows you're innocent, I'll be the first to say so."

"It's easy for you to talk big, ain't it, coming in here, packing a gun, giving me the business. I bet you wouldn't talk like that if it were just you and me out on the street, in a bar someplace. Boy, I'd like to—"

"Yeah, you'd like to what?" said Fulton, looking at him squarely. Howerton didn't answer; he just looked down at his desk. Fulton looked at the diploma again. "Did you know Jo Ellen in college?"

"No, sir."

"Howerton, when you gonna stop lyin'?" asked Fulton, reaching inside his coat. "Here's a photograph of you sitting next to her. I'm tired of these lies. Either come clean, or I take you to the sheriff's office and hold you for suspicion of murder."

"I-I knew her, yeah, we were friends."

"Who else did you hang out with?"

"She had a couple girlfriends, my best buddy, he's dead now, got it in Korea."

"What were her girlfriends' names?"

"I think one was Evelyn. She played tennis with her sometimes. She had another friend, Patty or something. She was in Reynolds Hall with Jo Ellen. Maybe that wasn't her name. That was ten years ago, doggonit!"

"Why didn't you mention any of this before—the client, your wife?"

"Look, do you need to talk to my wife? I was trying to keep her out of it. She's real touchy about Jo Ellen, old girlfriend and all. We can call her if we have to, but—"

"Let's call her."

"Fine," growled the lawyer. He dialed the telephone, angrily jabbing his fingers into the number holes and twisting the wheel around. "She'll straighten this whole thing out, boy!"

"Hello?" answered the woman.

"Liz, I got someone here that wants to ask you something."

"Okay, what, like a quiz? Like *What's My Line?* Oh, it'll be fun!"

"This is Mr. Fulton. He's a policeman, okay?"

"Afternoon', ma'am," said Fulton. He stood near Howerton so he could hear the telephone.

"Oh, good afternoon, Officer Fulton!"

"Now, tell this man about our first date—when it was, the month, the date and all."

"Oh, you know I'm terrible with dates, sweetie."

"Do you remember it being in November?" asked Howerton impatiently.

"I thought it was December—around Christmas?"

"Do you remember going to George's with me, doggonit?!"

"Sure!" she said cheerily. "That's the place built out over the water!"

The lawyer sighed. "Do you remember us getting a telephone call?"

"No, I really don't, honey," she said, trying to think.

261

"Do you remember the first week of November—around the second, Monday, we went to George's, and I ordered shrimp, and we got a phone call?!" asked Howerton, getting even more exasperated.

"If you say it was the second, then it was, dear. I just don't remember. I just remember my anniversary, birth dates, and so forth. Mr. Fulton, I hope you understand."

"Sure, I understand," he said cordially. Mrs. Howerton seemed like a nice woman.

Howerton slammed the phone down and cussed.

"When did you see her last, Mr. Howerton?"

"I told you!" he roared. People in the lobby looked up from their magazines, wondering what was going on in the lawyer's office.

"All right, what about the couple you visited at Wilson's Beach? How about it?"

"Bill Riordan, his wife, some others—they'll tell ya!"

"All right, call 'em."

"R-right now?"

"Go ahead," said Fulton, gesturing toward the telephone.

Howerton began to dial 0. "Bill's in Tampa," Howerton said. He paused, his finger above the dial.

"What's the matter?" Fulton asked, seeing the lawyer's bright red face fade to white.

"He-he's out of town, Mr. Fulton. I remember now. He-he's in Cuba, he likes the casinos," he said, stammering.

"Come on, quit stallin'. Are ya lyin' about him too?"

Howerton hung up the telephone angrily.

"Did you talk to Jo Ellen the week before she died?"

"No, I tell ya!" growled Howerton, turning red and flinging papers off his desk with the back of his hand.

"You know, you need to watch your temper. It'll get the best of you," chided Fulton, picking up one of the papers.

The younger man got ever redder. "Get out!"

262

"No need to get sore. We got a ways to go yet," said Fulton, putting the paper back on the lawyer's desk.

"I ain't sore, dogonnit! Ask your questions! Go ahead!"

"You sure you didn't blow your top about Jo Ellen, decide to pay her a visit?"

"No, sir!"

"You didn't decide to settle things with her once and for all and rush back to Tallahassee that night?"

"No!"

"You know how to reach this fella in Cuba?"

"No! He likes to fish down there! He's probably out on a boat—or drunk! I don't even know what town he stays in down there!"

Fulton wrote something down and paused for a moment. Howerton's complexion approached normal again. "How long was this Mr. Riordan staying at Wilson's Beach?"

"I don't know."

"Huh?"

"A couple days, I guess. I don't know."

"Come on, Howerton. Either stop lyin' to me, or I pick up that telephone and have Sheriff Sweat send a car for you, and we can do this over at the jail."

Howerton hung his head and ran his hands through his hair.

"What is it?"

"I'm ruined, ruined, if anyone finds out."

"Finds out what?"

"Look, I was with a dame that night—in Jacksonville. A whore."

"Oh," said Fulton, trying not to laugh. "What's the dear lady's name?"

"I don't know, we didn't exchange business cards."

"Where did you meet her?"

"At the Aragon, on Forsyth."

"All right, what did she look like?"

"Red hair, quite beautiful."

"What time?"

"I got over there about nine p.m., drove straight through from Tallahassee. I swear it. I stayed the night with her, caught a flight in the morning. I'm tellin' you the truth, honest I am." Howerton was sweating, breathing in gasps.

"Okay. I think you are telling me the truth—about that anyway."

Howerton's face flushed with anger yet again.

"Like I said, that temper will get you in trouble. Okay, it oughta be easy to verify this."

"Yeah, sure! Anything else?" he demanded angrily.

"Well, anything else I should know about?"

"No," growled Howerton. Fulton stared at him across the desk. Fulton had his legs crossed, relaxed. Howerton fidgeted with the pen and papers and the nameplate that was engraved with "Clayton Howerton, Attorney at Law," his hands shaking again. His armpits were damp with sweat, his bangs out of place. He slumped in his chair. He wasn't as cocky. He looked out the window, obviously distressed. He caught his reflection in the glass and looked away. "Are you gonna tell anyone?"

"I don't know. If your story—this version of your story—holds up, I may not have to."

"It's my tough luck, my rotten luck."

"Will you be in town tomorrow if I need to talk to you again?"

"Sure. Look, I don't mean to be a jerk about this thing. It's just like this, Mr. Fulton: I put Jo Ellen behind me. I got married to a nice girl. What good is it going to do anyone to dredge up all these old wounds? Let bygones be bygones." He wiped the sweat from his brow with his sleeve.

"Yessir."

"I didn't mean to blow my roof. You caught me at a bad time, that's all."

Fulton showed himself to the door. He reached for the knob and looked back, looking the attorney in the eye. "Have a good afternoon, Mr.

Howerton," said the lawman, noting how nervously the lawyer acted when he was forced to make eye contact.

Howerton looked down and swallowed. "Good-bye," he said softly.

Fulton rode the elevator down to the lobby. He crossed the street to the Barnett Bank; they had public telephones on the ground floor. "Let's see what your friend says, Mr. Howerton," he said aloud, dropping in a dime and shutting the door of the booth. It was a familiar number—Papa Topp's Bar.

49

Jacksonville
5:25 p.m.
Tuesday, 11/20/1956

Papa would indeed pass a message for his old pal. He'd do Fulton one better—he promised a cold beer, no charge. Fulton drove down to West Bay Street, near the old bus station, parking across from the old man's bar, one of many along the street. A mournful Kitty Wells song drifted out across the sidewalk from the jukebox at the Ajax, the competition across the way. Jacksonville was far different from the capital with its attitude toward liquor. A prostitute leaned out to look at his car then went back inside for another highball. Fulton turned to look though the passenger-side window. Papa's hadn't changed. The place was dark. The neon sign had burned out fifteen years ago. The same pawn shops and tattoo parlors were next door. Fulton got out, crossing the street and stepping through the open door of the little saloon.

"Can I get you a—say, True, I'm mighty glad to see ya!" The old man reached for his hand, smiling like he'd found the Prodigal Son. Marty Robbins's "Singing the Blues" was playing on the radio; Papa reached up to turn it down. "Sit down," he beckoned, filling a glass with the Jax beer on tap. "Yeah, I remember when you was a young cop, wearin' out shoe leather on those sidewalks."

Papa finished the mop job on the floor in front of the bar where someone had puked the night before. The place was small—a few stools, booths with torn Naugahyde, a staircase by the door that led through a dark, unlit passage to the rooms upstairs. They talked for a while about people they knew, crimes that happened nearby. As he sipped his beer, Fulton could hear the horn of a large ship heading out to sea and a couple sailors from Mayport laughing as they walked along the sidewalk.

A couple longshoreman came in for a beer. The barkeep flipped through his mail—bills. And a blue envelope. "Here," he said, handing it to Fulton. The old man glanced over at the door as a woman led a sailor upstairs.

Fulton tore open the note, reading the childish scrawl. He finished his beer. The old man shook his head at the sounds coming from the room above them. "Thanks for the *cold* beer," said Fulton. "So long."

He drove up to the corner of Laura and Forsyth, parking at a meter. He looked up at the old building again, chuckling. He took the elevator to the penthouse. The elevator man gave him a knowing look. He stepped from the car, drawn to the windows in the airy foyer. He took in the view: down to the streets and alleys, across at lofty upper-floor offices and hotel rooms. He could see a long way, the Main Street bridge, the river. The sidewalks were crowded with people leaving work, buses moving, people hurrying to catch the ferry, an old man sitting alone in the middle of Hemming Park.

The door to the penthouse opened, interrupting his look; it was Wendy, as striking as ever, even dressed in a conservative suit.

"What's with all the cloak-and-dagger? You'd think you were in the OSS or something."

"I can't be seen with a cop. I'm a respectable citizen."

"How'd you get a key to this place, I'd like to know."

Her coy smile indicated it was better he shouldn't ask. He looked at the marble on the floor and the furnishings in the three-bedroom "cottage" and took another look at the view from the twelfth-story windows.

"Cigarette?" she asked, a fresh one already between her lips.

"No thanks. Gave it up."

"Umm, what else have you given up?" she asked, tugging at his lapel.

He lit her cigarette for her.

"Thanks, fella." Wendy had been rousted a few times for prostitution, vagrancy; typically, she was able to pay off a cop or a judge—one way or another—and stayed out of jail. It cost time, money. She wasn't happy to see a blue uniform; she had little trust in the men that wore them. But she liked Fulton. When a customer tried to beat her to death in a motor court, it was Fulton who came to her rescue. After that, she was his best informant. He was one of a handful of men who knew her by her real name.

"I wanna talk to you about one of your friends—back three years ago."

"Gee, you think a lot of my intellect. I'm supposed to remember back that far, huh?"

Fulton nodded, sitting down on the long couch.

"Well, I'll try," she said, sitting beside him. "I don't keep a calendar, you know. I'm not like a library book. Men don't sign their name when they wanna—"

"Okay, okay. Just look at the picture." It was a photo of Clay with Jo Ellen at his side.

"Yeah, I seen him. Handsome fella, bit of a temper, paid with fives—all fives."

"Okay."

"Who's the squeeze?"

"She's dead."

"And handsome did it?"

"Maybe."

She took a drag on her cigarette.

"Do you remember—was it November three years ago?"

She didn't say anything.

He got up, looking out over the terrace. "Was it—"

"Don't crowd me, I'm thinkin'!"

"Okay."

"Don't know the date. But I got arrested the next morning, that I know. Clyde here is an early riser. Dyin' to get to the airport or somethin'. Wakes me up so's I can't go back to sleep. I'm hungry, so I drive to Kress's. I hit a parked car—some *jerk's* in the wrong spot. This cop starts hasslin' me about *dee-dubya-eye*. Hands me a ticket, carts me off to the city jail for three hours. If I didn't know the judge so well—and I do mean *well*," she said with a wink, "I don't know how I woulda got outta that jam. And you wonder why I don't care to be seen with you fellas." Wendy poured herself a drink. She nodded to the bottle.

He shook his head. "You meet him at the Aragon?"

"Where else?" she said, downing the whiskey.

"What time?"

"I Love Lucy was on."

"So, Monday night?"

"Yeah."

Fulton reached for the door. "Well, thanks for talkin' to me."

"Oh, it's no trouble. My days are usually free."

"Well, anything I can do for you, just say so."

"You could stay awhile," she said seductively.

Fulton twisted his wedding ring. "No, Wendy, gotta get back."

"You always were the responsible one. Bye, baby."

XXXXX

The long drive gave him time to think, his contemplation scarcely interrupted by the pines whizzing by, the occasional traffic coming the other direction. *So maybe Howerton was having a bad day earlier. His alibi is holding water. Every indication was that he was hours away from Tallahassee at the time of Jo Ellen's death. She crashed just after nine thirty. There's no way Howerton could have made it to Jacksonville in time.* Sometimes the evidence was like a roller coaster. It would have its ups and downs.

Well, Mr. Harbert had said he didn't think the boyfriend did it. That would be too easy, wouldn't it?

It was very dark along the highway coming into the capital, with the occasional filling station sign or porch light to interrupt the darkness. Fulton got into town at 9:00 p.m. Martin immediately sent him to DeFuniak Springs. It was 4:30 a.m. when he got home. He parked the Ford and shut the door, walking up to the front porch.

Marlene appeared, holding a book in her hands. "Hey, stranger."

"Hey."

"I've been sittin' here on the couch, wonderin' what time you'd come home and whether I'd finish this book or fall asleep first."

He dragged himself up the steps, his coat slung over his shoulder. He kissed his wife and collapsed onto the sofa.

She knew that glazed look. She put her arm around his neck, her knee resting on his leg as she curled up to him and kissed his cheek; he was quiet, but that wasn't unusual. "Catch something?"

He nodded.

269

50

Tallahassee
Wednesday, 11/21/1956

Chambord parked at the front steps of the capital in a brand-new '57 Mercury. The year before, the governor presented the highway patrol with the state seal design for the patrol cars' doors, making the black and tans much more distinct as law enforcement. Collins descended the steps to meet Chambord, the colonel resplendent in suit and tie and a brand-new Stetson.

"Say, that car looks nice," said Collins, shaking the colonel's hand.

"Yessir, the boys are putting them to good use too."

"I'm glad to hear it," said Collins, leading his guest up the steps and to the portico with its massive columns.

Small mountain howitzers rested on ledges beside them; they'd been there ever since Collins was a boy. He grew up in Tallahassee and well knew the lore, the history of the only capital east of the Mississippi that didn't fall to Federal troops. The men walked into the rotunda, under the dome, past the sacred battle flags—scarred with mini ball and shrapnel—that were hanging in the room. Chambord gave no notice to the flags; he began his campaign of schmoozing the governor, asking of Mrs. Collins, the children, telling him about his own boy making the football team at Leon.

They made their way down a corridor, through doorways and passages that recalled the countless additions to the Capitol since 1845. They reached a doorway with elaborate white trim, *Governor* in gold letters above. It led down a long hall, with Collins's secretary seated toward the middle and chandeliers suspended from the ceiling. "Good morning, Colonel Chambord. May I bring you some coffee?"

"Good morning, Irene. I appreciate that," replied Chambord.

Collins led him through the final doorway, into the governor's office. The room wasn't large, but nicely paneled with dark wood, high ceilings (a chandelier in the center), elegant blue curtains, and a patterned rug. The men sat down, facing each other across the rather simple desk.

"I'm hearing things about Fulton, his going around the state on this traffic accident."

"I know about it. Hal keeps me informed."

"It seems a waste of resources, a misuse of the authority of the bill that was passed last year. I have the resources to work the case, if there's anything to it—which I doubt. It seems like we're risking all we've worked for with an amateurish investigation at the behest of Milo Harbert."

"Fulton's hardly an amateur," replied Collins.

Irene entered with two cups of coffee on china and departed the room as quietly as she'd entered.

"I know he had a solid reputation in Jacksonville," continued Chambord, stirring his coffee. "But people are questioning why tax money is being wasted on this."

"Oh?"

"Yessir. Him driving all over, going to Jacksonville, sightseeing on the taxpayers' dime, acting like Wyatt Earp, here in our town."

"Is that so?"

"Yessir."

Collins let him go on with his indictment of the Harbert Case. It seemed to Collins that the colonel, with three hundred troopers under his command and a large budget, was a little quick to find fault with the paltry expenditures on behalf of the Bureau—which was living on donations. The Beverage Department and the AG contributed $100,000 in 1955. That was all they had to keep the lights on and salaries paid. There'd been no budget appropriation in 1956. Collins had to personally intervene to get their phone bill paid. But Chambord wanted FHP to take on the role of a state police.

"Our investigations section is doing really well, Governor."

"I know. I've heard good things."

"We've had some success against organized vehicle thefts farther south."

"I know." Collins kept track of such cases; he read most of the newspapers in the state.

"We got some good press on that. I think if the public learns more about this other thing, however, it could engender its share of ire. Harbert has always liked to throw his weight around. I hear he's trying to get Representative Austin to push forward his wild theories about his daughter. Boy, this is good coffee!"

"I'm glad you like it."

"We're duplicating our efforts, setting up an agency the public doesn't think we need. Even many of the sheriffs agree with that sentiment. If this gets out..." Chambord let the sentence trail off.

Collins knew that was a veiled threat. He sipped his coffee. Chambord was a good lawman, but he was also a politician—and he craved more power. And attention from the papers. One thing Collins liked about the Sheriff's Bureau—under Hal Martin—was that it worked behind the scenes, avoided the limelight. Its purpose was to help the local sheriffs, and if the local boys got the credit, that was okay. Collins knew Fulton was that kind of cop; he just wanted to do his job and didn't care about politics. Collins wanted professionalism in law enforcement to prevail over the personal kingdoms.

"Well, we appreciate all you've done for us, and I know the people will remember what you've done to make this state safer, to improve law enforcement—come election time."

"Thank you. Well, I do have that other meeting," Collins informed him. He held out his hand to Chambord, who took it with a firm grip and a hearty smile, "sawing" at it three or four times. The governor couldn't help but imagine what Chambord was thinking at that precise moment, underneath his mask of affability. Chambord was undoubtedly thinking that it would be he—in a few years' time—standing on the other side of this desk, shaking hands with officials, running a state.

Collins looked out his window after Chambord left. Florida was growing; life was becoming more complicated. The state needed a good coach. There would always be men criticizing from the sidelines, trying to push their own agendas, cheerleading for one thing or another, fellows that wanted to make touchdowns in front of the cameras instead of blocking like they should. There would always be another fellow gunning for his job. But this was a team; there's more at stake than a few careers. Collins hoped he'd call the plays right.

XXXXX

Fulton called Howerton and told him that everything checked out.

"I appreciate you callin'. I gotta admit, I was worried. You know, I *was* a heel all along. Thanks for letting me know."

"Like I said, we're not just trying to make a case. We wanna get the fella who did this."

"I realize that now. I got a fair shake from you. I was the one stallin' and being discourteous. I see I got a lot to lose. I got a good wife now, she's probably the best thing that could happen to a mug like me. I don't want to lose what I got. You made me see that."

"I think you'll be all right."

So another dead end.

"Hey, True," said Martin, stepping into Fulton's office, clutching his hat. "I gotta go see the governor. I think you should come along."

"Yessir?"

"Yep, I know you're busy, but he called me, and—well, I'll let him tell you."

They got in Martin's car, the latter steering silently as they passed the Capitol and continued north on Adams. They crossed Tennessee; Martin looked over at Fulton. "You know, I got a visit from Chambord today."

"Oh?"

"He had to stop by and gloat. He had coffee with the governor this morning."

Fulton chuckled at that.

"There's an awful lot of ambition under that fancy hat a his. He sure bears a dislike for you," added the old sheriff.

They parked in front of the old plantation home. They looked up at it, the giant oaks that surrounded it, before walking up the twelve steps to the door. They could hear sawing, hammering, coming from the new governor's mansion just across First Avenue. They knocked on the door, which was answered by the governor. Collins, in a suit and tie, greeted them with a friendly handshake and a "Happy Thanksgiving."

It was a lovely home with white paneling and a narrow but elegant staircase, which curved gently upstairs. The delicate spindles were white like the rest of the woodwork, save the handrail that spiraled to a finish at the bottom. It was very quiet, peaceful—the loudest sound the ticking of a grandfather clock in the hall and the sound of their shoes on the century-old wooden floors. The first family was living in Mary Collins's ancestral home while the new mansion was constructed. The old one had fallen into disrepair and was torn down last year—not before many furnishings were auctioned on the lawn to finance the new house. Some joked that Collins would hold a bake sale to come up with the balance; he frowned at that because it was uncomfortably close to the truth.

Collins led them back to the dining room. It was just Collins, Martin, and Fulton at the table. The children were in school, and the first lady was visiting a relative. A colored man in a white jacket and bow tie brought them sandwiches and coffee.

"Hal, you always warned about the smart criminal, how law enforcement would need the right training and coordination to solve that sort of case. I agree with you. I intend to do more to help the Bureau. What are the main items you have need of?"

273

Martin brightened like a kid offered a piece of candy. "Well, sir, I'd like to hire a polygraph examiner and a firearm's examiner and a latent prints examiner. I'd really like to be able to put on more training sessions for the sheriffs' offices."

"I know there's no money yet, but we'll work on it. Sheriff Thursby told me he really found your training session helpful last week."

"I appreciate him sayin' that. We've never had anything like that—formal training for our law officers."

"And you had some FBI men as instructors?"

"Yessir."

"True, how is your case going, the one involving the Harbert girl?"

"We've come to another dead end, Gov'nor. I got to go back to square 1."

"That's all right, you'll sort it out. I support you fellas looking at the case."

Fulton nodded.

"There are major cases we need the Bureau to look at," continued Collins. "The problem of unsolved capital crimes is one I'm really thinking about. I know you fellas already have a few—Chillingsworth, the disappearance of Charles Ferri and his wife from Miami last year. Listen to me, I'm starting to sound like you," Collins said, turning to Martin. "Rattling off names and all."

"Yessir," said Martin, grinning.

"All kidding aside, we need the Bureau working those cases."

The colored man filled up the coffee cups for another round. "Thank you, Clancy," said Collins. "We have something unique in the country here. You fellas come in and aid the local boys on a big case, like Scotland Yard does in England."

Fulton and Martin turned and looked at each other at that.

"How soon do you think you can get a crime lab in operation?"

"We can start as soon as we get money to pay salaries," Martin replied.

Collins drank some coffee. "I hope we can convince the legislature. I think the Bureau should provide technical assistance."

"We still need space to properly set up the equipment for the dark room that the State Racing Commission gave us."

274

"The house next to your office is empty. Maybe that could give us room to grow?" wondered Collins.

"That would be real nice."

Collins opened a file containing clippings of newspaper articles going back to the summer of '55. "I know you don't care about being in the paper, Hal."

"You're right! I don't mind stayin' in the background."

"But I'm real proud of this nonetheless." Collins held up a clipping. "'Murder of Gilchrist County Sheriff Mark Read Solved.' That was you fellas. I'm mighty proud of that and wanted to tell you so. Keep it up."

XXXXX

Fulton had a message to call Louise Davis at a Texas number. He dialed 0 to get long distance. The operator connected the call.

"Mrs. Davis?"

"Yessir, this is the Davis residence. I'm Louise Davis."

"This is True Fulton with the Sheriff's Bureau."

"Oh, yes, how are you?"

"Fine, ma'am, just fine. And you?"

"Oh, busier than a one-armed paper hanger. Trying to get settled in. It's the third time we've moved since we got married."

"Yes, ma'am."

"Were you ever in the service?"

"Yes, ma'am, during the war."

"Well, you know, after y'all left and my husband came home, we talked about it—my husband and I—and he reminded me of something I told him."

"Yes, ma'am?"

"Yes!" she said, excited about it. "I saw a man at that girl's house the morning after she died."

"Oh?"

275

"Yessir! With my own eyes, I saw him. It stood out because we heard about her passing. It was sad—we didn't even get a chance to say hello to her, hardly. We'd just moved in. But we heard about it. We saw her family packing up the house, and they told me what day she died, and later on I thought back to what I saw and told my husband. I thought maybe someone would come back and I'd mention it, but no one did. And to tell you the truth, it just slipped my mind until my husband reminded me."

"Can you describe him for me?"

"Well, let me see. He was fair-skinned. No hat. I thought that was unusual. He was balding—you know, his forehead bald or really thinning hair up on top. A little chubby. That's about it."

"Did he have a mustache, beard, anything?"

"No, nothing like that. Just a big belly."

"Hair color?"

"Uhm—not sure. Sorry."

"That's all right, Mrs. Davis. Do you remember what he was wearing?"

"He had a suit on—dark suit. Can't really remember anything more than that."

"Yes, ma'am. You sure about the date, Mrs. Davis?"

"Oh yes, it was early November, like I said, the morning after her accident. I was up about four thirty—I was up with the baby. Christine was an infant then."

"Now, you saw him next door—"

"Uh-huh."

"Could you tell what he was doing?"

"Well, I heard a noise. I walked into the front room and looked out the window. That's when I saw him on her porch. He reached back to do something, like he was picking something up or putting something there—I'm not sure. Anyway, while he did that, I was looking right at him. He was facing me. Then he walked across the lawn, kinda walkin' fast. I guess he got in a car, although I didn't see it."

"Would you mind helping us create a composite of the man you saw?"

"What's that?"

276

"Well, it's where we take your description and try to come up with a picture. There are artists that can do it, or we use a kit. Would it be all right if I had someone come see you?"

"Why, yes, sir."

"Fine. I have a friend with the Rangers that might help."

"I'd be happy to help in any way I can. You can give him my address."

"I appreciate it."

After Fulton hung up, he phoned a friend of his, a captain in the Rangers. He said he'd get in touch with Mrs. Davis.

Fulton sat in his chair, tapping his pencil. *Who was this fellow, and what might he know? Was he looking for something...or trying to get rid of something? Was he the killer?*

51

Tallahassee
Friday, 11/23/1956

The telephone rang. Captain Jacobs. "Hey, Fulton, what's doin'?"

"Howdy!"

Jacobs called from his office at the Department of Public Safety. He wore wire-rimmed glasses, had short dark hair under his fedora hats, and dressed in nothing but the finest suits available in Austin. They'd served together during the war. Jacobs retrieved a cigarette from his desk drawer. "I met with Mrs. Davis—that witness in the murder mystery of yours?"

"Yeah?"

"She's living at Bergstrom Air Force Base, which is just a stone's throw from me. Her husband is flyin' those big KB-29s. I drove over to talk to her yesterday," he said, lighting his cigarette.

"Uh-huh."

"She wasn't able to give much of a composite."

"Dang it."

"Yeah, I tried with the Identi-Kit, even tried with a sketch artist. She couldn't give us much—he was in his late thirties, receding hairline, kinda heavyset, round face. I'm sending you what we came up with. I'll have one of the girls put it in the mail."

"Well, thanks anyway, Bill."

"Sure. Look me up if you're ever out this way. We'd be glad to have ya."

"Will do." *So all we have is a balding, somewhat portly man.* Fulton carried his suitcase out to the Customline. He would have to make the drive to Jacksonville; they needed him on their bolita case.

XXXXX

Monday. Fulton couldn't sleep, even though he'd had scarcely an hour's worth of shut-eye in Jacksonville. Marlene lay beside him. He looked at her face, thinking of how beautiful she was, how peaceful she looked, each breath so quiet as to be barely noticeable. He dressed, trying not to wake her. Fulton had no leads on the heavyset bald man. He'd asked Janine about him, and he wasn't someone she was familiar with. He mentioned him to Carter, Martin, but no one stood out.

The lack of clues gnawed at him. It was like trying to think of a word, one on the tip of his tongue. The feeling of being right on the verge of finding the answer was much the same. He wasn't at a dead end. This was more like a cul-de-sac.

He drove to the depot. It was a little eerie around the station—the dark streets, the warehouses down Railroad Avenue, the silent woods, the black horizon stretching on endlessly as if there was nothing else in the world but the depot rising from the darkness and illuminated by the yellow glow of incandescent bulbs burning at intervals up and down the platform. An older colored man was off-loading boxes from a flatbed while the driver, a young white fellow, smoked.

Fulton walked over to the old man, Travis Bingham. He wore a bow tie and a gray work shirt, a railroad porter's hat over his snowy hair; he'd labored there as long as Fulton could remember. They'd met years earlier, before the war. He knew everyone that came and went.

"Howdy, Mr. True," said the old man, glad to see him. "How are ya?"

"Fine, Travis. It's been a while."

"Yessuh!" Travis grabbed a box from the back of a flatbed truck and lifted it over to the side of the platform. "I bet you workin' a case."

Fulton nodded; he buttoned his sport coat. There was a chill in the air.

"You like me, always workin'," said Travis, wiping the sweat from his forehead. It was cool, but Travis was working hard. "Yep, it seems like there's always somethin' left undone. A man don't git no rest."

"Yeah, workin' a case. Woman that died. Three years ago."

"White woman or colored?"

"White."

"Hmm. Three years ago. Long time."

"Well, I think whomever did it may still be around. Anybody suspicious come through lately?"

"No, suh—not lately."

"Anybody come through here a lot—someone that makes you wonder?"

"There's businessfolk. I git to know a few, none that seem like they bad folks," said the man, lifting another package and stacking it for the *Gulf Wind.*

"Anyone that seems odd?"

279

"Well, there is this one fella, suh. Now I don't want to talk bad 'bout nobody, you understand?"

"Sure."

"You got some smokes?"

"Sure," said Fulton, reaching for the pack he'd purchased at the Standard Oil at McCord Point. He handed Travis a Chesterfield—the old man's favorite brand.

"Thanks," said Travis, taking the cigarette and lighting it. "Tastes good, like a cigarette should." He laughed.

Fulton smiled at that.

"But I tell you, Mr. True, this fella is somebody I says to myself, if I was da *poe*-lease, I be watchin' that boy."

"Yeah?"

"Yessuh! I just get a feelin' inside like an icebox. My ol' cousin Lemoyne was like that. He'd be okay—nice and friendly most of the time—but inside him somethin' was mean."

"What makes you feel that way about this fella?"

"He kinda had a look in his eyes," said Travis, lifting another box from the truck.

"Yeah?"

"One time, a woman come and told me he was messin' with her."

"Uh-huh?"

"She was frettin' herself something fierce that he might be gettin' back on de train. I said ol' Travis'll watch and see which way he go. He kept on messin' with huh, and I told the conductor."

"Did he get back on the train?"

"Maybe he just mills about the station, or maybe he starts on into town. I know he didn't get back on. But I know he come through a couple times after that."

"Can ya describe him?"

"Well, he'as a white fella. Not as big as you—I mean, he tall, but not so burly. The boy don't have all this in the middle," said Travis, patting his belly and chuckling, indicating Fulton had a bulge in his waistline.

"Oh, that's fine, very funny!" said Fulton, shaking his head.

"I know dat's Miss Marlene's fried chicken and mashed potatoes!" He took another pull on the Chesterfield and grabbed another box.

"What color hair?" asked Fulton, trying to change the subject.

"Sandy, blond, kinda fancy-dressed. Musta thought a lot of hisseff. I coun'a see his face 'cause he was in the shadow. It was dark." Travis strained to get a heavy box down. The driver of the truck was in the phone booth, chatting up a dame, his back to Travis. Fulton could see the cigarette smoke swirling inside the booth.

"You recall the date?"

"Shucks, Mr. True. I cain't recall," he said, panting for breath. He grabbed the last crate from the truck and stacked it, clapping his hands to knock off the dust.

"Was it the week the gal died in the wreck? Do you remember that, three years ago?"

"Nuthin' stands out ta me. No, suh. Lord, that's a long time ago."

"That's all right, Travis. Do you know the woman's name from the train?"

The old man was thinking. "Well, to tell the truth, Mr. True, I ain't sure. Now that you say three years ago. It coulda been that long."

"Yeah?"

"Don't remember huh name. She a lady bidness woman though." He took off his cap, revealing a balding forehead glistening from the hard work. He sat on the bench by the terminal. "No train due for a while. I reckon we can take a sit-down."

"Sure."

"She used to come through here lots of times. Back there in forty-eight all the way through fifty-three, I expect. She married now, she settled down. Not a finer lady around, yessuh."

"Remember her name?"

"Well, suh, let me see. Just give me a minute, an' ol' Travis'll have that name fur ye, yessuh." He pinched his chin in his fingers, looking down the track, contemplating the name, calling to mind her face. "Lord, what's that

281

name? It's on the tip of my tongue!" He hummed a bit of a tune, trying to stir up his memories and bring up the name. Fulton let him think; he knew the old man would call the name to mind presently.

"There it is! Her name's kinda funny. Arr-uh Lee Dresser. I remember 'cause it's like the gen'ral. She was from Jacksonville. She done went back there, I 'spect. You got another one a them Chesters?"

Fulton handed him the pack. "So the letter *R*, middle name Lee? Last name Dresser?"

Travis took one and returned the Chesterfields. "Toll ya it was a funny name. Don't knows how ya spell it, but that be the way she say huh name. Arr-uh Lee."

"You've been real helpful, Travis," Fulton said, extending his hand to the old gentleman.

"I'm glad I can hep, Mister True. I know'd ya since ya was no bigger than a pup. Ya had hair then, mine wasn't white. We all gettin' older, I reckon."

"Yeah, don't remind me. If you remember anything else, call this number, will ya?" Fulton handed him a paper with the number to Gaines Street.

At 6:45 a.m., Fulton drove to the Motor Vehicle Commission. The sun was just starting to rise, lifting away the starry purple-and-black blankets that were draped over the town most winter nights. There was an FHP car parked in front; dew on the hood indicated it had been there overnight. Clevedale was nearly finished with his polishing. He let Fulton in the office. It was dark. Fulton found one of the switches and obtained enough light to make out the tags on the file drawers.

He rifled through the indexes. No "R. Lee. Dresser" was to be found, but there was an *Arleigh* Dresser that had lived in Jax. She'd had a '40 LaSalle registered to her, then a '48 Hudson. She'd lived on West Seventh Street. That was Springfield. After that she'd moved to Riverside. There, the trail ran cold. Fulton didn't know her married name.

He turned out the light, closing the door behind him. No employee had arrived yet. He drove to Gaines Street. Mary Ann was already there, coffee brewing, the stubs of two Chesterfields in her ashtray. At 8:00 a.m., he called a friend with the Clerk of Court in Jacksonville. Yes, there was an Arleigh C. Dresser in the records. She'd married a Collier Talken.

Fulton reached for the Jacksonville directory in the bottom drawer. *Talbet, Talbert, Talitha—there it was! Talken, C. E. and A. C. Skyline 9-7783.* It was 8:20 a.m. Fulton called the long-distance operator. She could get no answer at the Talken residence, nor could she reach Mr. Talken at Jacksonville University, where he worked. The operator connected Fulton to Talken's secretary. According to the latter, the professor had taken leave unexpectedly.

Fulton tried for three days. He phoned Spence to see if he could make contact. A neighbor told Spence that the Talkens left town; they'd be back at the end of the week. *We're still on that cul-de-sac.*

52

Tallahassee
Friday, 11/30/1956

Fulton called the Talkens'. No answer.

Then Martin handed him a note. "Sheriff Thursby's got something. Safe robbery. They thought they had a good suspect, but it's about to fall apart. Thursby said to give him a call."

Fulton reached for the phone. The Volusia sheriff gave him the lowdown on the case, and Fulton got on the road. They worked all night. Fulton lifted prints at the hotel; he helped them positively ID their suspect. Thursby had his man. Fulton slipped away before the New Smyrna reporter realized he was there. Like Martin said, "The Sheriff's Bureau works best when no one even knows we're around."

Tired and in need of a shave, he got on US 1. He stopped to use the pay telephone at Tony's Drive-In near the Flagler line. He dropped in a few coins, turning to look at a hawk circling over the pines and open country to the south. Talken was home; the professor would be expecting him.

XXXXX

Fulton stayed on US 1, the main road into town. He crossed the Duval line; there was just a small plain sign there. It was rural, pine trees along the highway, another twenty-five miles to the city limits. He was behind a truck carrying crates of tomatoes. The traffic was heavier southbound: cars pulling trailers, sedans with northern plates. Little motor courts were parceled out along the highway, catering to those tourists on their way to Marineland or Miami Beach. More pinewoods. Then the city limits sign, little motels clustered around it, three miles south of the river. Neon signs. Bright two-toned cars sitting around the little cabins.

The truck continued toward downtown while Fulton turned onto River Oaks Road, a quiet side street of modest homes built in the '40s near FEC Park. He made a left on Hendricks, lined on both sides with similar houses, each with a tidy lawn and shrubs. He veered off onto San Jose then turned down Oriental Gardens Road. Fulton well knew the area the Talkens lived in. It had once been the Oriental Gardens, a tourist attraction, popular in the forties. The entrance was the same, with palms and flowers—only now it was a subdivision with modern ranch-style houses.

He drove down the street. Remnants of the park—gates and fountains and white-painted wrought-iron fences—were sprinkled among the big houses and spacious lawns. The street ended in a loop around some large oaks and swanky homes with backyards overlooking the St. John's. The Talkens' house—930—was separated from the river by a very large ranch and a wide lot that remained yet unsold.

Fulton parked in the driveway behind a Cadillac, with its little rudder-like taillights. In his rearview mirror, he caught a glimpse of whiskers and circles under his eyes. He looked a sight. He got his briefcase, walking up to the front door of the modern ranch. There was a statue fountain in the side yard; it looked Chinese. Across the street, men hammered away at 2 × 4's, framing another ranch. A circular saw added to the racket, lumber going from flatbed to wall studs in an eye blink. Most of the men wore dog-eared fedoras or straw hats with their work shirts and tool belts.

He rang the bell. A tall attractive blonde appeared. She was in her midthirties, Fulton reckoned. She seemed a bit surprised, looking him up and down.

"'Afternoon, ma'am," said Fulton, tugging at the brim of his hat.

"Good...afternoon. Are you a salesman? You don't look like a salesman."

"No, ma'am, I'm True Fulton with the Sheriff's Bureau," he said, trying to be heard over the ruckus across the street.

"Oh, yes! How do you do? Won't you come in?"

"Thank you, ma'am." Fulton took off his hat and wiped his feet before stepping onto the sparkling floors.

"For a moment I thought you might be a salesman, the briefcase and all. This is my husband," she said, gesturing toward the man sitting in the living room.

He rose to shake the visitor's hand. "Collier Talken," he said with a friendly smile.

"Glad to know you."

The husband motioned toward one of the long sofas. Fulton found the couch covered by large books, opened to reveal photographs of various islands in the Pacific.

"Oh, you can move that," said Mr. Talken, gesturing to the large book about French Polynesia.

"Would you care for some scotch or wine perhaps?" asked Mrs. Talken.

"No, I'm fine, thank you," said Fulton, setting the book on a coffee table, which appeared to have been hewn from a giant teak tree. He paused for Mrs. Talken to sit on the big leather chair directly across from him before sinking back into the expensive sofa. Mr. Talken sat near his wife on the arm of the other sofa, which was at a right angle to Fulton's and just as large. He had a tumbler filled with tequila and ice. It was a very wide room with a large fireplace and numerous paintings from the Orient (Japan perhaps) and round brass tables from Morocco.

285

"I suppose you'll want to talk about that man. I had almost forgotten the incident. I was an auditor for several banks," said Mrs. Talken. "I'd travel between Pensacola and the capital and Jacksonville."

"Yes, ma'am?"

"He'd bothered me on the train," she said, leaning forward, her eyebrows squeezing together a bit. "You know, leering at me, making remarks. He started out wanting to talk, trying to act charming, but he just wouldn't stop. He was a real *masher.*" Mrs. Talken reached for a golden cigarette box on the table next to her. "Would you care for a cigarette, Mr. Fulton?"

"No, thanks. Do you need a light?" He removed the Zippo from his pocket.

"Thank you," she replied.

Fulton approached with his lighter. "Mrs. Talken, did he do anything to frighten you?"

She took a drag on the cigarette. "It was just something in the way he—something in his eyes really. It was more than just the usual man that gets fresh. You say something, and that's the end of it. Not with him."

Mr. Talken looked away, as if he was in serious thought about something.

"Did you report him to anyone?" asked Fulton, sitting down again.

"I did, in fact. I told the porter in Tallahassee about it. I'd had to stop there, of course, and I remember speaking to the gentleman there—a Negro—he, he must have noticed I seemed a bit apprehensive, and he asked if I was all right."

"Uh-huh. Was his name Travis?"

She looked up for a second, thinking. "That sounds right." She looked back at Fulton. "I told him there was a man that was bothering me. And he watched him leave the train, you know, kept an eye on him. And he didn't get back on. I thanked that man because it made me terribly fearful, him being on the train all the way to Pensacola, the possibility of the man following me to my hotel."

Mr. Talken continued to look away.

"Can you tell me what he looked like, Mrs. Talken?"

"Blond hair, tall. He was blue-eyed, good-looking."

"Did you have any occasion to see him again?"

286

"Why, yes! That was the strangest part of it. I ran into him again—here! He'd looked me up!" she exclaimed, gesturing dramatically with her hands. "He came to my apartment. I opened my door, and there he was. He tried to charm his way into...into getting me to let him in. I shut the door and locked it as fast as I could. That was one reason I decided to quit my job. The other, of course, was that I got engaged. When Collier and I got married, I left the firm."

"Mrs. Talken, do you know the date this happened?"

"I don't. I quit my job with the auditing firm in December 1953. It might have been in the summer before that. June. July."

"Are you sure?"

"Well, now, wait. Collier asked me to marry him in October. October 31, Halloween. And some people from the Barnett Bank in Jacksonville had a costume party. That was right before my last trip to Pensacola. So the man on the train had to have been in early November."

Mr. Talken looked over at his wife now.

"You're positive on the date, ma'am?"

"I am. In fact, somewhere, I have my calendar from then. Do you mind waiting while I get it?"

"No, ma'am, not at all."

"My wife is very good at remembering details, very responsible," said Mr. Talken proudly. He wore black-rimmed glasses and had dark hair and a turtleneck sweater. He had piles of books on the couch next to him, most of them about various Pacific locales: Formosa, Siam, other nations of the East.

Fulton nodded.

Noticing Fulton examining the books, Talken added something. "I have a lecture on Monday. This is some of my research."

"It looks interesting, sir."

"Have you traveled to the region?" asked Talken, his curiosity aroused.

"Some. During the war."

In a moment Mrs. Talken returned with a small book. "Look—November third, in the evening, eight thirty p.m. That's when I went though Tallahassee."

The dates match. So our boy was in Tallahassee, Fulton thought. "Do you mind if I get you to do one more thing?"

"What is it, Mr. Fulton?"

He reached into his briefcase for the Identi-Kit.

XXXXX

There was a grassy marsh along the south bank, lovely and green, the little Lobster House restaurant at the water's edge. New was the Prudential Building, looming over the river, the first skyscraper below the St. John's. Ahead, the Main Street bridge, its artful towers and steel trusses carrying the highway north into downtown Jacksonville, a lovely skyline of Klutho skyscrapers and tall hotels like the Mayflower and Roosevelt, their names in giant rooftop letters. Signs switched on one by one as the sky went violet, the sun slowly melting into the river.

The grand St. John's, fronted as it was by wharves and shipyards and mansions. His tires hummed loudly, rolling across the steel span, high above the water. Ahead, one couldn't miss Hubbard's Hardware Store, the Main Street Garage sign glowing at the foot of the bridge and Rhodes Furniture painted in giant letters on the side of their building up Main Street. Nor could one miss the Maxwell House plant, its sign glowing high above the riverbank.

McLanahan's Amoco was open all night at the busy intersection with US 90. Fulton pulled in to get a few dollars worth of gas. A long drive ahead. Four hours on two-lane roads. If nothing went wrong.

He shut the door of the phone booth and dialed 0. He gave the operator his own number and, when prompted, dropped forty-five cents. He told Marlene he'd be late. A black '57 Ford pulled in while Fulton was in the booth. The driver got out, walking to the men's room.

The man turned on both faucets and splashed water on his face. He combed his blond hair. He looked in the mirror. He had a long drive, but his expenses were covered. He lit a cigarette and returned the Southernaire Motel matchbook to his pocket. He eyed Fulton's car, the antenna and the Leon County ("13" prefix) tag.

Fulton turned around as he heard the door slam. He saw a man sitting behind the wheel of the black car. It was plain like a cop car, but he had no idea of the agency, nor could he see the driver's face. He said good-bye to Marlene as the car pulled away.

The pine forest seemed endless outside the city limits to the Duval line. There was no turnpike with 75-mile-an-hour speeds. The South's US 66 meant driving through little towns—slow. He passed the Old Spanish Trail building, an old rest stop. The little AM station he was listening to signed

288

off at sunset, playing a solemn rendition of "Dixie" before the power was switched off.

Baldwin. Tiny sleepy railroad town. The water tower loomed over the pine trees, the silver structure shiny in the moonlight. Headlights in his rearview. Was someone following? Near the water tower were two filling stations facing each other across US 90, competing for travelers along the route. He pulled into the little Sinclair. The headlights approached. The taillights faded away. Fulton pulled back onto the road, passing little farms with haphazard fences and low barns and woods. The sky was clear, the air crisp.

High beams on, he picked up speed again, toward the next town. Macclenny. County seat, courthouse with columns. Businesses closed for the night. When the glow of the last porch light faded, he got back to cruising speed.

The headlights again. In his mirror. He slowed for the next town, Glen St. Mary. Oranges and flowering shrubs grew in the groves and nurseries along the highway, countless acres of trees and plants. No people. There was an old gas station in the little town, closed for the night. The headlights were still back there.

He accelerated back to sixty, a good speed in the tired car on the dark, narrow road. The lights were still behind him. If he slowed, they slowed. They were in timber country, another part of Florida the tourists traveled through to get somewhere else. Dark. Isolated.

Sanderson. A tiny rail station—ten feet wide—was the noteworthy landmark "downtown." More dueling service stations: an Amoco and a Gulf, facing one another across the narrow street. Endless pinewoods. It was getting stuffy; he pushed the vent window open to let in the cool, clean air. He let the speed nudge seventy. The headlights faded in the rearview.

He was heading into the Osceola National Forest. He looked in his rearview mirror and saw nothing but the black of night. It was after nine o'clock. He thought he saw lights behind him, very far behind. He looked at his gages; the motor was getting hot. He slowed, letting the engine have an easier time pulling the car. He was coming up on Olustee Park, in the middle of a lonely stretch of the national forest. To Olustee the Union Army had marched from occupied Sanderson, trying to cut the rail lines, aiming to cut Florida in two. The high beams did their best to cut through the overwhelming darkness that loomed ahead.

Steam puffed from the edges of the hood. He stopped at the battlefield park along the tracks. The place hadn't changed in ninety years—pine forest in all directions. A road crossed the tracks, back into the park, where there was a large obelisk in a little clearing. Just past the monument, there was a little building with restrooms. Fulton retrieved a pail from the trunk and looked for a spigot; this he soon found behind the building, and he filled a pail for the radiator. Water was leaking out on the ground and spraying

289

through the grille. He'd let it cool. He wanted to call Marlene to let her know he'd be delayed. There was no phone. He turned on the Motorola. Static.

53

Olustee Battlefield
Saturday, 12/1/1956

The hum of tires on warm asphalt carried loudly over the night air. He watched as the lights approached, but the car went by in a hurry, the sound fading, swallowed by the overwhelming quiet. He reached for the hood. *Dangit! Still hot. Let it be a moment longer.* Another car approached— a faster one. He took a peppermint out of his pocket. He heard the car slow, the change in pitch of what sounded like a V-8. He saw the headlights turn into the park. They stopped, shining back along the drive, the car just sitting there by the tracks. Something made the hair on the back of his neck stand up. He got behind his car. The driver shined a spotlight toward Fulton's Ford. The car was close enough he could see it wasn't a sheriff's deputy, but the plain car could have been a detective's unmarked. But this wasn't the city with a lot of detectives running around.

It looked like a new Ford. He watched it; the car—whomever it was inside— lingered there a full minute, as if sizing up who might be present here in such an isolated location. Then for some unknown reason, it backed away and sped off.

He filled the radiator. He pulled onto the dark highway. The little town of Olustee was a mile ahead; he didn't want to miss it. One could do so very easily. The car was steaming again. He found the filling station. The lights were off; no one was around. He got water for the radiator using the hose lying on the ground.

Headlights! Slowly, they approached. He got back in the car, cranking the motor and taking off. The headlights disappeared down a dirt road. A freight train was coming the opposite way, its headlight blinding, just thirty feet to the right, the heavy rumble of the diesel pulling the Seaboard freight. He looked in his mirror, wondering if the car—if it was the same one—would follow. Now, to make matters worse, the ammeter was showing a discharge, indicating the generator was no longer working and the spark plugs and headlights were draining the battery.

There was no place to hide. One could see into the woods at a considerable distance—the same widely-spaced pines and floor of saw palmettos as present in the battlefield. Headlights were approaching fast. Was it a car? The sound of an air horn answered the question. The semi pulled around him, roaring past, giving the Ford a jolt. The radiator was steaming like a teakettle by the time Fulton reached the outskirts of Lake City, near the airport. He hoped the car would make it to town, and he wouldn't have to walk along the highway. It was midnight. The engine sputtered and died— just as he was able to make out the sign for the all-night service station at Main and 90. He coasted to the service bays.

Fulton called Marlene while the radiator was soldered. He hoped the Bureau would reimburse him for the repairs. It was still a hundred miles to

Tallahassee! Through rolling hill country with oak limbs hanging over the road, draped with Spanish moss, past tobacco farms with little wooden barns with old tin roofs, he kept going, not seeing another car. It was pitch-black through the ghost town—Ellaville—where a narrow bridge crossed the Suwannee.

Through sleepy little whistle-stops and county seats like Live Oak, the patched-up car chugged along. He hoped the tires would hold, traveling the dark stretches of country road. And the battery. It would be a long walk to the nearest porch light. No lights in his mirror—just a welcome and complete darkness.

It was 4:00 a.m. Marlene was asleep. Fulton turned on the light and collapsed into his favorite chair. He picked up Marlene's glasses from the side table. He sat, looking at the composite. Marlene stood in the bedroom doorway. She noticed he had her reading glasses on. He only used them when he was tired. She smiled, watching him. He looked up, sensing her presence. "I didn't want to wake you, darlin'. I was going to sleep out here."

"It's all right," she said, kissing him on the cheek, sitting on the arm of the overstuffed chair. "Still working?" she asked, yawning.

"Yeah." He sighed, wondering if he'd find this man. She cradled his shoulder in her arms. Fulton's eyes were tired from the drive, from reading through everything once more. He stared at the composite blankly. Marlene rubbed his shoulders and kissed his cheek. "Why don't you come to bed? I sleep better with your arm around me. He'll be there in the morning."

54

Tallahassee
Monday, 12/3/1956

The old man wiped his brow with the rag from his back pocket. He put on his wire glasses and looked at the composite photograph his friend had brought. "Now that's a funny picture." Travis held the photo a bit farther away. "There we are. Lord, that is a man I recognize! I didn't see him clear that night with the lady. But the other time, yes—the one time he spoke to me. That's him!"

Fulton grinned from ear to ear.

"Did I help?"

"Yessir. Gives us two ID's."

Travis nodded and looked down the track, as if to see what was coming. His look was serious, worried. "I'm glad I can help, Mr. True."

"What's the matter?"

Travis shook his head.

"When's the last time you saw him?"

"It woulda been the week of that accident. My wife come down ill that week, all kind of things happenin' then."

"Remember anything else?"

"You know how I said he was in the shadow, I didn't think he got back on the train?"

"Yessir."

"I saw him get in a car as the train was 'bout to pull off. A '49 Ford, don't know if it was a two-door or a four or the color. It was dark, you see. But I remember it. I always liked that car, and I ended up gettin' one a dem last year."

"All right, can I get you anything?"

Travis shook his head.

"Well, you let me know if I can ever do anything for ya."

"A Coke-Cola would be nice right about now."

"You got it." Fulton got two bottles from the noisy cooler; he sat there enjoying the drink, but more importantly, enjoying the moment in which he found himself—one step closer to finding a killer. Fulton talked to Carter, and they put out a want for the suspect.

XXXXX

Scrawled on the side was "US 27 crash, 11-1953!" It was evidence from the case!

"This was misplaced," said Carter, red-faced. "It was in a desk drawer, an old desk in the file room we don't use 'cause one leg's busted. This mornin' I was on a tear, son. I go, 'Either we fix this dadgum desk or we get it outta here.' That's when Penny found the box. The drawer was jammed shut, and we fooled with it 'til we got it open and—I declare—there it was. I thought you best look at it. I'm havin' 'em go over the old files from top to bottom. Everything in the little room where we kept the old cases."

"Yeah," said Fulton, wondering what was in the box.

Carter fetched his pocketknife from his trousers and cut the twine. He looked inside. "Well, doggone! This here was in her car," said Carter, pointing to the faded white envelope on top. "Underneath that...why, some of her clothes."

There was a small woman's jacket (from a suit) and what were white gloves, now a rusty brown.

"There's a lot of blood on the gloves," said Carter. "She had them on when she died."

Fulton took the end of his fountain pen and lifted the envelope. "It's got tape on it. And hair."

"Yeah?"

Fulton held it up so he could see.

"Blond! Like your suspect from the train! Son of a—" said the sheriff, letting the curse trail off. "We know Jo Ellen had dark hair—of course."

"Yep," replied Fulton, looking at the hair. He cringed in his stomach. He had that feeling he got in times like this, like getting punched in the gut. "This is clear evidence of who the killer was—that he was in Jo Ellen's car."

"It's somethin' to go on, that's for sure. Is there a way to *match* it to your suspect?"

"Maybe."

XXXXX

294

Fulton dialed the number for the hospital. Elston could meet him at the M&N in a half hour. Fulton walked over to the restaurant at 119 East Jefferson, sitting down at a booth. He was lost in thought, looking out the window, when Elston came and tossed his hat on the table, startling the lawman.

"Howdy, True," said the doctor, snickering and folding himself in the seat opposite. He wore his soft felt hat, that ubiquitous Camel hanging from his mouth. "I don't normally make house calls this time of day. What seems to be ailin' you, kid?" The waitress shoved menus between them, yellow with an outline of the capitol dome in red.
Elston already knew what he wanted and didn't open his.

"I know—the hamburger with lettuce and tomato and ice water," said the waitress.

"Thanks," said the doctor, lighting his cigarette. The "usual" was thirty-five cents.

"What about you, handsome?"

"Uh, I'll have an egg sandwich and a sweet tea, please," said Fulton. The sandwich was twenty cents; the tea cost a dime.

"As you wish," said the waitress, writing the order on a pad and darting away.

"So what is it, *handsome?*"

"Aww, cut it out, Doc."

"Seriously, you sick? You don't look too bad—about the same as always."

"Thanks—I think. Listen, I know you're always reading about the latest tests and scientific evidence—"

"I gotta have somethin' to do, sittin' around waitin' on you fellas, sittin' around waiting on someone to get sick or die."

"Ha! But have you run across anything where you can match hair follicles--say, evidence left at a crime scene, matching it to a suspect?"

"Well, it's not scientific per se, but each person's hair is a little different. It's common sense really. Some people got real thick hair, some real fine, different color, etc. And some of us hold onto our hair longer than others."

"Thanks," said Fulton, shaking his head.

"Haha. Anyway, I can look at the follicles under a microscope, and that tells us a bit more than just coarseness and color. You got something?"

"We got blond hairs left in the car."

"Well, you just got to find me something to compare it to, by golly."

Fulton nodded.

"I don't know if it would be admissible. Never been used in court before, I don't think," said the doctor.

"Yeah, the Frye test requirements?" asked Fulton, referring to the 1923 court case that governed admissibility of "new or novel" scientific evidence.

"Fulton, I think you know more law than some a them lawyers. Frye test is right."

They finished their lunch and paid their checks. "Thanks, Doc," said Fulton.

"I ain't done anything yet. You bring me that hair, and we'll make them bespectacled fellas with their vests and visors at the *Southern Reporter* take note!"

XXXXX

Fulton walked along the sidewalk. *We know he comes to Tallahassee on occasion. All right, where would he go? He'd have to eat, sleep, fill up his car. So restaurants, hotels, and filling stations would be the place to start.*

He began at the Gulf Wind and the Talquin Inn. Nothing. He worked his way back into town with no success. He pulled in the driveway for the glitzy Southernaire, a big motel with rooms facing a wide courtyard. A '49 Ford was parked across the courtyard, backed in toward one of the rooms. In the middle of the courtyard, there were two guests relaxing by the pool. Fulton shut the door of the car, looking back at US 90 and West Hall across the street. He showed the composite to the clerk. He didn't remember the man. Fulton asked if he could talk to the ladies that changed the sheets; two colored women did the work. He crossed the courtyard with its palm trees, finding the women cleaning one of the rooms overlooking the pool from the second story. Neither woman remembered the man. He asked about the Ford; it belonged to one of the ladies. Fulton even asked the maintenance man, an old man with a bow tie, bent over with arthritis. The face didn't ring any bells.

The Floridan. He went inside and talked to the clerk; he didn't remember the fellow. Fulton spoke to the bellhops and the girl making the beds. The same.

The Duval Hotel. It was being built in '53, but the suspect may have stayed there on subsequent trips. The clerks didn't recognize the man. Fulton even asked the barber that worked in the basement, showing him the

296

composite. "Say, this is like one a them TV shows, *Dragnet* or somethin'! Blond hair you say?"

"Uh-huh."

The barber looked at the photo, then handed it back. "No, don't know him. You need a haircut?"

"No. Thanks anyway."

Fulton went to every restaurant and café downtown. Then the Colonial Hotel. He tried the Motor Inn, the little stone cottages at Lake Ella. He showed the photo in the restaurant too. No one knew the fellow. He went on to Bowman's. Same story. The Ford was overheating, steam whisping from under the hood. Fulton wasn't sure what kind of trouble he'd be in if he burned up the motor, so he parked it at the Basset Dairy Ice Cream Parlor. He used the pay phone and called Marlene. She arrived in the Fireflite a few minutes later, getting out of the car in her wool jacket, her hands in her pockets as it was chilly today. They ordered "giant" twenty-nine-cent sundaes.

They drove down to the White House on Calhoun, an old firetrap converted from a mansion on the same order as the Dixie. "I've tried everything up and down West Tennessee and Monroe," said Fulton, getting back in the car and shutting the door.

"How 'bout the Cherokee?"

Fulton didn't think he would stay in the same place as the victim. But he'd seen stranger things. "Okay, let's check."

Marlene pulled away from the curb. She drove down Calhoun, with its antebellum homes and oaks, pulling to the curb beside the big hotel.

After he was inside awhile, Marlene decided to come in. Her man was still talking to the clerk, so she let him be, admiring the lobby. The bellhop's shined shoes clicked on the floors with their mosaic pattern. She went back outside. Fulton pulled the door open and got in. "Same clerk. Never saw the fella."

"Darn."

"You feel up to trying a few more?"

"Sure," said Marlene, starting the car.

"Let's try the GEM Motor Court."

Marlene turned around, heading back up Calhoun and making a right on US 90. The name quickly changed to Mahan, for the gentleman that planted crepe myrtles on that stretch of road. The GEM was the only motel out that way, at 2818 Mahan. Fulton came out of the office, shaking his head. "Let's try the Perry Highway and call it a day, darlin'."

Marlene took a shortcut down Magnolia and out to the highway, where they took up with the same routine. Again, no leads. Final stop: the Ship Lantern.

It was out in the countryside five miles from town. It had a tiny flat-roofed office near the highway surrounded by flowers. The motel rooms—six in all—stretched out in a row behind it, with windows that looked out on the highway and the pasture on the other side of the road. Cows grazed in the last bit of daylight that remained, one of them curiously watching the Fultons' car as Marlene slowed to turn into the driveway. It was getting dark quickly, as if someone was dimming a lamp, the air still, the sky a palette of gold, blue, and purple as is often the case in the winter in North Florida.

"Oh, you're a big fella. Must be six-three," said the manager, sizing him up as he walked in the door, Christmas bells jingling each time the door moved.

"Six-two," Fulton said, looking around at the little office, a Christmas tree in the corner. The woman wore a low-cut blouse and a tight-fitting skirt. Fulton showed her the composite.

"That's a funny-looking picture."

"Yes, I know."

"Got a light? I always get a little more talkative when I can have a smoke," she said, winking.

"Sure. You ever see this fella?"

"Let me think a minute," she said, looking him over, giving him a seductive smile.

"Sure...I remember him."

"Okay."

"The guy wasn't very friendly," said the manager, savoring the Chesterfield. "But more than that, he was weird. Something about him just wasn't right. And I see it all."

"How so?"

"He was evasive—where he came from, why he was here. Most people say, 'Oh, I'm from Memphis,' or 'I'm here to visit my sister,' or 'I'm here for the fair.' Not him. And then there was the argument."

298

"Yes, ma'am?"

"Yeah! And you don't have to 'ma'am' me, sugar," she said, touching his hand. "He scratches their car, see? You know, opens the door—he had a red Ford—he opens the door and hits that car. Then he gets mad at the *other guy*. I remember it because it was the morning that accident happened—the one by the lake. I read about it in the paper." She smacked today's paper on her counter. "I just love the houses on Lakeshore. If I ever came into some money, boy, that's where I'd live."

"Yes, ma'am."

"You're so polite. I got some mistletoe under the counter. You can help me hang it up, and maybe we don't have to be so formal with misters and ma'ams. That's what I like about Christmas—parties and presents and mistletoe, necking in front of the open fire."

Fulton laughed.

"You know, this fella's stayed here more recently."

"Oh?"

"Sure. He was here a few weeks ago. He plays cards with an old fella, a travellin' salesman, Mr. Alcott. He usually comes through every Monday night. He oughta be here soon. In fact, that looks like his car pullin' in past yours." She looked at the DeSoto and the woman sitting in it. "You're married?"

Fulton nodded.

"That's too bad," she said, showing a very sultry smile.

"Yes, ma'am," came his matter-of-fact reply. "What name did this fella use?"

"I knew you'd ask me that," she said, smiling. "Steve Hudson."

"That's the only name he's used?"

"Umm-hmm. That's your wife by the car?" Marlene had got out of the car, leaning against the door with her arms crossed.

Fulton nodded. He took down the manager's name and address. He told her to call him if the man returned.

"If you ever want to be less formal, you know where I am."

"See you later." Fulton walked out and introduced himself to Mr. Alcott. Marlene leaned on the roof of the car with her elbow. "This is my wife," said Fulton. She smiled and gave him a little wave.

"Wayne Alcott. Nice to make your acquaintance." The fellow had an old Zephyr coupe, the giant trunk full of sales samples. He remembered playing cards with a fellow several times. "I just need to get checked in, and we can talk some more," said the old man, delighted to have some folks to talk to. He invited them to his room, offering them ginger ale from the cooler that the manager had in the office.

Fulton wanted to see what the old man would come up with using the Identi-Kit. He got out the facial templates, and the man studied each shape, each feature, the three of them sitting in the little room. Fulton soon had his composite; it looked identical to Mrs. Talken's. He remembered the man's name was Steve, that he stayed at the motel on several occasions, going back to 1953.

"Merry Christmas!" said Alcott, seeing them to their car.

"Merry Christmas," the Fultons replied. Marlene got back behind the wheel, and Fulton settled in on the passenger side. The "one last stop" took sixty-five minutes. "I'll owe you a nice dinner," Fulton told her.

"Oh, it's all right—although in another moment I was going to walk in. She was giving off enough electricity, I could use it to light up half the town."

Fulton shook his head. "Just one more stop, baby."

"You betcha." Marlene backed away from the office. She turned around in the driveway, pushed the Drive button, then pointed the big car toward town. Back at Gaines, they parked and walked into the office.

"Hello, Marlene!" said Mary Ann.

"How are ya?"

"I just love that coat on you. Would you like some coffee?"

"Sure." Mary Ann was getting ready to leave. She poured fresh cups for the Fultons.

Martin looked at the composites, holding them side by side. "They're near identical. He looks like an actor. You know which one?"

"Yeah? I don't know."

"Well, let's update that want, get the latest information out on him."

"Yessir."

300

Tallahassee
Thursday, 12/6/1956

Another trip to Miami. Fulton packed his things and would soon leave for the station.

"I'd sure like to see that John Wayne picture," Marlene told him.

"I'll be back Saturday night. We'll go see it."

"And you owe me that dinner."

"We'll make a date of it," he said, giving her a kiss; she held on to him, drawing out the kiss as long as possible. But she knew they had to part. He grabbed his briefcase and bag and walked out to the car.

XXXXX

Marlene nearly tackled her husband when he got home. She grabbed him, pulling him toward her and kissing him. "I'm all ready to go on our date," she said. She had on a new dress.

He spun her around to look at her, whistling. "You look *wonderful!*"

"I know." She smiled. "Where are you taking me?"

"Joe's?"

"Mmmm, sounds nice."

"Let me shave and put on a clean suit. I gotta look presentable escorting a beautiful woman to Joe's Steak and Spaghetti House."

"Don't take too long," she said.

Fulton ran the razor over a day's growth; he noticed the dark circles under his eyes. He splashed hot water on his face and found his blue suit and one of Marlene's favorite ties. He put on a little cologne.

"Well, would you just look at my handsome husband! You smell good too!" she said, kissing his cheek. "It almost makes me want to forget the movie and just find something to do at home." She winked at him, brushing up against his shoulder. "But," she said, pausing, stepping into her shoes, giving him a coquettish grin, "you promised me John Wayne."

They drove to Joe's at 1713 Mahan Drive. The place was overflowing, couples in jackets and ties and dresses waiting to be seated; as quickly as one couple was done eating, another was led back to take their place. They waited their turn and got a table covered in white linen in a quiet corner.

They had their steaks and left, walking past a line of newcomers. They found a space near the courthouse and walked to the Florida Theatre, the big movie house near the corner of Park and Monroe. They had to wait in line for tickets to see *The Searchers*.

Kids cruising in an orange '55 Mercury stopped to talk to some of their friends, also in line. They were doing what kids did on Saturday night: go to a show, then Lake Jackson, then the truck stop—the only place that served food all night. People—the very young or the more mature—looked around to see who had a date with whom in line at the movies.

Fulton paid the young woman in the window, and they walked inside. Eleven hundred seats. Balcony. The giant screen in front of them—perfect for the new widescreen Westerns. Ushers in uniforms assisted them to their seats.

The movie began. The Duke was a Confederate soldier returning home to a desolate ranch. Fulton couldn't help it; he looked around at faces and body language in the theater. One man, a young fellow, was sitting between two gals a few rows in front. The fellow would smooch a bit with one girl, then turn and give the other a kiss. Fulton laughed to himself. He knew a few boys in the service that always managed to have two or three girls in every port. Fulton was always shy with women.

Nice suit. About thirty. Blond hair. Right age, hair color. Fulton shook his head. *It couldn't be.* He went back to watching the movie. John Wayne had just kicked a fellow in the butt and was wiping down a tired and sweaty horse; Indians had apparently raided some settlers.

Marlene looked over and smiled, taking his hand in hers. *I gotta at least try to watch the movie*, thought Fulton. Still, he caught himself watching the fellow. He couldn't stop being a cop.

The man turned his head. Fulton could see him in profile. It sure looked like the suspect. The fellow got up and walked down the side aisle. Fulton followed. The fellow bought some popcorn. Fulton watched from around the corner. The man finished paying; Fulton moved back so he wouldn't be seen. If it wasn't him, he could pass for his twin.

He couldn't make an arrest. And it would be unwise to try to corner him in here. It might not be him, but they would question him and find out for sure. Fulton watched as the man returned to his seat. Fulton went to the phone booth in the lobby and called the sheriff, but no one answered the telephone at Carter's home. Fulton dialed the dispatcher, Bobby.

"Oh, I like working nights, True. What can I do for you?" he asked in his melodious, radio broadcaster voice.

"You know where the sheriff is?"

302

"Yessir, he and the family drove to Havana tonight," said the man, standing on his crutches to reach the coffeepot.

"Shoot. You got anyone you can send over to the Florida Theatre? I spotted the suspect, the one we put a want out on."

"You spotted him! Why, we only have one deputy on duty, but I will get him headed your way."

"Tell him to come here in forty-five minutes. The movie's almost over. I figure we can set up and grab him when he comes out."

"Uh, 10-4."

"Thanks, Bobby." Fulton returned to his seat. Marlene could tell something was up, but she didn't ask questions. Fulton checked his watch. It was time. He told Marlene to stay inside and went out to meet the young deputy. On time, Cook had pulled his patrol car to the curb in front of the theater. He stuck his flashlight inside his Eisenhower coat and zipped it up.

The movie concluded with a final gunfight. People began filing out into the lobby. Cook and Fulton stood watch at the doors leading out to the sidewalk, observing the steady flow of hats and coats go past, ready to grab the handsome fellow in the nice suit. About three minutes passed when the two girls walked out, but the man wasn't with them.

Fulton squeezed his way back in, against the crowd, and saw the fellow's seat was empty. "Shoot!"

Marlene stood up and waved to him; he motioned for her to sit down.

Cook came in through the back door. "Mr. Fulton, I saw someone by the filling station."

"Let's go," said Fulton, unbuttoning his coat. He flung the door open, looking out into the alley that ran in between the theater and the Shell station and behind the post office. He didn't see anyone at the gas station; the lights were off. He drew his gun, turning the corner to look down the back wall of the theater. Nothing. He ran to the Shell station, Cook trying to keep up. Fulton looked around, standing near the two gas pumps, his eyes searching for a sign of the blond-haired suspect amid the trees, the cars parked in front of the Post Office, the doorways of the bank and Park Hotel across the street.

Suddenly, they heard a loud rattling. It sounded like garbage cans falling over. Fulton heard that sound enough in the River City. "Over that way," he said, pointing across the street. Fulton ran across Park, the deputy sheriff right behind him with his gun drawn; they took cover in front of the hotel, just long enough to glimpse around the corner. They dashed into the dark opening, the alley in between the old hotel and City Hall. Both men

303

stayed close to the brick wall of the hotel as they silently moved into the darkness.

To their right was a narrow opening between City Hall and the fire station. Fulton crossed the alley over to the corner of City Hall, looking down the dark path; no one was there. He motioned for Cook to keep coming up to the back corner of the hotel, where there were a couple knocked-over cans. They listened. It was dead quiet.

A little dog came out from the trash cans, startling Cook. The pup sniffed the garbage that had been strewn about then came up to the two men, smelling, hoping they had food. The dog started licking the deputy; Fulton grinned.

Footsteps! "Up that way!" whispered Cook. The men started moving, keeping close to the back wall of the bank as the alley narrowed and twisted and turned its way to the back of the Busy Bee and the old Ritz Theatre. It was dark, only the moonlight to illuminate the alley, the canyon of old brick walls. They came upon the back of the old movie theater, with its ladder and back door, the trash cans and boxes discarded behind the Monroe storefronts. They stopped at the corner—at the back of the larger State Theatre—where there was another alley that led out to College Avenue. The two men listened. A noise alerted Cook. He looked up, pointing his gun; it was just some laundry someone hung on the metal stairs that led to a little apartment, the wind causing it to rustle. Cook heard another noise coming from a stair landing behind some offices. He shined his flashlight. The glowing pair of eyes lurking in the shadows belonged to a restless tomcat.

The dome of the post office loomed over the walls of the alley, the strange glow of its lights set against the ink-black sky and the shimmering oak leaves and moss that blanketed Park Avenue. No one was about. They looked to the right, down to the end of the alley, watching the sidewalk busy with people leaving the theater and going to Bennetts. No sign of their man. He could be anywhere; he could have gotten inside one of the back rooms along the alley. He might have gone inside the State Theatre. They tried the old double doors on the side of the building. They were locked.

Most likely, he'd gone down College. They put their guns away, entering the stream of people on the sidewalk, scanning the faces moving along the street. Past the Baptist Church the street was dark, a mostly unlit valley in between downtown and the Westcott Building. Neither man saw the suspect on the street. They walked back, watching the rest of the moviegoers empty out of the State Theatre. Still no sign of him. Fulton called Bobby, dialing the number to the jail from the pay phone inside the movie house. He told him what happened. Bobby called the local radio stations to broadcast the suspect's description. He got word to the solitary state trooper and lone TPD officer that were working the night shift.

Fulton walked back to the Florida, finding his wife in front of the Shell station. "He's close," he told Marlene. "He's real close." He shook his head, mad that he let him get away.

Carter heard the broadcast. He came back from supper and stopped to talk to Fulton. He was dressed fit to kill. The Fultons got in his car, and the three of them went into the tiny communications room on the ground floor of the jail. Bobby had his large face near the microphone, his strong voice putting the killer's description out over the airways for the two off-duty deputies that had been called to look for the suspect. He stirred his coffee while he spoke. The telephone rang, and Bobby picked it up with his free hand. It was FHP. "All right, sounds good." Bobby wrote down the message to be passed along: FHP and LCSO officers could not communicate directly.

"This needs to go out across the state," said Carter. The sheriff wrote something down on a small piece of paper. Bobby was passing along a call for service to Cook, the night-shift deputy. Carter stepped over to him, patting him on the shoulder. "Hey, Bobby, would you put out an all points bulletin on this?"

Bobby took the note. He turned on their new teletype machine, sending the message just as it had been written—statewide.

56

Tallahassee
Monday, 12/10/1956

The new secretary, Mrs. Krenn, answered. "It'll be a moment. Mr. Austin just telephoned Judge Vaughn. Shall I take a message, or would you prefer to wait?"

"I don't mind waitin', ma'am."

"Very well, Mr. Fulton."

"What happened to Miss Welton?"

"Oh, she married, moved out of town."

"Oh, I see."

"Would you like to speak to Mr. Austin now? He's off the other line."

"Yes, ma'am."

"Surely," she said, pressing the button to put the line on hold.

Austin picked up presently. "True! How are you?"

"Good, and you?"

"I'm wonderful. What can I do for you, True?"

"I wanted to see if you'd heard from Mr. Harbert. We have a new lead, a suspect we're looking for, and I wanted to let him know."

"Is that so? That's really good news. I know Milo will be pleased. I haven't heard from him in a few weeks. Did you try calling him?"

"Yessir, and I couldn't reach him. I thought you might be able to get in touch with him."

"Sure, I'll call him this morning. If I can't get him, I'll try Janine. What about this suspect?"

"We put out an APB for him. We don't know his name yet, but we have his description."

"Okay!" replied the lawyer, enthused. "I'll let the Harberts know right away."

"Fine."

Fulton and Martin met the sheriff at the latter's office. They were joined by Cook and the sheriff's right-hand woman, Penny.

"We know we got someone from out of town. None of us know this feller," said Martin.

"Ain't got no wants matchin' him, do we, Penny?"

"No, sir."

"We got him in town same time as our girl, Miss Harbert," Carter added.

"I think he's a professional," said Martin.

"Professional killer—here? Why?" asked Cook.

"That's what I don't know yet," replied Fulton. "I don't know what Jo Ellen had that mattered to anyone."

"Who's got the money for something professional?" asked Cook.

Martin just said one word. "Bolita."

Dreggors parked beside the courthouse. He walked in the front doors, down the hall to the sheriff's office. He opened the door. Fulton had his entire file—which by now was three inches thick with notes of conversations and photographs—opened on a desk, with the latter, Carter, and the others gathered around.

"You want some coffee, hoss?" asked Carter.

The big fellow nodded. Carter began pouring from the pot Penny had just made. He handed the cup to Dreggors. "All right. Let's get to it then."

"Who do we know in Leon County with a link to organized crime?" asked Cook.

"Wallace Paxton," said Martin.

"The lawyer?"

"Marlene just went to work for him," said Fulton, concerned.

"But we don't really know what he's involved in," said the sheriff.

"He lives here. His wife owns a lot of property in Atlanta. He takes frequent trips to Mobile and Tampa. We haven't any more than that," said Martin.

307

"I hear he carries money for the bolita fellers," said Dreggors.

"I guess that's the next link in the chain," replied Martin. "Maybe you get Marlene to quit."

Fulton looked up at him, nodding his head.

XXXXX

Marlene wouldn't quit. She thought she could help. There was no arguing with her. Fulton pulled through the Spanish gates at Los Robles, in between the Y where Thomasville and Meridian Roads went their separate ways. It was a nice neighborhood of estate homes built in the twenties. The Paxtons' house faced the large grassy park in the middle. Fulton parked the Ford out of view, on the other side of the park, masked by large azaleas. A white '53 Lincoln coupe sat in the driveway. It fit in with the perfectly trimmed lawn and squared-off boxwoods, gleaming paint, and spotless windows of the lovely house.

There was a For Sale sign in the neatly maintained lawn next door. It was quiet in the neighborhood, the only sound the Velda Dairy truck farther down the street, the driver finishing up his deliveries. The place seemed perfect. A movie set. Fulton wondered what skeletons lurked behind those paneled doors. He poured from the thermos and enjoyed a cup of hot joe. It was cool this morning.

The door opened, and a distinguished-looking man emerged in a Brooks Brothers suit and briefcase. The man looked up at the sky—it was a pretty day—and examined the lawn, noticing a few leaves that had fallen from a dogwood. He frowned. *Lori will have to call the yard man about that.* His smile returned, seeing the mums still in bloom. He reached for the door handle and gave it a tug, settling behind the wheel of the elegant car. Fulton recalled that he'd seen this man, and the Lincoln, downtown a month ago.

Paxton drove down to the gates; he waited for a truck to pass, then made a right on Thomasville. Fulton crept along, saw traffic clear, then followed onto the main road, keeping six car lengths between his car and the Lincoln, the white car travelling five blocks to the Y with Monroe.

Fulton coasted along slowly while he watched the Lincoln come to a stop at the traffic light. It turned green, and the Lincoln continued. The light was red by the time Fulton reached the corner; he watched as the Lincoln disappeared below the hill, farther down the street. Green again, he mashed the accelerator to catch up, the flathead moaning as the car pulled along in second gear. He spotted the Lincoln at the bottom of the hill, approaching Tennessee Street.

The light went green, and the Lincoln glided across the intersection. Fulton kept his distance. They went on a couple blocks, and Paxton swung across

308

the oncoming lanes, making a U-turn and parking in an angled space in front of Capital City Bank. He dropped a dime in the meter and walked inside. It was just after nine, according to the round clock that hung over the sidewalk.

Fulton parked a few spaces up the street in front of Grant's and followed Paxton inside the quiet marble innards of the bank. Fulton acted like he was filling out a deposit slip while Paxton waited in line.

"May I help you, sir?"

Paxton stepped up to the counter. "I'd like to withdraw a hundred dollars, please," he said. The teller provided the cash, which Paxton placed inside a large wallet, shoving it in his inside coat pocket and starting for the door.

Fulton crossed the lobby, watching the lawyer open the door and go outside. Fulton held the door for a woman in a fancy hat; he saw Paxton get in the big car and back out. Fulton waited for a car to pass, then followed. He kept the Lincoln's taillights in sight as it travelled up the street and turned left on Tennessee.

Okay, where you going? Fulton thought as he turned the wheel. He stayed several car lengths behind, unnoticed. In a moment, the man held his hand out the window to signal a turn into the parking lot of the Jitney Jungle, nosing the car into a space by the door. Fulton parked around the corner, along the side of the store. He slipped inside, watching Paxton go up and down the small aisles, browsing. Finally, the lawyer picked up some Jax Beer. He carried the paper bag to his car, setting the beer beside him on the seat. He drove back to Monroe Street. Fulton hung back, pulling into the Shell station by the post office as the lawyer parked in an empty space along Park; he looked around for a minute before getting out of his car and making a beeline for the little doorway, carrying the brown paper bag under his arm. He disappeared inside, up the straight flight of stairs to his office. Fulton walked over to Capital City and asked for the manager, Conley.

"I can't reveal anything about our customers."

Fulton pulled out his badge and opened it, showing Conley the small star.

"Oh, I see. Well, Mr. Paxton has three or four accounts with us."

"Uh-huh."

"Nothing seems unusual about any of them."

"Pretty routine?"

"Yessir, he makes normal deposits and withdrawals. He's real meticulous about his business accounts—client money and retainers and such."

Fulton thanked him and walked back to his car. Paxton's Lincoln remained where he'd left it.

At 12:14 p.m., the lawyer came outside. He got in his car, driving down to the Silver Slipper. Fulton went in and ordered a cup of coffee, drinking it at the bar, reading a newspaper and watching Paxton in the mirror. An older man met him—a short fellow with white hair. It was the defense attorney, Ingleside. They seemed to discuss something serious, the old man leaning in and nodding, listening to the young lawyer carefully. The younger man paid the tab, leaving an eighty-five-cent tip, before donning his hat and getting back in the Lincoln. He retuned to his office at 1:45 p.m.

Fulton sat in the Ford, watching through the windshield. No one visited the law office. He saw Marlene looking out the second-floor window, but nothing else. *We might need to wire that office*, Fulton thought.

Paxton went home at 3:30 p.m., Fulton tailing him. A gardener was raking the leaves. Fifteen minutes later, the lawyer came out, his family with him—an attractive wife a bit younger than he, two boys, about six and ten years of age respectively, a girl about thirteen. They got in the Lincoln, heading north on Thomasville. Fulton followed as the white car pulled into Killearn Gardens and drove toward the lake.

Fulton parked unobtrusively and approached on foot along one of the secret paths in the park. The family relaxed along the shore of the lake, enjoying a snack. Father and children began playing a bit of catch with a baseball. The wife sat alone, looking out at the water. She seemed worried, lonesome.

Fulton checked with the Southeastern Telephone Company, the main office on Adams Street. The Paxtons made few long-distance calls, all to Mrs. Paxton's grandmother in Birmingham. The law office was another story, but Fulton was able to account for most of the calls—a handful of clients Paxton had in Georgia and Alabama. Fulton checked with the Georgia Bureau of Investigations and the Alabama Department of Public Safety. They had nothing on Paxton.

Fulton drove back to Paxton's office, watching Marlene leave at 5:15 p.m. When he got home at 6:45 p.m., she was making dinner.

"He's real secretive, sneaky even," she told him. "Always shuts his door. Whatever he's working on he puts aside soon as I come in with something to sign. He has a file cabinet he keeps locked. He doesn't let me go near it. He'll take a drink, but he doesn't want anyone to know about it. I hear him put the bottle away when I knock on his door. He'll be tough to catch."

57

Tallahassee
4:00 p.m.
Tuesday, 12/11/1956

Paxton's morning routine was identical, down to his frowning at another round of leaves on the lawn. He arrived at work at 8:30 a.m.—thirty minutes after Marlene. Again, he went to lunch at a quarter past twelve, driving down to the Slipper, taking the same table. *All right, who's joining you today?* Fulton wondered. It turned out the lawyer was dining alone. He seemed preoccupied. He left his money and drove back to the office. No visitors. At 3:30 p.m., he returned home. Fulton sat in the Ford across the little park. Fulton got a peppermint from his pocket and waited. *If only he had a girlfriend on the side, something interesting.*

A half hour passed before the door opened. "Okay, here we go."

Paxton walked out and smoked half a cigarette. He seemed worried. A station wagon pulled up; Mrs. Paxton and the kids got in. The lawyer leaned inside; for a second it looked like he would get in too. Then he shut the door, the car pulling away. He got in the Lincoln.

The Lincoln moved with little haste; it was easy to keep it in sight as Paxton drove down to Park Avenue and found a space beside the Fireflite. The lawyer walked over to the Midyette-Moor building. Fulton followed, just close enough to keep an eye on him. The sidewalks were busy, folks leaving work. Paxton went into the main lobby of the insurance company. Fulton paused by the door long enough to see him sit down with an insurance man. Fulton browsed in front of the window at Grant's, across College. In a moment, Paxton reappeared on the sidewalk, crossing Monroe, shoving what appeared to be a folded policy into his pocket.

He was just another man in a hat, invisible to Paxton, to the people going about their business downtown. It felt as if he was from some outside world, looking in on people's lives, those people unaware. It was strange yet comfortable. Perhaps the work dovetailed with his introversion. He was good at taking things in, putting together random shards of information— little links that people didn't want strung together. Things that people trying to get away with crimes hoped would be lost in the background noise of ordinary life, like the movement, the random errands of a Tuesday afternoon.

Paxton walked down to Fleet's Clothing Store at 106 E. Jefferson. Fulton hung back at the corner by Butler's Shoe Store. The lawyer eyed the cars parked along Adams, the state troopers at the Martin building. Maybe he was meeting someone. He went inside the store.

Fulton got a paper at Hick's Drugstore and hung around, watching. After a few moments, Paxton came out, looking around some more. The lawyer walked along the sidewalk, passing the windows of the Public Loan

Corporation, turning the corner. He seemed relaxed. He paused at the hardware store, looking in the window, then went inside. Fulton followed.

Paxton checked his watch and left the store, crossing the street to the Martin building then down the steep sidewalk to the parking lot behind. Fulton stopped at the corner of the building, in the shade. Rascal's Hill was a pretty spot with all the flowers and the birds singing. The lawyer moved slowly down the row of cars. He kept looking around; he glanced back up the hill, at the building, his head turning toward the corner where Fulton was; the lawman took a step back so he wouldn't be seen.

Satisfied no one was watching, the lawyer slipped behind a Ford and opened the trunk. He quickly removed something, shut the lid, and walked up the hill on the north side of the building this time. His pace was brisk, the unknown item wrapped in the lawyer's wool overcoat. Fulton used his little Bolsey C22 to snap a few photographs of the lawyer reaching into the trunk and carrying the item. He pulled his small Japanese binoculars from his coat pocket and read the tag on the Ford. He trailed Paxton as the lawyer crossed the street and turned onto Park. Once he rounded the corner at City Hall, the man resumed his nonchalant pace, continuing to his car then driving home.

XXXXX

Wednesday. Paxton kept to his routine. He came out of the house just as before. Same briefcase. It seemed heavier; maybe it contained yesterday's package. He went to work. Carter ran the tag on the Ford, radioing Fulton with the information. It came back to a familiar character: Reynolds Johnson.

One could set his watch by the lawyer's movements. At four, he left the house again. Fulton followed, keeping the Lincoln's taillights in sight as the big car crossed the river into Gadsden County. Fulton wondered how far the lawyer was going. He got his answer when he saw the taillights of the Lincoln glow as Paxton turned down a dirt road.

Fulton could not stay close and remain unseen. He had to let him go on. The road was primitive. *It would be nice to have a Jeep*, he thought, the car bouncing and rattling and scraping its muffler over the ruts and bumps that seemed barely fit for horseback travel, let alone wheeled passenger cars. Up ahead was a pool of muddy water; it appeared rippled, stirred by the passage of the Lincoln. The smaller Ford nearly sank to its axle. He spun the wheels, sawing at the wheel until the worn tires bit into the shallower sections of the hole. He got it through and turned down an unused side trail, the road all but consumed by the dry stalks of last summer's weeds.

Fulton opened the trunk, retrieving his boots, an old jacket, and fishing hat. These he put on, leaving his sport coat, Florsheims, and fedora behind. He put his camera and a long lens in the pocket of the baggy coat.

312

He grabbed the large binoculars, with "Property of Jacksonville Police Department" stenciled on their case, before he quietly shut the lid.

He moved along a path through the woods until near the edge of the thick brush and trees, he was able to see a big house overlooking the river. It was wood-framed with a tin roof and porches encompassing the upper floor. He got to a place where he could use the binoculars. He was well concealed in the woods, grateful to have the thick jacket in the midst of the greatest concentration of poison ivy he'd ever encountered. Four or five cars were parked in the clearing around the house. Paxton's Lincoln was there, muddy from the dirt road. A couple Cadillacs and a new Ford 500 were parked near the Lincoln. The little Ochlockonee behind the house was no more than fifteen feet wide and muddy. An alligator sunned himself on the other side. He was as still as the many oak branches that lined the river on both sandy banks.

Men were drinking but also engaged in serious discussion, leaning forward in their rocking chairs, facing each other at the far end of the second-story porch. A couple tough-looking boys hung out by the cars, their arms folded, beer bottles in their hands and guns slung from their shoulders, guarding the approach to the house.

Another car drove up, a Ford coupe. It too was covered in mud from the hole. A portly man got out. He had a sharply receding hairline, was well-dressed. He carried a leather bag—like a doctor. He could be the fellow Mrs. Davis saw!

Fulton pulled his Leica from his pocket, attached the 90 mm lens, and snapped a few photographs, steadying the camera on a low branch. He got a good shot of the bag. He knew the bolita men carried the lottery balls in bags like that. One of the big guys began moving toward him; he must have seen something, perhaps a glint from the lens. Fulton stepped back. The big fellow neared the tree line. Fulton retreated another step and froze. The man's glaring eyes scanned the leaves and branches like searchlights.

He kept coming. The man continued his search. No more than ten feet separated them. Fulton stayed behind a large sweet gum tree, watching quietly. Bugs buzzed loudly. A giant grasshopper—as big as Fulton's index finger—rested on a dilapidated old fence post, "singing." A frog croaked in a marshy spot behind him. A mockingbird sang from a branch of a dead tree over to the right, the little gray bird letting the human visitors know this was his territory. A squirrel scurried up an oak with a pine cone. The man looked over at it; he listened, trying to isolate any sign of human presence. The sounds of the woods overpowered the senses of the city fellow. Someone called him. "Hey, Jonesy, quit foolin' around. I gotcha 'nother beer." The man turned around and got his beer.

The sun was going down. Fulton was able to get closer to the house; he read tag numbers and was able to overhear a few things. It was clear these fellows were in the bolita racket. The man with the bag came outside. He got back in the coupe.

Fulton quickly made his way down to his car. Mud had caked all over the fenders and doors; she'd sunk into the soft sand. It was getting dark, the temperature falling fast. After a few pulls of the choke knob and a few shoves on the gas pedal, it started. Fulton spun tires for a second or two before retracing his path out to the highway.

Did I lose him? He saw taillights to the south. He accelerated, the car flinging mud for a few miles. He kept the taillights in sight as the coupe made its way into Glendale. The coupe stopped at a little house near the corner of Florida Avenue and Thomasville Road. Fulton parked just north of the intersection, by the furniture store, and came through the woods with his camera. The coupe sat in the driveway, the engine running. A porch light came on. A man came out. The men looked around, making sure no one was watching, and the bag was handed over. Fulton snapped a photograph with the long lens.

Fulton watched the coupe drive away before returning to his car. Back at Gaines, he developed the photos in the closet (the Bureau's "darkroom"). He put them in an envelope and closed the front door behind him. He drove home with the manila envelope beside him. He came in the house and dropped the envelope and his hat on the coffee table. He ate dinner and did the dishes for Marlene after she fell asleep in front of the television.

58

Tallahassee
Thursday, 12/13/1956

Fulton set the envelope on his desk. Carter and Dreggors had come in and were sitting in the old man's office. Fulton picked up the envelope and opened it, looking at the photos again. He walked down the hall. He handed the old sheriff the pictures. Mary Ann and Dreggors gathered around. Martin handed the first photo to the chief deputy. "I wasn't sure who it was," said Fulton.

"Well, that's old Reynolds Johnson—he did his time, and he's back at it," said Carter.

"That one was kinda blurry," said Mary Ann, kidding with Fulton.

They flipped to the next photo.

"I think I may have my bald fella," Fulton said.

"Shoot, that's Carlton Lanier!" exclaimed Dreggors.

"I can't believe it," said Mary Ann.

"Well, I heard that name before. Milo Harbert mentioned him. He's a friend of the Harberts, I believe. Maybe the bolita ties in to Jo Ellen somehow, I can't figure it." The significance was lost on Fulton, not a native Tallahasseean.

"I don't know about that, but...hell, should I tell him?" Carter asked, looking at Dreggors.

Dreggors just shook his head. Mary Ann could not contain herself. "Why, it's Ben Austin's uncle! State Representative Ben Austin—his uncle!"

XXXXX

Fulton drove to the Old Supreme Court, the fancy three-story. The phone company girls showed him the records of Lanier's calls. He'd made only a couple long-distance calls from his home. They were easily tied to relatives in Georgia. The records for his freight company were a bit more interesting. There were daily calls—dozens of them—to Lake City and Jacksonville coming from Lanier's office. The records had names and telephone numbers and how long the calls were. Fulton returned to his office and began going through the list, one by one.

Most were simply businesspeople that had shipped with Lanier, who ran a truck from Jacksonville to the capital. He telephoned Rex Sweat, asking about some of the names.

"Nothing jumps out at me, True," Sweat told him.

Fulton talked it over with Dreggors. "You know Lanier has a garage. Ya might wanna check those records too."

Fulton went back to Adams Street. More long-distance calls to Jacksonville. A few more names. One in particular stood out. He called Sweat.

"True, we put out a want for him a while back. For the bolita case. We think he has somethin' to do with the disappearance of an informant that used to carry the bolita balls for the crew over here. He's got blond hair. The name we have is Jim Boyette."

Fulton called Carter. The sheriff walked in with a piece of chicken, tore off the leg, and handed the rest to Fulton. "Let me see that *com*posite foe-toe," he said, his mouth full. Fulton got it for him. "Yeah, could be *our* suspect from three years ago."

Fulton got phone records from the house on Florida Avenue. It showed a number of calls to Jacksonville. But service was disconnected. When Fulton drove to the house with Carter, they found it empty, just a telephone cord lying on the floor in the hallway, scattered bits of straw packing material, and empty boxes in the back bedroom. The owner had died a few months earlier. The real estate agent had no idea who could have been in the house this past week. The sheriff put out a want for Johnson.

XXXXX

Dust was floating in the air as Dreggors turned down the drive, noise from the factory overwhelming the otherwise quiet morning. The Elberta Crate Factory was the largest employer in town.

Over at the loading dock, three men were loading a flatbed. Dreggors put his coffee cup on the dash. A thin almost unhealthy-looking man saw Dreggors's '51 Ford out of the corner of his eye. He looked up. He saw the signal. He excused himself and began walking toward the train track.

Dreggors drove up Lake Bradford Road and pulled into the woods by the track where he waited for the thin fellow. The man appeared presently and got in the Ford. Dreggors looked at him. "I want ya to tell me all ya know about Carlton Lanier."

The man swallowed and got wide-eyed, looking down the track. It took him a moment before he could speak.

XXXXX

Dreggors called Fulton. "I think I got somethin'. Don't wanna talk about it over the phone. Can ya meet me?"

316

They met at Centennial Field. Dreggors handed Fulton a coffee in a paper cup, and they sat in the empty stands. "I got this informant I been cultivatin'—I knowed he did some work for Lanier and for the Austins. But I never talked to him 'bout that before. This feller was a moonshiner across the county line and not far from the river house built by Lanier's daddy. He's reliable. I have no reason to doubt what he says."

"Uh-huh?"

"This feller is none too fond of the Laniers. Ol' Carlton's son got drunk and tried his damnedest to rape this feller's wife. The Laniers got it swept under the rug with the sheriff in Gadsden County. But this ol' feller's never forgotten it. He's sayin' there's a friend of Carlton's—a blond-haired feller."

"Yeah?"

"Says this feller will stop by Lanier's house from time to time, well-dressed, always drives in there and talks to Carlton. From bits and pieces he's heard, he thinks this feller's got a girl in town."

"Oh?"

"And that ain't all. Ol' boy done some repairs at Lanier's house last Saturday. This blond-haired feller's probably comin' back this way, from what he hears."

XXXXX

Fulton stayed on Lanier the rest of the day, hoping he'd meet with his pal. When Fulton had to go home, he handed it over to Dreggors or Cook. The three men kept up an around-the-clock tail with their unmarked Fords. Giving up his lunch, eating sandwiches while he drove, Fulton checked the hotels again. He turned up nothing.

59

Tallahassee
6:00 p.m.
Friday, 12/14/1956

It was dark, the stores about to close. Lanier hurried inside the National Shirt Company. Fulton browsed the windows up the street.

Lanier came out with a box—new shirts—then dashed inside the Capitol Café. Fulton slipped in, overhearing Lanier order a coffee. Fulton got some coins from his pocket and quietly entered the phone booth. "Long distance please." It still didn't make sense—what could Jo Ellen have had on the Laniers or the Austins? What could she have known about bolita?

He called Janine. "I'm trying to fit some things together. Did Jo Ellen ever gamble?"

"No," she replied, surprised.

"Not even bolita?"

"No—I don't think so."

"Do you know who she might have had contact with in Jacksonville?"

"No, I don't."

Lanier sat by himself, drinking his coffee. Finished, he drove to the Jitney Jungle on Monroe. Fulton followed, pulling in behind the store alongside Dreggors, cranking his window down.

"Anything?" asked the big man.

"He's made a few stops. No sign of our suspect."

"10-4."

Dreggors left to follow Lanier. Fulton picked up something for Marlene before the store closed. Paxton gave her the day off; that suited Fulton just fine.

XXXXX

Saturday. Evelyn Madgison worked at the Savings & Loan at 115 East Park Avenue. She was at the teller's window, busy with a line of farmers in for their Saturday banking and haircuts. She smiled when she saw Fulton. "I get a break in a few minutes," she told him.

He nodded and glanced at the paper. He wondered how Dreggors had made out last night.

They walked around the corner to the Busy Bee and ordered a couple coffees. "I know she used to go down to the coast a lot," the woman told him. "She'd drive down there with friends of hers. She had a boyfriend."

"Do you know who it was?"

"No. She was mysterious about it, kept things real private."

"You sure it wasn't Howerton?"

"No, I'm sure of that. He went with another friend of mine, Suzie. He was crazy about her then."

"Did she know Carlton Lanier?"

"I don't know."

"Do you know him?"

"I've heard of him. Don't know him."

XXXXX

Fulton trailed Lanier to an apartment house near the stadium on St. Augustine Road. The little apartment block was in a low spot where water collected after it rained. Lanier had to wade through a giant puddle to approach the door. He'd backed his Ford around the side of the house. Fulton parked where he could go unnoticed, up the street. He watched through the long lens of his camera. "Well, Carl, who you goin' to see?"

The door opened; long legs and a silk slip, Fulton brought the lens a little higher. "Okay who are you, gal?" He focused on her face. *Miss Madgison!* She grabbed Lanier, and they began kissing, arms around each other, Lanier letting loose of Evelyn with one hand only long enough to shut the door behind them. Fulton could have sworn Lanier's bow tie and Madgison's brassiere ended up on that door stoop.

60

Tallahassee
Monday, 12/17/1956

Lanier opened a beer and went in the office, a back room at his garage at 922 South Macomb near the tracks. The place had a stepped design to the top of the façade, the walls soundly made of terracotta block in the twenties and whitewashed. Two service bays had been added on over the years; a couple police cars were getting tune-ups. Lanier had met with no one—except the Madgison girl—in three or four days.

Fulton drove to a public telephone, placing a call to the manager at the Ship Lantern; she'd left a message for him. But she hadn't seen the fellow she knew as Steve—not in quite a spell. She seemed like she just wanted to talk. He hung up, chuckling and shaking his head. *He has got to be close. I can feel it.*

When Cook took over, Fulton drove around to the motels but didn't see the blond man. He showed the composite again, with the same results.

Cook called Fulton at home. "I saw Lanier stop at a phone booth at a filling station way out North Monroe. Only talked a minute."

XXXXX

Dreggors met his informant at the isolated stretch of track west of the factory. "That stranger was in town day 'fore yesterday," he told the big lawman. "He's changed his 'pearance some."

"Yeah?"

The informant spit tobacco on the ground. "Yeah, I was up at that river house, two or three cars up there. Six, seven fellers, I reckon. They had me in the kitchen, fixing the gas stove. They had a colored lady cookin' 'fore 'em, but the stove wouldn't light. Lanier was careful I didn't see who all was there, just kept me in the kitchen and kinda watched over me—makin' sure I didn't get too curious, was how I took it."

"What was this blond feller drivin'?"

"He had him a new car—a black Merc'ry. Hey, you got some smokes?"

"Sure," said Dreggors, handing him his pack of Chesterfields.

"The talk I heard from these boys—wudn't much I could hear—was that this feller was carrying money—a lot of it."

"Okay."

"That ain't all," said the man, striking a match. "I fix the stove, and I'm takin' a look out the winder now and then. And I see this feller out by one of the cars. Well, I reckernized that car." The man took a long drag on the smoke. "It was a Lincoln. I seen Mr. Paxton drivin' it one of the other times I was up there."

"Yeah?"

"So it kinda caught my 'tention. Paxton rolls the winder down. He hands this feller somethin'. Looked like a doctor bag, black bag, big as a loaf of bread," he said, holding up his hands to show Dreggors. The money had to be for the bolita, or perhaps the bag contained bolita balls. "The blond-headed feller goes inside. Then I hear Paxton drive off." The man finished the cigarette and threw it out the window.

"Okay," said Dreggors, reaching for the ignition switch.

"There's more, Mr. Will."

"You really got after it," said Dreggors, turning loose of the key.

"Well, it just kept on comin'! You best hold on to your hat for this next part. I was 'bout scared to death what happened next."

"Uh-huh?"

"After I fix the stove and the nigra woman starts cookin' for these boys, Lanier tells me to come on and git in the Merc'ry. And they get in—this feller'n him—and start drivin'. And they keep going on and on. And this feller's drivin' but ain't sayin' much. So I ask Lanier where we goin' anyhow. And he ain't sayin' much about it. They carry me out to the Perry Highway and start drivin' fast. And I'm tellin' myseff, 'Oh, Lord, they fixin' ta kill you and dump you out in some swamp off Ol' Saint Aug'stine Road or down by the nachrul bridge' 'cause we ain't stoppin' noplace. But 'parently this feller likes to stay at the Ship Lantern. We pull in there and go back to this feller's room. There was an old man there that come over, and we all commence to playin' cards."

Dreggors smiled.

"Yeah, ain't it somethin'? My hands were shakin', and they thought I needed a drink, so they had an ol' gal there, and she poured me one."

"He had a girl in his room?"

"Yeah. Come to find out, she's the dadgum clerk a that motel. She was real friendly towards this feller."

Dreggors looked out through the windshield, down the tracks, thinking. He looked at the informant. "You caught up on your rent, son?"

"No, sir, I owe 'em ten dollars for this month."

Dreggors handed him seven dollars—all the money he had; he backed out of the little clearing and raced away in the Ford. He screeched to a halt in front of the Sheriff's Bureau; Fulton got in, and they headed for the Ship Lantern.

XXXXX

They walked the manager into the jail. Dreggors and Fulton questioned her. She maintained her denial. Dreggors left the room and spoke to Carter in the hall. The big man returned and tried once more. "You've been lyin' to us. We talked to the girl that cleans the rooms. We can 'rest ya right now."

She broke down and admitted she did know the suspect, that she spent time with him. She was crying. She kept repeating how lonely she was. They drove her home and called a friend of hers to stay with her.

Fulton watched the river house while Dreggors sat in a room at the Ship Lantern to see if the man would come back. They watched three days. He never showed. Cook told Fulton that Lanier kept up with his normal errands, with one trip to that telephone on North Monroe.

61

Tallahassee
Friday, 12/21/1956

Fulton parked in front of the Westcott Building. He waited outside the dean's office. The man arrived momentarily; he was about fifty, Fulton reckoned. He wore glasses, seemed bookish, but had powerful hands; he had boxed in his youth, judging from the photos in his office. The dean took Fulton to a room filled with wooden file cabinets. "We have records that go back to 1851 in these cabinets. let's see…1947, here we are. Yes, by golly, we have a Benjamin Austin right here."

"How long did he attend?"

"Give me a moment, and I will tell you." The dean looked into another cabinet, pulling out the dusty drawer. "Two years. We have a transfer here, looks like he transferred to our illustrious rival in Gainesville."

So young Ben Austin had been a Seminole—at the same time Jo Ellen was playing tennis and basking on the shores of Lake Bradford.

"Was that all you needed, Agent Fulton?"

"Yessir, thank you."

XXXXX

Fulton called the sheriff. "True, I don't think Ben ties into this thing with Jo Ellen. I just don't see that. Lanier always tried to be a big dealer. He probably knows people that would kill for the right price. And he'd be fool enough, brave enough, when he's drank a little, to say the word."

Fulton stopped at Terry-Rosa Hardware on South Monroe, near the Lincoln dealer. He picked up some extra locks. The clerk thought he was crazy; no one locked their doors in Tallahassee. Fulton didn't want to take any chances when Marlene was by herself. She sensed he was worried, watching him put the locks on, the way he had that look—his mind turning, going over a hundred different things, his eyes blank, like he wasn't really in the room.

"What is it? Talk."

"I'm not sure who I can trust, baby."

She shook her head. "This entire thing's crazy. I just see this exploding in your face."

"These people were born here, raised here. They got their spiderwebs, they're like poison ivy—or…or…kudzu—growing through everything. This

323

isn't Jacksonville or Tampa where you got a whole department trying to fight it."

"It's all right, don't worry."

"I will too worry. You have only three or four men, and you don't even know if you can trust all of them, except Sheriff Martin."

"He's worth three or four men in a pinch."

"But he's getting to be an old man."

"I'm more worried about you working for Paxton."

62

Tallahassee
1:30 a.m.
Saturday, 12/22/1956

"What's wrong, True?" asked Marlene, rolling over and putting her arm around her husband.

"I'm just thinking about you. This thing with Paxton. I don't want you to go to work this week."

"Maybe I can help. For one thing, he always sends these boxes to an address in Jacksonville about once a week. A truck comes by, you know, the green trucks from the shipping company at the old Coca-Cola building?"

"Really?"

"Uh-huh. Maybe I can try and see what's in them."

"No, baby. I don't want you to go anywhere near this."

She started kissing him. The telephone rang. Marlene sighed, getting up to answer it.

Fulton looked at the clock and yawned. She returned to the bedroom. "You've been summoned."

Fulton got up.

"It's me!" exclaimed Carter cheerily. "We found Johnson. I'm fixin' to question him. See ya in a few minutes."

Click.

"Okay," said Fulton, yawning. Marlene handed him a cup of coffee.

XXXXX

The sheriff had Johnson brought into the interrogation room. The room was about seven feet across, with barely enough room for a table and chairs for the suspect, the sheriff, and Fulton. Haywood—who found Johnson while on midnight patrol—stood. Bright fluorescent lights hung from the high ceiling, making 2:00 a.m. feel as bright as the noon sun. The feeling was magnified by the white walls. There was a small window that had metal grating on it to keep suspects inside, seven layers of white paint framing the blackness outside.

Three pairs of eyes focused in on Johnson. The man looked around nervously, trying to avoid eye contact. The sheriff put a pack of cigarettes down but didn't say anything. Johnson—shaking—took one. "I'd like to help you boys, I really would. I've been out of town, I've been gone a couple months."

Carter stayed quiet; Fulton just sipped his coffee. Johnson filled in the silence. Little by little, he crafted an alibi. They let him talk. They listened politely. Then Carter and Fulton began to ask him, "Well, how can this or that be?" He soon began to contradict himself with dates, people he saw. After a few minutes, Johnson knew he'd driven himself down a dead-end street. He hung his head and spilled everything—enough to send Paxton to prison. "Look, you got me. I'm a little fish. I got paid well for it, but I ain't nowheres near the top. Paxton's picked up the cash from all the tickets. He'd get it to someone in Tallahassee—medium-size fish. They'd send it on to a bigger fish in Jax. I swear I don't know those names." The bolita man talked a lot—but he wouldn't dime out Lanier.

Penny typed Johnson's statement, and the fellow, exhausted, signed it and put his head down on the table.

"Take him to his cell, Charlie."

Haywood got the jailer, and the two men led the prisoner down the hall.

"Let's bring in Paxton," said Carter.

XXXXX

They only had to play the first reel of tape recordings.

"Look, boys, you got me. I'll tell you what I know," said Paxton.

"Okay."

"Got a cigarette?"

"Sure," said Carter, handing him one.

"Bring a stenographer in here, and I'll tell ya all about Carlton Lanier."

XXXXX

The lights were off at the Paxtons'. The Lincoln was in the driveway. *They're asleep.* He knew the back door was unlocked. He crept through the kitchen, into the hall. He heard snoring coming from upstairs. He began to pour the gasoline around on the hardwood floors.

Footsteps. "Who's down there?"

Frantically, the intruder tried to get his Zippo to work. Someone was coming down the stairs. "Stop, I'm a deputy sheriff!"

326

The man dropped the gasoline can and ran for the back door. Cook stayed with him until they got to the first high fence. The man was more agile than the big deputy. He slipped around Lake Ella, past the cabins, and back to the highway.

XXXXX

At the big house at the corner of Park and Gadsden, they could hear music playing as they pulled up—loud jazzy music. There was a car parked in the grass. Fulton touched the hood as they walked past it; it was cold. They walked up to the door. Carter took his hat off and knocked. The lights were on, curtains open in the windows that overlooked the veranda. They could see Ben take his mother by the arm, circling around her in the Rueda de Casino–style salsa. Carter knocked again. They could see other people in the house. It was a party.

A colored girl opened the door and led them inside. Mrs. Lanier was standing near the steps in an apron.

"Evenin', Margaret," said Carter, holding his hat.

"Evenin', Sheriff."

"This here's Mr. Fulton."

"Ma'am," said Fulton, taking off his hat.

Mrs. Lanier had a strange look on her face.

"You all right?" asked Carter.

"I'm okay. Just cooking supper."

"Your husband here?"

"All night."

"You sure he didn't go noplace?"

"Sure, I'm sure."

"Can you get him?"

Ben approached them. "Well, how are ya? What brings you fellas over this way?"

"We wanna talk to your uncle," replied Carter.

Lanier came down the staircase. He lit a cigarette and leaned against the railing, looking askance at the law men, hiding none of his contempt.

327

"Got somewhere we can talk private?" asked Carter.

"We'll talk here," said Lanier. "You won't be here long. Say your piece."

"All right. Were you over in Los Robles tonight?"

"Ain't been noplace. I don't understand why you boys are questionin' me."

"You know Paxton. And y'all were into bolita real heavy."

"Why, Sheriff, I can't speak for the esteemed attorney, but I was into no such thing—bolita! Ha! That's funny, huh, Marge?" he said, turning back to his wife.

"You drive here?" asked Carter.

"Ben drove."

"Mind if we look at your car, Mr. Austin?" asked Fulton, nodding toward the garage.

"He does mind. You ain't said what this is about," answered Lanier.

"Has something happened?" asked Ben. "We've been here all night. My car's been in the garage the whole time."

The colored girl appeared and summoned the lawmen to the parlor, which was lavishly furnished with antiques and papered walls. Voncille Austin was in her fifties but looked considerably younger; she wore an elegant sleeveless dress. She'd been drinking and was angry.

"Miss Austin?" Carter asked, sensing she was upset. "What's wrong, ma'am?"

"I don't understand why this is happening. Whatever do you mean to imply by these questions?"

"We don't mean ta imply nothin', Miss Austin," the sheriff assured her.

"I have a mind to speak to Grant Wilkinson about this in the morning."

"Somethin' happened at Wallace Paxton's house—somethin' serious. We're just trying to clear it up."

"How is Lori?"

"A mite shaken," said Carter.

"Oh?"

"Would you care for some coffee?" asked Mrs. Austin.

328

"Yes, ma'am, thank you," Carter replied.

Mrs. Austin nodded to her servant. "Ida." The young woman quietly left to get what was requested. Mrs. Austin noticed Fulton looking at the mantel clock. "That was my cousin Harland's. My cousin was governor and was given that clock for his efforts to establish many of our state parks before the war."

Fulton asked the questions. Mrs. Austin reiterated the same story as provided by her guests. No one left the house. She was polite but annoyed by the questions. She looked at Carter like he'd just run his patrol car through her azaleas.

"Ida will show you boys out," she said, rather upset. The young woman escorted them back through the house, the central hall that led to the front door. Fulton paused for a moment; he noticed something in the small powder room under the staircase. It was a gold butterfly, quite large and ornate. He had seen it before—*in the photos*!

Lanier smirked. "Leavin' so soon?"

"Now, look here," said Carter, getting mad.

"You go for a drive tonight?" asked Fulton.

"You must not hear too good."

"Someone tried to burn the Paxton place. You know anything about that?" asked Carter.

"Yeah, you do business with Paxton, don't you?" asked Fulton.

"Unless you boys got more, I think we're done talkin'."

"There's other things, but I ain't gonna go into it in front of your wife. She's a good woman—better than you deserve," said Carter.

"I'm sorry you feel that way about me. Good night, Frank!" With that, it became obvious who the guests were.

Grant Wilkinson walked into the living room. "I think the steaks are done, Carl—say, what are you fellas doing here?" His eyes were bloodshot, and he was staggering, close to knee-walking tight.

"Just a little police work," said Carter.

"Well, if you fellas need help, if you need someone to explain the law to you, you just let me know. If you'll excuse us, our dinner is ready."

Carter was red-faced. Fulton walked him back to the patrol car. "I ain't never seen you this mad."

"I'm all right. Dadgummit, these fellers got all the answers, all the cover in the world."

He sighed. "You know, Marg'ret is my cousin."

"Didn't know that."

"Makes me mad how he's runnin' around on her."

Carter started the car.

"I stood right by the garage door. I didn't hear ticking," said Fulton.

"Huh?"

"Ticking—the sound a car makes when you shut off the motor."

"Yeah. Well, he mighta caught a ride with someone."

None of Mrs. Austin's neighbors remembered seeing Ben's Lincoln leave the house. Carter raced north on Calhoun. They talked to Ben's neighbors on South Ride; then they canvassed Lanier's neighbors in Indian Head Acres. Nothing. Carter cussed. "We'll charge Johnson with possession of gamblin' paraphernalia and illegal lottery tickets. That's that law that passed last year. That's about all we can do right now."

XXXXX

Marlene sat up in bed. "I'm wondering if there's another woman."

"Didn't mean to wake you."

"Glad you did. The only time I get to see you is three o'clock in the morning."

He laughed and pulled her close to him; she fell asleep in his arms.

XXXXX

Jeanne Craine was explaining how good her new DeSoto was. "Almost a foot lower than I am, and I'm only five-foot-five. My DeSoto is fun to drive—even in heavy traffic. This new DeSoto is the most exciting car I've ever had."

"Drive a DeSoto before you decide," enjoined the announcer before flashing the address for Mayo-Mingledorff DeSoto-Plymouth, 808 North Monroe Street. The commercial ended, and opening music for the *Jack Benny Show* began, followed by an ad for Lucky Strike cigarettes.

330

Marlene opened the paper. "'Voncille Haynes Austin, Society Matron, Restores Family Home,'" she read. The article had photographs of the grand home. "Say, isn't this the family?"

"Yeah, does it mention bolita?"

"I doubt it. This says, 'Austin family in Tallahassee goes back to 1844, the year before Florida's statehood, when Judge Thomas D. Austin established a plantation east of the capital. Mrs. Austin is proud of her family's accomplishments which include electing a representative to the first state legislature and bringing the first Cadillac to Tallahassee in 1907.'"

"I remember the fancy wallpaper," said Fulton, noting the shot of the parlor.

"Yeah. Get this—her father, Milburn F. Haynes, owned holdings in Gadsden County and invested in the original Coca-Cola stock in the 1920s. It ends by saying, 'Mrs. Austin's husband, of course, is long-time US Representative Brock Austin. Son Ben, following family tradition, will take his seat in the State House when the new session begins in April. Her youngest son, Donald, followed family tradition by attending the University of Florida and is finishing a three-year tour of duty as a naval aviator.'"

"Does it say that her cousin was governor?"

"No—but it figures."

63

Jacksonville
Monday, 12/24/1956

Fulton pulled to the curb near Papa Topp's. The joint was quiet this time of day, before the after-work rush. Fulton ordered a beer and sat on a stool, the only customer in the place. The old barkeep, Papa, paused to talk to him while he wiped down the bar. "Have you noticed we've been getting a lot of rain lately?"

"We always get a lot of rain in the spring," said Fulton, knowing the code.

Papa nodded and went into the back room. Fulton moved to a booth. It was dark, no lights on, a shadow cast over the beat-up table. He sat there, his hat low on his forehead.

He finished the beer, waiting. The old man refilled the glass. In a moment, a woman in a green jacket with velvet trim, a matching hat, and veil appeared at the door, carrying herself gracefully as a movie star. Papa watched her glide in. She could probably double Gene Tierney; she had *mysterious* down cold, walking into the dark barroom like she'd come back from the dead. She sat in the booth adjacent Fulton's, her back to his. Her face he couldn't see. He recognized the perfume. Underneath her hat was red hair that matched her temperament. She lit her cigarette and continued to face the opposite way. Finally, she spoke—low, almost out of the corner of her mouth, the way Marlene Dietrich might deliver a line in such situations. "The park...by Riverside Hospital."

"Yeah?" he whispered.

"Take a cab. Meet me there, opposite side from the hospital." She got up, quickly disappearing through the front door. Fulton waited a moment, said good-bye to Papa, and walked back outside. There was no sign of the well-dressed woman. It was a strange meeting—but that was Wendy.

XXXXX

The driver made a U-turn and pulled his '55 Plymouth to the curb. "Where ya headed, boss?"

"Memorial Park."

"You got it!" They drove down Riverside Avenue, the meter clicking over ten cents at a time. They neared the entrance of the park with it's wrought fence and the high-rent apartment building across the street. Fulton leaned forward. "You mind turning here?" said Fulton, pointing to the next street.

"Sure thing." The driver steered the car down Memorial Park Drive, the shady side street that ran alongside the park. "Okay, you can let me out. Keep the change," said Fulton, handing the man $1.50.

"Thanks, mister." The driver took the money and sped away, down to the river shore, hanging a left on Lancaster Terrace. The street was dark; the sky threatened rain.
Fulton saw a sports car—bright red with a white hard top—parked near the river, along the fence, low-hanging oak branches and Spanish moss almost obscuring it from view. He approached. The driver—a woman—held her hand out the window. She had gloves on, a large hat, the brim of which partially hid the side of her face.

He walked slowly, watching for cars or anyone that might be milling about. There wasn't a soul on this side of the park. Riverside Memorial was on the opposite side, the top of the three-story building rising above the surrounding oaks. Next to the hospital was a tower-like apartment building that went up in the '20s at the river's edge. It rose into the gray sky, the yellow glow from a few windows the only sign of human presence there. Lifelike bronze eagles kept an eerie watch over quiet paths. There wasn't so much as a parked car on Lancaster Terrace, which followed the river back toward downtown, fronted by some of the grand homes Riverside was famous for. A motor
yacht bobbed lifelessly at the dock.

He had to wait. He pretended to read his paper, leaning against an oak. A maid came out with one last item for the dry-cleaning man at the house on the corner, hurrying back inside before the clouds opened up. The woman in the sports car ducked down. The maid disappeared up the walkway, the delivery truck pulled away, and the woman resumed her scanning.

Fulton put his hands on his hips, the look on his face begging the question, "Are we done?" Presently, she patted the door, the signal for him to get in. "You satisfied no one's around?" he asked, squatting down by her window.

"Can a girl be too careful?" she asked, lighting a cigarette. "Get in."

He folded himself in the little Simca and flicked the door shut. "Some car," he commented, looking around the cozy interior. The two-seater had the look of a Thunderbird someone left in the dryer too long. Wendy adjusted her floppy hat and sunglasses; she seemed determined no one would recognize her.

"It cost me four G's at Gateway Motors, the crooks."

Fulton whistled at the lavish cost. She noticed a man carrying a paper sit down on one of the benches in the park, facing the river. She started the motor, tipped the gear lever in first, and pulled away from the curb. She looped around Lancaster then got back on Riverside Avenue before running up Margaret toward Riverside Park. She kept looking around, wary of every car, of every Joe walking down the sidewalk in a suit and tie and a copy of the *Times-Union* under his arm.

"Wendy, I was wonderin—"

"My name is officially Diamond Page, you know."

"All right, Miss Page, would you mind takin' a look at this?" He pulled the composite picture as she drove around the park, looking for a space. She looked down at it while she shifted gears. She nodded quickly and looked back at the road. She stopped at the north end of the park, away from the old people, the kids, and their mothers who were trying to enjoy a few minutes of exercise beside the lake before the rain arrived.

"Did you meet him at the Aragon?" Fulton asked.

"It's a classy place, isn't it?"

Fulton knew she met most of her "friends" there. She'd left behind the days of the Patio Motor Court. The Aragon was a ritzy air-conditioned high-rise at 230 West Forsyth.
"I'm tryin' to find him."

"Well, he ain't in town. Least, I ain't seen him."

"Okay."

"He was pretty careful what he told me. But men talk about things they enjoy, and they tell a girl about things they're good at. He liked to shoot. He showed me a rifle he had. He offered to take me shooting. Someplace out on the highway."

"Yeah?"

"It was a motor court with hunting and fishing. I don't like waking up with the chickens and bathing in a washtub, so I said uh-uh."

"Do you remember where it was?"

"What's the town that's a tree?"

He looked at her, unsure what she meant.

"Say, let's go, there's too many cars coming by." There was a bit of traffic coming across the Fuller Warren toll bridge. She drove up Park Street and stopped in front of a large house. She put a cigarette between her lips and answered her own riddle. "Live Oak—that's it."

"Okay."

"Light me up, will ya? Also, he liked to fish. He always talked about some bridge in Tallahassee," she said as he held the lighter for her. "Thanks." She savored the Chesterfield.

"On the river?"

"No, something about pools of water in the woods. Sounded creepy to me."

"Natural Bridge?"

"That's right."

"What name did he use?"

"Jim. He always paid, he minded his manners, I didn't ask questions. He talked a lot but didn't really say much—if that makes sense?"

"Sure."

"Oh, another place he mentioned was a motel near the capital, travelaire, comfortaire, something-aire."

"Southernaire?"

"Yeah." She started the car. She drove up and down side streets with porches and shade trees, making sure she wasn't followed, before turning back on Riverside Avenue and driving down to a secluded spot by St. Vincent's. "No one would know me here," she said, looking around. A nun walked by in a gray habit. "One other thing," she said, flicking the cigarette out the window.

"Yeah?"

"His wife's name is Jackie. She lives in Tallahassee."

"Oh?"

"Yeah, I saw a check he had with her name on it—Jackie Younkins. Funny name. Y-O-U-N," she spelled. "He told me he was married to her, but not for long." Wendy put the car in gear again, rolling along slowly, stopping near the corner of Goodwin and Riverside, looking up at the apartments to make sure no one was watching. The rain was beginning to fall in large drops that rolled down the windows of the car. "All right," she said, nodding toward the door handle on his side.

"You can't drop me closer to my car?"

"This is the best I can do. I can't be seen with the likes of you."

He frowned.

335

"Well, don't get sore about it. We can go back to the Aragon. Could you handle it?"

"Never mind." He watched her disappear up Goodwin Street. He turned up his collar, walking back along the river. *So maybe the wife will tell us something.*

64

Tallahassee
4:30 p.m.
Monday, 12/24/1956

In a little country store east of town on US 90, they sold everything from bread to tupelo honey to homemade fishing poles. There was a '46 Ford in front; a wrecker driver was hoisting it up for a tow. Dreggors pulled in right after Fulton.

A woman came outside, her face red from crying. "Are you Jackie Younkins?" asked Dreggors.

"Yessir."

"Is there something wrong?" asked Fulton, seeing she was distraught.

"This ol' heap won't start. I ain't got no money to get it fixed," said the woman, beginning to cry again.

"Why don't you come inside, Mrs. Younkins," said Fulton, opening the door for her. The place was open, but there were no customers. "You own this place, ma'am?" Fulton asked, looking around at the sacks of rice and flour, canned goods, and canned meats.

Mrs. Younkins had a simple ring on her left hand that probably cost $20, no other jewelry, a plain dress. She had dark hair and was thin, average in appearance, save for her very light blue eyes. Both men took their hats off.

"No, sir, I just work here. The owner ain't got much money, that's why I ain't got much neither, I reckon."

"Yes, ma'am. Here," said Fulton, handing her a Kleenex from the box on the counter.

"Thanks," she said, drying her eyes.

"Mrs. Younkins, we's wonderin' if you might know where your husband is," said Dreggors.

"I don't know. Course, I don't think *husban'* is the word for him anymore. He told me he'd been a-workin'. Had a little cash money. I seen it and asked of it. He comes home drunk, gets his clothes, and he's gone again. Don't give me nothin' for the light bill or the rent that's overdue. Barely got anything for baby food. My mama had to buy food for the baby last month. Ain't right. No, sir, I ain't got a husban'. If you're talkin' 'bout Plummer Younkins, I don't know where he is."

"Do you know where he might go?"

337

"He's got a woman in town. I don't know where she lives, but she works at one of the banks. Her husband has something to do with the ball field, although she doesn't live with him, ain't for some time."

"Do you happen to know her name?"

"That sow's name is Evelyn Madgison. Jezebel is more like it."

Fulton and Dreggors looked at each other. Miss Madgison again. Both wondered what else she was hiding under her feathered hats.

"Do you know Plummer to frequent anyplace else?"

"Hotel rooms and barrooms in Jacksonville. He'll go himself and do the town, whenever he gets a little money. The only thing he likes as much as his women is his huntin' and fishin'. There's someplace in Live Oak he's partial to, and out there at the nachrul bridge."

"Yes'm, thank you for your time," said Fulton. The men excused themselves but paused outside the door. Mrs. Younkins watched, wondering what they were doing. She saw the men reach into their pockets and, in a moment, the big fellow came in and handed her $4. "This here's for the young'n, ma'am."

She thanked him, practically bursting into tears again. They sped toward town, pulling up in front of the Savings and Loan. They found Madgison filling in behind the counter, cashing a check. When the customer left, they approached.

"Mr. Fulton this *is* a surprise!" she purred, a flirtatious smile on her face.

Dreggors leaned over the counter. "We're lookin' for Plummer Younkins. We ain't got time to play. Where's he at?"

Her smile faded. She grew sullen, angry, refusing to answer.

"Maybe you better get your coat and hat then," said Dreggors.

"I ain't got a hat. My coat's in the cloakroom," she said, her eyes flashing their disdain for the lawman.

"All right, get it."

XXXXX

At 5:45 p.m., they walked her back to the interrogation room in the jail. They sat the woman in the oppressive little corner, the oak table hemming her in, the two lawmen crowded around her in their wooden chairs. Dreggors questioned her for a half hour, but the woman wouldn't talk. They stepped out of the room and talked it over with Carter, speaking in hushed tones in the booking room while keeping her under observation

338

through the open door. The woman sat in her hard oak chair, smoking, a contemptuous expression on her face.

Dreggors took another crack at her. "Aiding and abetting's a felony, you know it?"

"You tryin' to scare me?"

"We got your record. You ain't never done more than thirty days at a time."

She seemed surprised. Dreggors held up a teletype from Miami, Madgison's birthplace.
"You think the new women's prison's a summer camp, where you'll get to do your nails, maybe some nice girl will help you do your hair?"

She scowled at him.

"They'll chew you up and spit ya out."

"Shut up!" she snapped. "Shut up, you don't scare me, cop! You haven't any proof against me."

They traded barbs for another ten minutes. Her stomach was rumbling in between protests as to why she shouldn't be there. Fulton hadn't said anything, just listened. He got up and walked over to the coffeepot in the booking room, where wanted posters were displayed. "Miss Madgison, would you care for a cup of coffee?" he asked, pouring himself a mug.

She didn't say anything. He put in a little sugar and shook in some Pream. She hadn't eaten, and by the look in her eyes, she clearly wanted a coffee. "You sure? It's no trouble."

She looked away, at the wall.

"Sure is good coffee, Will. Ya want a cup?"

"Well, I take that very kindly. Sure, I'll have a cup of coffee," replied the big man, smiling broadly. "Just a little sugar and cream," he said, indicating a small amount with his large fingers.

"Yes, sir! You got it." Fulton handed the mug to Dreggors, who returned to his seat, opposite Madgison.

"Gee, this is good coffee," said Dreggors, sipping it loudly.

"Isn't it?" replied Fulton.

"Yessir, it sure is," said Dreggors, taking another loud sip.

The woman squirmed, unable to hide her desire for the coffee and an end to the lawmen's seemingly limitless conversation about the same.

"You sure I can't get you a cup, ma'am?" asked Fulton, standing in the doorway. She looked down, the scent of the jailer's fresh brew drifting across the table.

"Forget it, True, she doesn't want any."

The woman looked up, anger flashing under her long lashes. "Sure I do. A cup a coffee would be swell," she retorted, glaring at Dreggors.

"Okay," said Fulton, pouring a third cup. "Would you care for any sugar or cream?"

"Just sugar."

Fulton brought it over to her. She held the mug—stained inside and cracked on the rim—with both hands, taking a sip.

"Good?"

She nodded.

Fulton sat down. "Don't get sore at us, Miss Madgison. We're just trying to find a killer."

Her expression changed. He could see her shiver at that word. "I'm not sore. I don't know nothin' about a killing."

"Okay." Fulton watched her drink the coffee, watched her thinking, worrying. "You know, you got a job, things are going pretty well for you. Then a fella comes along—sometimes a gal will do a lot because he tells her things. Sometimes he asks a lot in return. Things that make it tough for a girl." He could tell she was thinking about what he was saying. She looked up at him; the anger had left her eyes.

Fulton continued. "Only sometimes this fella is sayin' the same things to more than one girl. And sometimes he's told the same things to a wife, put a ring on her finger, had a few kids."

The anger flashed across her brown eyes again. "All right, he's a heel. But I ain't a snitch."

"I get that, honest, I do. But things would get a lot easier for you if certain things got said, accidental-like. For instance, if we was to find out where Younkins might be."

She finished her coffee. "You got any food?"

"I think we can get you something to eat."

"I'll rustle something up," said Dreggors, leaving to go get her a tray. Miss Madgison was silent for a moment.

"Miss?"

"I'm thinkin' about what you said."

Dreggors brought in the food—eggs and bologna and an orange—all from the kitchen across the hall. She attacked the tray with a vengeance, cleaning the tin plate.

"Miss Madgison, where's Younkins at?" repeated Fulton.

"Well, I know where he should be—he should be at work. The bum was supposed to save up. Supposed to leave his wife. We were gonna go away together, start over fresh."

"But?"

"He took off for Jacksonville. He called me from there. I know he has his women over there. He's coming this way for sure—to see me."

"You supposed to meet him?"

She nodded.

"Where?"

"The Southernaire."

"When?"

"Day after Christmas."

"Okay. How's Lanier tie in with this?"

"Don't know. They do some business together. There's a lot of money mixed up in it. That's all I know."

"Okay," said Fulton. "You'll have to stay put while we go get him. We don't want you gettin' ideas about warnin' him, you understand, of course?"

"I get it."

The jail matron came and escorted her back to her cell on the west wing of the jail. There was only one other lady prisoner that week.

341

65

Tallahassee
6:20 a.m.
Tuesday, 12/25/1956

Fulton and Dreggors drove to the jail in the latter's shoebox Ford. On the fraying cloth of the backseat were a couple casseroles and plates of food, toothpaste, and soap for the three inmates that were unlucky enough to get themselves locked up for Christmas. They could see their breath when they got out of the car. The sun had been a faint glow on the horizon a moment ago; vigorously, it stepped up from behind the trees over Myers Park, sending rays of light into the little valley and warming their faces as they gathered the food and parcels in their arms.

Bobby met them on his crutches. Fulton shook his hand. The man took a bullet a few years ago, losing mobility but not his strong, clear voice. One plate was for him. They watched the sun rise over the valley. The Spanish celebrated the first Christmas in the New World below. There had been a waterfall and a pool. When Florida was a territory, parties set out from Pensacola and St. Augustine, meeting in the middle of the future state by the tiny falls. So enamored were they with the spot, they decided the capital should be built nearby. Later, Union troops camped in the bottom of the valley. The pool became a trash dump, the stream diverted by man's desire to channel everything into tidy, efficient outlets. Now, the jail sat high on one side, Myers Park, with its canopy of oaks, on the other. The old power plant, red brick with a brick smokestack, sat on the southern end of the valley, and the shacks of Smokey Hollow marked the north, the fog and smoke from woodstoves resting like a blanket on the peaks of the metal roofs and trees. Fulton and Dreggors brought Miss Madgison her food then returned to their families.

XXXXX

Marlene was asleep. Fulton started breakfast—just eggs and grits, since they would probably stuff themselves worse than the turkey that Marlene would soon have in the oven. Marlene's sister was coming for Christmas dinner; so was Spence. He sipped his coffee and looked at the front page of the *Times-Union*. There was an article by Bill Dufour. About Ben Austin. There was talk he might run for the US House when his daddy retired. He heard Marlene wake up and carried in her breakfast.

She smiled, taking the tray. "Looks good! I forgot you knew how to do stuff like this," she said, teasing him.

"Haha."

She tasted the eggs. "Not bad!"

"Glad ya like 'em, doll." He figured it was the least he could do, bring her breakfast in bed, since she would be cooking and serving the rest of the afternoon. He looked at the boxes wrapped under the tree. Marlene's smile was the best present he could ask for.

66

Tallahassee
Wednesday, 12/26/1956

Miss Madgison remembered a phone number. They got her to make the call. She shook her head. "Out of service." Dreggors got her a room at the Southernaire in case Younkins tried to contact her. Fulton warned her that they had enough to send her to the new Lowell Correctional Institution for Women.

"How long?"

"Five years, I expect," Martin answered. The young woman shivered. She admitted she had been passing information to Younkins all along. She promised to stay at the hotel and do what they asked.

The manager let Fulton and Dreggors use an adjoining room, the windows looking out over the driveway and US 90. They could see who came and went and keep an eye on Madgison. They stayed put eight hours, waiting for Younkins to show. The lawmen drank coffee and waited. Madgison filed her nails and did her makeup and looked at television and bummed cigarettes from Dreggors. Fulton breathed their secondhand smoke and chewed peppermints.

"You reckon that heifer lied to us?" whispered Dreggors.

"No, I think this fella's real cautious."

"Reckon I oughta go get us some more coffee?"

"Sure."

After a half hour, Fulton heard a knock at the door. He peered through the curtains and saw Dreggors in his big hat, holding two cups from the lobby. "My nephew just told me something. I had him watching for cars at his fillin' station on 90—the one at the GEM Motor Court?"

"Uh-huh."

"Well, he just saw a black Merc'ry come in and fill up." Dreggors's "intelligence network." "I called Frank and got him to go out there. He was long gone. He called me back, cussin', tellin' me he had to miss half his lunch because of it."

Fulton laughed.

The phone rang. Mary Ann. She had a sixth sense of where to find Fulton. "Mr. Fulton, I got a call from a Jackie. She said you'd know her."

"Yes'm?"

"She said her husband had come by and got some of his clothes. She overheard him mention the Flagstone Motor Court. She thinks he's going there."

XXXXX

Dreggors had his foot on the floorboard, running eighty out of town. The clerk had a guest matching Younkins's description in cabin 14, at the back of the court. The man gave them the key to the room. Silently, they moved in on the cabin. The black Mercury was still there. Dreggors went around back with a shotgun in case anyone should come out the window. Fulton pushed the door open, pistol at the ready. His eyes scanned the dark little room, ready for a fight. Cook looked too. They saw no one. They went inside, Fulton training his pistol on the closet door. No one. He checked the bathroom. He holstered the Colt.

"No one's here, Will!" Cook hollered.

Fulton noticed the shower head drip. And then it dripped again. "Shower's still dripping. It's hot in here like someone just took a bath," he told Dreggors, who had walked in the front door.

"Yeah?"

"Towels are wet," said Fulton, feeling the white towel hanging on the wall rack. "So is this toothbrush. He was just here."

"Doggonit!" said Dreggors.

They went through the Mercury, from nose to tail. Cook looked in the trunk. "Hey, look at this."

"Yeah?"

"He's got a plywood panel behind the seat. Looks like a little access panel in the middle—" He stopped, pulling it open. "Look at this," he said, pulling out license plates from various counties in Florida and Georgia.

"Dadgum. Who is this ol' boy?" Inside the car, under the seat, were matches from the Aragon Hotel.

Carter arrived in his patrol car. Fulton dusted every surface of the Mercury; he shook his head. It was wiped clean. Dreggors went to talk to the clerk. He learned that a gray Chevy had been parked next to the Mercury.

67

Tallahassee
Monday, 12/31/1956

Carter's reserve deputies were watching the Jacksonville and Perry highways, his plainclothesmen at the bus and train stations. So far, not a sign of Younkins or the '55 Chevy.

The green and white flashed its headlights. It was Cook. Fulton rolled down his window. "We got somethin'. Follow me." Cook's Chevrolet roared away, flying down Tennessee Street, flashing red blinking and siren shrieking. They made their way past the detours out to the Perry Highway. No emergency equipment on the Ford; Fulton just hung onto the wheel, trying to keep up.

Cook cut his flasher and siren just west of the Chaires crossroads, by the Tung Oil works. Fulton could see the fencing, the large tanks, tall cylinders that held the oil, the structures rising in the shadows, the orange light of the impending sunset reflecting off the silver metal. Fulton's radio was nothing but static this far from the transmitter. Cook's brake lights came on; the patrol car pulled into the dusty driveway at the plant.

Cook paused for Fulton to come alongside at the edge of the groves. "True, I didn't want to draw attention to it on the radio, case our boy's listenin'. We got word from the manager at the plant. Someone saw the Chevy."

The manager came over to the patrol car with the witness, a fellow wearing a fishing hat. "I'm a retired cop from Savannah. I saw the Chevrolet described in the local broadcast you boys put out. It turned down W. W. Kelly. I didn't try to follow, but I thought I should call you fellas and let you know."

Cook fired up his car and picked up his handset, adjusting the knobs on the radio. "Bobby, can you see if the highway patrol has someone out this way?"

"10-4. I have informed Leon One," came the static-filled reply. Bobby meant he had called Carter. Cook dashed to the fourway intersection. The road to Chaires ran north; south ran W. W. Kelly. The deputy squealed his brakes, the car heeling over, turning south. The sun was going down, the road dark, a narrow path cut through the pines and saw palmettos, shaded by the oaks and Spanish moss. Fulton tried to keep up with Cook. He couldn't call anyone. Leon County's reception did not extend much farther than the crossroads, the frequency weak, the bent-up antenna on the Ford having little effect.

They came to the spot where W. W. Kelly crossed Tram Road. Cook cleared the intersection, continuing south on Old Plank. It was getting dark in the woods; Fulton tugged the light switch. Old Plank Road was once paved with logs from Newport to Tallahassee. The logs had long since rotted, leaving a bumpy narrow path of loose sand.

Fulton struggled to see, all the dust raised by the green and white. Cook turned left on Natural Bridge Road. Fulton saw a man loading a car with fishing tackle; he looked up, surprised by the headlights and fast-moving cars. It wasn't Younkins.

Cook drove toward the battlefield. There was a gray '55 Chevy not far from the entrance to the state park. Both men got out with their pistols drawn, walking over to check the car. No one was in it, the hood cold. "We need to call the sheriff, but my radio ain't workin'," said Cook.

Cook got in Fulton's car. They rolled toward the small obelisks that stood on either side of the road, marking the entrance to the park. Past the markers, a couple loaded their rods and reels into the backseat of a Hudson Wasp. Fulton stopped, watching. A man came walking out from the same direction as the couple. "That's him," said Cook. He had a fishing rod. He seemed relaxed. Then he noticed the Ford. His expression changed. He flung rod and reel and the fish he'd caught, running toward the couple's Hudson.

"We gotta take him, now," said Fulton, mashing the accelerator, the tires chirping as the car accelerated in first gear. "You! Get away from that car, and git your hands up!" hollered Fulton, pulling the handbrake and diving out with his shotgun. Cook was right after him with his Winchester pump.

The man dove into the car and started it. Fulton and Cook fired as the man accelerated toward them. Fulton dove into the saw palmettos as the wanted man tried to run him down, sideswiping the rear fender of Fulton's car, snagging the bumper, the metal groaning and squeaking, the red and blue paint mixing where Fulton's legs would have been if he hadn't moved. Younkins accelerated toward the entrance. Fulton hit a rear tire and shot out the back window, causing Younkins to run off the road. The car bogged in the wet sandy ground. He spun tires in the sand as Cook and Fulton sprinted after him. The couple took off running back inside the park.

"We can't let him git to the main road!" shouted Cook, blasting the Hudson with his shotgun.

Younkins saw he was stuck. He bailed into the saw palmettos, firing back and dashing farther into the woods. Cook could hear him running and fired into the pines. Younkins neared the two obelisks, heading back the way he'd come. Younkins ducked behind the monument and fired at Cook.

The couple lay on the ground, terrified. Younkins took off again, sprinting to get behind a large pine as Fulton and Cook closed in on the obelisk on the south side of the road. The lawmen dashed to the big pine tree Younkins had just left. Younkins hid behind another, banging away with his .45, the rounds hitting the pine bark, little pieces peppering Fulton's face like confetti, rounds whistling over the officers' heads. Fulton fired

347

back with his shotgun, buckshot peppering the pine tree the killer hid behind.

Younkins reloaded and fired again then ran farther into the woods. Fulton loaded two more shells into the coach gun. Cook had joined him with his pump-action shotgun as they gave chase deeper into the woods. They couldn't see Younkins; they could only hear him running. They ran for quite a distance, stopping to listen. The woods were nearly silent. Younkins stopped. They couldn't tell if he was in front of them or somewhere at their flanks. He fired again, the rounds passing over Cook's head. They heard a rustle as Younkins brushed the saw palmettos. They listened, hearing the killer take off again. He was moving toward the big monument and public restrooms in the state park—back toward Natural Bridge Road, which ran through the park.

"We can't let him grab a car. There might be more people fishin'."

"Yessir," replied Cook, alert and ready to do what had to be done.

Younkins turned and fired again. They could not see him in the shadows, but they could see his muzzle flash and hear him running away from the road again, deeper into the woods. They could hear the crackling as he stepped on the saw palmettos that covered the ground.

He paused to shoot at the lawmen. Fulton stepped behind a pine as a round struck, sending bits of bark flying, sap sticking to his sport coat as Fulton tried to shield his body behind the tree. The wanted man kept moving, cutting back toward the road. There was a station wagon pulling a little trailer parked on the edge of the blacktop.

Fulton took a step forward and fired toward Younkins's footsteps. He could see--out on the road--a man and woman crouched behind the car, holding on to each other. They had fishing tackle. The man dropped it and the large striper, the man's jaw open, shocked by what was unfolding. They didn't know which side of the car to duck behind, hearing shooting and running and hollering echoing in the woods. The couple had merely hoped to catch a few fish! Fulton motioned for them to get behind their trailer.

Fulton sprinted forward and crouched behind a large pine. He listened. There was hardly a sound except for a squirrel squawking, alarmed by the gunfire. The trees were getting black, the dusk magnified in the woods with the tall ceiling of pines. Cook reloaded. They heard movement, Younkins was moving around to the left, back toward the Ford and trailer. Fulton and the young deputy blasted away at the tree line with their shotguns. The wanted man rapidly returned fire with his .45 and headed back into the woods. The people were ducking behind the fender, their mouths open in disbelief over this battle raging on this hallowed ground.

Quiet again. Fulton and Cook listened carefully. Fulton motioned for the people to get out of there. He led Cook back into the woods, toward the spot where their suspect had fired last. They could see where their buckshot had hit the trees, and casings from Younkins's gun.

They took cover behind two pines and listened; it was hard to tell where sounds were coming from. A shot could ring out any minute; the suspect had the advantage. He could be hiding behind the very next tree for all they knew.

"Ha!" Deputy Cook jumped back at the sound of a squirrel scurrying up the pine beside him, the animal startled and confused by all the noise. The lawmen looked at each other, Cook shaking his head at how jumpy he was. The squirrel chattered away, disturbed from his nest by the gunfire. Just then, a twig snapped—up ahead. "Come on out! You can't get away in these woods," Fulton hollered.

Younkins was but yards away. He put another magazine into the .45. They heard it click. He soon found himself with his back to one of the sinks. He was disoriented in the thick dark pines, in front of the cool water of that pool. *Which way?* He listened too.

"Come on out a them trees, and you won't get shot!" came the same voice.

This hick cop isn't giving up. I may have to kill the SOB. He sank into the mud, trying to swim across in the darkness. He struggled to climb out on the other side, grasping the saw palmetto fronds. His pursuers were coming. He got to his feet and began running in his soaked clothes. He came upon another murky pool. He tried to skirt around the soggy edge.

The lawmen made their way around the large sink. Fulton stopped and listened. He heard splashing, struggling, somebody trying to move in the pitch-black; Fulton started moving forward again. Younkins had slipped into a sink and was struggling to get out of the deep pool of water.

Fulton ducked behind an ancient pine. Cook moved up to a tree just behind him. It was quiet again. A scaly lizard on the tree flicked his tongue and darted away, startling Cook.

"There he is," whispered Fulton, seeing the man crawling out of the water. "Drop that gun!" Younkins was trying to gain his footing and aim the pistol. He fired at Deputy Cook, narrowly missing him.

Fulton knocked the gun out of Younkins's hand. The fight was on, both men standing in the muck at the edge of the pool, both ready to see this long cat-and-mouse game put to an end. Younkins landed a hard punch to Fulton's head, holding a pocketknife in his hand like a brass knuckle. Fulton fell back into the saw palmettos and slid down into the water.

The wanted man dove for the gun lying in the dirt; prone, he aimed at Fulton, ready to kill him. Deputy Cook lunged for him, wrestling with the young killer; the suspect drew back his fist, hitting Cook in the face with his augmented hand, knocking him back. The killer hit the lawman again and again as Cook tried to get up, tried to push himself back. He ended up with his back against a tree. Younkins lunged for him, grabbing a hold of the black-haired deputy, raising him up, beating his head against the tree trunk until Cook was knocked unconscious.

Fulton recovered his senses, got to his feet, drawing his gun and firing a shot at the again-fleeing murderer. Younkins forgot his gun; he took off running as fast as he could. Fulton propped the unconscious Cook against the tree. He checked to see if the young man was breathing. He took off after the suspect. Younkins had just tried to beat a law officer to death. He had to be stopped.

They ran through the brush and palmettos, down to the St. Marks River. Younkins was running like it was the Olympic 100 meter in Melbourne. It took every ounce of wind for Fulton to keep him in sight. Younkins sprinted through the pine straw and sharp edges of the palmettos, jumping over branches and fallen limbs. The river was in front of them. A bull gator grunted and splashed into the water.

Younkins paused then took off running along the riverbank. *I can't let him get back to the cars*, Fulton thought. *If he gets one, I'll never catch him.* He was moving quickly. Fulton leveled his pistol again, firing, the shot echoing in the night air, the expansive forest, the round creasing Younkins's shoulder. The killer knew he had nowhere to go. He stopped, his back turned to Fulton, thinking of a way out.

"Git them hands up!" Fulton hollered, advancing with the revolver trained on the bad man's chest.

"You shot me. Why'ja wanna do that? You were chasin' me. Ya scared me. I didn't do anything," said the man, taking rapid breaths.

"I'm fixin' to shoot ya again if you don't get them hands up, and this time I won't be so careful where I aim."

Slowly, Younkins turned around and raised his hands in the air. "I didn't do anything. I didn't know who you were, just some fella shootin'—no uniform. You never said who you was."

"Get movin'." Fulton, breathing heavy from running, held his pistol on him, marching him back toward the road. His heart was beating fast; he felt pains in his chest. He felt he might pass out. He looked around. The people in the trailer had driven away. There was no telephone out there. It was completely dark. He made Younkins sit down on the road and cross his legs.

Younkins watched Fulton gasping for breath. "What's the matter, cop? Outta shape?"

Fulton's chest felt like it was in a vise. He gritted his teeth and kept the cocked gun on Younkins. About ten minutes later, he saw headlights coming down the road—fast. Red light on top. It was a sheriff's car. Another car was right behind—the state trooper.

The bright lights enveloped them, the lead car pulling beside Fulton, and a familiar voice he heard—Sheriff Carter. "You glad to see me?"

"You know it," said Fulton, still breathing heavy. "We gotta get Cook. He's hurt. Will you stay with him?" Fulton nodded toward the suspect.

"Yeah, son." Carter trained his carbine on Younkins's middle, while Fulton and Weiss went to get the downed deputy. The sheriff waved the barrel of the gun. "Look here, you try to get up, and I'll put a hole in ya, stick some antlers on ya, and hang your head on the wall in my office."

Fulton found his shotgun along the way and Cook's gun and the young deputy under the tree just beyond. They got him on his feet and walked him back to the road. With Cook coming to in the backseat of the trooper's car and the prisoner secure in handcuffs, Fulton got some water from an old wellhead where you raised the handle to turn on the water. He was muddy, his clothes torn and dirty, his tie nearly off.

"Now you didn't have to go to all that trouble. Get yo'self cleaned up and slicked up like 'at in anticipation of seeing me," said the sheriff.

"Yeah," gasped Fulton. "I must be a sight...but I got the ol' boy."

"Yeah, you did. Another Southern vict'ry right here in these woods!" Carter laughed, slapping the trooper on the back. Weiss helped take the names and addresses of the witnesses and put the owners of the Hudson—still shaken—in his car with Cook. They put the prisoner in the backseat of Carter's car. Fulton rode beside the killer on the way to the jailhouse. The car had no cage. Fulton's heart was still beating fast. It felt like a fist squeezing his insides. He wiped some of the dirt from his eyes with a handkerchief.

"You got my whole backseat muddy and smelly, son. I reckon I'm gonna have to get it cleaned. The county commission's probably gonna have a dang fit."

"Yeah," said Fulton with a chuckle, silently enduring the pain. He kept a careful eye on Younkins, his index finger on the trigger of the Police Positive.

"Well, it can't be helped. We fixin' to take a ride to the county." Carter raced back to town on the Perry Highway. He turned onto Gaines. Across the street was a row of shiny GMCs, the trucks sparkling in Carter's headlights when he pulled up to the jail. Younkins remained sullen, calculating. *He's a smart one*, Fulton thought.

"Well, we gonna have to book him in, son. I got to call ol' Thurlow and wake him up to come down and fill out the form. Now I got to listen to the

351

ol' boy complainin'. He's terribly ornery when he don't get his forty winks."
Carter brought the jailer down from his second-floor quarters.

"What the hell is goin' on, Frank? I'm coming already! Give a fella chance to
wake up! Dadgum!"

"We got some work for ya. You can go back to sleep in a minute," taunted
Carter, walking with him down the hall.

Thurlow had pajama pants on and a wifebeater undershirt, and he'd put
his fedora on his head, down over his eyes. "You damn right I'm goin' back
to sleep." His eyes were sunken in his face, highlighted by dark circles that
looked like mascara. He was fifty, a little heavyset, and the top of his head
bald.

"Hell, it's only a quarter 'til eight. Why you gotta go to bed so damn early?"
asked the sheriff.

"I've gone to bed when the sun goes down all my life. That's how it was on
the farm. You get up at four in the morning, work three hours before you
see the sun, and you're in bed when the sun goes down. Wasn't no
'lectricity. No entertainment at night. You worked, then you went to bed.
But then you wouldn't know about work. You never did none a that."

"I wasn't around when Florida seceded neither. You ain't gotta be up at
four no more. Who says ya got to?"

"I get up and help the missus feed all these yea-hoos you got here." With
his giant key ring, he opened the doors for the booking room, and the
trooper shoved Younkins inside and into a chair. The jailer got out some
forms and a ball-point pen. He stood over his table, arranged his forms,
and began to fill it out. "What's your name?" he asked gruffly. The prisoner
said nothing. "So we got a friendly one, ay?" asked the jailer, turning to
Carter.

"Maybe it's the way you ask, Jim."

"This is as good as I get this time of the night. *What's your name, hoss?*" he
repeated impatiently. Silence again. The suspect glared at the sheriff and
Fulton, who stood by silently, pistol in hand, his arms crossed as he leaned
against the wall, watching.

"Yeah, neither one of ya are night people," said Carter. "Me, I'm pleasant to
be around all the time."

"You're full of horse manure all the time," replied the jailer, who happened
to be the sheriff's second cousin. He left to open the doors for the
photographer. The latter appeared momentarily, dark fedora, pajama top
tucked into his trousers. He set up his camera so they could photograph
the killer. The jail's camera was broken, and there was no money to get it
fixed.

352

Mr. Nash loaded film and screwed in a flashbulb.

"Look at the camera," barked Thurlow.

"I know the drill, mister."

"Good, then I won't have to tell ya."

The photographer snapped the mug shot. The suspect turned to his left.

"Hey, Fulton, ya got a light?" asked Thurlow. Fulton handed him the Zippo while Nash put in a new bulb and snapped the side shot.

"Good night, boys," said Nash, leaving as quickly as he'd come in.

"Good night," said Carter.

"Still won't tell us your name?" asked Thurlow.

"You figure it out, buddy."

"All right. Fingerprint him and send him back to his cell," said Carter.

Fulton rolled the killer's fingerprints on a card. The prisoner held his hands stiffly but more or less cooperated.

After Younkins was locked in a cell, Fulton pulled a small envelope from his pocket. "Some stuff I picked up out there." They emptied it out on the table: .45 shell casings, brown leather wallet. Carter looked through the expensive billfold. "He tried to throw it in the woods when I got him," Fulton informed them.

"We got his IDs here," said the sheriff, pulling them out of the wallet. Fulton took them. Florida and Georgia driver's licenses in the names of "Graham Forrest, Kurt Jensen, James D. Boyette, Plummer Younkins."

Mary Ann came down to the jail when she heard that they'd got their man. She was as happy as the rest of them. "You want to know his record?" she asked.

Fulton nodded. "Let's send the teletypes."

"This late?" asked Carter.

"Yeah."

"What's the matter, you tired?" asked the jailer.

"Don't you worry about my lack of sleep, son. You can go to bed now."

"Oh, thanks," replied Thurlow.

"Come on. I'll drive ya over there then," said Carter.

"If it's no trouble, I appreciate it."

"I'm just missing a nice dinner, that's all. Fried chicken tonight."

"You have fried chicken just about every night," said the jailer.

"Ya dang skippy," said Carter. "While you snorin' away, I'm eatin' my supper."

"Bye," said the jailer mockingly.

"Pleasant dreams, son."

At 8:30 p.m., Carter drove Mary Ann and Fulton to the Sheriff's Bureau. The secretary helped them look through the Raiford files, sitting on the old orange crate she used for a seat. "There's nothing on him, not under any of those names," she told them.

"Well, he's never been to the big house then," said Carter.

Mary Ann sent teletypes to the GBI and the police departments in Atlanta, Jacksonville, and Tampa and to Hillsborough sheriff, Ed Blackburn.

"We can go home now?" Carter asked.

"Yeah."

"You sure? 'Cause if there's anything else you need, son, now's the time. Once I get into Miss Myra's fried chicken—hot or cold—I ain't gonna be disturbed shorta that ol' boy getting loose from his cell or something serious like 'at."

"Okay." Fulton laughed.

"Now you go home and get Miss Marlene to fix them cuts you got and get you some soap and haul out the washtub," said Carter, slapping Fulton on the back. "Take it easy now, son."

Mary Ann got in her car. Carter waved to her as she drove off then reached for the door handle of his Chevy. He looked back at the porch. Fulton had turned white, collapsing to his knees, dropping his bottle of nitroglycerin. "Hell's bells! What's wrong, True?" Carter ran to catch him from falling on his face; gently, he laid him down on the porch. Carter ran to his patrol car and called Bobby. "Call Culley's, send 'em over here now!" He ran back to Fulton. "You gonna be all right, son!" he exclaimed, distressed at seeing Fulton like that. He'd seen only one other person have a heart attack—his daddy—and the elder Carter didn't make it.

354

68

Tallahassee
Monday, 12/31/1956

New Year's Eve at the hospital. Three car wrecks. A brawl. Brains pickled by a copious amount of who-hit-john. One fellow jumped from a second-story window at the Elk's Club, thinking he could fly. A patient on the fourth floor under the influence of too much "Auld Lang Syne" flooded his room, which in turn flooded the entire hall. As if that wasn't enough, in walked a deputy sheriff with a concussion. The hospital was full of walk-ins, accident victims, and sick folks that had to be moved from rooms that had an inch of water on their floors. The janitor was busy with buckets trying to bail it out, and more patients were arriving.

Dr. Clayton took a puff on his cigarette and started to throw it away. "Here comes another one," he sighed, watching the long Packard drive up Miccosukee Road, siren blaring.

"Don't waste that. I'll take this one," said Elston. Linton backed the ambulance in, the siren slowly winding down after the driver switched it off, the emergency light flashing on and off, giving a strange red glow to the ER's entrance. Linton's son was using the only medical equipment they had—oxygen—and trying to keep the patient alert by talking to him. Linton swung the back door open, and an orderly helped him pull the stretcher out. Elston approached. "What the hell! True?"

XXXXX

Marlene flung the door of the car open and ran into the building. The young nurse, intently filling out her forms and trying to keep up with the onslaught, didn't look up. Marlene continued down the hall to the Emergency Room desk. The nurse's back was to the desk, the tired woman pouring herself a coffee.

"Where's True Fulton? I'm his wife."

"He's in the morgue," said the nurse, stirring the cup.

Marlene nearly cried. She fought back the tears. "What?"

The nurse turned around. "Oh no, Mrs. Fulton! He's fine. Dr. Elston has him in his office. He's just putting in a few stitches. I'll show you the way."

XXXXX

Fulton woke up with Weiss at his feet smoking nervously and Elston leaning over him with forceps and gauze, cleaning wounds on his forehead. "This can't be good," said Fulton, a little woozy.

356

"You're right, I've only had one other patient wake up on my table," said Elston. The ME had brought an ECG down, the wooden box sitting on the table. Fulton could feel all the wires attached to his body. "Your heart sounds fine. How's your head feel?"

"Hurts."

"Well, I'm pretty good at sewing. I think these stitches will hold. We'll need to keep you overnight. I'll get you a room when they dry one out."

"Aww, Doc, I'm all right," said Fulton, trying to sit up.

"Now that's why I like my regular patients—they don't give me any arguments."

"I'm okay," said Fulton, getting up off the table.

"Take it easy now."

"You listen to the doctor, Truitt Fulton, or I'll knock you silly myself!"

It was Marlene! "Yes, ma'am."

"So stubborn!" Marlene kissed him on the uninjured side of his head. She looked at his cuts and the bandages. Tears ran down her cheeks; she left the room. That was the one time he'd seen his wife cry, full-on tears and all. She was always brave, even when he'd been shot—perhaps more so than he. Marlene came back in. "I thought I lost you. I don't ever want to feel like that again."

He put his arm around her. "I'm fine, baby."

"That's what you always say," she said, smacking his arm lightly. She turned to Elston. "Are you sure he's going to be all right?"

"Well, I've never had a patient come back and complain yet."

"Your patients don't come back at all," said Fulton, chuckling.

"Yeah, I guess they do have a rather low recovery rate."

"Y'all stop!" said Marlene, scolding them. "I suppose you're all right, if you can cut up like that. How long's he gonna be here? A long time, I hope?"

"He was having chest pains. I think it was that arterial spasm again, but he needs to see a cardiologist. So you should plan on stayin' a while," he said, turning to Fulton.

"How's Cook?" asked Fulton.
"He's fine," replied Doc. "He asked Nurse Jones to the movies, if that tells you anything."

357

A nurse brought a tray of food, including key lime pie. Fulton tasted the pie. "Not bad—want the rest?"

Marlene snatched the fork away and took a bite. "You make me so mad I could spit."

69

Tallahassee
Friday, 1/4/1957

Click-click-click-click-click. In came the teletypes. Boyette was his real name, place of birth New Orleans, according to Chief Canefield's kickback.

"Another stone to turn," said Martin, looking at the rap sheet. They'd send a separate communication to the New Orleans PD.

Fulton stayed out two days. He was moved to a room, Marlene with him every minute. She fell asleep holding his hand, her legs stretched out on a chair. At 9:30 p.m., the telephone rang. They looked at each other quizzically. "Who could that be?"

"Mr. Fulton," came the familiar—but unknown—voice. "I heard about the arrest you made. I'm impressed. I hear you're doing better. I wanted to wish you a speedy recovery."

"Thanks."

"You'll want to speak with Ben Austin's former secretary—she talked to your suspect. And she took a message from Jo Ellen when she called Austin at his office."

"What's your name?"

"You'll meet me soon enough." *Click.*

XXXXX

At 3:00 p.m., Fulton dressed and walked out to the taxi. Darley drove him to the jail. Cook was back, his head bandaged. "Your wife know you here?"

"Never mind that," said Fulton.

Cook had the teletypes. "His record from Jacksonville: Assault. Gambling. Arrested for rape, but the charges dropped. Atlanta: Assault, Petit larceny. Tampa: Breaking and entering, assault, peeping. No convictions. Hillsborough SO has a couple aliases: Graham Randolph, Graham Fenderson," he said, reading from the paper. "New Orleans, he's got an arrest for assault. Skipped bail on that charge in forty-eight."

Fulton called Canefield. The chief informed him that Boyette had been arrested in Saint Augustine. Gambling offense in 1952. The St. Augustine PD didn't have a teletype, so Canefield called down there when he learned that Younkins—Boyette, whomever—owned a house in the old city and a coupe de ville registered in St. John's County.

Boyette had a key to Bowmans Motor Court. Carter checked the room. He called Fulton from the court. "He's got $7,500 cash in here. No wonder he can afford a Cadillac."

The jailer led Boyette into the interrogation room. Fulton entered with Dreggors. The special agent had a thick manila folder under his arm. He sat down opposite the prisoner. "We went to Jacksonville. We got your record from there, from Atlanta, Tampa, you name it. We know who you are, Boyette. We know everything about you. And we know what you did to the Harbert girl."

Boyette smirked.

"You think you're pretty smart. But we got you. We know what you did."

"You ain't got nothin' on me. I won't talk. I won't crack. You hear me, cop?"

"You'll crack, and you'll talk," Fulton said calmly, quietly. "You act tough because you ain't done any hard time. We'll send you to Raiford for motor vehicle theft and attempted murder of two law officers. That'll get you fifteen, twenty years." The suspect remained sullen, arrogant. "What do you think, Will?"

"Well...maybe fifteen, yeah."

"You'll be wearin' lipstick in three months," said Fulton, smiling. "A man as purty as you."

"Listen, I—"

"Shut up," said Fulton, smacking the table.

"I'd like some water. I ain't drank anything all day," said Boyette, looking at the men.

"They'll paint you up with mascara and pass you around," continued Fulton.

"I'd like some water. I'm thirsty, I tell ya."

"Shut up. You better start talkin', or it'll be a long time before you see any water."

"Who were you working for?" asked Dreggors.

Silence.

"Who's your contact here in Tallahassee?" asked the chief deputy.

"I'll tell you who it is," said Fulton, looking the killer in the eyes. "It's Carlton Lanier. We're wise to ya. Start talkin'."

360

The suspect looked away. *I won't be made to talk. They can only ask so many questions before they take me to my cell and I'll call my lawyer. I know the score.* The suspect began edging off the side of the chair. Fulton grabbed him and yanked him back toward the table. *What the hell?*

"Get it through your head! We know you were in town November second, fifty-three. We know you arrived on the *Gulf Wind*. We know you left the depot in a '49 Ford. We know you were up on North Monroe that night. The night that Jo Ellen Harbert was murdered. We know you were in her car, you beat her, you shoved a bottle in her mouth. You let her car roll into the trees. You killed her! Now start talkin', Boyette. We know ya did it!"

Fulton getting so physical took the man off balance, but he quickly recovered. "Y'all ain't got nothin'!"

"We know you left town on the bus the morning after. The clerk remembers you buying a ticket on the Dixieland route. Ticket to Jax. You made an impression on her—handsome fella, nice suit. She thought you looked like that movie star. Remembered a bandage on your face, below your right eye. I see you got a scar—below your right eye."

"What of it?"

"She hit you with the dish, didn't she?" said Fulton, putting a photograph in front of the killer. "She got it the day she came to town at the Standard Oil station."

"You're nuts. I got that a long time ago, fightin' the gooks."

Fulton pulled out another photo. "Your booking photograph from the Saint Augustine PD: December 17, 1952. No scar on your mug. We got you. They'll give you the chair, boy. You ever think about that? What that must be like? Think about it."

"I don't have to think about nothin'. I don't have to say nothin'."

"Sure, you can sit there and act like we're a bunch of idiots down here. But you know I'm talkin' sense. You tell us who hired ya, and we might get ya life instead of that appointment with ol' sparky down at the state prison."

"I got the word of a couple cops for that?"

"Look, if ya play it straight with us, we'll be straight with you," said Dreggors. "Life is a long time, but it sure beats getting it that other way."

"Neither one a them that good."

"No, but it's always easier on a man what comes clean," said the chief deputy.

"Y'all ain't got nothin', I tell ya!"

"Sure, keep thinkin' that. Keep thinkin' it right up to when they throw that switch," said Fulton.

The suspect scoffed at that.

"Sure, go ahead and laugh. You got one chance to tell us what you know. You killed that girl. You got one chance to show you deserve some leniency. Now get with it!"

The suspect turned away again. Fulton slapped a photograph in front of him. "Look at her. You like killing a pretty girl? You like beating them? No, you like raping them, is that it? Yeah, you look like the type. Maybe little girls? You know what happens to guys like that in the joint?"

"Shut up! I ain't never touched no kid!" he roared, lunging at Fulton, his hands out to grab the lawman's sleeve.

"Sit down!" Fulton ordered, slugging him in the chin, sending him falling over the chair and onto the floor, the little space in between the table and the door. "Get back in that chair!"

"You socked me, you sure enough socked me," said Boyette, rubbing his chin awkwardly with the bracelets on his wrists.

"You just sit there. We ain't through. I gotta calm down before I really lose my temper with you, Boyette." Fulton picked up the photo again. "This is what she looked like to her friends and family. Look at her! This is how she looked when you got through," said Fulton, dropping the autopsy photo on the table. "You wouldn't even know her. That's what you got paid to do, wasn't it?"

"You don't know nothin', pal."

Cook came to the door; he had something for Fulton. The special agent left the room. The prisoner turned toward Dreggors. "What the hell's with him?"

"That's just him. Now's your chance to he'p yourself. The guys you're protectin' ain't gonna do the time for ya. Look, you got a girl or somethin'?"

Boyette smirked.

"All right, maybe you got a few of 'em. Use your head. Ain't no chance of holdin' a woman in there. Only thing you get are letters or visits across a table. After a while—ten years, fifteen years—they stop comin'. Women wanna be held. They don't want a man they never can touch without a guard saying something."

"I won't be anyone's *lady friend* in there. I don't care what he says."

"Maybe," said Dreggors, looking up at the ceiling, exhaling smoke from his cigarette. "I seen guys go in there tough—like you—but they all come out old men, gray hair, hollow eyes. I tell ya, ten years made 'em look like they went away for thirty."

"They won't make a jail wife of me, no sir!"

"I hope *not*," said the chief deputy.

Boyette relaxed his clenched fists and leaned back in the chair, tipping back to the wall, the corner that seemed to close in on him.

"Yeah, relax a little. We still have our questions. We gotta do our jobs, see?"

"Sure."

"You from Lose-ee-anna, right? You got family?"

"Just my mother. One brother. Old man died a couple years back."

"How old was he?"

"Forty-seven."

"And you're twenty-six now? You got a lot a years ahead. You need to think about that. You cooperate, we can talk to the state's attorney."

"I ain't talkin'. I don't have to say nothin'. I keep clammed up, and that friend a yours ain't got nothin', see? I was in Korea—name, rank, serial number. I know the drill."

"I was in Korea too. In the army. What about you? Army?"

"Army, yes, sir."

Fulton opened the door. He set a glass of water on his end of the table. Boyette's lips were dry; he began licking them, looking at the water. Fulton sat at the end of the table, staring at the young killer. "I just got off the phone. You like living it up, parties, good booze, expensive suits. Detective in St. Augustine says you just got a new Cadillac. I wonder how a guy supports all that with no education, no skills?"

"What would you know about it? My family's got plenty of dough."

"It's gonna be rough, going from all that to a cell at Raiford...on death row."

Condensation dripped down the glass of cool water. Boyette could hardly take his eyes off it. He reached toward it.

"Not yet!" barked Fulton. "The Jacksonville detective tells me you're a real ladies' man. You like Bay Street, upstairs rooms over the Ajax bar. Got girls at practically every whistle-stop from the River City to Miamuh. Yessir, a ladies' man," said Fulton, smiling. "And just like I thought—he said you enjoy hurting them. You're a *sadist*. That's the word, ain't it, Will?"

"Yeah."

The suspect rolled his eyes.

"You think I don't know what I'm talking about. But you better listen. I do this for a living, and I know what I'm talking about. I know who you are, what you are, and what you've done. So unless you start talking, things are gonna start happenin' real fast, and you ain't gonna like the place you end up."

"I ain't confessin' to nothin'. I ain't even confessin' to bein' in this room. I was out there in the woods hunting, minding my own." He turned to Dreggors and motioned with his hands toward Fulton. "This ape comes up there with a gun. I didn't do nuthin'. He starts shootin' at me for no reason."

"I take it you were huntin' elephant with that .45 then?" Fulton replied.

"Whatever you say, chief," Boyette spat out.

"We know who the Chevy belongs to."

Boyette smirked.

"You think Mrs. Conley isn't spilling her guts out?"

His face turned white.

"Yeah, like I said, we know what we're talking about. Think about it." Fulton opened the door. "Get him back to his cell," he told the deputy.

"How about that water, friend?" asked the suspect.

Fulton picked up the glass and flicked its contents against the wall.

The two lawmen walked out after the prisoner was removed. "Damn, son, you seem so easygoing and even-tempered all the time. You were scarin' *me* in there."

"Let's have some coffee." It was 2:35 a.m.

XXXXX

They walked back to Boyette's cell and had the jailer open it. "All right, wake up," said Fulton, yanking him from the bed. "Let's get him in the interrogation room."

"What's the idea? You gotta let me sleep. Shoot, you can't go at me all night. I know the score."

"Shut up," barked Fulton.

"I got my rights protected by the Constitution a these United States," he said in mocked seriousness.

"You'll be afforded your rights, you'll get a trial a lot fairer than the chance you gave Jo Ellen Harbert, and then you'll get a free bus ride to the state prison." The deputies took him back to the interrogation room.

"I ain't no lawyer, but I know I can have an attorney if I want one. You ain't denyin' my rights to phone my attorney, are ya?"

"You want a phone book?" asked Fulton.

"I wish you'd take the cuffs off me for five minutes, and you'd see where I'd put that phone book."

"I'll take the cuffs off, and he can leave the room," Fulton replied, nodding to Dreggors. "Still want it?"

The prisoner glared at Fulton.

"Will, why don't you go get some air?" said the lawman, watching the young man's face. "No?"

Boyette looked away.

"Yeah, I thought you might change your tune. What happened to the guy that was there a minute ago? That talked so big? You're real tough with women though, huh, Boyette?"

"What *were* ya doin' out in the woods, Boyette?" asked Dreggors.

"Well—I was fishin'."

"Why did you start shootin'?"

"It was the moccasin—I was shootin' at that. You boys didn't see it?"

"Afraid not," replied Fulton. "I guess we're done for now. Deputy Raffield, you wanna step in here."

The deputy came in with shears and a paper envelope.

"Say, what are ya doin'?"

"We need a lock of your golden hair," Fulton told him. Fulton got in the car. His chest hurting, he drove anyway. They were too close to stop. Fulton drove the hair to Elston's house, knocking on the door.

"Who the devil can it be!" Doc hollered.

"I don't know," said Mrs. Elston.

"Aww, hell," said Doc, peering from the window. He opened the door, wearing a T-shirt and his drawers, a cigarette hanging from his mouth. "Let's go to my office. You look like hell. You shouldn't be out of bed." Doc cussed and grabbed his trousers and a shirt and got in the car with the Sheriff's Bureau man, speeding along the vacant streets to the deserted hospital, the parking lot dark and empty.

Doc switched on the light in the morgue, and Fulton handed him the hair they had in evidence. Doc prepared a slide. Fulton gave him the clipping from the jail. The doctor prepared a second slide. He leaned over the microscope. "So maybe they struggled in the car, he leaves a bit of hair," he said, studying the slides.

"Yeah, that's what we think."

"Umm-hmm. You got a cigarette? I forgot mine."

"No."

He frowned and looked up. "In any event, it's a match."

XXXXX

At 5:30 a.m., Dreggors wanted to take a break. Fulton waited with him outside, the big fellow going through three Chesterfields.

Marlene pulled up in the DeSoto. She wasn't mad. She hugged Fulton. "I know you're going to keep going until this is done. But please don't overdo it."

"I won't, baby."

"Call me, and I'll come pick you up."

366

70

Tallahassee
Saturday, 1/5/1957

They took another break at 10:00 a.m. They had him brought back to the interrogation room. They walked in, finding Boyette dozing in the chair. Fulton shook him by his shoulder. The suspect woke, lunging at Fulton. The lawman grabbed him by the collar and slammed him against the wall. "You want to take a poke at me? Be careful what you wish for."

"Look, he's crazy, you know he is. Get him outta here, will ya?" he said, pleading with Dreggors.

"I am crazy. Crazy enough to believe that girl didn't deserve what she went through with you. I think maybe I slam your head against the wall a few times until you know what she felt."

"You can't do that. The law doesn't let you do that."

"What? There's a law that says you can't have an accident and hit your head? There's a law that says we can't defend ourselves if you attack us in close confines?"

"I'm so tired. I'm so tired."

"Who paid ya?" demanded Fulton.

"You got a chance. You can help yourself out, son," said Dreggors.

"I-I-I don't. I ain't talkin'."

"Who wanted Jo Ellen dead? What did she know?" asked Fulton.

"I ain't gonna—I'm so sleepy." He began to nod off again.

"Wake up!" barked Fulton. "We ain't through. You got one chance. That electric chair ain't gonna wait for you to take a nap."

Boyette smirked, the expression on his face hiding none of his thoughts— that Fulton was a stupid hick cop and beneath him. "I want a lawyer, understand? You can't keep me here forever."

"We'll keep you here as long as we need to," replied Fulton.

"We know you were in town November second a fifty-three. We have two people that put you on the train from Jacksonville," Dreggors told him.

"We know Lanier paid ya. Here's the bank records," said Fulton, laying them in front of the prisoner. "He withdrew $2,000 the day before you got to town. We know you talked to Austin's secretary around the same time.

Get wise. They won't protect you. You think the Austins would spend one night in a cell if it came down to them or you? They'd sell their best friend."

Silence.

There was a knock at the door. The deputy handed Fulton an envelope containing a typewritten report from Elston. "We got a match on your hair that was found in Miss Harbert's car. ME ruled it a match. Whaddya say to that?"

"Lots of people got blond hair. I'd like to see you make that stick."

"We'll make it stick. Look here—more bank records. Your friend Lanier took out another $1,500 two days before Wallace Paxton's living room got splashed with gasoline. How about it?"

"I don't know no Wallace Paxton."

"We got a witness that'll say otherwise."

"Look, you got me on assault. Yeah, I took a shot at ya. You got me in town three years ago. But nobody's pinnin' a murder on me. Prove it, I tell ya. Prove I did it. I ain't talkin'. I ain't no stool pigeon. I'll take my chances on assaultin' a coupla cops. That's all you got that can stick," he said, sinking to the table, exhausted.

"So you're saying you tried to kill me and Cook?"

He looked up. "I wished I woulda run right over you two big ugly sons-a-bitches."

"And you shot at me?"

"I sure did."

"And you missed—didn't you?"

Boyette let his anger get the best of him. "Yeah, and it bothers the hell outta me that I did. You damned hillbilly cop."

"All right, let's get Mary Ann over here." She was at the office and drove over. She typed the statement. Fulton read it back. "All right, sign it."

The suspect signed the paper, then flung the pen against the wall.

"So you ain't confessin' to nothin', huh, tough guy?"

Boyette spit in Fulton's direction.

"Get him back to his cell," barked Fulton.

Two deputies dragged him down the hall and shut the door behind him. Boyette collapsed to the concrete floor.

Dreggors walked out with Fulton, breathing the cool, fresh air outside. "I guess we done for a while."

"Yeah."

71

Tallahassee
Wednesday, 1/16/1957

Another trip to Miami. He boarded the *Gulf Wind* alone, in pain. He returned feeling even worse. Too close to stop. Darley let him out at the telephone company in the old Supreme Court building. The gals brought out the records for long-distance calls from the booth on North Monroe. He looked them over. Calls to Jacksonville and Tampa. Pay phones.

XXXXX

Monday. Wilkinson made no effort to hide his annoyance. "So I'm having to clean up your mess, Fulton. Attempted murder of a police officer. Phone calls about your gunplay out at the state park. We've imported you into our city—people are wantin' to know are we importing a bunch of crimes right along with you. This Boyette wasn't wanted for anything locally—wasn't a suspect in *anything* except this supposed plot to kill Miss Harbert—and you got to go after him with a gun!" He shook his head.

Fulton laid out the whole case. "There was something in the past that tied Jo Ellen to the Austins."

"Okay," said Wilkinson, reluctant but listening.

"Ben went to school with her, yet pretended like he didn't know her."

The prosecutor shrugged.

"Then there's the matter of the strange photographs, the basement, the identical butterfly in the Austin mansion."

"They could have got that thing in a yard sale."

"But they didn't. His mother got that in France. It was in the paper."

"Even so, there are probably a hundred houses with basements in the city."

"Ninety-two. And the Austin's is one of them."

"There's no evidence the Austins are into anything illegal. No reason why they'd kill this girl."

"We got his uncle tied to bolita."

"You have no proof of that."

"Recordings from Paxton's office," replied Fulton, laying the reels from the tape recorder on the desk. "He calls a mechanic at Lanier's. They talk in code—it's about the weather. Raining or sunny. Took me a while to figure it. Some days it would correspond, other times it would be sunny outside, and he'd talk about rain. Then I followed the trucks—tracked some of the money pickups. Got the photos right here. Paxton was in bolita up to his neck. So was Lanier."

"That may implicate *Paxton*, the mechanic—but not *Lanier*, not *Austin*. I can't go around accusing men like that. Lanier's from a good family. He owns two or three businesses. Ben's the most highly-regarded lawyer in town."

"We got their associate, Boyette, ID'd by four people. All his contacts with Lanier are in my report."

The lawyer flipped through the pages. "What else?"

"Bank records. Lanier took out $2,000 the day before Boyette arrives on the *Gulf Wind*."

"Circumstantial. He owns businesses, what were his expenses? His purchases? How do you know the money wasn't for some repair?"

"No one I talked to remembered him making any big purchases."

"Still, he owns businesses, a home. There's always expenses. Last week I had to reshingle my roof. Cost three hundred dollars. I couldn't prove that now if I had to. I paid cash. The money doesn't link Boyette to the Austins at all. No evidence putting the money in his hands."

"He bought a diamond watch in Jacksonville a week later. Here's a statement from the jeweler. Five hundred and seventeen dollars. Here's his tax return. He paid twenty-three dollars in taxes last year."

"Maybe he's a tax cheat. Doesn't prove he murdered for the Austins or even has any dealings with them."

"Boyette is related to Alton Austin. That's his uncle."

"So?"

"We got Alton Austin at meetings where Boyette and Lanier are present."

The lawyer shrugged. "There's no crime in being kin to Alton. Frank here is related to him."

"Lanier matches Mrs. Davis's description—the heavyset man at Jo Ellen's house. That was the same time someone rifled through Jo Ellen's office."

"You got a fat guy wearing a suit that may or may not have tossed the office. Could be a lot of people."

"No, sir. The links are there. We have Boyette in town the day someone tries to burn Paxton's house. We got Lanier withdrawing cash—fifteen hundred—just two days before. There's more—"

The lawyer ignored him, turning to Carter. "Why's he even in on this?" Wilkinson asked, nodding in the direction of the special agent. "Couldn't your department have cleared this up?"

"My boys don't have as much experience working a 'who dunnit.'"

"Huh?"

"A homicide with no suspects at the scene," answered Carter.

"I see. Well, it's still a *whodunit*. I'll repeat, we don't have direct evidence that either Lanier or Austin was involved."

"We got the busboy that saw a man matching Lanier's description drop off something—possibly a bottle of whiskey—at the Cherokee. According to the kid, she threw away that bottle, still full, later that day."

"Meaningless. Let's focus on Boyette. You say he killed her."

"Yessir."

"I've looked at your file on him. There is no direct evidence to substantiate your *theory* that he murdered Miss Harbert."

"We got a hair test."

"Inadmissible. Look, we don't have anyone saying this is homicide. You want me to go to the jury with Elston saying he thought it was an accident?"

"He really didn't say that."

"He can't say *anything*, that's the problem. Cause of death. I'm certain you've heard that term before and know what it means in a murder trial. Look, nothing ties this boy—Younkins, whatever his name is—directly to Miss Harbert."

"The ID's. We got Mrs. Talken on the train. She puts him in town for the murder."

"So you got a blond fella on a train, but it's hours before the crash, miles away from the scene."

"We have the manager from the Ship Lantern."

"Who was romantically involved with your boy. What else have you?"

"Mr. Alcott. He played cards with our boy."

"So he played cards. What else?"

"Travis from the freight office."

"You want me to base a case on that? A *colored* man."

"I've known Travis my whole life."

The prosecutor raised his eyebrows, as if to say, "And?" "Any defense attorney worth his salt is gonna tear your case to shreds. First of all, you have a victim that liked to bend her arm."

"But was sober for five years."

"Well, you put her history of alcohol use in front of the jury..." He shook his head. "Jurors here are decent folks. They're not going to like a lush that comes over here, driving recklessly on our roads and gets herself killed. I'm sorry, it's not enough. I think we have better things to focus on. You know the Austins, you're close to being part of their family, Frank."

"She had a family that cared about her too," said Fulton.

"Sure. I just don't want us wasting our time. I think you boys spent a lot of time on it. You did good with what you had. But any more time spent on this thing is gonna be counterproductive. Don't you agree, Frank?"

Carter shook his head. "If it's a homicide, we investigate it until we figure out who done it."

"It's an irresponsible fishing expedition," Wilkinson retorted. "I have real responsibilities for law enforcement in this town. Now, I need to get going. If you men will excuse me?"

Carter started to say something, but Wilkinson cut him off. "You can investigate all you want. I'm not filing charges." He stood, gesturing toward the door. "Good day, gentlemen."

Carter, face reddening, rose to his feet. "Grant, you wanna crush an ol' boy for running a stop sign or stealin' a pack of cigarettes, but let a bunch of crooks conspirin' murder go on about their business."

"All crime's serious—if there's proof of what was done. Do you disagree? You let people get away with running stop signs and throwing newspapers on the sidewalk, pretty soon you'll have no-tax whiskey proliferating, pickpockets and professional gamblers moving in. People will wake up to bars and dirty movie shows on Tennessee Street and whores walking down *Mun*-row—a dadgum carnival of crime! And they'll wonder what the hell happened to their town, who the hell let it happen! It ain't gonna happen while I'm the chief law officer around here."

Carter was livid. "Now you wait a minute," he said, pointing his finger. "You ain't the chief of nothin'. You don't have cases to prosecute unless my boys bring 'em to ya."

"And no one gets prosecuted unless I say so," said the lawyer, raising his voice.

"Shoot!"

"And we don't let some outsider from Jacksonville come over here and decide to railroad the leading citizens of this town. Now, if you'll forgive me, I have Rotary," he said, picking up his jacket.

"Don't forget, you gotta go in front of the people, just like the rest of us! Don't forget that! Let's git the hell outta here!" roared Carter, reaching for the door. Fulton followed him out.

Wilkinson shook his head, shutting his door and pouring himself a glass of whiskey.

XXXXX

Fulton stopped at Los Robles. Judge Anderson's house was in the English Tudor style—elegant, but not ostentatious. Mrs. Anderson welcomed Fulton inside and brought coffee for the lawman and her husband. They chatted for a few minutes. The woman left, leaving the men to discuss the legal matter that was obviously on the detective's mind.

The judge led him into his den, a room with high ceilings, timber beams, a fireplace, and overstuffed leather furniture. He had a gun cabinet with glass doors and an old grandfather clock in the corner. It was quality, but not so you couldn't live there, not dainty. It was comfortable, masculine. The room fit the judge's personality completely.

Fulton settled into one of the big armchairs and explained the entire case to the judge. Anderson sipped his coffee. "He's right, True. I hate to agree with him. But I'm afraid it's not enough to get past a judgment of acquittal. The coroner's jury found there was no foul play. Elston would be honest— he cannot give an opinion that this was homicide. You've got to find the motive. That, I think, will be the key to successfully going after the Austins, Laniers, whomever."

374

72

Tallahassee
Monday, 1/28/1957

A tearful Mrs. Younkins begged for mercy for her husband. Anderson twisted the cap on his fountain pen, listening. "All right, thank you, we'll come back to this."

The Harberts watched from the gallery—the same seats as the inquest. They wondered what Anderson would do.

He waved for Wilkinson to proceed. The prosecutor made a skillful argument for the forfeiture of $200 seized from a moonshiner. The hearing concluded, and the arraignments began. It was a full docket—five felony defendants. Two pled on the spot. The courtroom emptied out after the thief and the colored moonshiner were sentenced.

Fulton walked in, taking a seat beside Janine.

"All right let's go back to *State of Florida vs. Boyette*," said Anderson. Wilkinson announced the terms of a plea. Anderson's brow wrinkled. "How long?" he demanded.

"Five years."

The judge waved for the prosecutor to approach. Old Man Ingleside came up as "friend of the court."

They talked for several minutes—Anderson forceful, Wilkinson getting frustrated. He hoped to wrap the case up before lunch. Ingleside was nodding and offering suggestions. Finally, Wilkinson relented. Ingleside talked to Boyette at the table while Anderson left the courtroom. The old man whispered to the accused, "You'll be out in four. You don't want to go to trial with Anderson." Boyette nodded.

Anderson returned presently. Wilkinson announced the terms of the deal as if the previous scenario never occurred: ten years in Raiford. Boyette was led away; he looked back at his wife and laughed.

Harbert shook Fulton's hand. "*Criminal* justice," said the old man.

"Partial justice. We know who killed Jo Ellen—just not why."

XXXXX

Fulton wore a Centel uniform. He wired a bug into the telephone booth. He got back in the truck. He had to return it to Carter's cousin. Fulton came back in the Ford, parking in front of a little house off Lang Drive. The real estate agent—another cousin of the sheriff—let them use the vacant home. Fulton retrieved the heavy suitcase from the trunk and carried it through

375

the back door of the house, setting up his equipment. He could see the gas pumps and the phone booth from the window. He didn't have to wait long. Here came the familiar coupe.

Lanier dropped a dime and dialed a number. Fulton put on his headphones to listen. "This guy's sure stirring up some trouble."

"Fulton's from some of that *hardworkin'* white trash down in Eastpoint," said the other man sarcastically. Fulton recognized the voice—none other than Grant Wilkinson.

"We got any other loose ends?"

"One."

What does he mean by that? thought Fulton.

73

Tallahassee
Tuesday, 1/29/1957

Fulton's telephone rang. He recognized the voice. "I'd like to meet with you. Someplace private."

"Okay."

"I'd prefer to be as discreet as possible."

"Sure."

"Centennial Field in a half hour?"

"Fine."

Mr. Yancy slipped out the back door of Leon High. He got in his car, looking around, making sure no one was watching. It was eerily quiet. A semi broke the silence, the staccato diesel beat that poured from the open stacks sounding a little sinister as the Peterbilt shoved its way past on Highway 90. Quiet again; the teacher started his four-year-old Ford and drove down Franklin Boulevard, taking side streets down to the ball field.

Fulton walked over from Gaines, the ball field just around the corner. From the back door stoop of the house, one could hear the games, practically watch the outfielders at work farther down the hill. Fulton looked around; there were no cars. He walked through the opening in the fence. The grandstands were empty. He heard brakes squeak as a car slowed, very slow, as if they were looking for something. Fulton watched from behind the corner of the fence. The car was a Ford—plain. It took off.

Fulton found a seat. He heard a car pull up along Bloxham Street—another Ford. He could see a man behind the wheel; the fellow got out, walking hurriedly toward the entrance of the ball field. He wore a windbreaker, tie, and a ball cap; he spotted Fulton and smiled, climbing up into the bleachers. Fulton chose a spot where they would not be visible from the road, under the covering in the cool shade.

"You a ball fan, Mr. Fulton?"

"I am. You're the coach, the high school baseball team."

"That's right. Football too."

"You sent the pictures?"

"I did. I think you know from whom I obtained them."

"Austin."

"From his trash. You may ask why I would be going through Ben's trash, and that's all right. I want to tell you a story."

Fulton nodded.

"Voncille and Brock Austin have always been important boosters. Especially when their boys went to Leon and ever since. Ben is an alumnus, of course. He was a heck of a pitcher. Needless to say, the Austins have a lot of pull at the school. Ben was Jo Ellen's boyfriend for a while—in college. I was a student there. This was right after the war."

"Uh-huh."

"So Jo Ellen gets a job at Leon. Ben's still in school. They have a falling out. It's not long after that there's rumors of a party, Jo Ellen drunk, carrying on, taking her clothes off."

"Yeah?"

"I knew her. She wasn't a lush. Someone was really trying to make it look that way."

"How do you know?"

"I saw Carlton come up to the school and meet with Dr. Truston. I heard them mention pictures. I knew Ben was behind it. His uncle has always run interference for him."

"Okay."

"Truston said she could either leave town quietly, or there would be a firing, a scandal. So she left. She disappeared, really. I never heard anything about her. Not until her death."

"Do you know why the Austins wanted her out of town so badly?"

"She kept a journal. Wrote in it religiously. I bet the reason's in there."

"Mr. Yancy, were you ever romantically involved with Ms. Harbert?"

"You get right to the point." He shook his head. "Sure, I was interested. She always said no. She said she needed time because of how things ended with Ben, and the boyfriend she had after that—both of 'em treated her badly was what I gathered. She was cautious after that."

XXXXX

If only I could piece together what was in her journal. Got to find that book! Fulton telephoned Mrs. Lindgren. "Is there anything still in the office? Any of her things?"

378

"I don't think so."

"May I look?"

"Surely."

Fulton drove to Fort Walton. He parked on Main Street. He looked around, turning things over. He even checked behind the Art Deco lamp shades on the walls. It was all very curious to Lindgren. There were two desks in the office. Fulton opened the drawers.

"There was a drawer that I never could open. Jo Ellen locked it, and we just left it. That's right, that one," she said.

Fulton removed a tool from his pocket and had the lock open in short order. Nothing.

"Well, I didn't think there'd be anything," said Lindgren.

Fulton began feeling underneath the drawers of the large desk. Nothing. He took everything out of the middle drawer. Lindgren looked at him like he was mad. He pulled it all the way out and examined it. He turned it around, looking at the back panel. Taped to the back was a key.

"Well, what in the world!" declared Lindgren.

"What do you wanna bet that goes to a safety deposit box?" said Fulton, his Hank Williams smile broad on his face.

Fulton raced to Crestview. He slid to a stop in front of the bank just as the manager was locking the front doors. The manager was a little perplexed but agreed to take the strangely-behaving man back to the boxes. "There it is, number 14!" Fulton inserted the key. It was rather stiff. Would it turn? *Click.* The box unlocked. The manager pulled it out. Fulton didn't even wait for him to set it down. He grabbed the little booklet from inside.

"Much obliged!" he said, dashing out to the Ford. The journal had been copied on a Photostat machine:

zzzzz
24 August, 1947

We went to St. George's Isl., Ben's uncle took us on his boat. Ben, Clay, and I. We camped there. We found bullets from the Air Corps gunnery range, when the pilots practiced there. Quite a few cattle on the island. No houses, except the old lighthouse keeper's place. We had lots of fun. Ben said if they ever built a bridge over, it could be some kind of place, like Coney Isl.! His uncle brought this Cuban rum—in copious supply, I might add. We roasted a chicken and drank and danced.

We ended the trip in Carrabelle, at a house. Spent the night. More rum. It was fun until it came time to leave. It turned out that Ben's uncle really didn't know the owner of the house—and the man was coming back! Ben insisted we go. He was acting crazy! He insisted he drive my car. I thought he shouldn't. He was drunk. I was so drunk I fell right to sleep. I woke up when Ben slammed on the brakes. He hit a man! He was still alive, but barely, they stood around him, not knowing what to do. It was awful! He was a deputy sheriff. I saw the motorcycle he was riding. Ben must have been speeding, must have came upon him too fast and clipped the back fender of the motorcycle. They were scared. We argued about what to do. They decided to leave him. I screamed for them to go get help. They made me get in the car. His uncle said I better not tell! They took my car to his shop and I never saw it again!

XXXXX

29 Feb., 1948

I said I'd tell what happened. They went to my boss. Either I leave Tallahassee or the pictures get out. No one will believe me! Ben took those pictures, when we were alone. I didn't know he was taking them. It wasn't at a party, in front of people. But no one will believe that. They own this town. His uncle reminded me that it was my car that hit the sheriff. I don't know what to do!

Zzzzz-end

Fulton knew who the deputy was. He gave the operator the Apalachicola number. Lexie Fulton taught at Chapman High and knew everyone in the county. "Well, hello, son. I was just about to go outside and bring in my washin'. You doin' well?"

"Yes, ma'am. And you?"

"Just fine."

"Mom, does Clara Jamieson still live in Apalach?"

"Oh, no, son. You know, she came back here for a while. About four years ago. Then she took off again."

"Do you know where?"

"No, I sure don't. Her oldest daughter got married and moved to Panama." She meant Panama City, Florida. "I know she had cousins in Eastpoint. I can ask of her."

"Would you, Mom? I'd really appreciate it."

"You bein' good to Marlene, son?"

380

"Yes'm, I try."

"My brother sure tried to solve that case. He never could find who killed that boy."

"No, ma'am."

Fulton called the Franklin County clerk and Sheriff Marshall. To the dismay of both men, the Jamieson files were nowhere to be found.

74

Tallahassee
Wednesday, 1/30/1957

Fulton called Bill Dufour. "What do you know about Austin? Finances, things like that."

Dufour nearly dropped his pipe. "Uh, okay. Wow. You wanna know about that, huh?"

"Yeah."

Dufour coughed. "True, I can't talk about this over the phone. I can meet you somewhere. Umm, out by the dam, maybe."

Fulton looked at his watch. "That far?"

"I'm serious, True. This is heavy stuff."

"Okay, okay," replied Fulton, relenting. "I'll meet you out there."

XXXXX

The reporter tiptoed though the woods, the pines like shadowy awnings overhead. He found a spot by a clump of live oaks along the riverbank, on the bluff. There was no one about. Not one fishermen. Not a single worker in the windows of the red-brick powerhouse nor the walkway over the dam. He lit his pipe, comforted by the solitude; he listened to the birds, the water cascading down the face of the dam, as the Ochlockonee flowed gently past. Perhaps a few deer were watching in the woods that surrounded. He chuckled at that prospect nervously.

He watched warily as a gray sedan slowed to a crawl in the middle of the little Highway 20 bridge downstream. It was too far to see who was inside. He ducked behind a low-hanging branch. He breathed a sigh of relief; the car was moving again. He heard an outboard motor on the lake. He listened to it, louder and louder as it approached. Thankfully, the boat turned, the motor fading into the distance.

Snap! Someone was there; he was certain he heard a branch break! He turned around, nearly dropping his pipe. A black form was moving in the shadows. "Bill Dufour!" It was a very deep, ominous voice calling his name. "Bill Dufour!"

"Uh, who-who's out there?" He saw the shape move closer, through the trees. He thought about running. That's when he heard snickering. "Doggone it, True! What the heck's wrong with you?"

"Sorry," replied Fulton, laughing, pulling the collar of his coat back down.

Dufour was wearing a ball cap and a ridiculously large quilted coat. Smoked glasses that he'd probably picked up while a correspondent in the Pacific Theatre a decade ago completed his attempt at incognito. "My disguise didn't work at all, did it?"

"No, sir."

Dufour puffed at his pipe nervously, shivering in the cold.

"So, about Austin—"

The man put his finger to his lips. "Shh. Ya gotta whisper, True. Dadgum!"

"Okay."

"No one knows where Austin got his campaign money, True."

"Was it that significant?"

"He outspent Howerton five to one. Not just mailers. All them TV ads— practically every station in South Georgia clear to Jacksonville. They cost money."

"Sure."

"His family owns a lot of land. But they don't have cash flow. They owe a lot of taxes on those properties, you see? They own a business or two, but they don't generate much income. Not much *cash*. Ben does, maybe, one big case a year? See the problem?"

"Yeah."

"Don't repeat this, but I know for a fact that he didn't touch any of his stocks during the time he ran for office. Not one share."

"Oh?"

"I got that from someone that handles his account. Please, do not reveal that."

Fulton nodded. "So where do you think he got it?"

"Has to be bolita. I've heard things about his uncles for three years. Ever since Carter raided the Johnson farm and sent him and his brother to Raiford. Lanier can be ruthless when it comes to his nephew. Watch out."

XXXXX

Carter leaned back in his chair, holding his coffee cup. "Be careful with Austin."

Fulton nodded.

"He ain't dumb. And his money buys him a lot of friends. He can make things rough for us all if we get cross ways of him. He inherited a million dollars worth of stock from his grandmother. Every now and then he'll sell some—oh, to buy that Lincoln a his or that house down at Alligator Point. He don't have to work and doesn't for the most part. He don't 'practice' law in the true sense of the word, not like someone practices something and really works at it. But he knows how. It's funny how he can get the court system turnin' for him when he wants it. He knows his hocus pocus, what to say to a jury. But that's all window dressing. He knows how to get up under it and grease those ol' gears—get the result decided *before* he walks into court. It's knowin' everybody, and it's money."

Fulton nodded.

"I played football with his older brother, Henry. We graduated Leon together. All of us was in the same company in the army. So was Grant Wilkinson, Carlton Lanier."

"Oh?"

"Yeah." Henry's killed in Okinawa. Ben pretty well avoided the front lines, despite the ribbons the newspaper likes to talk about. His contribution to the war was in the way of morale-boosting activities, you might say. Always had a poker game going, always had a line on gettin' the boys whiskey. So he was popular, stayed drunk most of the time, and came home with about ten thousand in cash. He was always Brock Austin's son. Never could tell him nothin'. When we got sent to Korea at the end of forty-five, for occupation..." Carter paused, chuckling. "Son, you'd never know it the way ol' Ben sits at the front row of our church, but he spent most of his time in a monkey house—whorehouse. Him and Lanier set it up near our base. Now, Wilkinson was too pure to go up there. He did his share of drinkin', but no whores. But Ben, the boy practically went AWOL. He spent most of his time over there. Then we come back, all of us come back from the great World War II in our nice uniforms, and they pat us on the back, and it was time to start paying bills and raising kids. Hung up my uniform, put away my captain's bars, and I was pumpin' gas at Dan Johnson's fillin' station before I got hired to ride a motorcycle, writin' tickets and collectin' rent for Chief Jarvis. But Ben was the big hero in the papers."

75

Tallahassee
Saturday, 2/2/1957

Fulton watched as the Eastern Airlines Connie lifted off the runway and faded into the gray sky. He didn't want Marlene in town for what was coming. The Laniers and Austins were laying as low as the paver bricks on Monroe Street. All they did was go to work and church and stopped using the phone. Calm before the storm.

Southeastern Telephone Company was installing new phones in the Midyette-Moor building, going from office to office. Fulton put on a uniform and rode over in the work truck with the sheriff and Carter's cousin, the foreman for the company. "They just finished up the sixth floor," he told them, pulling to the curb on College Avenue.

"Don't worry. He won't be in today, son," assured Carter, letting Fulton in the back door, the special agent making his way through the dark passages inside, entering Austin's office. He worked quickly. He put the bug behind the barrister's bookcases. Carter's cousin helped string wire all the way to the courthouse using the telephone poles, running it into the sheriff's office. Fulton had but one more connection to make.

XXXXX

The governor stopped at Grant's Furniture across the street. People gathered around. Including Austin. Ben shook Collins's hand and did a little politicking with Saturday shoppers; that finished, he crossed the street.

"Oh, shoot!" exclaimed Carter, watching from Bennett's. He rang the telephone in Austin's office—the signal for trouble. Fulton heard the elevator coming. He hurried, pulling the wires through, taping the microphone.

XXXXX

The ornate brass doors of the elevator opened, and the lawyer stepped off into the small vestibule. Austin reached for the doorknob for his office; it was unlocked. He pushed the door open and looked around the unlit space. *That's right, the phone company was in here.* He looked at the new phones, retrieved a tumbler and his bottle, and settled into a chair.

XXXXX

Fulton breathed a sigh of relief, watching from his hiding place on the landing. He continued down the stairs with his tools, passing the men working on the third floor, out to the crowded sidewalk.

XXXXX

Austin poured himself a second whiskey; he hadn't turned the lights on. Sunlight illuminated a square in the corner where the blinds were halfway open. His campaign posters hung in the shadows.

XXXXX

They could hear Austin's secretary, Laurel Krenn, come in, flip on the lights, and begin typing. Fulton turned on the Revere reel-to-reel tape recorder they'd borrowed.

Austin barely greeted the secretary. He certainly didn't thank her for coming in on a Saturday at a moment's notice. He cussed to himself and crumpled the small pink paper with the telephone message, angrily tossing it in the trash can. Drink in hand, he watched Krenn through the open doorway as she leaned over her typewriter with a pencil in her mouth and a half-smoked Pall Mall in the ashtray beside her. Krenn examined the work—yes, that was how you spelled *Ochlockonee*. She resumed punching the keys on her IBM Model A electric; it was much better than the manual machines Krenn relied on as a young typist, but one mistake, and the entire document may as well be deposited in the large metal wastebasket beside her desk.

Efficiency was the hallmark of Mrs. Krenn. Ben listened to the steady *tick-tick-tick* of her typing, watching her, an efficient automaton, completing her task. She was the perfect secretary. She made no mistakes that he could see. Perhaps she made mistakes in her personal life, in her youth, but none showed in her work. He looked at her, for the first time considering that she was more than "equipment" for the office. That perhaps she had feelings, dreams. She dressed attractively: mauve long-sleeve blouse and a gray skirt. It was the first time he'd noticed what she wore. Her dark hair she'd pinned up. A few streaks of gray were present, but her figure was still good. Nice shape to her hips, her shoulders; she was undoubtedly a looker fifteen years ago. He wondered if she was happy. He finished his drink.

In a moment, she'd bring the paper for him to sign, and she'd drop it in the mail slot out in the hall, and the letter would fall to the brass box that was built into the wall of the ground floor foyer, ready for the postman to collect. It was all so perfect, wasn't it? Perfection was possible; he was a witness to it. Ben wondered if there could be a perfect crime. He had defended criminals; it seemed they always got caught sooner or later.

Krenn brought him the letter, correspondence on behalf of Talquin Electric. He signed it and told her that was all he needed done, that he was going out. He left without further explanation and shut the door behind him. *Gotta get outta here. I'm thinkin' too much.* He looked back at the smoothly polished oak door, the frosted glass center with gold lettering: Law Offices of T. Benjamin Austin, Esq. He smiled.

A corner office in the Midyette-Moor building evidenced his success. It remained the tallest office building downtown. His could look down on the

386

busy College-Monroe intersection, the activity that flowed past on those brick-paved streets, politicians walking to the Floridan Hotel, the shoppers circling to find a parking space. A block from the courthouse and little more to the Capitol, it was at the center of life in Leon County.

From the landing he could see clear to the flatlands of the Gulf of Mexico. He let his hand graze the smooth handrails as he wound his way down, floor by floor. He walked outside, down College Avenue. Some men were loading a chair into the back of a wood-bodied station wagon at Grant's. The slam of the tailgate made him jump. The sidewalk was steep. Ben descended beneath the four large windows that defined the first floor of his building. He was startled by the "Ow!" that came from the open windows of Dr. Strong's office a few floors up. He was startled again by jackhammering at the old employment office, the place coming down to make room for a parking garage. He turned down Calhoun.

He didn't pay attention to the man getting out of the car. "Howdy, Ben!"

Startled, the lawyer turned to look. It was Fulton! "Uh, hello. Sorry I didn't return your calls. It's been hectic in the office. Getting new phones and all."

"That's all right."

"Have you...have you learned more about the case?"

"Boyette gave up some information. It's led us to a new suspect. Someone from her past. Someone with skeletons. And I think she knew where those skeletons were."

"Who?"

Fulton opened up a peppermint. "Don't know yet. But I'll figure it out. I'm patient."

Ben looked away at the half-demolished wall of the employment office across the street, the telephone repairmen loading their equipment on the back of a Chevy truck.

"You have a nice day, Mr. Austin."

"Yeah, sure. You too."

XXXXX

Everywhere Austin went—to lunch at Holland's, to the country club, even to the Jitney Jungle—Fulton was there in that Ford, saying, "Howdy" and talking to him about what a nice day it was.

Ben drove home to South Ride. He sat by the pool and got himself liquored up; every few minutes he'd peer around the corner of the modern ranch, looking to see if Fulton's car was there. Then he'd pour another drink with

387

unsteady hands. At 3:00 p.m., he noticed Fulton's car was gone. It was his chance to get out of the house. He was going stir crazy!

He got in the Lincoln, racing down South Ride, turning onto Meridian Road, down the treacherously narrow two-lane at breakneck speed. He slammed on the brakes to turn down Bradford.

The tires squealing, the car leaning over, he turned onto Monroe, racing away from town. He crossed the county line. He slowed and spun the wheel over, bouncing down the long dirt road. Ben's family had enlarged the river house several years ago. It was a place for family gatherings, a place to hunt, drink, and talk in private, away from the help—and the law. Ben had hunted in the woods near there more times than he could count.

Ben pulled behind the house. Entering through the back door, he found his uncle Alton—gray hair, wire glasses, and a fresh jar of moonshine— seated in a wingback chair, his head bowed, in front of the large fireplace and his favorite dog. The mantel was bare, a large beam thicker than a rail tie ten feet across. When the family gathered for Christmas, Uncle Carlton would have the kids hang their stockings from that mantel, and they'd all go to the kitchen and get cans of Jax Beer and cookies to leave for Santa on the big coffee table adjacent the fireplace.

"That big cop, Fulton, has been following me too," said Lanier.

"Every time I turn around he's there. The fream. Every time I go buy a pack of smokes. Or open a can of beer. Or go see Sally, that son of a bitch is there in his hat, chewing his damn peppermints," said Ben.

"You sure he didn't follow you just now?" asked the elderly man.

"I'm sure. He left my street. Didn't see him after that."

"He had to leave town apparently."

"Yeah?"

"Yeah. I still got a guy watching 'im. Just called me. Let's get you a beer," said the fat man.

"I'll get it," Ben replied, getting up and walking in the kitchen. He came back with a can of Jax. "He's been asking about Hattie. He's asking people why she left town, *all of a sudden-like*," said the lawyer, mocking Fulton's accent.

"I heard. Ol' Billy Davis said Fulton was asking about her," said Uncle Alton.

"I'm worried about that," replied Lanier.

"We need to meet with your pappy. I hear Fulton has been asking questions about him too," said Alton.

"You know Dad won't want to get mixed up in this."

"Yeah, my brother-in-law has to keep his hands clean. But if this thing gets out of control, he ain't gonna smell like no Dove soap neither," said Lanier.

"Can't we get Carter to influence Fulton?" asked the old man.

"Yeah, you'd think the high sheriff would play ball with us," said Ben.

Fulton could hear it all—faintly—over the crackling speaker in the car. He was getting pretty good at electronics. He'd replaced the antenna with a big one from Ramm's Radio Shop on College Avenue. The car looked like it could pick up stations from Alaska. Posing as a TV repairman had worked nicely.

XXXXX

Ben left, driving down the dirt road under its canopy of oaks. His heart was beating fast, like that time Claiborne almost caught him with Sally, and the lady had to climb through the window. No sign of Fulton. He neared Monroe, dark from the tall pines.

"Son of a—!" Headlights! Coming out of the little dirt road that veered off to the neighbor's—Fulton! Ben pulled over, waving the Ford around. He lit a cigarette, his hands shaking with rage. The lawyer cussed and flung the cigarette to the ground. Fulton waved as he passed, smiling. The plan was working.

XXXXX

Voncille Austin telephoned the sheriff. She asked him to come over right away. The young black woman opened the door for the sheriff when he arrived. Mr. Ben Senior (Ben's grandfather) was sitting in the back parlor, looking at television. The colored woman led Carter down the hall to Miss Voncille's Florida room.

"Ida, get the sheriff some coffee," ordered Mrs. Austin from her throne-like chair.

"Yes, ma'am."

"How are you, ma'am?" asked the sheriff cordially. She waved for him to sit down opposite her on a shorter chair. His leather belt squeaked, and he awkwardly squeezed in with the Colt holstered at his hip. He wore his black windbreaker and a plain tan shirt.

"I wanted you to come here and explain why you're investigating my son—why your office and this Agent Fulton are accusing my boy."

"Fulton's been gathering information. He ain't accused nobody, Ms. Austin."

"Gatherin' information? From whom?" protested Mrs. Austin. "Jail trash and negroes?"

"Anyone that knows something, I reckon. But like I said, it's an investigation. True ain't accusin' nobody."

"Well, you see to it that he *doesn't*. Who is this Fulton anyhow? I hear he's from Jacksonville. What's an outsider coming here, stirring all this up?"

"Miss Austin, Fulton's a good man. He's just doin' his job. He'll find out who did this, and these questions right now will be forgotten."

"We don't betray family. We don't let outsiders come in and tell us how to live. That isn't how things are done. Tell this Fulton to lay off my boy."

"Yes'm."

76

Tallahassee
Thursday, 2/7/1957

The Austins couldn't make a move without Fulton showing up. It went on for a week.

Ben whirled the Lincoln down Lakeshore Drive, stopping at a white two-story colonial. He tried the door. No one was home; he forgot Alton was in Atlanta. Ben got the bottle from under the seat; he sat on the lawn behind the house, drinking and looking out at the water. It was dead quiet along the shore. His uncle had just built the pretty home. There were hardly any neighbors; the lake looked scarcely different, Ben was certain, from the time Indians built burial mounds around it and the first Spaniards explored the hilly landscape that would become Leon County. Ben eyed the johnboat tied up at the dock. It might be nice to fish a little.

Ben had a big trial tomorrow. This business with Jo Ellen would take care of itself. He walked back to the driveway. He took another swig and put the bottle away; he felt better. He cussed as he noticed the blue Ford approaching from down the street. Fulton stopped, waving for Ben to pull out.

Angrily, Ben stomped the gas, the car bouncing where the driveway met the street, squealing tires as he headed toward Monroe. He turned left, careful to avoid speeding down the hill with the blue Ford in his mirrors. He stopped at the Standard Oil at McCord point—he looked out at both roads—Thomasville and Monroe, the oaks that spread out behind the filling station, shading both routes as they ambled north to the capital's sister cities. He could take one of those roads and be across the state line, and this would all be over. He cussed. A young man filled the Lincoln with .29 gasoline. He noticed Ben smelled of booze and offered him some coffee. Ben declined. "I'm fine," he muttered. He tossed the kid seven bucks and drove home.

Ben slept poorly. Despite the good rye in his belly, he kept waking up, tossing and turning, going over the "problem" again and again. He shaved and dressed and went in to work.

"I have a message for you, Mr. Austin," said Krenn. "And I poured you a fresh cup of coffee."

"Thanks," Ben said tersely. Next to the coffee cup was a message—another one from Fulton. *Damn!* Usually, he'd ignored problems and they'd gone away, worked themselves out. Not this time. He crumpled the message and tossed it in the wastebasket, on top of the last one.

He walked to the courthouse, making it there by nine thirty as Judge Baker had wished. He met his client—old lady Patterson—and tried the case. He walked back along Monroe, smiling. Fulton pulled up to "congratulate" him, and his hands began shaking again.

Ben drove to the old Coca-Cola bottling plant on St. Michael—a brick, two-story, Art Deco structure. His uncle just got a new sign for the place. The shipping company was doing well—supplemented by bolita money they laundered through his accounts, of course. Ironically, all this took place in the "All Saints" neighborhood. Some of the little houses around there dated to the 1860s.

Men were unloading boxes from a delivery truck. Lanier painted his trucks green, since his main competitor used brown. He normally worked out of the second-story office. Ben went up the front steps. The foreman was inside, looking over a clipboard, rifling through papers. "It ain't on here, son," he said, handing the clipboard back to the driver. "Oh, hiya Mr. Austin!"

"Lookin' for my uncle."

"He ain't here. Reckon he's at the shop."

Ben got back in the car and drove around the corner to the body shop on South Macomb. One of the guys worked a grinder over the fender of a poor, wrecked Buick.

"Hey, Benny, how's my handsome nephew?" asked Lanier, slapping him on the shoulder.

"Worried."

"Yeah, ain't you a little brazen driving down here?"

"I don't know, he might have my office wired. Look, see his car up the street."

"Yeah, that cop. I'd like to..." He let his sentence trail off. "Anyway, let's ignore him. What's up?"

"He's found Hattie. She didn't say anything. She called from a pay phone and let me know. But he found her. That son of a bitch found her. I don't like it."

"Me neither. I'll call someone. Uncle Carlton will take care of it."

"If she wants more money, I'll pay."

"She's a good girl. She'll do right by ya."

XXXXX

392

Voncille Austin instructed her driver to park at the curb alongside the Lewis State Bank. He squeezed the long car into the spot, jumping out to open her door. In hat and gloves and a navy Dior suit, she stepped from the Cadillac and over to the bank's side entrance. She ascended the stairs and pushed the door open. She walked right past the secretary, flinging Wilkinson's door ajar.

"Are you going to let these Jacksonville types walk all over us?" she asked, dropping her purse in a chair.

"No, ma'am."

She rearranged his lamp, moved a file, and pulled a chair close to his desk. "Is he deciding to prosecute people on his own?"

"No, ma'am."

"Frank isn't helping at all. He's taking Fulton's side. Has that hillbilly cop got you by a bit and bridle?"

"No, ma'am. I'm the chief law enforcement officer in this circuit."

"Then act like it."

XXXXX

Wilkinson dialed the sheriff. "Hello, Frank. Do you have a minute?"

The sheriff told him he did and would be right over. Carter walked in, set his hat in one chair, and settled his frame into the other.

"Coffee?"

"Sure."

Wilkinson poured two. Carter thought the lawyer seemed tense, the lines on his forehead deeper than usual. "I'm sorry about the other day, Frank. I can be a little—well, arrogant. I know it. But I think we both gotta get our hands off this tar baby. People are cornerin' me about this at the country club. I don't have to tell you the Austins are one of the oldest families in Tallahassee. They started the biggest bank in town. They helped fund the library. Heck, they opened the movie theater I used to go to when I was a kid. They're not a gang of criminals."

"I know all that. I grew up with Henry same as you."

"Well?"

"I think he should lay off too. I'll talk with him."

"You'll tell him to lay off?"

"Yeah."

Wilkinson relaxed. "I'm glad to hear it. Smoke?"

"Thanks," said the sheriff, accepting a Fatima.

"I'm getting calls from people—folks you and I grew up with. They're concerned about someone coming here from outta town, running roughshod over people that have been here their whole lives. I'm sure Fulton was a good cop in Jacksonville, but this isn't the same thing. We don't have murderers on every corner. We got folks that grew up together and care about one another and care about their town." Wilkinson lit his cigarette and inhaled.

"I see what you're sayin', but True's a good man. He ain't really an outsider. He's from Eastpoint, probably knows as many people up here as I do. Shoot, he's a sorta hero to a lot of people down in Franklin."

Wilkinson scoffed at that. "Well, that explains a lot of things—if those folks like him, there's gotta be something wrong somewhere."

"Huh?"

"I'm sorry, I know he's a friend of yours. But people are concerned—people that vote. Folks are going to start hearing about this case and wondering why the taxpayer is on the hook for Fulton's joyriding."

"There's probably not much of a bill. Hell, True's driving his own car half the time. They ain't got much money to work cases over there."

"Well, if he doesn't want to be reasonable, we can cut that down even more. If he wants to help his bureau, he's got to play ball. I've already talked to Collins. There's plenty of folks that feel we don't need to be giving power to an agency that's not accountable to anyone. If Fulton's not careful, the Bureau's opponents will fan those flames, and he'll be out of a job. I think the Bureau's a good idea. I really do. And if Fulton wants to be reasonable, so will we. Or he can go back to shuckin' oysters. His choice."

"Now wait a minute—"

"He can go back to it and leave law enforcement in this circuit to me—"

"Now hold on—"

"*And you*, of course—the people *responsible* for it. We understand what matters to our community. He doesn't."

"I'll talk to him. Is that all?" Carter was angry, more so because he thought Wilkinson was right and Fulton was stirring the pot a little too much.

Carter dialed Fulton's number. "Maybe you oughta take it easy on this for a while."

"He had her killed, I know it," Fulton replied.

"Wilkinson's saying he's gonna go to the governor about ya. That he'd cut ya off at the knees."

Fulton laughed.

"Ol' Wilkinson ain't no fan of yours, son."

"I know."

"I tell ya what, I was 'bout ready to jerk a knot in that boy's tail," said Carter. "Arrogant cuss. *Chief law enforcement officer.* Shoot!"

"I'm not worried about him."

"Anyway, something to think about."

"Okay."

"It just stands to reason."

"What's that?"

"What I keep tryin' ta tell ya."

"Yeah?"

"Workin' too hard ain't good for ya."

XXXXX

The telephone rang a second time. "It's Mr. Wilkinson," said Mary Ann.

Fulton picked up.

"Now before you go off half-cocked, maybe you oughta listen. You oughta talk to Ben," said the prosecutor.
"He won't talk."

"He's willin' to talk. He wants to cooperate. I'll have him call you. Then you need to think about what you're trying to do here. Make a name for yourself or do the right thing."

The next call was from Ben. "I have been avoiding your calls. I'm sorry. I'm willing to talk to you."

395

"Why don't you come by my office."

"That'll be fine. I'll be right over." Ten minutes later, Ben pulled up in front; Ingleside was with him.

"My client is willing to answer any questions. He's nothing to hide."

"That's right, True. I want to cooperate so we can put this behind us."

"Okay," said Fulton, gesturing for the men to sit down.

"I had court that morning. Judge Baker could verify that. So could Mr. Delford, the clerk. He's retired now, but he's still in town."

"You knew Jo Ellen was in town?"

"No, sir."

"She never called you at your office, saying she was in town?"

"No. If you talk to Hattie, I'm sure she'd say the same thing."

Fulton nodded, opening a peppermint.

"I went to the Point after that. My neighbors saw me."

"Did your uncle meet with her?"

"No."

"Did either one of you have anything to do with her death?"

"No, sir, we most definitely did not."

Austin's a smooth liar, Fulton saw. It would do no good to try to get him to deviate from the script he'd devised.

"You knew Jo Ellen?"

"In college."

"Were you romantically involved?"

"No. We were friends."

"Have you ever seen this photograph before?" asked Fulton, showing him the bruised creepy photo of an approximately twenty-two-year-old Jo Ellen.

The lawyer didn't even flinch. "I have not."

"Never saw this butterfly?"

"No—well, my mother has one like it. A lot of GI's brought that stuff home." Ben was cool, looking Fulton directly in the eyes.

"Do you have anything else you wish to add?"

"No. Well, other than I hate how this whole thing's gotten out of control. Jo Ellen was a good friend, so is her father. I got to know him since her death, of course."

"Well, thanks for coming in," said Fulton.

Ben extended his hand confidently. "No hard feelings, I hope."

Along US 98
Saturday, 2/9/1957

Behind the wheel of the white Cadillac convertible, a bottle of Straight
Eight in his hand, the top down, the gulf's warm breezes flowing in—Ben
had the world by the tail. He'd beaten the frazzled lawyer Tallahassee
Memorial had retained. He won the Patterson case! He sure could sweet-
talk a jury. The settlement would enable his client to have a surgery she
really didn't need and landed Ben enough dough to buy this car—brand-
new—from Proctor's. Most importantly, he had beaten that oyser-shuckin'
redneck cop.

Claiborne just loved the car. It surprised her that he'd splurge for
something like this. Then he'd called his dad and made plans for all of
them to spend a few days at the beach! So with the congressman, wife and
son, he set out for their vacation home.

"Hand me another beer, son."

"Sure, Dad," said the eight-year-old, reaching behind the seat to get a cold
beer from the ice chest. The boy, named for Cliff Holland, had black hair
and brown eyes like his father.

"Thanks, buddy." *He's a damn good kid*, Ben thought, taking a swig. Ben
didn't notice the DeSoto behind them. "Here, have one," he said, handing
Cliff one of the ham sandwiches he stashed under the seat before they left.

"Thanks, Daddy," said the boy, taking it, unwrapping it, and biting into the
white bread, ham, and mayonnaise.

Ben looked over at him and smiled. He glanced back at his wife, sexy in
her sleeveless top, sunglasses, and the scarf around her hair. Ben
recognized the intro to "Hey Good Lookin'" and turned the volume up. It
was a corny song, probably something his hick clients would love, but it
was fun to listen to on a ride like this. His wife laughed, and so did the
congressman.

They were about to cross the bridge at Ochlockonee Bay. George's Cafe was
on the left, of course, a low-roofed building that rested on wooden pilings.
The restaurant had been built over the water in the days when Wakulla
was a dry county; liquor could be served at George's for the place was
across the Franklin County "line." White beaches and pine trees stretched
out along both sides of the wide blue bay. Ben steered the convertible onto
the bridge, over the body of water that was formed where the Ochlockonee
flowed into the gulf. Fulton was three car lengths behind.

Colored fishermen leaned over the whitewashed concrete railings of the
bridge, dipping their lines into the blue water below. One of them was
putting his catch in a silver bucket beside him. The bridge was narrow with

no safety lanes; Ben steered the Caddy into the oncoming lane to give the men room. He caught a glance of a sailboat coming down river. The large motoryacht *Josephine* was visible to the left, coming back home from an excursion in the gulf. A few small motorboats with outboard motors also plied the waters around the bridge. The water was calm, visibility limitless.

Ben unwrapped a sandwich and took a bite, washing it down with a little beer. "There Stands the Glass" blared from the speaker. At the south end of the bridge, white folks were fishing, a man in a fedora and a woman with a scarf over her hair.

Making sure there wasn't a trooper's car lurking amid the pines south of the bridge, Ben took another swig. The cool beer sure was nice. It was safe to take a drink; ol' Sam Tucker and his black and tan Pontiac were nowhere to be seen. Ben was just swerving a little bit, but staying well on his side of the road. What was the big deal about having a cold brew—or two or three?

It was wonderful just enjoying the beautiful day, driving down the coastal highway, through the pines and lowlands, listening to the one station they could pick up. Both father and son had grins that were, like the bay, a mile wide.

Fulton decided to make his presence known. He mashed the accelerator, quickly closing in on the shark-finned Cadillac.

"Fulton!" growled Ben, his veins popping, looking back in the mirror. There it was, that Fireflite, the gray fedora behind the windshield.

Not a care in the world should rest upon my mind. But there he is, that damn Sheriff's Bureau nosebleed in the rearview. It was a ways to go—a mile and a half to the turn off for Alligator Drive. Ben thought about this day—three generations of Austins in the car. *All of us together. No one will come between us.* Ben swung the wheel over, making the turn onto the little strip of pavement that went down to the beach. The DeSoto turned too. "Ignore him," growled Ben.

"Do you think you'll have any competition next year, son?"

"No, Dad, not that I've heard. I don't think Clay will run again."

"I'll be in the same boat. That's the thing about the house—you got to face the people every two years. If we can get the presidency in '60, we can make some progress."

It was a short drive down to the middle part of the cape, a narrow, fishhook-shaped strip of land that jutted out into the gulf.

"There's the house, Daddy!" said Cliff, pointing to the peach-colored block house on the right.

Ben spun the large steering wheel, pulling into the oyster-shell driveway that ran to the front of the flat-roofed one-story. The sparkling water of the bay was right at their back door. This beautiful spot was Ben's escape. He used some of his inheritance to buy the lot, clear a few pines, and build the house—the first vacation house on this stretch of the Point. Claiborne didn't want to spend so much money on the place, but Ben insisted on the long dock, insisted on making the house a three-bedroom so there'd be plenty of room for his friends. They only had the place three years and already had made some great memories. It was worth every penny.

The Point was starting to build up, with several houses going up on the gulf side since '55. People realized this was the perfect escape from the sweltering summers in the capital. Ben could see the azure waters of the gulf from his front door; the cape was barely 175 feet wide.

Fulton parked on the opposite side of Alligator Drive. Ben looked over at him, a scowl on his face. "Cliff, wanna carry this down to the boat, son. We'll get out in the water soon as we can," said Ben, patting the boy on the shoulder.

"Oh boy!" exclaimed the young man, grabbing the ice chest and lugging it around back, heading toward the dock as fast as he could manage.

Ben telephoned his mother. "Yeah, he's here."

XXXXX

Gunsmoke was about to begin. Carter had enough time to take a bath and get a spot in front of the television.

Voncille Austin dressed in a green Chanel suit, white gloves, and a fancy hat, a lily pinned to her lapel. The new outfit she'd obtained from the Diane Store at College and Monroe. She had Roland drive her down to Georgia Street. She instructed him to pull down the driveway that ran to the back of the little house at the corner of Georgia and Talaflo—a 1930s cottage on the slope of the hill. Her Cadillac berthed in the driveway, she approached the door, finding a young boy with a baseball glove taking out the trash.

"Is your daddy home?"

"Yes'm. He's inside fixin' to take his bath," answered the boy, the sheriff's youngest.

"Well, get him. I need to speak with him."

"Yes'm." The boy went inside as requested. He left the door a crack, and Mrs. Austin walked in, a family room added on back.

Myra came out from the kitchen and greeted Mrs. Austin deferentially. The boy was running down the hall to the bathroom. Carter was in the tub, the water up to his navel, a cold cloth over his eyes and another behind his

400

head, where he leaned back against the wall. He had an ashtray and cigarettes on the rim of the tub. The door was ajar, and the boy leaned in. "Daddy, Miss Austin is here to see you. She seems mad, sir."

"Well, now *I'm* mad. Dadgum!" he muttered. He cussed under his breath and shook his head. "Hand me a towel, boy."

"Yessir. You want I should tell her you're mad?"

"*No*, son. Don't say *that*. Doggone. Go find me another pack of cigarettes."

"Okay, Daddy."

Myra excused herself and came back to talk to Carter as he wrapped the towel around his waist, the half-smoked cigarette between his lips. He was cursing, fit to be tied. "Ol' Voncille Austin is out there madder than a wet hen," said Mrs. Carter.

"I know, sweetie pie. She's 'bout to drive me crazy. Shut the door, darlin', I gotta put my britches on, and I'll be out."

"Okay, sugah."

The sheriff came out, undershirt and trousers on, but no belt or shoes. His boy handed him a cigarette. His girl handed him his lighter. "Thank ya, darlin'." He stepped into the more formal living room, where the lady of the house had taken the visitor. "Ma'am," said Carter, acknowledging Mrs. Austin.

"I want you to end Fulton's involvement in the investigation—right now."

"All right. I've been contemplatin' that very thing."

"You know my son had no involvement in any crime. Why, he's like a little brother to you, he looks up to you. He was in your company in the war and all. It would break my heart to see him lumped in with criminals, his good name sullied by a *white-trash* deputy from Eastpoint. No Austin has ever been *investigated* in this town, not in a hundred years!"

"Yes, ma'am."

"I've heard 'yes, ma'ams' before. No, what are you going to do?"

"First, I'm gonna finish my bath. And I'm gonna study on this here, figure out what I *should* do."

The woman started to say something rude but calmed some, observing the children eager to look at the television show and have the dessert Myra had fixed. "I'm sorry to come over here like this. I'm sorry to be so direct. I know you'll do the right thing, Frank. Say hello to your mother, and tell her to come see me sometime."

401

"Yes'm, I'll do that."

XXXXX

At 8:30 p.m., Martin drove to the Fultons' home. Fulton offered him a seat on the porch, which he accepted, settling on the swing that hung from one side. Fulton sat facing him on a rocker. The old man was quiet, lazily rocking. He set his hat beside him and lit a cigarette. He looked Fulton in the eye. "Maybe you need to take it easy on this thing."

Fulton nodded.

"I'm getting calls from the sheriff, state's attorney, you name it, wanting me to get you to ease up. Carter's close to asking you to come off the case."

"He said that?"

"He did. He didn't want to come out and say so because you two are friends, and he knows you're just doing what you think is right. But he's getting all kinds of pressure."

"I figured."

"Well, you may just want to think about taking the back door into this thing instead a playin' the bull coming through the front door at the china shop. Sometimes you back a man into a corner, he's gonna bow up, do something."

"That's what I was countin' on."

"Well, it may have other consequences beyond this case, tryin' to stir up these Jacksonville and Tampa boys, these aspiring mafia boys, whatever you wanna call 'em," said Martin, rising.

"I always was direct, boss," said Fulton, getting up and facing Martin by the steps.

"Yeah you was," said the old sheriff, chuckling. Martin put on his hat and walked back to his car. "See you later."

"Yes sir, boss."

About a half hour after Martin left, Fulton heard a car outside. He got that feeling someone was watching.

78

Tallahassee
Monday, 2/11/1957
The pastor of the church on Miccosukee Road—Sheriff Carter's pastor—called him. Carter hung up the telephone and cussed. He drove down to the Sheriff's Bureau. "True, I've decided it would be best to close the investigation into Jo Ellen Harbert and any conspiracy to bring about her death."

"Okay," said Fulton quietly.

"We got Younkins. Let's let it go at that."

"I talked to Milo Harbert. Ben Austin never let on that he knew Jo Ellen."

"True—"

"Don't you think that's suspicious? He agrees to represent Harbert, help him try to get something done on the case—yet never mentions they'd been acquainted?"

"We spent a lot of time on it. We followed a lot of leads. But we ain't never gonna make a case against Austin that's gonna hold up—not for murder, nor conspiracy to commit murder, we ain't."

Fulton said nothing else. He just nodded and stared out the window. After a moment, Carter rose to leave, going back to his office. Dreggors was quiet and didn't speak to Carter when he walked past. Carter picked up the telephone and called Carlton Lanier, telling him the case was concluded.

XXXXX

Fulton looked at the heavy file. He sighed. The missing piece was out there, somewhere. He put the file in the drawer and closed it.

XXXXX

In Tallahassee, no establishment had served liquor since 1904—at least not legally. The Austin family saved the mahogany bar top out of the old Leon Bar that stood at the corner of College and Monroe (before Bennett's came along). Now at the river house, the long polished woodwork was as beautiful as the day the ordinance banning spirits passed the city council.

"I'm not so sure Fulton will quit this easy," said Ben, making himself a bourbon and Coke.

The state attorney agreed. "He's a stubborn son of a bitch. I guess he gets tenacity from his time shucking oysters."

"Can't we get him canned for good?" wondered Ben.

403

"I tried," said Wilkinson. "But Collins thinks he's splendid."

"Can you get some dirt on him?" asked Ben.

"We're trying," said Lanier. Wilkinson didn't have to ask what that meant.

"I still wonder if he's following me," Ben remarked, taking a drink.

"I got a man watching him," said Lanier. "He ain't followin' you—not the past coupla days."

"You said that once before."

"Yeah, but this guy's from Tampa, used to be a cop. He's good."

"I didn't hear that," said Wilkinson with a grin.

79

Tallahassee
Wednesday, 2/20/1957

Fulton took a few days off. He rested—and watched for the mysterious car to return. He drove into town at noon; he went to see the records girl at the telephone company. She left to pick up lunch from Holland's, turning a blind eye while Fulton looked through the long-distance calls to and from Ben Austin's law firm. A call had come in, person to person, from Hattie Welton in Tampa. He looked at the telephone records for Lanier's garage—he got a call from Miss Welton too.

XXXXX

Evelyn Madgison hugged Dreggors and told him good-bye.

"I know you been cryin'," he told her. Her mascara was running, blue lines down her cheeks. She had a bruise under her seven layers of makeup. "You wanna tell ol' Will what's gone on?"

She shook her head.

"You got family in *Miamuh?*"

She nodded.

"You call me if you ever need somethin'. You hear me?"

She nodded. She smiled and left. He watched her car pull away and went back inside, penciling in some paperwork on a bond he was going surety on. The telephone rang. "Yeah, I can meet you. Just hang tight."

The big man drove to the secluded spot by the tracks, and the gaunt fellow got in the car. He reeked of sweat and cigarettes. Dreggors handed him a fresh Chesterfield to mask the stench. "I was playin' cards with Lanier again. Out at the Ship Lantern. Old Ford pulls up, and it's Ben Austin in the car—drunk as a skunk. They talk about a few things. Money mostly. Then they talk about Lanier's girl—Evelyn. He talks about how he beat hell outta her for talking to the *poe*-lease. And that he gave her gas money and told her she best git on the road, or things were gonna get real sporty for her 'round here."

"Yeah?"

"That ain't all. They git to laughin' 'bout the sheriff. They cuss him every which way and say how he's got a tenth-grade education and dumb as all get out."

"He ain't gonna like that."

"No, sir. Then they cut up some more, and they says they get away with what they want in this town."

"Which one said that?"

"Both of 'em."

XXXXX

The sheriff turned red and threw his coffee mug, Dreggors ducking to avoid getting splashed by flying coffee. "No, sir! They ain't above the law! I don't keer how far they can trace their selves on Calhoun Street. No, sir!"

"You want another coffee, Dad?" asked Penny, looking at the empty mug on the floor.

"Thank you, darlin'. Doggone! I'm madder'n a hornet," he said, getting his mug from the floor and handing it to his daughter. He called Fulton. "I ain't stoppin ya from workin' that case no more. You solve it. I don't keer who they daddy is, cousin, or mama. I don't keer what Miss Austin or anyone else says."

Fulton smiled. "Sounds good, Sheriff."

"Well, finish your coffee and git after it."

80

Tallahassee
Friday, 2/22/1957

Fulton paid $40 for the old pickup; a tattered jacket and straw hat completed the look. He watched Lanier leave his office and drive to the Tallahassee State Bank at Calhoun and Jefferson. Fulton stayed in the truck, not sure who might be around. In a moment, Lanier walked out, stuffed an envelope in his inside pocket, and got back in his Ford.

Where's he going? Fulton kept his distance. Lanier pulled into the airport parking lot. No luggage. He bought a ticket and boarded an Eastern DC-3 bound for Tampa. Miss Welton now lived in Tampa. One more piece. She'd spoken to Jo Ellen. She was a link in the chain.

Fulton looked in his rearview. Seemed like that Crown Victoria was following. He ducked down a side street to get away. Fulton thought he might have been spotted. He'd deal with the consequences later.

XXXXX

The private eye continued to watch Fulton. He drove to Fulton's home and sat all evening. On his way back to his motel, he parked the Crown Victoria in front of Mutt n' Jeffs. He finished a burger and shake. He shut the door of the phone booth and dialed Lanier's number. The phone rang. *He oughta be back by now.*

"Hello."

"He was watching when you went to the bank," said the PI.

"Son of a bitch! What about the airport?"

"Yes."

"Why didn't you do something!"

"And draw more attention? All he knows is you got some money and took a trip. Nothing illegal about that."

"You're right. But this son of a bitch ain't gonna stop until he knows too much for his own good."

"Sure."

"Well, what are we gonna do?"

"That's not what I was hired for. I'm just here to watch."

"Thanks for the report!" Lanier snapped, slamming down the receiver. "Son of a bitch!"

The detective stepped out of the phone booth and paused to light a cigarette.

"Howdy!"

The man turned around quickly. "Damn!" *Fulton!* The game of cat and mouse had been won by the man from Eastpoint.

81

Tallahassee
Monday, 3/25/1957

The azaleas were in bloom, and it was hot. Fulton answered the telephone. It was a familiar voice. Soft, sexy, almost a whisper. "I want to be with my husband. I want to be with him right now."

"Well, hello."

"Hello, stranger. Can I come back from my exile?"

"I'd feel more comfortable if you didn't."

"I know you just wanna protect me. But I wanna fall asleep with a smile on my face, baby doll. If you miss someone, the best way to stop missing them is to go where they are. Unless...you don't miss *me*."

"I miss you...like I did in the war. Everything's just...empty without you."

"Oh, baby doll, that's nice," she purred. "So you want me to come back?"

"Uh-huh."

"Good, 'cause I'm at the airport right now."

"Huh?"

"Yeah. Come pick me up."

No AC in the Ford. He was sweating by the time he got to the terminal. She hugged him, holding on and not letting go; it didn't matter how sweaty they both were getting. He cranked down all the windows and took off, trying to get a breeze flowing in. She held his arm with both her hands, looking up at him. "Don't worry, I'm a Franklin County girl. Anyone comes in that house, they'll find out what 'double-ought buck' can do."

By the time they crossed the overpass that ran past the stadium, the car was boiling over. "She's steaming like an old Model T," said Marlene.

Fulton turned down Gaines. It sounded like someone turned on a faucet under the hood. Water was spraying up from the hood seams.

"Am I gonna have to walk?" Marlene asked.

"We ain't far from the Texaco." He pulled in the driveway of the German's garage. "*Ja*, head gasket," agreed the mechanic. "*Sie kommen.*" There was a fan on; Marlene sat in the chair beside it while Fulton looked out the window. He saw the Crown Victoria drive past, parking down the street.

Marlene got up. "They're going to kill you if this keeps on. These people, whoever they are. I know they won't stop. I know you won't either. So you get them first." The look in her eyes he hadn't seen in a long time—probably not since she'd run Dollie Tyson off from her front yard when the latter tried to get Fulton to go for a ride in her new convertible. "You hear me?"

Fulton nodded. He picked up Bayerlein's telephone. "Yeah, he's down the street."

XXXXX

Fulton and Dreggors walked up to the private eye. "You kinda gettin' tiresome," Dreggors told him.

"I'm mindin' my own business. Why don't you?"

"Surly characters *are* my business," said the big man.

The fellow found himself rather crowded with Fulton and Dreggors surrounding him. "Listen, I don't have to stand for this. I think—"

"I think you're gonna amble on over to the Seaboard office and git you a ticket."

"Maybe my business interests require me to stay a while."

"Maybe your business interests gonna find you runnin' afoul the law," said Dreggors, an intimidating look on his face. "Around here, that's me," he said, jabbing his thumb back toward his chest.

"I'm a licensed PI. You can't push me around."

Fulton reached in the man's coat and snatched his gun. "Now, wait a minute. I have a client."

"Carrying a concealed firearm. Judge might give jail time for that," said Dreggors.

Fulton nodded.

"Yeah, I think you just quit workin' for your client," said Dreggors.

"You hold on."

Dreggors pushed him against the wall. "This kind of work is stressful. I don't think it agrees with you. What do you think, True?"

"I think you got something there, Will." Turning to the PI, Fulton said, "You tell Lanier you ain't working for him anymore. You tell Austin I've set in like the bad weather. Then you gonna leave town."

The man lunged toward Fulton. Dreggors grabbed him by the collar. "Now, you fixin' ta git your bag packed over at yo *hoe*-tell—yeah, I know you stayin' at the Cactus Motel—room 4, by the pool," said Dreggors, nodding. "You gonna drag that bag down ta Pensacola Street and git that ticket. Then you gonna go sit at the depot until the train gets here tomorrow mornin'. If you don't, you fixin' ta find Tallahassee sorta unpleasant as we get close to summer. It's *awful* hot."

82

Tallahassee
Tuesday, 4/23/1957

"Can you come over here? I'm ready to see him. Bring your tapes." *Click.*

Fulton, lugging the heavy Revere, met the sheriff in front of the courthouse. The two men crossed the street to the Lewis State Bank.

Carter laid the warrants in front of the lawyer. *Carlton Lanier* was written in Penny's lovely cursive. Three separate gambling offenses. Fulton spread the photos on the prosecutor's desk and switched on the suitcase-size machine, giving Wilkinson a sampling of the conversations. They had Lanier on bolita—cold.

Wilkinson shoved the papers away from him.

The sheriff leaned across the desk and handed Wilkinson a pen. "You'll sign it. Unless you don't need my help come election time."

Wilkinson pulled the papers toward him angrily; he looked at them, contemplating.

"Just put your John Henry right there on that line," said Carter.

Wilkinson scratched *approved* and penned his initials in large flowing letters and slid the paper back across the desk. He cussed. He knew the sheriff held the cards this time.

XXXXX

Lanier wasn't home. Carter had been looking all day. Fulton doubled back to Lanier's shop. The lights were off. He walked around back and looked through the window. A Pontiac was on the oscilloscope, hood tilted open. No one was around. Just then, he heard someone crying—a man. Lanier was sitting in the backseat of that car. Fulton called Bobby from the pay phone.

Quietly, they entered the office and slipped into the shop. The only light was the dome lamp in that Pontiac.

"All right, Carl. Put down the bottle. Let's go," said Carter.

Lanier gave him the dirtiest look imaginable and took another drink.

"I said put it down," the sheriff repeated.

"I'm gonna finish it!" he screamed.

"Come on, Lanier," said Fulton, leaning in the other side.

"No!" He reached into his coat.

Fulton grabbed his arm and yanked him from the car. He was clutching something. "Drop it, Lanier!" He did so, fifty or sixty bolita tickets scattering as Lanier turned loose of them. He began bawling, sinking to his knees.

They took him by the arms, dragging him to Carter's Chevrolet. They shoved him against the fender. They patted him down, finding his pockets full of tickets.

"I ain't saying a damn thing, I'm calling Ingleside."

XXXXX

Friday. He walked down to Centennial Field. He paid for his ticket for the baseball game, the Tallahassee Pirates playing the Moultrie Phillies. Austin smiled, hearing the announcer, the applause from the crowd as the players took the field. *Minor league, but good ball. And that fream Fulton wouldn't follow me in here. A few hours of relaxation.*

XXXXX

Fulton got his ticket and a hot dog and walked in, finding a seat in the wooden grandstands. He spotted Austin near the top of the covered bleachers, overlooking third base. Austin looked happy, made in the shade under that tin roof. Men approached him deferentially, shaking his hand; one bought him a Coca-Cola. He smiled, enjoying the perks of public service. When he thought no one in the crowd would notice, he took a drink from the flask he carried in the side pocket of his suit, hiding his actions with his hat. Fulton saw him chase the hooch with the bottle of Coke.

The Moultrie hitter was up to bat, the loud pop announcing the first homer of the day. The hitter paced around the bases, the ball flying up over the Seaboard Line—just as a westbound freight rumbled by—rolling somewhere into the woods on the other side of the tracks.

Austin happened to look up to his right. His smile faded, seeing Fulton in the front row by the catcher. The lawyer looked uncomfortable, Fulton saw. *Good.* It wasn't long before Austin got up and left. Fulton followed him out to Bloxham Street.

Ben drove down the hill, away from town. He grinned when Fulton turned around just outside the city limits. He turned on the radio, whistling to himself. He checked into the lodge at Wakulla Springs. He made a phone call and heard a friendly voice; it would be a nice afternoon after all. He waited around outside. His smile faded and he cussed when the big DeSoto turned in the driveway. He flung his cigarette down. He went back inside

413

the hotel. Sally arrived a moment later; the lawyer sent the clerk to tell her today wasn't a good day to meet.

XXXXX

Fulton called another number, trying to track down Hattie Welton. Her old landlady said she'd moved, left no forwarding address, and owed her ten bucks. He hung up the telephone, crossing off another lead.

XXXXX

Sunday. Austin drove to church, smiling the entire way. No DeSoto in the rearview. The country church had added a larger building—whitewashed, big columns, and a steeple that was visible from downtown. Austin sat with his family and friends and relaxed, enjoying a nice sermon from Dr. Garland.

The service concluded, and piano sounds clanked out the open doors, an enthusiastic rendition of "Victory in Jesus." Austin shook the pastor's hand and paused on the steps; he looked out at the quiet country road, the oaks, the pretty spot. Claiborne looked lovely in a new dress; their little boy was in a suit and bow tie. He smiled. The next couple came out, Grant Wilkinson and his wife. Austin patted the SA on the back, and they casually walked toward their cars, parked along the road for the church grounds were filled with automobiles. They chatted about going down to Holland's Restaurant.

"Good morning!" came the cheerful greeting.

Austin turned around. His grin faded; he nearly cussed right there in front of the church. Fulton leaned against the bumper of the DeSoto, smiling. "Good day, Mr. Fulton!" the lawyer growled. Voncille Austin came down the steps, her glaring eyes locked onto the lawman.

Carter, the deacon, leaned out the door. He made eye contact with Fulton, shaking his head as if to ask, "What are you stirring up, son?"

Fulton tipped his hat to Claiborne. "Ma'am," he said, excusing himself. He got in the car, disappearing down Miccosukee, leaving the politician to fume.

Ben slammed the door, firing the motor and yanking the lever into drive in a single angry movement. His head on a swivel, he looked for Fulton all the way home. He said nothing to his wife. They'd been arguing.

He tugged the blinds closed in his den, picking up the phone to call Jim Burke. The reporter. He'd steered Jim a few stories over the years. Perhaps Jim could return the favor.

XXXXX

414

Monday. Marlene brought in the paper and sat on the couch. She crossed her legs and lit a cigarette, spreading out the paper over her knees. "Oh, baby doll," she sighed.

"What's the matter?"

"'Is Sheriff's Bureau, Collins's Pet Project, a Waste of Money?' it says. "I don't see how—they haven't given it any money," Marlene quipped. "Why, the dirty—listen to this. 'Special Agent Fulton has spent more than a year investigating a case ruled to be accident by highway patrol.'"

"Aww, don't worry about that."

XXXXX

Tuesday. Fulton continued his surveillance. Burke continued his editorializing. Marlene got her newspaper, took one look at it, and shook her head.

"What's wrong?"

"They're out to get you. This story talks about you getting in a car crash in Jacksonville. 'Does Fulton have a drinking problem?' it asks."

"Baby, don't pay attention to that."

XXXXX

Wednesday. Fulton got ready for work. Marlene was smiling.

"You seem awfully happy. Was it last night?"

"That too," she said, continuing to paint the front door. "But how do you like these headlines?" She noticed him trying to read the spattered front page. "I take the editorials and put them underneath the spot I'm painting."

Fulton laughed.

"Frankly I find the paper best suited for such uses," she said, carefully brushing on the paint. "And take a look at my flower beds." He stepped out on the porch, looking at fresh pine straw around the flowers. "I found something else the paper is good for."

"Uh-huh?"

"Sure. I put it underneath the pine straw, keeps weeds down, and then no one has to read *what's in that cheap rag.*"

Fulton laughed. "You really are enjoying yourself. I like that color, by the way."

415

"Yes, I think it'll do nicely. I can't wait to paint over tomorrow's headlines."

"Bye," he said, laughing.

"I'd kiss you, but I might get paint on your suit."

"I'll get two kisses tonight."

"Hmmm, that'll give you something to look forward to, won't it?"

83

On US 27
5:30 p.m.
Saturday, 11/2/1957

It was cold and drizzling. "Walkin' After Midnight" played from the speaker of the Ford. The Motorola—tuned to the SO's frequency—was quiet. Fulton pulled to the side of the road, the spot that looked down at the blackness that was the edge of the lake. He had the newspaper on the seat beside him. The surroundings were as black and gray as that paper.

The summer of '57 had been hot and long. Fans and window AC units blowing, jackets off, and cigarette smoke swirling in back offices at the capital. The kid from Holland's Restaurant bringing cold drinks and sandwiches for the politicians in committee. Martin was called over to Appropriations. Collins made a few phone calls. A good bit of horse trading and some statesmanship, the legislators arrived at a budget for the Sheriff's Bureau: $534,495. Compared to other spending bills, it was small. It was a start. Martin hired two more special agents and began putting together a crime lab. He was able to rent the house next door for his new chemists and document examiners. The firearms experts got the cellar of their first "home," Mary Ann nearly jumping out of her chair every time Halligan test-fired a weapon below her. Ben Austin had been the most prominent vote against the "extravaganza." Ben's happy-go-lucky demeanor had returned over the summer. He'd ridden out the storm—he thought.

Fulton hoped he'd think that. He kept up surveillance from the alleys, the shadows, driving another old pickup. Austin was spending a lot of time at Alligator Point after the session ended in June. He'd meet Sally over on St. George Island. Fulton watched him take the ferry. He was drinking a lot. And when he got to drinking, he was talking a lot. *Sooner or later he'll slip up.*

Then Martin had to pull the plug. Despite the extra manpower, Fulton was needed on other assignments. And the listening devices were needed for new cases. Summer was over.

Fulton didn't give up, even if the Harbert case had to be confined to the time he could spare while eating a sandwich or grabbing a cup of coffee. He kept after Austin's bank until they revealed they "lost" the records from his account that pertained to the fall of 1953. Mr. Conley was able to tell him that Clara Jamieson had an account opened for her on October 31, 1953. He knew Mrs. Jamieson, and it wasn't she who opened the account. Although he could not positively ID Jo Ellen's photograph, he did say she resembled the woman that made the initial deposit.

He'd presented the information to Wilkinson this morning at the golf course. He gave him a copy of the journal. Wilkinson wouldn't touch the case. "It says Ben—Ben who?"

"How many Ben's could she possibly be acquainted with?"

Wilkinson shrugged. "It probably doesn't matter much. As evidence goes, it's hearsay—inadmissible."

Conley thought Mrs. Jamieson took her girls to Dunnellon. Maybe there'd be time to follow up on that lead. If it took another year, he wasn't quitting. He looked at the paper; the article said Senator Reynolds was retiring.

"Political analysts believe this would be a great opportunity for up-and-coming member of the House, Ben Austin. Some experts discount Austin for he has served only one term in the House. Reynolds himself says, 'Don't underestimate Ben. He's a fine speaker, a good campaigner. People like him.' The four-term senator believes Austin has a brilliant future in politics. Even Governor Collins, some say, believes Austin would be a formidable candidate for his own post in a few years."

He opened the paper to C9. There was a small article below a giant spread for the Rambler dealership. "Tallahassee Man Sentenced. Carlton Lanier was sentenced to three years in the state prison, yesterday ... gambling ... racketeering." Fulton folded the paper and put it back on the seat. Faithful to his word, Lanier had remained silent.

Fulton stared down the hill toward the lake. It began raining harder, the drops tapping the roof of the car. He sat there, watching the clouds roll, listening to the rain fall.

Part IV

84

Cape San Blas
Friday, 10/24/1958

Sultry would be charitable. It was hot. The kind of humid, furnace-like hot that only exists in North Florida. Summer didn't end with Labor Day. It would fight the onset of autumn to the bitter end.

Dr. Fowler's beach house nestled amid dunes of sugar-white sand and sea oats, half-facing St. Joseph's Bay, the other half catching the hot breeze from the gulf. Fowler didn't know about the party taking place at his house. He certainly didn't know his eighteen-year-old son was there, nor two dozen kids from Panama City and the capital, the high school and FSU students arriving in a veritable motorcade of '55 Chevys, foreign sports cars, and hopped-up '40 Fords.

Three girls from Chapman High—in Apalachicola—came. Shorts and sleeveless tops. Pretty. One of the girls—Kay—caught the eye of a college boy. A real doll. Nice legs. Sixteen. He got her a Coke; it had a little whiskey in it. He danced with her. He kissed her. At first she liked it: attention from a college boy, a judge's son from Atlanta. He led her into one of the bedrooms, continuing their necking; he tried to roll on top of her. She told him no; she didn't like him *that* much. He relented and cooled off, and they sat on the bed and talked. He got her another drink. It made her head buzz. He had his arm around her. They began kissing again; he walked her into the bathroom. *She's getting to where she kisses pretty good*, thought College Boy. He'd try for more.

Her back up against the sink, his hand went up her shirt, touching her back, her soft skin. He let the hand drift around, farther up, lifting her shirt and touching her breast. "No," she told him, pushing his hand away. He had a good hold on her. Kay had to fight him off in the bathroom. He was strong. The Buddy Holly was so loud no one heard her yell. She was able to slip from his hands and ran down the hall, out onto the beach.

"Boy, what a wolf!" she said, sitting down on the sand. She sat there, her arms folded across her knees, looking up at the house, listening to the party. Careful not to be seen by the wolf, she got up and looked in one of the windows. She didn't see her friends. She asked a boy on the deck if he had seen Kathy and Liza. The boy—drunk—shook his head. Her friends had left her. She walked along the dark road, back to her grandfather's car; she'd borrowed his '31 Plymouth. She'd parked a fair distance down the road, embarrassed by the jalopy, what with the sharp-looking Austin-Healeys and Bel Airs sitting in front of the house.

A flash of white light interrupted the intense darkness—the beacon of the old lighthouse that stood sentry at the southern tip of the cape. It was near midnight. She was a little woozy from the drinks. She climbed into the Plymouth, praying it would start. *Thank God I got away from the boy. I didn't know he would be such a masher.* The little four banger spun and settled into a comforting clatter. She shoved the clutch in and put the car in gear, retracing her path down Cape San Blas Road, the dark waters of the Gulf of Mexico reflecting the pale three-quarter moon that was struggling to come out from behind the clouds. The headlights may as well have been flashlights taped to the battered fenders. State Road 30 was black and gray and seemed to fade right into the thick, jungle-like woods. She had trouble seeing. She was weaving, her head spinning, her reflexes messed up. She drove on for a few miles, but it was only getting worse. She had no idea how far she'd driven. She stopped on the side of the road. "Boy, I'm *drunk!*"

XXXXX

He was drunker, and he'd used a little dope. He saw a girl with a summer top—pretty— on the side of the road in an old heap. Maybe broken down. He pulled alongside her.
"You all right?"

She was sitting with her feet on the running boards out the open door of the car. She got down, leaning in his window to talk. "I'm ashamed to say it, but I had a little to drink. I'd never drank anything before," she told him. "I had trouble driving, so I pulled over."

"You should get in. I don't want you to get in trouble. Driving while intoxicated is a crime, you know."

"Okay. If you think that's best. I don't want to get into trouble. I don't live far. I'm from Apalach."

He let her in the car and started driving. It was dark woods on both sides. After another mile, he began slowing down.

"What's the matter?" she asked.

"Nothing. This is a nice quiet spot," he said, turning down a dirt road.

"I can get out from here. I can walk, it's no trouble," she said, her heart beating faster.

"It's not safe to walk," he said, grabbing her arm as he flicked the lever into park. She tried to writhe free and open the door. He grabbed her by the back of the neck, pulling her to him. "Have some of this," he said, putting the bottle in her mouth, forcing her to drink. She tried to scream; he covered her mouth, squeezing her face. "Just shut up," he told her. He said it calmly, softly even, yet his words, his clammy touch, made her blood run cold.

He shoved her facedown into the seat cushion, pinning her to the seat, his hand running over her thigh and in between her legs. How casual he was, yet completely in control; she tried to pull herself up, reach for the door handle, but she could do nothing. He unbuttoned her shorts and put his

421

hand down her panties, touching her; he yanked her clothing down her legs with one violent movement, his other arm continuing to pin her to the bottom of the seat. He flipped her over, raping her on the front seat of the car.

He made her sit up, shivering, naked on the front seat. He made her drink some more bourbon. She faded in and out of consciousness. She came to on the side of Highway 98, at the Y where State Road 30 joined the highway.

XXXXX

She was still woozy. She heard a loud motor. Someone was trying to get her to drink. Something was pinching her legs. Her face was burning. Her eyes focused; a man with a gray cap and necktie was standing over her; he began dragging her by her arms toward a truck. She tried to fight him.

"It's okay! It's okay! I ain't gonna hurt ya." He picked her up, putting her on the seat in the cab of the idling Dodge tractor. She closed her eyes, still woozy. "Are ya all right? Can ya hear me?" He was a truck driver; he noticed her leaning against the road sign and had stopped. "You all eat up by ants. What were you doin' there?"

"I don't know," she told him.

He put a blanket over her and radioed for the highway patrol. They summoned the sheriff, who met the semi farther up the road, near the airport. The green and white carried the young woman, still wrapped in the blanket, to the hospital.

85

Weems Hospital
2:00 p.m.
Saturday, 10/25/1958

The heat of this Indian summer hadn't let up. It was almost unbearable in the one-story brick building at 135 Avenue G. Despite John Gorrie's invention of air-conditioning right here in Apalachicola a century before, the innovation had not been fitted to the little hospital. The nurses had the windows open in Kay's room, trying to catch the little breeze that made it inland from the gulf.

Sheriff Herbert Marshall drove his '55 Ford—the car fitted with a siren on the fender and gumball light on the roof—around the circle driveway, pulling up underneath the canopy. He got out, dressed in a plaid long-sleeve shirt and a black necktie. He slammed the door and walked inside.

Marshall was sore distressed over what happened to the little Byers girl. That kind of thing didn't happen here. Heretofore, his biggest worry was Collins's visit on Harbor Day, whether there'd be enough fried mullet. He tapped lightly on the door and walked in. Kay's face and hands were swollen and red from insect bites.

Marshall pulled a chair up to her bed. "Hey, darlin'. Can you talk to me a minute?" he asked gently. She nodded. "How ya feelin'?" She didn't answer. "You let me know if I can get you somethin', okay?" She nodded. "Can you tell me anything about what happened?" She started crying, gasping for breath, carrying on about her friends leaving, the dark road. Marshall tried but couldn't get much in the way of details out of her.

"I couldn't find my friends," she cried. "I couldn't find them! I couldn't see!" She cried into her pillow. The sheriff couldn't make heads nor tails of anything she was saying. He tilted his Stetson back, rubbing the sweat from his forehead. He waited for her to settle down enough that she could talk. "Did someone touch you, darlin'?"

She nodded then started crying again, burying her face in the pillow. Marshall looked over at her daddy.

"I can't git nothin' out of her neither," said Mr. Byers. "She went to a party with some friends. They done left her alone. That's 'bout all."

"All right, let her quiet down," said the sheriff.

Marshall called the daddies of the two girls that were with Kay. They had seen a boy talking to her at the party. The sheriff returned to Kay's room and tried to get her to talk again. "Was it the college boy that done this?" She started crying into her pillow again, almost to the point of hyperventilating.

Marshall called his friend, Frank Carter.

"And I thought you might be invitin' me to go fishin'. Damn, son, this is bad. She ain't said nothing yet?"

"No."

"Maybe we can get Hal Martin in on this."

"I'm not sure...about that," said Marshall, wiping his face with a handkerchief.

"Whatchyu gonna do?"

"Don't know. The girl's daddy is 'bout ready to drive over to the cape and kill the boy that had the party. I talked to the boy's daddy—he's a doctor up in Montgom'ry. I talked to the truck driver and the patrolman that was out there that night. They don't recall seein' nothin' suspicious, no cars out where she was found. Mr. Byers has the clothes Kay was wearin'. We ain't got no way of testin' 'em. I talked to Doc Milligan. He ain't got no way of testin' 'em neither."

"You best call 'ol Hal Martin, son."

"Yeah, I reckon maybe we oughta call in the Sheriff's *Bue*-row."

Carter gave him the new number. Marshall dialed 0 and got the long-distance operator.

"Number, please."

"Tallahassee 7000."

"Hold please."

The call was connected to the director's office. "This Hal Martin speakin'," answered the director, the sentence coming out like one word.

"Sheriff, I got a problem," said Marshall. He gave Martin a rundown on the rape.

"Well, Sheriff, I think there's only one fella for this case. I think we both know who that is," said Martin.

XXXXX

Fulton returned from Bonifay, parking at the curb on St. Augustine; he rode the elevator up to the third floor, finding Carter in the director's office. The old man had just moved in, the building only recently completed. Martin's office looked out over the new parkway. "Ya'll look like you got something serious on your mind." They told him.

424

Fulton and Martin drove down in the latter's new Ford. They met with Marshall in a stuffy office at the hospital. They talked for a minute then walked down the hall to Kay's room.

Marshall asked a lean fellow with a crop of black hair to step into the hall. The thin sunburnt oysterman looked at Fulton, curious about the stranger in suit and tie. "I'm her daddy," said the man. He was perspiring heavily; nervously, he clutched a pack of Camels.

Fulton shook his hand, which was damp with sweat. "My name's True Fulton."

"I heard a you."

Fulton knew of Byers too, but the last time he'd seen the fellow was before the war.

"She's sixteen. Just a junior in hah-skoo," said Byers. "A lot of people tell me not to tell y'all nothin', not to let her talk to you boys. That it'll ruin her life."

Fulton listened to what the man had to say. He ultimately decided, "No, I don't want you fellers to talk to her anymore."

"Maybe we should take a look at her clothes. You still have what she was wearing?"
asked Fulton.

"I do, but I don't want my girl to go through all that."

Marshall drove Fulton to the spot where Kay had been found. There was nothing there. Only tire tracks from the semi. Not even a cigarette butt was to be found. Fulton dusted the pole that held the sign. Marshall nodded, impressed with the special agent's thoroughness. "I was hopin' he touched it when he left her," said Fulton. "Nope. Nothing."

The Sheriff's Bureau men got back in the car empty-handed, disappointed—a feeling that made the two-hour drive back to the capital seem even longer. Silently, Martin steered the black Fairlane across the long bridge. Fulton looked out over the choppy water. Monarch butterflies were fluttering across Apalachicola Bay on their journey south, smashing on the windshield of Martin's new car.

86

Apalachicola
Monday, 10/27/1958

Kay was out of the hospital. Her father called. "She will give you the statement, Mr. True."

Tallahassee, despite being the capital of a large state, despite the university and the government offices, was still a small town. It turned quite rural just three miles from downtown. Tallahassee folks, for the most part— whether it was in regard to the fellow pumping gas on the corner or a Supreme Court justice—knew a good deal of everyone else's business. Apalachicola was a whole order of magnitude smaller; barely three thousand people, insulated by water on three sides, and hemmed by dark woods and wilderness on the fourth, it was a world unto itself. *Everyone* knew about the attack by now. As much as they tried to protect her, it would be rough on poor Kay, Fulton knew.

The drive down the coast was beautiful, peaceful; the task facing him would be neither. Much of the countryside along US 98 was wild country, remote beaches and bluffs. It would be a long walk indeed if the Ford's bent-eight motor quit shaking. He made it to the bridge by 10:00 a.m., the narrow roadway stretching seven miles across the bay. A lone shrimp boat was coming in from the gulf, the deckhands tired from a long night; soon the bridgetender would swing the bridge around for her.

XXXXX

The deputy read his bulletins and savored his fourth cup of coffee for the day. The pot sat on the table nearby, steam rising from the stainless steel. The Franklin County sheriff's office was in the tiny yellow-brick building that sat behind the courthouse. The office— dispatch/investigations/patrol/missing persons/everything—was on the bottom floor, below the jail cells. The deputy had a young woman and her father waiting in the interrogation room/lunchroom/file room.

Fulton pulled up to the front steps, the Customline steaming as much as the deputy's coffeepot. Walking into the crowded front room, the deputy handed him a coffee and nodded toward the doorway of the interrogation room. Fulton could see the young woman, sitting no more than two arm lengths from where he stood. She wore a simple cotton dress, a catatonic expression on her face.

He stepped inside the little room. "Miss Byers?"

She nodded.

"Glad to know ya, Kay," he said, offering his hand. She—her expression still blank— shook it. He took his hat off and sat down. "I'm a police*man*," he said, showing Kay his star. He said the word the same as locals would say *oyster*man.

She nodded.

"I hear you were born in Eastpoint. So's I."

She smiled weakly.

"And I hear you're doing pretty good at school—Chapman?"

She nodded.

"You may know my mama then—Mrs. Fulton?"

"Yessir...got her for English. She's my fav'rite teacher."

"Okay. Good. Well, you know why we here. And I know this ain't easy. I know a little bit a what happened. But I need to hear it from you, from the beginnin'. I need to know so's I can catch him and he don't do this again. I need your help catchin' him."

She nodded.

"So, do you wanna tell me about it?"

Tears welled in the girl's eyes. The words came pouring out. "He stopped like he was wantin' to help me. Stopped and acted like he was worried about me bein' out there alone. He let me in the car, and I thought he'd take me home. He seemed nice. Asked me about school. I thought he was gonna keep goin' to Apalach. Then he stops. I ask him why. And he says something. And he's just got this look, and I get scared. I try to jump out. He grabs me. Before I could even holler, he shoved my face into the seat cushion. I couldn't hardly breathe with him pushin' my face into the seat. He was kissin' on me. He wouldn't let go. He was over me. I couldn't get up. He pulled my shorts and panties down." Kay wiped her cheeks with the back of her hands. "He was holdin' my arms, my neck, had me pinned. I tried to yell. He told me to hush up and pushed my face down harder. I kept trying to yell. That's when he turns me over on my back, and he laughs. He says, 'Fine, scream all you want, bitch, no one can hear you. That's when he—" She stopped talking. She was sobbing hard.

"It's okay. He had you under him?"

She nodded, crying, large teardrops moving down her cheeks. "I cried and cried. I kept hollerin', hopin' someone would come along. He wouldn't stop," she said, her face in her hands, tears falling onto the table.

"Okay. We talked about that enough. I won't ask you any more about it."

She nodded, quieting a little.

"Do you know this fella?"

"No, sir. I ain't never seen him before."

"Can you describe him?"

"He was big. Not as tall as you. He was skinnier. But bigger than my daddy."

"Okay. How old?"

"Old, like you. Sorry."

"That's all right. So let me be real clear—he wasn't your age, he wasn't maybe college age, he was an older man?"

"Yessir."

"What color hair?"

"Dark brown, I reckon."

"Anything unusual about him?"

"No."

"What kind of car was it?"

"I don't know cars. It was a new car. It smelled new."

"Can you describe the color?"

"Uh—no, sir."

"Was it a family car? Sports car? Station wagon?"

"I don't know. It was big."

Fulton got out the Identi-Kit. He worked with Kay to create a composite. He took it outside and talked to the sheriff.

"That could be anybody—even you," said Marshall.

"That's as specific as we could get," said Fulton. They went back in. "I just have a few more questions. You're doing fine."

Kay nodded.

"Can you describe where it happened?"

"Woods, out by the road. I don't know. I reckon I could tell ya if I was to see it again."

"Well, do you feel up to it now?" asked Fulton, looking at her father to see if it was all right. Byers nodded. Fulton showed them to his car, letting Byers sit in back while Kay rode in front.

Marshall followed. They crossed into Gulf County, driving to the cape and retracing Kay's steps. Kay picked out two spots she thought it might be, but she wasn't sure. One of the spots looked like someone had pulled over, the grass bent over, but there were no tire marks.

"We'd have a problem charging any suspect. Which county was it in?" asked Marshall. "We don't know if it happened in *Guh-uff* or Franklin."

"Let's drive back towards town," said Fulton. They headed toward the Franklin line. "Kay, was it before you crossed the line—before the sign?"

"Umm—I'm not sure." They kept going, the windows down; they were all perspiring in the heat. They drove past the sign, Kay very quiet, looking out the windows, the windshield, trying hard to remember.

"Over there, that spot. That dead tree kinda looks familiar." They pulled to the side of the road and got out. She looked around, trying to remember. "I don't know. It could be."

"Are you positive?" asked Fulton.

"No, sir." There were no tracks; it didn't appear that even a blade of grass had been disturbed. They were about to get back in the car when Fulton stepped into the tall grass. They wondered what he was doing. He pushed aside the weeds and got out his handkerchief, pulling something up from the ditch. It was a small bottle of whiskey.

"You think it might tie in?" asked Marshall.

"Not sure," said Fulton, setting it on the hood of the car and getting his fingerprint case from the trunk. He dusted it. They all watched him go over the entire bottle. He shook his head. Nothing.

They got back in the car, driving slowly. Kay continued looking. About a quarter mile later, she leaned forward, her face near the windshield. "There—that dirt road!" she exclaimed, tapping her finger on the glass. "He turned down there, I know it!"

"You sure?"

"Yessir."

Fulton turned down the sandy trail, the thick vegetation about ready to swallow the little Ford.

429

"This is it, are you sure?" asked her father.

"Yeah, Daddy, this is the place! This's where he stopped."

Fulton got out. There were tire tracks from a dually truck—any tire marks that the suspect left were gone. Fulton took a photograph of the area.

They drove back toward town. At least they had something. They'd take Kay and her father home and try to interview the kids at the party. They drove down Palm Drive, where Avenue E (US 98) was lined with tall Mexican fan palms, to the corner of Avenue E and Market Street and the Standard Oil station.

A diminutive old man in overalls was reading the Tallahassee paper on a bench in front of the station. Fulton pulled in by the pumps, and the sheriff pulled alongside, cranking his window all the way down. They talked quietly about dividing up the witnesses; they'd canvass anyone that may have driven by that way and saw something. They ignored Kay. She kept looking at something. Staring at it. She had a funny look on her face. She began trembling.

"All right, boss man, let's do it," said Marshall, starting his car.

Fulton looked over at the girl. She'd turned white. "What is it, Kay? What's wrong?"

"That's him!" she gasped. "That's him!" She pointed.

Fulton leaned down so he could see through the passenger-side window. In the hands of the little old man was the *Democrat*, which he'd turned so as to read the sports page. Facing Kay was a big picture of a man's face. A familiar face with a familiar tagline: "Ben Austin, State Senate."

XXXXX

Fulton talked to the doctor at Weems. Based on his examination, he was of the opinion that Kay was raped. They got the clothes from Mr. Byers. Fulton rushed them to Elston. The ME examined Kay's underwear under a microscope, determining sperm was in fact present. "We can still do a test for the clothes, underwear—for blood type."

Fulton stood by while Elston did his test. The doctor shook his head. "We can't get blood type—about 20 percent of men do not secrete antigens or proteins of their blood into their bodily fluids. Your rapist is a rare bird."

XXXXX

Franklin county folks, including Mr. Byers, wondered what *Wilkerson*—as they pronounced the lawyer's name—would do. Martin and Fulton went to see the state attorney at his house. He wasn't very pleased but offered

430

them a seat in his den. His breath, Fulton noticed, revealed the state's attorney had been drinking.

He listened for a minute. "It's not enough. She's not given many details. You don't have blood type."

"We got as positive an ID as you can imagine," said Fulton.

"She was drinking—so much she couldn't drive. She'd been at a party with college boys. She lied to her daddy, sayin' she was going to spend the night with friends in town, but ends up at a party with booze. The jury won't like her. And they won't believe her."

"Now, I talked to her. She's credible as hell."

"We can't try a man for rape with so little evidence. There's holes in this case big enough to run the *Sunshine Special* through. She can't really remember this fella. She can't give you a composite. You drive her around, she wants to ID someone, she's impressionable, she wants to help out. She picks the first face she sees. If I'm the defense attorney, I'm gonna jump all over that."

"No, sir, she really saw him."

"I think she let things go too far at the beach house. It scared her. She knew she'd have to face her old man, so she cries rape."

XXXXX

Fulton left and called Byers. He told the father that it would be a few days before an arrest was made. He'd have to get more evidence for *Wilkerson*.

431

87

Apalachicola
Thursday, 10/30/1958

Fulton canvassed downtown with Marshall. They dropped by every store on Market Street, stopping to talk to everyone they saw—from men packing crates at oyster houses, to the gal working the counter at the A&P, to the boy cleaning windows at the Rancho Tourist Court at the outskirts of town. They talked to truckers and oystermen and people driving to work at the paper mill in Port St. Joe. Fulton's feet hurt, and the sheriff was down a half tank of gas. No one saw a damn thing.

Fulton went to check on Kay at their little house in Two Mile. Her father kept her home from school. "Some of the girls picked on her. She ain't said much today. Maybe it'd do her some good ta talk to you. She's real takin' to ya. She's out back."

The back door stoop overlooked a weather-beaten fence, a clothesline, and the alley. Kay was sitting on an orange crate. Fulton squatted down beside her. Her face was still swollen from the ants. She was sad, quiet, her arms around her knees. She looked over at him. "Mr. Fulton, do you believe me?"

"Yeah, Kay, I believe you." Fulton told her that Marlene tried to have a baby, miscarried. The girl would have been about Kay's age. She wanted to talk some more.

"I remember he started the car. He drove past Thirteen Mile, I remember that. Then he stopped. It must have been right after Thirteen Mile when he stopped the second time. And he done it again. After he's through, he let me put my shorts back on and put my shoes back on."

Fulton shook his head, hating what the girl went through.

"And I opened the door and fell out on my knees—that's how I skinned them. And I'm pretty dizzy. He props me up against the sign and leaves."

"Remember anything else?"

"No, sir."

"We're gonna get him."

She nodded.

Fulton left, driving through town, past the courthouse, toward the bridge. He sped across, making it through before they swung the center span around for a sailboat. There were hundreds of monarch butterflies in the air as he ran the causeway at seventy miles an hour. By the time he reached Eastpoint, his windshield was streaked with yellow and orange from the pretty creatures, their attempts to cross the bay, their winter homes in Mexico, cut short. It was a shame, but their migration path did not bend for the needs of modern vehicular traffic.

88

Alligator Point
Friday, 10/31/1958

Hangovers somehow felt more tolerable at the Point. The place was just so damn relaxing. If he hadn't obligations in the capitol, he'd spend all his time there. He told himself the days he spent in the city—shaking hands, making deals, putting up with the people about which he had to feign concern, fake interest in their problems—was what let him afford a place like this. Barefoot, Ben walked across the lawn, out to the dock. He opened a can of Jax and enjoyed the lovely, unspoiled view of Alligator Harbor.

The sun was warm on his face, the water like glass. There wasn't the sound of another living soul. The *Sine Qua Non* bobbed gently at the dock, eager to put to sea. He smiled. Claiborne out of his hair, nothing to worry about, it would be a nice relaxing day on the water. His "ball and chain" would be asleep for hours. The wine last night saw to that. He just got off the phone with his campaign manager. He was ahead of the bumbling Republican by a good 40 percent.

He stepped aboard the Wheeler Sportsfisherman; his most prized possession was thirty-six feet from prow to transom, a real battlewagon with bamboo outriggers and a flying bridge. She wasn't new, but she was kept immaculate: her hull bright white, a smart red stripe band extending just above her waterline, everything repainted just last year in Carrabelle. Her teak decks were regularly polished, her stainless and brass fittings shining like jewelry in the morning sun. He'd come by the boat as settlement for payment from a client. He'd got the fellow off on a gambling charge, but he didn't quite have the cash to repay the trial fee.

Ben stowed his rod and reel. A fellow he knew made the expensive tackle down in Miami, the best in the business. One reel cost more than the jalopies most of his clients drove. Cliff lugged out the Coleman full of Jax and Straight Eights. Ben had everything he needed for the day's sortie into the gulf.

He nodded to Cliff; the boy worked the starter buttons and fired up the big Hall-Scotts. The boy adjusted the throttles so they burbled pleasantly at idle, the swish of water from their exhaust soothing Ben's headache. "Cliff, you're getting to be a good little sailor." The boy smiled; he even had his own deck shoes and a captain's cap on his head.

Ben wore shorts and went bare-headed. He reached for the bowline but paused when he noticed two hats approaching. He cussed at the sight of Fulton and the high sheriff. He took a swig of beer. "What do *you* want?"

"We wanna talk ta ya," said Fulton.

Austin signaled for Cliff to kill the motors. Angrily, he stepped ashore. "You have no jurisdiction here," snapped the lawyer.

"He does," said Fulton, nodding to Marshall.

Austin motioned them toward the screened porch, which overlooked the harbor. Fulton sat down very comfortably, crossing his legs, looking at Ben. The lawyer was annoyed; he seemed tense. "Whaddaya want?"

"Where were you nine p.m. last Friday to two a.m. Saturday?"

"What's this about anyhow?"

"Please answer my question."

"What right have you to—"

"Where were ya?"

"Here."
"You sure about that? You sure you didn't drive over to Apalach, maybe around the airport?"

"I was nowhere near Apalachicola. Never left the Point. I ain't been across the bridge in months."

"You have someone that can vouch for that?"

"I don't have to have someone do that. Are we done?"

"You're done when I'm through, or we carry you to Apalach," replied Fulton, his response firm but relaxed and confident.

"Look, I haven't the time for this," growled Ben.

"I got lots of time. We can sit here all day," said Fulton, leaning back in the chair.

"Is this about Jo Ellen again? I know you wanted to pin it on Howerton. Then you wanted to pin it on me."

"Who were you with? Should I ask your wife?"

"Shut up."

"Are you afraid your story's not gonna hold up?"

"Get out!" roared Ben.

Fulton just looked at him.

"You ever seen this girl?" asked Marshall, holding up a photo of Kay.

435

Ben didn't react. "No. Who's she supposed to be?"

"Girl that was attacked a week ago," replied Marshall.

"I heard that was a college boy. Why you roustin' me about it?"

"I don't think it was a college boy. Do you, Herb?" asked Fulton, looking over at the sheriff.

"No."

"I'm calling my lawyer," said Austin. "Now get the hell off my property."

"Don't go anywhere," Fulton told him.

"You're the one that's going somewhere," retorted the lawyer.

"Oh?"

"Next year, when I introduce a bill to disband the Sheriff's Bureau. I'll pull the rug right out from under ya," said Austin, jabbing his finger toward the special agent.

Fulton smiled. "Have a good afternoon, Mr. Austin."

It was personal at this point. Austin thought the world owed him a living and the rules didn't apply to him. In reality, he was just another lowlife. Fulton would do what he had to do to see him carted away in handcuffs.

They walked back through the yard, to Alligator Drive, where Marshall had parked. They could hear the motors of the *Sine Qua Non* turning over behind the house. Fulton walked around the front of Marshall's Ford; he started to get in but paused. He stood in front of the car, staring at it. The sheriff had opened his door to get in but stopped, noticing Fulton's strange fixation on his patrol car. Fulton looked at all the torn wings stuck in the grille—the chrome mesh that resembled the business end of an electric razor.

"Oh," said Marshall, grinning. "I reckon I oughta git the car washed. If it ain't lovebugs or dirt roads, it's the doggone butterflies."

Fulton ran over to the Cadillac sitting under the carport. He inspected the shark fins, the whitewalls, the white paint and top. It was all spotless. He walked down the side of the long car; the fenders and chrome were, likewise, without a speck of dirt. He got around to the front bumper, the massive chrome bars that framed the air intake for the burly V-8. He bent down. Marshall had walked around, wondering what Fulton was doing. They could hear the *Sine Qua Non* idle away from the dock.

Fulton ran to Marshall's car, getting his camera and running back to snap a photograph. He snapped another then another. Marshall bent down to look. *Fulton sure is acting strange.* There was a piece of orange wing lodged in the grille. There were yellow streaks on the bumper and on the headlights. There were more pieces of wing in the parking lights and stuck in the gold Cadillac crest. Fulton pulled out a wing, ragged but nearly whole, and photographed it beside a small-scale ruler.

"I'm a mite bumfuzzled, True. What's this prove?"

Fulton looked up. "It proves Representative Austin has been across the bridge."

Marshall smiled. "Oh, so that's it. True, I don't believe I've ever been so happy to see a bunch of dead bugs."

The steady growl of the *Sine Qua Non* faded as she approached the tip of the cape.

Tallahassee
Saturday, 11/1/1958

A storm was coming. It was already raining in Apalach. The weather would be in Tallahassee in a few hours. Marlene read the paper. Burke was still at it. The article mentioned Special Agent Fulton and "girlfriend" Wendy—a known lady of the night. Marlene read the article aloud. "Well, I know this isn't the truth. My man doesn't need another woman, not with my lovin'. "

"Right, honey. And...he's scared."

Marlene threw a pillow it at him. "You had better be. 'Traveling on state funds to see the woman, who uses the alias Diamond Page,'" Marlene continued. "What a pack of lies. You spent your own money to fix that broken-down heap. Where do they get this? What can we do about it?"

"Front page kinda crowds out the truth—after someone's filled it with a nice neat lie."

XXXXX

Fulton drove to Proctor Cadillac and spoke with the young man that washed cars there. During his surveillance of the lawyer, Fulton had learned that Austin took his car to the dealer to have it washed. He found the boy working on a Fleetwood. "You remember the last time you washed that Eldorado?"

"No, but we keep a calendar, right here. Mr. Ben had his car in for an oil change and a wash on Tuesday, the twenty-first."

XXXXX

Sunday. It was raining. The telephone was ringing. "Fulton speaking."

"This is Byers."

"Yessir?"

"Ben's chief of staff offered me money."

"What?"

"Yessir. He said I needed to think about how five thousand could help my family. All I had to do was leave town for a while, and the money would be sent my way. My head is spinning. That's so much money. I told him to leave us alone."

"When was this?"

"Last night. He come to our back door."

"Okay."

"I'm scared that this feller come to my house." Byers was calling from a pay telephone in Port St. Joe. Fulton could hear the fear in the man's voice. Martin had brought in a small television he'd put by the fireplace. The local news was on.

Fulton stood so he could see it. The WCTV reporter, standing out in the rain with an umbrella, was doing an interview. Standing alongside was none other than Austin's chief of staff. He was hosting an event at a local church.

"Don't worry about him, Mr. Byers. We know where he is."

XXXXX

Monday morning. Marlene sighed, turning on their televison and handing Fulton the editorial page. He took a bite of his eggs and read the column.

zzzzz
Jim Burke, Ed.
When the votes are counted Tuesday night, Representative Austin will surely advance to the Senate, that small yet hallowed chamber on the second floor of the Capitol. Polls show the handsome lawyer comfortably in the lead. A term in the Senate, and he'd be in the lead for Governor in '64. Zzzzz-end

Fulton folded the paper. The telephone rang. It was Cook calling from the pay phone at the Standard Oil at Monroe and Tennessee. "Yeah, Austin's back in town, campaignin' in his daddy's ol' farm truck. He's down at the Elks Lodge."

The truck was a symbol of the campaign. It was a recession year. Politicians were sensitive about their image. Additionally, to cement his "of the people" status, Austin had been photographed driving a used Rambler to work and buying groceries at the Jitney Jungle. The newspaper carefully omitted photographing the Cadillac.

"Thanks, Jim." Fulton looked over at the television, the familiar face filling the screen, the announcer reminding folks to "Vote for Ben Austin."

XXXXX

The two men got out of the DeSoto and knocked on the door. Wilkinson sighed. His wife was clearing the table from breakfast. He led the visitors to the back porch. He was upset, apprehensive, about the warrant. "You sure he did it?"

"As sure as hell," said Martin.

439

Fulton nodded.

Wilkinson looked down, thinking for a moment. He raised his head, looking Fulton in the eye, nodding. "Okay." He put his initials on the paper, handing it back to the lawman.

XXXXX

The rain was pouring down. Fulton and Martin sped through the gates at Los Robles. Mrs. Anderson led them back to the jurist's den. The room was warm, oak burning in the fireplace. The judge offered them seats and returned to his desk. He read the probable cause report, his face grave. There wasn't another sound in the room but the crackle of the fire and the ticking of the clock. "No one is above the law," said Anderson, signing the warrant and handing it across the desk to the special agent.

XXXXX

Cook flagged them down. "Austin done stopped at the bank, drew out a wad a cash. Then he got him three cans a gas."

Fulton gunned the motor, racing toward the coast, the red line touching 110 on the big DeSoto. They met Marshall and his deputy at the turnoff for Alligator Drive. "Ol' boy's plannin' on makin' a run for it. Saw him loadin' up his boat."

XXXXX

Ben finished stowing the gasoline aboard the *Sine Qua Non.* He checked his carbine. He leaned it against the console by the throttles. He drained the last mouthful of his beer. The water was rough, the boat rocking, tugging at the lines. He looked at his chart. He had enough gas to get to Tampa then make a run for Cuba. A Huckins slowly idled through the harbor, 100 yards from shore—otherwise no one was around. No one would stop him. He cussed, realizing he'd forgotten the cooler. He ran back to the house.

XXXXX

Jo Ellen's picture was clipped to the front of the file on the seat. Fulton looked at it and shut off the motor. Fulton and Martin unbuttoned their coats; they could get their pistols in a hurry. Marshall got out of his car. Fulton handed him the paper signed by Judge Anderson. Silently, they approached Austin's house.

Austin dashed for the boat, mashing the starter buttons.

Marshall and his deputy moved around the far side of the house. Quietly, Fulton walked towards the carport, his pistol in hand. Martin was behind

440

him. Austin continued his efforts to coax the cold motors to life, the groan of the starters drowning out the steady rain.

A woman came out from behind the Cadillac with a pistol. "Look out, True!" cried Martin. Voncille Austin's gloved finger squeezed the trigger. Martin pulled Fulton back. The shot went wide. The shell casing rolled off the hood of the Cadillac. Coolly, Mrs. Austin levelled the barrel. The old man aimed his Police Positive. Simultaneously, they pulled triggers. The report was defeaning against the concrete block of the house. A red dot appeared on Mrs. Austin's dress. Furiously she jabbed at the trigger. Her small automatic had jammed. Martin grabbed the gun, wrestling it away from the woman as she shrieked, "you're not taking my boy!"

Marshall and his deputy ran down the long, narrow dock. Ben fired his carbine wildly as he yanked the bow line untied. The men returned fire with their Colts. Fulton ran down the dock, leaping for the deck of the boat, and missing, falling into the water as Ben backed away. Safely away from the dock, Ben spun around and shoved the throttles forward. Marshall and his deputy fired at the stern of the *Sine Qua Non* to no avail.

XXXXX

Ben rounded the tip of the cape and shoved the throttles wide open. That hick Fulton and that bumpkin Marshall would never catch him. The boat pounded over the waves, water spraying past the side windows as the hull slammed against the chop at full speed. He got a can from the Coleman and relaxed. *They'll never find me in this weather.*

XXXXX

The Huckins Sportsman had turned around, coming alongside Fulton. A hand reached down from the gunwale of the low-slung boat—Sam Nowak in a captain's cap. He ran the throttles up, the boat rising on plane, speeding towards the gulf. Sam steered towards the sandbar, the shortcut; the water seemed scarcely deep enough to clear the props. They made it, the boat heeling over as Sam turned to pursue the fleeing Wheeler, the sea growing darker beneath them. A deep bellow rose from underneath the engine covers as the twin Chryslers pushed them faster and faster.

The gulf was an endless, formidable gray. Clouds hung low, the rain masked the horizon. There was no sign of the *Sine Qua Non*. Sam kept the throttles at their stops, skimming the water at thirty knots. Would it be enough? Both men scanned the rolling sea for any sign of Austin. Soon a dark, gray form appeared in the distance, but only for an instant. The *Sine Qua Non* seemed to pull away. Perhaps Austin was too fast. Sam kept the engines screaming. Little-by-little Sam reeled him in.

Sam nodded for Fulton to go below. In the cabin were empty crates of Sunny Brook whiskey and a Browning automatic rifle. Closer and closer they came. Water splashed up from the sides of the *Sine Qua Non* as the

441

battlewagon sheared the tops off the whitecaps. The wind was howling. An orange dot blinked on the deck of the *Sine Qua Non.* Muzzle flash.

Bullets passed by the windshield. Fulton fired a burst with the BAR. Ben fired again, a round splintering the glass of the Huckins. Sam eased off the throttles. Another burst with the heavy BAR. Smoke poured from the engines of the *Sine Qua Non.* She began to slow.

Another burst. The Wheeler ground to a halt, flames lapping from her deck. Sam maneouvered close. Fulton leapt aboard.

Ben looked at Fulton and sneered. He was out of ammunition. He swung the carbine and missed. Wildly he threw fists. One connected. Ben tried to get over the side. Fulton pulled him back; down into the cabin they wrestled, Ben at the lawman's throat. Fulton broke the lawyer's grip, knocking him backward. The lawyer swung again. Fulton landed the sole of his Florshiem on Ben's forehead.

The lawman locked his handcuffs and dragged Ben onto the tossing deck of Sam's boat. Sam steered for the Point, the rain intensifying. Ben looked at Fulton and smirked. "What does the State of Florida have in the way of evidence? Nothing," the lawyer said smugly. "You boys'll be letting me out in an hour, you'll see. Two years you've been after me. Is this the best the you can do? I must be real dangerous. They send an old man and a washed up cop. You'll be back on an oyster boat with the rest of the white trash when I'm through." Ben watched the orange flames fade out behind them. When he could see them no more he grew quict; he hung his head and sobbed.

Milo Harbert was standing on the dock as Sam brought the Huckins in. "Justice," he said, shaking Fulton's hand. Ben cussed.

Martin showed them the gun that Mrs. Austin used. *J.H.* on the grips. Mrs. Austin was sitting in the back of Marshall's car, holding a towel to her shoulder and fussing about her hat. "I hired Boyette," said the woman. "She had it coming. I'm a good mother." They sat Ben beside her and shut the door.

They heard screeching brakes in front of the house. Two newspaper photographers dashed into the backyard, snapping photos as quickly as they could change their flashbulbs.

The reporters fired questions like a machine gun. "You got any comment, Sheriff?"

"Boy, that's quite an arrest!"

"Did he have a gun?"

"Did he try to run?"

Martin handed Fulton his fedora. They buttoned their coats and slipped around the other side of the house, back to the DeSoto. *The Sheriff's Bureau works best when no one even knows we're around.*

Made in the USA
Columbia, SC
14 December 2021

51462983R00264